REBEL

LAST CHANCE BOOK TWO

KT HANNA

Author: K.T. Hanna
Cover Artist: Sleepy Fox Studio
Layout & Design: Caitlin Greer

Ebook ISBN-13: 978-1-948983-26-6
Paperback ISBN-13: 978-1-948983-28-0
Hardcover ISBN-13: 978-1-948983-27-3

ALSO BY KT HANNA

Dedication:

The Oldies
For getting me through so much. Thank you.

1

SECRETS

Electricity can make you feel alive. The body acting as a conduit as it peppers through your system igniting fear, potential damage, and an overwhelming sense of power. Fueling the mind, speeding up the body's natural defenses. All of it pushing through to new heights.

But power can corrupt the mind, the body, and morals along the way and leave but a husk of a person in its wake if it leaves anything at all.

As soon as the swirling stopped around me, I dropped to my knees, retching up my dinner and bile as my stomach cramped into positions I didn't know it could reach. Next to me, Wick studied my actions with a curiosity only canines could manage, his tongue lolling out of his mouth like he found the whole thing hilarious.

Considering I was fairly certain I'd traveled by teleportation or instant relocation before—or whatever they called this thing—I didn't understand why

I felt so ill. Although if memory served me correctly, I'd also been partially asleep at that time.

Shane crouched next to me, cringing. "Sorry 'bout that. I'm not nearly as smooth at displacement as Nya is."

"You don't give yourself enough credit." The voice was familiar enough that I looked up to see the eternal seventeen-year-old. She seemed so out of place in this stark stone surrounding.

A wry smile adorned her mouth, and she inclined her head ever so subtly. "Keep your thoughts to yourself for now. Direct everything there so we are safe." She leaned down to scratch the top of Wick's head fondly.

Even as she spoke the words I felt like it triggered an immediate reaction. If I funneled my thought process into the tiny safe haven I'd created, it would help. I got the distinct feeling the program wouldn't want me to be here. Just like the last time.

Shakily, I stood up and brushed myself off, trying not to look down at the mess I'd made.

Nya leant forward and put a hand on my arm, her smile less mischievous than I remembered. "It's okay. Happens a lot when people first travel using displacement." Wick smiled up at Nya like she walked on water, pushing his head up for more pets.

"You two know each other?" I raised an eyebrow, mildly upset that it didn't seem I'd have a dog after all. Although, how I thought I'd manage a pet when I was barely home anyway had crossed my mind, not to mention I wasn't even sure if we could have pets.

Nya shook her head.

"No, but I've always had a way with dogs. Not a cat person, mind you. I think he likes me." Her eyes twinkled with happiness for a moment before her demeanor turned serious. "I'm sorry. They've escalated your assignments since we last spoke. I had no idea where they were sending you on that last mission before they actually did."

She made it sound like she could have altered that fate, could have prevented me from seeing my best friend turn murderer.

The vision began to repeat in my head again, and my stomach threatened to betray me yet again. "Can't refuse a mission."

She shook her head slowly. "No, you can't right now, but sometimes I can influence the type of mission you'll be sent on, occasionally with whom."

Her wording struck me as odd, and I studied her face. Not a hint of mirth to be found. "But you can refuse a mission?"

Nya laughed, and even Shane chuckled. I'd never liked being on the receiving end of inside jokes, and I scowled, suddenly angry.

"Look, I just saw my best friend blow a guy's head apart. Now you've whisked me away to Oz. So can we just suspend the inside jokes, or send me and Wick home now?"

My insides churned at the memory of Orion's actions, at the audacity to speak to these people who had a hell of a lot more experience than I did. But I stood strong. It helped that I wasn't short and didn't look like a tantruming child. Even Wick had stopped his wide doggy grin.

"Sorry." Nya ran a hand through her gorgeous blonde hair. Suddenly, she looked older than her appearance by decades. A bone-weary sort of presence lingered about her for a brief moment before disappearing.

Her gaze sharpened, and she looked me over with renewed interest. "Did you sense that?"

Sense? Did she mean the weight of the world on her shoulders? "Yes?"

"Interesting," was all she said before walking back purposefully to her desk, the one she'd sat on when I first met her a couple of weeks ago. Was that all it had been? The cold of the stone blocks that made up the building seeped in through my feet, sending that chilly wave through my body. I had no idea where we were, after all.

Nya shook her head like she needed to clear her thoughts and gave me a small smile. "People like Shane over here are outside of the system. For all the system knows, Shane died on a mission." She watched my face intently, like she was looking for understanding, or else for my reaction.

In truth, I had no idea how to react. Shane wasn't in the system any longer? How even the fuck?

"But you're alive." You know, because stating the bloody obvious always went over so very well. "Like in the system, I mean. Explain, please."

"You're not quite ready for the full concept, but…" Nya hesitated, eyeing Shane like she was weighing him. "I can let you know it's possible to remove yourself from the system. With a lot of dedication and practice of your abilities."

"How does the system react when it sees his face then? Because I know for a fact he was there while it was calibrating in my head." Because he had been. Right there in the ambulance.

Nya bit her lip, like she was figuring out just how much she could say at this time. Maybe she didn't trust my control over my safe space yet. "It doesn't quite work like that. The system runs on electrical frequencies and brain signature. Not on visuals."

Well, that was eye opening, and made a ton of sense. I mulled that over for a few moments before realizing the true stumbling block for me.

"How am I supposed to practice my abilities when the system doesn't know anything about them, and even more so without the system noticing that I'm doing it?" The words came out more heated than I'd expected, the emotion of the day beginning to wear me down alongside the fatigue.

Shane spoke this time. "You learned energy distribution all by yourself. Much sooner than any of us. Probably because you're a long-distance runner. I can see how that might have made it click sooner. You've partitioned your own mind, you can use your ability to heal…"

I nodded, understanding the correlation but felt the need to correct him somewhat. "It's not really healing. It's sort of rejuvenating, like boosting the natural healing mechanisms within the body."

Shane's grin widened. "Just know that as you push your abilities, you'll need to keep them from the system that woke you up. In that separate place."

"We don't need the system to use the abilities?" I didn't quite understand how that worked. The system had saved me for a purpose; how did I detach from it?

This time the medic hesitated, another brief glance thrown at Nya. "Look. Just…the system that saved you has many components. The one you've met is its persona for you, and it's legitimate, but it's also an evolution of different elements of the program over time. It's—not what it was."

Sure, that didn't sound ominous at all. As I let that sink in, Shane's eyes took on a brief but distant look. "Sorry, I have to go for a bit. I'll be back to send you home."

And he was gone, just like that, leaving me with Nya and my stolen pup. Okay, so he wasn't stolen, but my mind was honing in on weird stuff right now.

Nya reached down and scratched Wick's head like she'd been doing it forever. She gave me a pointed look and continued. "Anyway—if I'm correct, and I am, you can also sense auras."

"Auras?" I mean, I'd played enough RPGs to know what an aura was, but how did that apply…oh, yeah. The age thing. Apparently, that was something she kept hidden. I wondered why. "Never mind. I know what you mean."

"Excellent." She folded herself back up onto the desk and looked at me. "Yes, I've been around for a long time. Long enough that I've done things. Long enough that I've seen things. Long enough that I knew I had to do something about it."

I listened, wanting to know where Shane had disappeared to. Yet curious enough to stay here and listen. Besides, Wick liked Nya, and I had to confess to liking her too. People not liking dogs was one thing, but dogs not liking people was always a sure warning about that person.

Nya seemed to be the only person so far who'd even remotely led me to useful information, who'd talked to me with what I could only surmise was actual truth. Sure, maybe she hid some of that behind riddles and a convoluted way of speaking, but maybe she had to.

"What did you do?" I didn't realize I was whispering until I spoke. It felt like sacred information, things only I could know because I was a fellow eel.

Nya sighed, and for a brief second I saw pain flit across her expression. The desperation to know why was real, but I was pretty sure I was going to be told what I needed to know when I needed to know it. Call it a hunch.

"I faked the loss of my power."

"What? How? Why?" I couldn't help ask as incredulousness overwhelmed me.

"That's a story for another time. Right now, we need to go over what skills you have and work on the skills you need." She eyed her watch critically, a frown on her face. "We only have so much time we can pull you off the grid right now. So each minute counts, and I need to attune you to the Timewarp before I can let you use it. I've already wasted too many minutes reminiscing."

"Timewarp?" I asked, but she waved the question away.

"Shane will take you through it."

I nodded, sort of understanding, and, at the same time, not at all. Part of me screamed wanting to know how to fake the loss of our power. Because dang if I wouldn't like that.

"Second Chance loses a lot of eels early in their training due to overloading their system, due to drawing in more power than they can hold and having it take over. The electricity overloads them and burns them out from the inside." Nya sighed and looked impossibly burdened for a second before continuing. "The power is tempting, reckless, and difficult to control. We can't reach everyone in time."

I gulped as I listened to her speak, understanding what she meant with overwhelming clarity. I tried not to envisage myself exploding like that guy's head had earlier. And oh, how I didn't need my thoughts to go full circle to Orion. He was why I was here. Shane mentioned getting to know more about him and why he'd become what he'd become. So I waited for Nya to continue.

"But that isn't true for all the eels. Those who master the ability generally discover that being an eel comes with potent power. We can heal the body, we can energize the body, we can manipulate information and tech through computers and the mind. We can kill with just a touch. And," she paused for moment, locking eyes with me, "as long as we act before brain death, we can revive the dead."

She smiled tightly at me as I attempted to digest her words.

"Like human defibrillator?" Which would make a lot of sense, considering the origins of the power, but also sounded so fantastic that it didn't belong in the real world.

Nya nodded, an eagerness entering her eyes. "Exactly. Now, we won't ever have a lot of time. Keeping you here is risky, but necessary. Shane is just finishing some stuff up, and I have a meeting to get to." She glanced at Wick with a small frown. "Have you decided what you're going to do with him?"

I started to answer but stopped myself. How was I going to keep him in our apartment? Hell, when would I even be home? I hadn't thought about a multitude of things including if he was house trained, where I would take him to the vet and all that sort of stuff. "I'm not sure. I was going to take him home and then see what happened?"

She raised an eyebrow skeptically. "You just had to save him, didn't you?"

It sounded like she understood, so I nodded, trying not to let the emotions attempting to overwhelm me get the better of my demeanor.

"You know, I do love dogs, even though they don't live very long. They live their best lives while they're here, and I think that counts for something." Nya paused, and knelt down to pet him on the head again.

His eyes closed and his tongue lolled out again, like he was the happiest dog in the world who hadn't just witnessed his sketchy owners getting murdered in cold blood.

"I get the feeling he likes you and likes it here. Will you take good care of him?" I found myself asking before I could lose the most rational decision I'd made all day.

Her face lit up, and for a second I could see loneliness underneath and it made me wonder how many people she'd lost over the years. How many, if any friends were still around for her to talk to. "Yeah. I think he likes you too."

At least I'd be able to visit him when I came in for my sessions.

I glanced around at the stone walls, at the huge bookcases and screens. To the right of me was the couch I'd been resting on last time I was here as we'd moved into the less crowded portion of the massive room. It still felt cold and impersonal, almost like a facade.

The squash ball in my hand was wearing down. I'd fired so much electricity through it, I think it was degrading from the inside out. But at least I was getting better at controlling my impulses.

Better at digesting the information Nya gave me? Perhaps not. Shane was a good teacher, though, and didn't hesitate to put me through grueling drills. Everything surrounding this still felt surreal. Like maybe a dream that had gone on for a long ass time.

Holding the ball in one hand, I focused on the feeling of the currents running through my body. If Shane hadn't given me a brief example, I'd never have realized that some of these strands were hostile, just waiting for a lapse in my judgement or control so they could burn up all the energy I had. Most of the currents flowed with me, not against me, but I needed to train those to police the others and heighten my awareness of all of them.

It sounded a lot easier than it was. I closed my eyes and reached down through my body, following the sparks as I went, keeping an eye out for snakes in the grass. Zings rippled through me, echoing past each layer of skin until I sweat. The whole time this looming clock hung over my head. I only had so much time I could spend here. So much leniency from the program.

Each zing caused me pain, but I realized it was much less than it might be for someone without my abilities. Still, though, mapping out the paths in my body was excruciating pain and speed-wise.

"Dare." Shane pulled me out of my concentration, lending me some blessed relief. I wasn't about to tell him that, though.

"That's what people call me. Your point?" Perhaps too much sarcasm peppered there.

He smiled but his expression grew serious. "I'm going to need to divert some of your energy in order to attune you to the Timewarp chamber."

"Come again?" I blurted, the ear worm now stuck in my head.

Shane's smile became somewhat strained, but he took a breath and carried on. "Timewarp chamber. Cannot be used unless you are attuned. Hence, I will attune you."

"What happens if you're not attuned?" Because of course I had to know, but Shane didn't answer me, and the expression in his eyes made me swallow the repeated question. Instead, he changed the subject.

"Remember." Shane's words were even, and soft, easy to calm any nerves that might be fraying, even my patience. "Knowing your own currents helps you more than anything else. Know them inside and out and any which way. Practice it constantly. Recognize the power that is your own, so you can expel any outside interference."

It took me all my restraint not to snap out that it was easy for him to say. He wasn't electrically shocking himself in order to map them. I bit my lip instead, knowing he'd done this whenever he'd broken free too. It didn't make it feel any better, just gave me hope that it'd be over eventually. "Outside interference—you say that like someone is going to try and hijack me and my eelness."

Shane raised an eyebrow. "After everything you've witnessed, you think that's strange?"

"Fuck!" I encountered a particularly nasty thread of electricity and glared at Shane like he'd sent it.

Wrestling it caused more pain than I'd endured so far. It didn't want to yield. Wiry and wriggling like the eel I was, it challenged me to take control. Pain shot up my arms and through to the base of my skull, and I gasped out again, falling to my knees with a crunch. The carpet beneath me did little to soften the blow of the stone below it. Breath came to me in short rasps, but I thought I'd done it. Grinning widely, I didn't stand up; my panting lungs just wanted another moment.

Shane chuckled. If I'd had any energy I'd probably have punched him, but I'd literally zapped myself of it.

"Hey. I get it, trust me." He offered a hand to help me up, and I gladly took it. "I think we'll call that enough. We can only fiddle with time so much before it gets angry with us."

"Fiddle with time?" I managed to ask between gulps of air.

"You know when stuff slows down? That's time reacting to our imminent need." Shane shrugged like he'd just told me the sky was blue.

"So we can control time?" Because that seemed ludicrous to me.

Shane hesitated and shook his head. "It doesn't work like that. Time lets us return to our bodies and finish our stint here. It allows us glimpses. The electrical power we get only assists that. While other abilities might experience some time glitches, an eel can eventually extend the windows time allows us.

Does that make any sense?"

I shook my head. "Not really." Because nothing did, and I was far too tired to process more than I already had.

"It will, though." He glanced at me with a frown. "Which is why I've been attuning you to the Timewarp while you work. Without that, you can't enter. Without an understanding of just how powerful electricity can be, you won't understand the sheer miracles you can pull off."

Before I could say anything, he switched the conversation again. "We need to work on your shielding."

"Wait, what?" I was too tired for these terms that sounded like I should be at home on a Friday night playing a campaign with my friends.

"You can use currents to reinforce the layers of your skin and sort of give yourself a shield. Maybe you're not quite up to that yet, though." He studied me, and then his eyes grew distant for a moment. "We have to call it. I have to leave shortly."

"Sure. My body welcomes the chance to sleep," I mumbled in reply.

"Next time I think we can move onto electrical current manipulation, if you don't manage to figure it out on your own. You're a fast learner, like I was." He winked at me before biting his lip. "Okay, so you know the system is active in your body all the time, whether we like it or not. And you've realized you can portion off a part of your brain so you can keep your thoughts to yourself. You are, and will always be, linked to the system, just in its background operations. But the defaults from however old this thing is are still in place."

"What?" There were two systems? Or two halves of a system? I was starting to get so confused.

"You're still getting updates, right? Like," he looked me over critically, "probably portent ability warnings?"

"How did you know that?" The words escaped almost before I'd thought them.

Shane laughed. "You can sense auras. Goes hand in hand. Anyway, I know it's a lot to take in, and I realize we've only given you more questions than answers, but it's a process, and you just have to protect yourself."

"Sure. Yeah. Of course." Because that was the perfect response.

He laughed and looked at his watch. "Okay. We have to get you back home."

"Wait." I didn't want to go. I didn't want to see Orion. It was the first time in my life that I'd legitimately no idea how I was going to talk to him when all I wanted to do was fling myself at him and rip away his skin to see what pesky old person was hiding underneath it. "You told me you'd tell me about Orion."

Shane eyed me thoughtfully. "I'm not sure how much I can tell you right now. We can't remove you yet. It takes a while. Besides, they have their eye on you, and we need to know why. Keep practicing your skills so we can expand on them next time. Oh, and here." He tossed me a cylinder. "To help you practice."

I opened the top of it to find black squash balls inside. "Thanks," I said with a grin I didn't one hundred percent feel.

"Those are a heavy duty, specifically for channeling excess. You don't want to go home, do you?" he asked, surprisingly insightful for someone I'd known all of forty-five minutes.

I shook my head. "I don't, but if I don't help him, no one else will. I have to make sure his partition stays in place."

"What?" Shane snapped around to me, his eyes suddenly alert. "You did what?"

"I partitioned Orion's mind, so he could think away from the system." I wasn't sure what was so bad about that, but apparently I'd broken some unwritten rule.

Shane appeared to visibly hold himself back. "Don't refresh it. Use an excuse, say you can't. I'll talk to Nya about this, but Dare—don't share your abilities in the future. Not with a non-eel. SC can see what you do, and if you're not actually an eel, which Orion isn't, I swear it can see more. We have to be careful, no one should know what we can do."

"Okay." I didn't know how else to respond. Why couldn't I help my friend? But then again, my friend had been acting like a different person now we were in SC together. He'd killed a man, like he'd done it a thousand times already.

Maybe he had. Regardless of how much I wanted to help him, Shane's warning made sense. I wasn't about to make it easier for Orion to kill, or easier for SC to control us.

Shane placed his hand on my shoulder only briefly, giving it a quick squeeze in solidarity. "Sorry. That's just not something we encourage, and it's probably something that shouldn't be done again, at least not until we understand why we can do it. And while I know you don't want to hear this— we also can't afford to apply our own skills to a non-eel brain. There could be dire consequences for that."

He had a point. I'd dived into Orion's mind with abandon and little concern for any consequences. I'd been so sure there was a way to do what I wanted: a way to protect my best friend.

But how did I protect my best friend when he was apparently his own worst enemy?

LIKE USUAL

The disorientation as I landed in my room wasn't nearly as bad as it had been to land in Nya's office. Granted, I landed on the bed, which was ten times more comfortable than the stone floor of her place, but still. I counted it a win that I didn't empty the rest of the bile in my stomach. There wasn't any more food in there, that's for sure.

I should have asked Shane when I could learn displacement myself. There was no way I could be as rough as him at it. Come to think of it, was it an eel thing? Because if so, it made sense that SC didn't just drop us into missions individually with a bit of a teleport. Okay, so I had a lot of questions for Shane next time.

The house seemed quiet. I knew it was late, almost midnight by my watch. I'd been gone a lot longer than I thought. Perhaps time passed differently where I'd been, on top of the weird eel time thingy I still didn't comprehend.

Damn, I'd have to ask more about that next time. It really felt like I'd come away with a thousand more questions than answers received.

Next time? I guess I'd already made up my mind. While I still felt like they were keeping secrets from me, I think some of that might have been because they wanted me to get used to my powers gradually.

Fuck it. I didn't have time for that. I needed to get used to things now and be able to do everything now. I wanted to know more about this skill and ability I seemed to possess. That had been given by a damned electrocution. Electricity wasn't pretty or tame, it was full of rage, it fed off rage. And if I even had a moment of indecision when utilizing my power, I was pretty sure I'd be burned out like all the eels before me.

I'd never been very good with taking directions. People telling me not to do something made me itch to do it even more.

Whining in my head wasn't going to get me anywhere. And I sure as hell didn't feel like seeing if Orion was home at the moment. Instead, I crept into the bathroom to clean my teeth before bed.

Orion's door was open, with no sign of life in there. As I brushed my teeth, I peeked into the living room. No one there, and no-one in the kitchen beyond either. Maybe he'd had to be debriefed. Maybe I shouldn't have run, even though Adam knew and had okayed me to. At least, that's what I thought the nod meant. That or he was saying: *I know right? That's so fucked up!*

Whatever it was, I quickly finished up and headed into my room so I could continue being oblivious. At least for one more night.

Sleep, though, seemed to have different plans for me. Firstly, that poor guy's head featured prominently in my dreams. Exploding icicles kept tormenting me from behind my eyelids, so much that I feared Orion might walk in and do the same to me. Was that the real reason, though?

Frankly, if I was being honest with myself, I think I was more concerned that he had changed so much. If he could become what I saw last night, then so could I, right? Wasn't it possible that part of me was scared I could kill in order to keep myself alive?

Self-defense was one thing. Burning those strange shadow creatures had been in self-defense, and even then I was quite certain they hadn't been killed. Instead, I'd let them flee. Why couldn't Orion and that Driver dude have just knocked those people out? Which was the crux of my concern. I couldn't figure out why the hell they'd had to kill those people. Had the system ordered the actions, or was that the way they'd chosen to execute the orders? Lives weren't expendable. Hell, ours weren't. We were brought back for a specific purpose, which I was pretty sure didn't include killing random petty drug dealers on the street. So why?

Of course, I didn't have any answers because I directed my thoughts to myself, and no one answered me. Not even my little friend checked in on me, which didn't surprise me, considering SC probably had no idea what to say to actual sentimental people.

Sleeping through my alarm hadn't been on my list of things to do the next morning, but it happened. For the first time ever, though, I decided to just let it be. I sent a text off to Coach Marth to let him know I'd had a bad night and wouldn't be at practice that morning. It was only when I finally got an answer five minutes later that I knew the man hadn't had a heart attack when he got the message.

Train twice as hard tomorrow was all the answer I got.

I lay in my bed staring at the ceiling like maybe it could rain down answers on me. But it remained stubbornly silent. Funny, that. Also funny were my attempts at avoiding the thoughts I least wanted to have.

Couldn't do that forever, so I got up and changed, trying to think on how I'd approach Orion.

You're being awfully silent, and you're awake late. Are you not feeling optimal?

No, I'm not feeling optimal, I snapped back at it.

Okay. Just wanted to check.

It sounded offended and maybe a bit sad. And while I wasn't a huge fan of what I'd witnessed in the last two missions, the voice that spoke to me was never anything but polite. Well, most of the time.

Finally dressed and utterly not ready to make my way to class, I finally left my room to clean my teeth and whatnot, only to find Orion exiting the bathroom.

The expression of shocked surprise on his face when he looked up to see me there was priceless. Seems he'd been trying to avoid me almost as much as I was still trying to avoid him if the bleeding dark red aura around him was anything to go by. Perhaps I could plead temporary blindness and just walk straight past him.

Warning: Aura Detection not optimized.

Fantastic. Here we went again with the notifications. Just what I needed.

"Hey, Dare, missed you last night." His words were hesitant, forced almost, and he wouldn't look me in the eyes. And I had no doubt at all that he was lying through his teeth.

Not that I particularly wanted to look into the eyes of a killer. I'd say I was being harsh, but he had in fact killed a person in cold blood. I was there, and my brain wouldn't stop reliving that very concrete moment in time.

"Sorry about that." I pushed past him, trying not to be too rude, but unable to make myself stay too close to him. "Have to run. Slept through my alarm."

I closed the bathroom door behind me before he could say anything and gripped onto the porcelain sink stand to stop myself shaking. It didn't work as well as I wanted. My anger boiled, the uncertainty in my gut intensified, and I could feel the electricity beg to sizzle my insides, battling to escape. I once again found myself close to throwing up. That was getting to be a bad habit.

Breathe. In the everlasting wisdom of Mom, just breathe.

It helped to calm me down at least. The storm inside me reduced down to sullen static shocks instead of lightning bolts, but I could sense it wouldn't stay that way long if I didn't do something about it.

I was sure Orion was still standing outside the door, so I busied myself with brushing my teeth. Didn't want to face the day with stank sleep breath now, did I? My stomach was doing that thing again. I tried to push it down, but it wouldn't go away, and I could feel the panic rising in me. The breathing needed to help more. Perhaps I should meditate.

Warning: Portent Ability unstable.

You think? I yelled to the self in my head. But there was blessed silence in return. So that portion of the system was constantly monitoring my body's actions and reactions. Like a dormant guard of my inner powers. What was odd was how much I missed the personality of the other voice.

Failsafes were fine by me. Okay, I could work with that. I could probably build on that, too. In a way, knowing that separating my thoughts to keep them for myself still allowed me access to the failsafes of the system was reassuring. At least in a way that wasn't totally focused on the fact that I was the living embodiment of undead. Dr. Frankenstein, eat your heart out.

Taking a deep breath, I opened the bathroom door and bolted for my room, grabbed my backpack after checking for my tablet, and began the trek to school.

It was always a weird sensation for me to walk through the front gates of the school instead of heading directly to the athletics field. If I had time, people-watching might be something I'd enjoy, but I didn't really have someone I could share those observations with right now.

What Orion had done seeped into my very core. It separated us. I didn't think I could put my life above someone else's in that situation. Maybe I was being idealistic, but I had no intention to develop my powers into a usable weapon before I could make myself disappear.

"Dare!" Cyan's bright and cheerful voice broke through my thoughts, and I had to admit to the genuine smile it put on my face. It was like all the stress and irritation flooded out of me and let me relax.

"Hey there!" I grinned at her as she flung her arms around me like she hadn't seen me in months. She was such a hugger. Extricating myself took time. Sometimes I didn't mind the contact as much, but today I definitely needed minimal.

"What you doing? Didn't you have training this morning? Have you injured yourself?" Suddenly an aura of complete concern flickered across her face, like she thought I might have hurt myself. Standing back, she frowned, looking me up and down so much I almost felt like an antique being appraised for auction.

"Well, you don't *look* injured…" She paused, eyeing me expectantly.

"I'm not injured. I just had a really bad night's sleep and slept through my alarm." I shrugged, like it wasn't a big deal, even though we both knew the only time I'd ever missed practice since coming to college was when I managed to get pneumonia and was down and out from everything in freshman year for about two weeks. A memory flickered past me so fast, I couldn't quite catch it. Me standing drenched from head to toe, cold and shivering. Probably hadn't helped that flu.

"Are you sure you're okay?" she asked as she fell into step beside me, pulling me back to the conversation. At least I wasn't going to be late for the lecture we were going to.

"Of course." I glanced at her, wondering why she was so concerned. Was she a part of the program as well? After all, her friend Sam was. What if I was surrounded by people who were all in the program, which was why they'd picked me to be electrocuted? "I'm just tired. It's been a trying few weeks."

A thought occurred to me.

Hey. I want you to scan every person I come into contact with, and tell me if they are in the SC program. Okay?

There was a pause, so long that I wasn't expecting an actual response by the time it came. Just as I was about to push the door open for us to go into the lecture hall, it spoke.

Done. Please do not disclose the nature of your predicament to Cyan. She is not a part of the SC program.

Thanks. And I didn't realize how much I'd been hoping it would tell me that. Not that the delay it took to give me information didn't register. That in itself was odd. Another thing for marginally future me to worry about.

Future Dare was going to be so pissed.

We found our usual seats and got ready to sit through yet another lecture that I already knew the content for. I liked reading. Doing so about subjects that genuinely interested me was an even better way of studying for me. I glanced around the entire hall, wondering if it would trigger the system to react to other people who were in the program. Apparently, it didn't see anyone until Orion wandered in.

My breath caught in my throat, but just before he made it over, Neale dropped into the seat next to me a wide grin plastered on his face. Sometimes I wondered if the basketball player had a sixth sense. He always seemed to be around just when he was needed, even when I didn't realize until he was there.

"Hi there, practice ditcher." He grinned at me, and I groaned.

"It's like the first time I haven't been bed-bound and missed a practice. I was tired last night, okay? Slept like shit." I grimaced, hoping they'd think it was because of the bad night and not the fact that Orion had made his way over to us.

Neale grinned, pulling out his tablet. "Sure, sure. Any excuse, am I right?"

His wink was as disarming as his smile, and I couldn't help but grin back. Of course he had no idea what Orion and I were fighting about, but it helped that his presence eased my tension.

Neale is not a member of the SC program. Please refrain from any forbidden information sharing.

Another relief for me, and yet again hesitation by my inner companion. It felt so much better to know I wasn't surrounded by people who were sent to keep an eye on me. Orion and Levi dropped down next to Neale, and I completely avoided looking at him. I wondered if our friends noticed anything off about us, but the lecture began before I could follow that train of thought any farther.

My notes practically took themselves, but wedged in between Cyan and Neale, I didn't even mind. As long as I kept my gaze directed in front of me, I could avoid Orion's eyes and everything he was trying to say with them.

3

QUIET

My ability to avoid Orion throughout the day proved legendary, but I knew he'd cotton on sooner or later. Apparently it was sooner, because when I finally got home, he was sitting on my bed.

I wasn't expecting him to be there when I pushed the door open, but he sat on the edge, his arms resting on his knees, hands gripped together, and looked up from where I assumed his gaze had been riveted on the floor when I entered.

"We need to talk." He spoke the words with a distance in them, between us. I didn't like the tone and had to suppress the shudder doing its best to run through me. I could feel the electricity begin to build within me, reacting to my thoughts and emotions, to the very anger I knew was at the core of how I felt right then.

We'd always been so close, but the last two years were full of lies, forced on us by the system. They were full of changes I'd known nothing about, that he couldn't share and that he took in stride to preserve the rest of his existence. I got the desperation all too well, and I could see it from different angles, but

I'd never thought he could be the sort of person to put himself before another's life. Especially not after losing his mother.

Maybe he thought himself above the law; perhaps he felt his life was worth more than the people he struck down because he wanted to help others. I got that strange logic, even if I didn't agree with it. So maybe I could hear him out.

I crossed my arms and tapped my foot, raising an eyebrow to indicate he could continue. My patience was thin and my temper fraying at the edges. Electricity nibbled at the barrier, trying to push through when I least expected it to. I tried to make it appear casual, but I walked over and pulled out one of those heavy-duty rubber balls to help.

If I tried to speak now, it was going to devolve into a shouting match, which would, in turn, give way to electrical discharge that I likely couldn't control properly. Though I probably couldn't avoid that for too long at this rate at least I could temper it.

He cracked his neck from side to side before looking up at me and speaking. His voice sounded like nothing I'd heard from him before. Calculating, yet tinged with sadness and a side of righteousness. Maybe he was still convincing himself.

"You've received one punishment so far, correct?"

I wasn't expecting that question, but I nodded my answer, probing, trying to see if his aura indicated where he was going with this. But it didn't. Instead, it wavered like old TV stations and their static screens.

Warning: Aura Detection unstable.

Oh, joy.

He seemed put off by the fact that I wouldn't commit to a verbal answer, but he continued on anyway. "I've had a lot more than one, and since the punishment fits the ability, I can tell you that ice can get so cold that it burns. That water can make you *wish* you were drowning. And air is stronger and more brutal than tropical storms make you believe."

"Fantastic. So that's worth the price of human lives, right? I mean, not having to put up with shit yourself?" My tone could have stripped bark from a tree, but I couldn't take the words back, and to be honest, I didn't want to. I was angry, and I had a right to be.

Orion actually flinched when I spoke, but then a scowl crossed his face. "You have no idea what the last two years have been like for me. Being the person my friends knew, keeping up this charade and pretending the whole world hasn't completely changed for me. Not changing your life means so much, and I did it. I managed to do it without anyone—including you—suspecting a thing. So yeah, I fucking deserve to be alive."

He stopped, blinking, seemingly surprised by what he'd just said. And if he was surprised, I was fucking reeling. Other lives were worth him not having to suffer? Not even him dying like originally intended, fated or whatever. I waited a moment, trying to conquer the wild electricity that fed off my anger with glee. I needed to speak and have a partially rational conversation. Since none of the whole mess of Second Chance was a rational thought, it was difficult to call it that.

Warning: Electrical Discharge necessary.

No shit, Sherlock. Arg. I'd been saying that so much lately. I took a deep breath and forcefully eased the tension out of my shoulders, shooing the power through my system and into the palm of my hand. I wondered if the faint scent of burning rubber was me or my imagination. I wondered if Orion could hear my body crackling with the force just waiting to break free.

"So," I began quietly, a complete rush of calm suddenly overcoming me even as the power zinged so loud I swore it was audible to everyone. "You've obviously killed before. How many people, exactly, have you murdered?"

I'd never heard my voice that cold before, that calculating. It was like a side of me had taken over that I never knew existed. The kind that wouldn't let simple things interfere with my emotions, that wasn't about to make me lose my temper. My power bubbled just under the surface like it was lying in wait but listening to my commands.

Orion sat there, a stunned expression on his face. I wonder if he told himself they weren't murders. I mean, since the system portrayed this to be in the greater scheme of life on the planet and all, maybe he did feel righteous in what he was doing, in the execution of people.

He didn't say anything, and that only fueled me more. Without the words to back up his intentions, the sadness in his eyes could have been about anything.

"Sure, they might not all be innocent, but that doesn't mean you're not affecting lives that are. Did you stop to think that some of them might have children, wives? Mothers, fathers, people who will care that they're gone." I tried to remember how this place I was speaking from felt, so I could harness it again. It gave me this strange clarity to my words, to my thought process. It was exhilarating.

I continued, not letting him speak yet. Actions spoke. Icicles through the head spoke too. Without even meaning to, I initiated the trick Shane had mentioned I needed to practice. I used the power that was itching to escape the confines of my body to reinforce my own body, protecting myself because the person in front of me wasn't the Orion I knew any longer. I couldn't trust him, not fully, not anymore. The power had to go somewhere, and I was pretty sure I was already down one heavy duty electro ball.

"So tell me. In your best, rational argument. What justifies you killing someone and going on living like it never happened?"

He clasped his hands together, fidgeted in a very unlike-Orion manner. I almost wondered if he was in fact Orion or a clone who'd been placed there to take his place. When he finally spoke, I barely recognized the voice. It was heavy with guilt but also confidence that he was in the right, like he'd convinced himself—perhaps he'd had to do so.

"I realized too late that the icicles I'd developed could be used for far more than I ever intended. At first they were a great lock pick if I made them strong enough. But then…melted ice leaves no evidence. Once they realized what I could do, the first order came in. I tried to resist, but…" He looked off into the corner of my room like he was remembering what had happened.

A sliver of sympathy entered my heart for a moment, because yes, the punishments we received weren't pleasant, nor warranted. Taking away our freedom of choice was fucked up. They'd taken away his freedom of choice, and I got that, I did, but that still wasn't an excuse. Using our own abilities against us by removing our natural resistance to our own elements? That was fucking cruel.

"Look. I did what I've done to be here, to stay here, to attain my dream and be here for my family and friends. I don't like what I do, but I would do it all over again if it meant I got to live, to stay in this world with the people I love, to help the people I love." He paused, looking directly at me. "Like you."

I blinked. What a very odd thing to say. So pointedly directed at me. Don't get me wrong, I'd told him I loved him several times, and received the same in return, but now those words were weighted with so much baggage, and so much obligation that I wasn't sure how to deal with them. I certainly wasn't about to question their origin to his face. Yet.

"Sure. Of course. How do you think those friends would feel to know that you made the decision to call their lives more important than the person you're killing?" I shook my head. His logic was flawed, out of a need for self-preservation and selfish goals. Yet I could see some of his reasoning, see how he came to it in desperation.

"Look. Maybe the dude you killed was a dick. Maybe he tortured people for a living, perhaps he didn't have a family. Maybe he was planning terrorist actions; I wouldn't have a clue. But he was a human being, and he had a life. You aren't a judge and executioner. You had no right to take that from him, from his family, from anyone who knew him. Definitely not without knowing more about it, without knowing that he might blow up a school tomorrow, or that all he was guilty of was packaging some blow." I stepped to the side of the door, leaving his path to it clear. "I have to study now. I don't have time to talk anymore."

Orion looked up at me, some surprise showing on his face. We never left things hanging in the air. It wasn't my style. But you know, I'd died recently, and I was beginning to take a lot of things seriously, including how I saw myself as a person.

No messages came in, nothing. Not even a mission. Nothing from my friends, no noise in the house. The door had closed earlier, close to slamming. I guessed Orion had left the house.

Perfect timing to dig a little deeper. I stretched back on my bed, accessed my own mind, and attempted to pull up SC's interface.

To my ever-growing surprise, it actually worked. Except it didn't look like I remembered. It wasn't as streamlined and glowy and gave me pause. Had I somehow gotten a system virus?

Nya and Shane's words came back to me, clamping down on my phantom panic. There was a rudimentary system or something, always available if you'd been brought back. Buried under all the complexities layered over it.

Except to me, as far as information went, this one seemed far more in depth and complex and apparently accessible through the little haven of solitude I'd created in my head. There was no reassuring robotic voice to comfort me as I navigated it. But the more I delved into it, the more apparent it became that whatever had caused SC to splinter like this had left out a plethora of information. Stuff I needed to know. Hell, stuff everyone needed to know.

Eels weren't an unknown factor, but over time it had changed through necessity. From what I was reading, this whole system dated back as far back as Mesopotamia, maybe the Big Bang. It all seemed a bit far-fetched to me. Like some great hoax, or hidden camera show.

But the information was there. Each fall of a great empire: Minoan, Mycenaean, Egyptian, Sumerian…they were all sprinkled in here. References, reports I couldn't figure out how to access or else didn't possess access to. Oh, how I wanted to. The only thing I could see was that they were all related. When civilization became too unbalanced, the system stepped in.

I remembered a comment from SC's representative in my head. That WWI had been the best outcome they could choose from. Chills ran through me, sparking electrical reactions that actually hurt a little. Just what was this thing I'd tapped into and how was I supposed to figure out its motives?

If I got stuck on the history of it all, I was never coming out of the rabbit hole. Right now, wasn't the time for this. I slapped my cheeks, willing myself to focus on digging out information I could use right now. I'd try to stop history repeating itself once I had a handle on my own abilities.

The one thing the two variances of the system had in common was progression. The Portent ability flickered at me every time I looked at it. Like it thought it probably shouldn't be active, but that it had occasionally reached activation. It hadn't been available to me in the other screen, which seemed like a barren wasteland of eel abilities.

Energy Distribution
The ability to manipulate energy to suffuse and rejuvenate anything organic.
Current Skill: General

So that *was* what my healing power was called. I liked healing better; it sounded nicer. Displacement was listed, but so blacked out I could barely read it. That didn't surprise me. Either I wasn't strong enough to use it yet or else my abilities weren't geared in that direction. Of course it was probably the latter because having my own teleport pad would be too cool to give me.

Electrical Current Manipulation, however. That was a different thing. And just the place I wanted to start learning more. I needed distraction, and what a perfect way to combine some of my real-world learning with my underground super abilities.

Electrical Current Manipulation
The ability to maneuver currents outside of the user's body, including but not limited to: any type of creature, or thing that conducts and utilizes electricity in a communicative form. Finesse depends on practice.
Current Skill: General

Electrical Pulse Control
Current Skill: General

Electrical Shock Application
Current Skill: Rudimentary

Timestance
Current Skill: Incomplete

Power Absorption
Current Skill: Rudimentary

Electrical Grounding
Current Skill: General

Aura Detection
Current Skill: Rudimentary

Displacement

Portent Ability
Current Skill: Warning
Fine line electrical control.

To name a few…

The information splayed in front of my eyes like I had contacts on that were tiny computers. Only the screens were mostly transparent with a weird sort of script used that I couldn't define the color of. I wasn't sure how they made this possible, and it made me think it was always present in humans, but not activated unless the system chose you. Again, even with accessing the system and researching, all it gave me was more questions.

As I opened the ability to attempt further research for, I don't know, information I could actually use, something flickered in the corner of my vision. But every time I attempted to look at it head on, it escaped into the peripheral again. Yeah, that wasn't spooky at all. Taking a moment, I closed my eyes briefly and counted to five before opening them again. Nope. There it was, still there, like a blur at the corner of eyes. Like a…

Shadow.

I don't think I've ever stood up so fast in my life. Back against the wall as I stood at the head of my bed, I tried to catch an actual glimpse of the thing. Of course I hadn't thought to ask Shane or Nya about the shadows, because I was utterly stupid. Okay, I wasn't stupid and had been put on the spot and out of my element at the time.

But this was something I *had* to ask them about, and I had no idea how to contact them.

So, like I was talking to Wick or any other cute, fluffy dog, I did what any almost sane person would do when confronted by a shadow creature of indeterminate origin.

"What can I help you with?" I spoke the words in cutesy, that strange tone that everyone uses with babies and puppies when they speak nonsense. Maybe it even disguised how nervous I was.

Perhaps I was imagining it, but the shadow flickered. Encouraged, I attempted to speak to it again. "You're such a persistent fella, aren't you? Why do you hang around me?"

Again, it flickered, but this time it grew in size, and I had to bite back the initial fear that flooded through my system. I was too old to be jumping at shadows, so I stayed as perfectly still as I could.

For the first time since finding that strange laboratory that I still needed answers for, I got a good look at once of these non-robotic shadows. Try as I might, it wouldn't let me look at it head on, perhaps that had to do with the lighting in my room, maybe it didn't. But staying still was my best option. It slowly leaked out a little more, taking on a vaguely humanoid shape until it stood just in the side of my vision like a person you can't quite look at.

The edges weren't defined but instead blurred like a page that had been ripped from a book. Finally, it blinked its eyes open, as if curiosity had gotten the best of it, leaving soft red globes in place of the black eyelids. My skin prickled, but not just with electricity, with a sense of foreboding and familiarity rolled into one, like I should know what it was.

Out in the house, the front door slammed open—or shut, I couldn't tell—but the shadow dissipated like smoke in the wind. Electrical charge made the hairs on my skin stand on end, and my power threatened to spill out as the shock rushed through my system. I'd almost been able to talk to it, to be able to ask it what it was. But for some reason, I had the distinct impression that it couldn't speak for itself.

Which only made me determined to speak for it.

Good morning. You've been quiet for several days, but your presence is requested, and I have to wake you up.

I blinked my eyes open at the noise in my head, the voice in my head. My drool and I didn't appreciate being woken up that way. Even though I was barely awake, the churning in my stomach began, making me want to retch before I'd even stood upright.

What? I asked it grumpily, not liking where that feeling of dread I already had was about to take me.

Assignment Notification.

Location: Biomedical Research Building

Objective: Retrieve a brown paper package, placed in the top-rightmost drawer in the main desk in laboratory seven.

Time Limit: By midnight tonight.

Reward: Dependent on the mission's success.

Caution: Guards, medical staff, and the lab supervisor. Being detected is not an option.

Research building? I mean, I knew where they meant, but that wasn't even on campus. That was over the road and down the street, at the hospital. Perhaps I could stop and see Dr. Caroline at the same time. There were so many questions that needed answers. Yet the thought in the back of my mind kept telling me that the only place I'd find the actual answers was back at Nya's office.

Not to mention my logical brain yammering at me. Why couldn't the person who'd obviously put the paper bag there deliver it to its final destination? I mean, that seemed a bit suspect to me.

Still, all the unanswered questions in the world weren't going to help me right now. At least I had until midnight tonight. I should be able to sneak away and grab this at some stage during the day. Though my stomach seemed to be feeling the anxiety far more than I'd ever done before. Perhaps it knew nothing good could come of this sneaky and covert stuff.

Warning: Portent Ability shifting.

Great. That was a new one.

There was no mention of target elimination, so I'd have to call it a tentative win, right? Electricity zinged between my fingers, like it didn't agree with me. My control had to be getting better; I was pretty sure it would have done more than that only a couple of days ago.

It was Tuesday, and I still had enough time to make it to training. At least there I could run over all of the facts I had in my head. Sure, I realized what knowledge I possessed could fill a thimble, but I needed to be a glass half full of any information I could glean if I was going to survive until my next meeting with the others.

You don't have any questions?

I balked at my friendly neighborhood voice speaking to me. It never sounded mechanical, just distant for being so close to me. And I didn't really think it would have the answers for the type of questions I wanted to know. I shrugged, aware it could feel that as long as I wasn't actively blocking the connection. *I dunno. What do you want me to ask? I don't have to kill anyone, do I?*

It took a few seconds to respond to me, which told me more than I think it realized. Great. I never *had* to do anything, right?

We are preserving the human race. You never have to kill anything.

Nice phrasing, asshole. I was proud of my restraint in directing that thought to myself. *Sure you are. Saving us from ourselves, yada yada. Look. I'm not so sure we deserve saving. But I will not trade my life for another's. Just so that's clear. Ever.*

There was no response as I raced across another intersection, enforcing my body, holding my speed at a believable level regardless of knowing instinctively that I could go much faster.

Noted. The system is aware of your inclinations.

Oh, great. I didn't like the sound of that, and the sudden lack of presence in the back of my mind alerted me to the fact that it wasn't open for discussion. Oh well. Making my own bed and all. I should be used to it. I'd been doing that since I could remember.

4

PORTENT

My black clothes itched. I knew I'd washed them, so it had to be psychological or something since it's what I wore when Orion…I took a deep breath. Dwelling and rehashing it wasn't going to make it go away or feel better.

I was dealing with enough trepidation considering the knots my stomach was trying to contort itself into.

Warning. Portent Ability unstable.

No shit. I sighed, trying to calm my mind and therefore my stomach. This didn't strike me as a good thing. Instability wasn't about to help me right now, not to mention that I still wasn't sure what the ability involved. I swallowed, counting to ten slowly, and allowed a little of that excess electrical charge to flow into the ball in my hand. I wanted to attempt releasing it into my skin, to create that barrier Shane had briefly mentioned, but I didn't have the skill yet, and the temptation to let too much out and fry myself was too real.

As I passed it, the hospital was doing what hospitals do, but it didn't appear to be overly busy. People bustled about as they entered and exited the building, and no one really paid attention to anyone else. Toward the end of the day, with the sun setting, the concrete jungle was still a hive of activity. But then in a house of healing, the sick never really stopped entering.

Just down the street, the lab loomed in the darkness. Such a stark juxtaposition. Even with the trees planted in concrete surrounds, the effort for fake nature failed abysmally. I managed to hide in an opposite doorway and time my entry. Security patrolled the perimeter every twelve minutes. That should give me plenty of time to gain access.

Lower left-hand side of the building has a basement entrance with a loose lock on the window. Some small applications of force should open it for you.

Great, I said, while not feeling it at all. They wanted me to jiggle the window open. Fantastic plan. I'd have to check for any security systems along the way and disable it if possible. It had to be a basement grate, didn't it? The way in always felt like it came from the basement. Did people never learn to lock those properly or check their security?

Flashes of Dave being shot—of his face exploding over mine, of the blood that dried into flakes I had to scrape off—flooded through my head, assailing my senses. For just that split second, I found myself back in that instant, witnessing my first SC death.

Maybe it wasn't a second chance at all; perhaps it was punishment. Our last chance to do over for something in the past. It had to be. Knowing we could die for any misstep, or for refusal…that was emotional torture.

I needed my brain to shut up and stop working me into a frenzy of fear and doubt about what I needed to do. Right now, as long as it didn't come down to my life in exchange for someone else's, someone innocent, someone who had no clue that we existed? I would do what I needed to in order to survive.

Breathing calmed me. Barely. Get in that window, get the nondescript brown paper bag of oh, I don't know, probably a bribe. Overactive imagination, go!

You seem on edge today. Is something wrong?

There was a thread of underlying concern in those words, and I felt, just for a moment, a pang of guilt at having to deceive the voice in my head. But it lasted the blink of an eye, and I pushed it away.

Yes. Brown paper bags are synonymous with shady dealings, and frankly, I hate shady shit. If you're going to be evil, you should at least be upfront about it.

Second Chance is not evil.

It sounded defensive this time. I wondered if that meant I could milk it for information. It wasn't procrastination, not at all.

I didn't say the program was evil. Why would you assume I'd implied that?

It hesitated. If I thought about it, the system had been doing that a lot lately. Like it had to choose its words more carefully around me. Although I didn't know how it operated in other people's heads. Maybe it always lagged. Just like video games that used the internet, or how video streams would sometimes pause and need to load a cache to catch up.

My mistake, then. With the comment of being upfront about evil, I assumed that you implied that. I'll adjust my literal understanding constraints.

Are there things you're not allowed to talk about? I feigned surprise, knowing full well that the whole thing kept way too much from me and others in the program.

Of course. The answer came immediately, without any hint of shame or subterfuge. *Each participant in each mission receives exact instructions as to what they must accomplish. No more and no less. Very little leeway is permitted, else the assignments needlessly endanger our operatives.*

I swallowed. Somehow it didn't seem to make me feel any better to know that Orion had been directed to kill. I frantically searched for something else to say, to extend the conversation. *Sort of like a need-to-know basis then.*

Of course. You are told what you need to know in order to complete the assigned task. It's not only for the program's protection, but for yours as well. We invest far too much time in all of our recruits to have them killed due to poor timing or an overactive sense of knowing better than the system.

There was a momentary pause, like it was letting me take a moment to digest all of the information it had just given me. Somewhere in all of those words was a warning that made my stomach try to double over in its knot tying.

Warning: Portent Ability strained.

Oh, for fuck's sake. What I needed was a way to shut off the damn notifications like I could in a video game.

I attempted to clear my head of any distracting thoughts and gather up my power so I could boost my speed enough to get to the grate undetected. I wasn't expecting the system to speak again, so I jumped when it did.

For what it's worth, I hope that you're with us for a long time. Your view of the program might assist us in bringing it into the twenty-first century. We've been lacking from a cohesion and motivational standpoint. Knowing what comes after the fear and uncertainty that besets most fresh operatives is a good thing.

You're not telling me I'm the only person who ever raised concerns about the way the system conducted business, are you? Because I find that damn difficult to believe.

No, I'm not. I'm telling you we haven't listened before.

A chill ran down my back, and it took all the strength I could muster not to ask it why they were listening now.

Twelve minutes seemed like a lifetime when I had to wait for the full window all over again. That the system was listening to me caused profound discomfort. If they were listening to my feedback, then were they paying super close attention to me?

If so, how were Nya and Shane going to spirit me away and teach me all the secret eel-jitsu I needed to know? I pushed that thought back. It would work; we would figure it out. We just plain had to. Forcing the thought only helped me calm down a fraction of what I needed. Midnight was approaching, and that fraction would have to do.

Finally, the patrol passed me again. Taking a deep breath, I allowed power to suffuse through my body, lighting up my adrenaline, lending me speed and accuracy. Like fuel flooding pistons, I could feel my ability to accelerate come alive. Alive like I was, like me, as if I'd never died.

Timestance activated.

Pushing off, I could feel the insane speed I reached, leaving me breathless. It took me but seconds to cross the entire distance, but in that strange Timestance way, it felt like I'd been floating through the air.

Timestance deactivated.

Crouching down at the grate, I breathed, appreciating the endurance I'd built through running and practice that allowed my heart rate to stay virtually the same. The bars on this basement entrance had no signs of rust, and was only marred by some splattered tree gunk and water stains left over from the rain.

In the interests of fire safety, the grate wasn't locked. I didn't need the tiny ladder attached to the side; I just jumped down lightly and closed the grate behind me as softly as I could.

Talk about cramped spaces. This one set me on edge, even more than I'd been while talking to my little brain friend. Two by three feet or something like that, and only six deep. It felt like a concrete, bar-lidded coffin.

I shook my head and told my imagination to get lost. It laughed at me. At least the system seemed to be right about the state of the window lock itself. How did this sort of shit happen constantly to important buildings? No maintenance budget, perhaps?

A tiny wire bridged the connection between the side of the window and the actual frame. It had to be connected, or the entire system wouldn't be armed, and I could, in fact, tell that it was.

Finesse still wasn't my strong suit, and neither was knowing what I was doing. But I pulled up the strangely comprehensive eel manual in my other mind. At some stage I'd have to stop jumping between them because my naming abilities were only so advanced.

Okay, so this one was important.

Fine Line Electrical Control

Current Skill: Rudimentary.

Origin: Developed due to mankind's advancements.

Use: Manipulation of delicate currents interfacing with electronics.

Guidelines: Some knowledge of electronics required. In order to avoid backfiring, do not rush these procedures.

Note: Feel the system out before handling the actual current. Make sure to:

1. Follow the current to its source.

2. Engage only when you understand how the system works.

3. Allow the current free flow once released.

4. Make sure the flow is adjusted accordingly.

5. Do not burn your surroundings to a crisp.

Sure. No pressure there. I sighed, hoping that I didn't have to roll a natural twenty. Perhaps this was something I should have learned earlier? My brain friend was oddly quiet, although I wasn't saying anything to it, so I couldn't really blame it. But it felt like the sort of moment in time that it should be trying to give me advice. Clearly, I was wrong.

Closing my eyes, I reached out with my ability. Electrical energy now appeared with a glowing blue undertone to it. I could trace the tiny charge that would trigger the alarm—should I open the window before disabling the system—all the way to its origin. Understanding that charge and how the system interpreted it was the difficulty. There appeared to be cameras hooked to this system too, which made complete sense, but made my task and how I targeted it far more complex.

The thing was, again, that the whole macro ability with electricity still wasn't my forte. My mouth went dry, and my hands felt like they would begin sweat like a torrential downpour any moment.

Calm it down. I breathed the words in and out, forcing myself to ignore the time as it passed, making sure that I went carefully and slowly. This wasn't the time for unnecessary risks.

Keeping my eyes closed, I ignited the tiniest spark of power on my left pointer finger. Toning down the current, I shifted it to match the frequency of what I could feel from the alarm system and placed my finger closer to where I'd need to expel said charge.

Holding my breath so I didn't move a muscle, I fervently hoped I wouldn't twitch. I released the charge.

Opening my eyes, I looked at the window. I couldn't sense a shift at all in the alarm center, nor could I hear sirens. But I could see that the wire I'd been aiming to disconnect was no longer live. It was deader than I'd ever been.

To say I breathed in a sigh of relief would be an understatement. I opened the window carefully, fully aware now that it had taken me all of eight minutes to get to where I was. Gingerly, I hopped down and into the room beyond the frosted basement window.

The room was dark and filled with shelves. Their silhouette showed me beaker upon beaker, and Bunsen burner upon burner. Protective goggles looped around every single post of the shelving, gloves and aprons, too. Storage rooms were so fun.

Remembering my last major break in, I glanced at the ground, but this room was clean. No dust to show my footprints. I guess in a lab people had to be more careful about dust interfering with and contaminating samples or whatever they did here.

Okay, so if I were a high-profile research facility, where would I put laboratory seven? Brown paper bag. I still couldn't help laughing at the audacity of this one. Maybe it was someone's lunch, and this was just one huge prank. I doubted it, but it was fun to think of it like that. Better than letting my imagination run wild with the potential start of the zombie virus theories that I know it wanted to bring up.

Laboratory seven is on level two.

That was disconcerting. How had it known to speak? *Thanks*, I said, just to make sure it knew I'd heard it. The timing was eerie and only served to heighten my already-over-the-top anxiety about this task. Maybe I'd grown too comfortable running with a team instead of alone.

Level two it was, then. Desk drawer, right hand side. Before leaving the good ole storage room, I pushed out my ability, trickles at a time, to see if I could sense any living things on this level. Aura sensing had to be worth something right?

Aura Detection Activation Complete.

Please direct your enquiry appropriately.

Current Skill: Rudimentary.

That's all I had to do to activate a skill? Considering people ran on electricity, I should technically be able to sense a person in my vicinity. Maybe I was getting too comic book logic about this all though. I wasn't even sure it would work, but it did find a few mice, locked in cages all together, and a few insects that I don't think were the subject of tests.

More people milled about the building than I'd anticipated, but if my positioning was correct, there were only a couple around the lab I needed to get to. Research labs and their fellows. All hours of coming and going.

There were, however, a lot of computers. Of course there were. Electrical energy shone off all of them. Tests being run through the night even without the manpower.

Hell, I wanted to let those little mice free but worried it might leave more of a footprint behind than was wise. The basement was clear, at least of human life forms. Thanks, brain.

I assume this is the basement level.

You'd assume correct.

I detected a hint of humor behind the statement. One day I'd figure out the voice in my head. Some days, like today, it seemed all over the place.

Just because I'd determined that only lab mice and insects were down here didn't make moving through it any less terrifying. If I got caught here, my scholarship was toast. If I got caught here, I'd probably give my mother a heart attack.

None of us needed that. I approached the stairs to the ground floor. Just a few more levels and I'd get to the bag. I'd be almost done. The cold of the steel railing sang through me, and I clenched my teeth.

After the shock wore off, I realized I heard footsteps. Which wasn't a good sign. Not good at all.

5
BROWN BAGS

Shit.

I could hear a walkie talkie going off and pulled myself out of the line of sight from the ground level just in time for the inner guard to walk past the opening at the top of the stairs. Talk about pure luck. I guess one of those people near the lab was the damned guard.

My breath caught in my throat, and I had to steady myself. No time like the present to reevaluate my afterlife.

The footsteps began to fade as the guard continued on. Those were the most excruciating ten minutes I'd ever spent. Because I had to wait and see just how long this guard's rounds took.

Are there guards on the other floors? I asked my not so helpful brain guide.

Ground and first floor should have a guard. Second and third will have one as well.

I took the information in, trying to map out the times in my head. *You realize that's pretty pertinent information, right? Like maybe something that should be included in future mission parameters.*

There was a pause before it spoke again. And when it did, there was genuine puzzlement to its tone. *This should have been included. I'm not sure why it wasn't.*

Didn't you *give me this mission? How could you not know why it wasn't included?* Irrational anger tried to grip a hold of me, and I knew the electricity was fueling it. It wanted out, wanted to destroy, just wanted to break free. Clamping down on it was the only way to push it down. For now. I needed more control techniques.

I apologize. It won't happen again.

It definitely seemed contrite, but that didn't make me feel any better. I took another deep breath and refocused myself as best I could. I was on a tight schedule. There'd be plenty of time to rant and yell later on.

This was how operatives died. David had died due to my not knowing how to use my abilities. Due to us not having the full information about the staff at the location. For a brief moment I couldn't help but wonder if that had been this mission's purpose. Surely, not, right? Wasn't my ability a rare one? But perhaps, because it didn't seem to be fully supported or understood, maybe they didn't like having operatives who they couldn't fully control after all.

Perhaps Orion had told someone about the partition.

As I waited for the guard, I swear I saw a flicker of a shadow out of the corner of my eye again, but as usual I couldn't look directly at it. It was probably just my imagination.

I needed my thoughts to stop wandering. Finally, the guard passed by, his flashlight swinging at his hip as he strolled along in the dim lighting with no sense of urgency. I pulsed electricity through my body and flashed up both sets of stairs and waited closer to the second level, scanning for the other guard now that I knew what to look for.

The sooner I got out of here, the sooner I'd have to deal with Orion again. My stupidly irritating brain reminded me of the thoughts I'd been avoiding.

Second level reached and my heart raced so fast I thought it might jump out of my chest. Labs seven through nine were on this level, and my destination stood right in front of me.

Glass walls gleamed in the low light. At the far end of the lab, I could see the supervisor's small office area and a very large desk. The supervisor sat at it, a gentle gleam of yellowed light reflecting off their glasses. Why didn't electrocution grant me invisibility, eh? I knew there'd be a supervisor, I just didn't envision having to dodge both them and the guard and retrieve the package without being seen.

The wandering guard was due to head my way shortly. Moving as quietly and quickly as I could, I slid through the corridor and into the lab through the secondary door on the far side.

Luckily, the lab benches ran all forty feet of the lab. Several of them, and if I crouched, there was no way anyone would see me. Luckily, they didn't have those reverse mirrors and I'd disabled the cameras on my way in.

Shadows sat with me, my only company. This time I could sense them next to me, see their fuzzy outlines in my peripheral vision, gone if I tried to swivel my head. Silent and solid in their contemplation, I really needed my mind to stop trying to trick me. Of course there were shadows; the bloody lighting was dim.

Think. I made myself focus on the task at hand and moved slowly across the floor to the other side of the lab bench. I could hear several of the experiments I passed whirring in their calculations as the servers worked on the information load. The whole sound was a bit unsettling, like a snoring bear.

When the timer went off, I nearly shat my pants. My heart jumped into my throat and threatened to choke me to death. The only saving grace was the soft sounds of movement coming from the supervisor's office. Trying to calm myself, I watched them through a crack in between two of the workstations. They exited their room with a clipboard in hand and walked to the desk closest to their office and began checking results and noting down whatever it was they had to note down.

If I timed this right and managed to be stealthy enough, I should be able to get into their office and then back out before they were finished with the front row and moved to the middle one where I was hiding. After a couple of quick time calculations in my head, I was mostly certain that my exit from the supervisor's office should just coincide with the guard already finishing up their patrol of this floor and heading down to the first.

Maybe.

You seem worried.

Yeah. No pressure here at all. I don't have to keep up appearances, which means maintaining my scholarship which would get taken away if I got caught here. I snapped the words and sort of regretted it, but in the end, I didn't have time to care.

I'd have to execute this pretty much exactly or else I was going to run into one or the other of the people I was trying to avoid.

That does seem like an oxymoron. I shall bring that to their attention.

Seriously? In the middle of all this? I sighed softly, not voicing my incredulous thoughts. There was too much at stake for me to bother with the rest of the conversation. I calmed myself before launching a dive roll into the office.

Misjudging just how much power I needed to fire through my system in order to make that roll as fast as I could was just the icing on the cake. How I stopped just before my foot went smashing through one of the filing cabinets, I'll never know. This assignment was getting chalked up to my second least favorite so far. Granted, it would have to get messy quickly if it wanted to take that first spot.

I was doing a lot of deep breathing. Too much. Settle. I told myself. Thing is, I rarely listen to my own advice.

The drawers on the desk opened slid open with a whisper. Lo and behold, there sat a nice crispy brown bag, just waiting for me to take it. As much as I wanted to reach in, grab it, and run, I didn't. First of all I looked it over. It was a plain brown bag, the sort you get to pop your sandwich lunch in so you can throw it out at school.

I scanned it briefly, making sure it didn't have any hidden wires or signs of electricity around or in it. But it didn't seem to be connected to an alarm or anything. It was, in fact, a plain brown paper bag. And this whole thing still felt entirely too sketchy. Reaching in, I pulled it out.

Nothing happened, just the soft sound of the paper being pressed in on itself. I handled it gently, and shoved it in the large zip up front pocket of my hoodie. I had no clue what I'd do in a few weeks when it was too hot to wear the damned thing.

Object obtained, I turned around to make sure the supervisor was still doing their lab results thing. As I did so, I realized I must have tweaked my ankle or something when I superhero rolled into the office. Damn. I hoped it wasn't serious, and I shot a spike of electricity into my system, willing it to speed up the healing process, to make it possible to escape and possible to complete this stupid mission.

It might just have been my imagination, but it felt a little better already. Supervisor Clipboard was still taking down notes half way along the middle row. With luck, I hoped to make it out in time.

I noticed the night supervisor didn't seem chuffed about what they were looking at. Perhaps the experiment went wrong. Maybe the building was about to explode. For once my overactive imagination was going to help me speed out to freedom.

Creeping out of the lab, I let the door fall closed behind me, softly checking that the tumbler fell into place.

I crept along the outside of lab seven again, letting the relief at being done wash over me. In hindsight, relaxing too soon can be dangerous. Lesson learned.

Suddenly, the guard turned the corner I'd just come from. I barely managed to get around the corner to the corridor of shadows between the two labs. Crouching there, I tried to control my breathing, but my heart wouldn't shut up. Shadows milled around me, part of my imagination, yet close enough to feel the hairs rise up on my arms.

His footsteps echoed across the floor with agonizing slowness, like death knocking at the door SC had closed in his face.

Counting to five, I opened my eyes and saw the guard finishing off the last steps to meet me. But there was no recognition in his eyes. It felt like he looked straight through me. The shadows touched me now, cool and wispy, not there yet somehow visible. Had they protected me or was it something else?

The guard's unexpected appearance shook me more than I liked to admit. His apparent inability to see me didn't help either. Him, the shadows around me, I knew deep down that wasn't my only problem right now. There was too much going on, so much it was starting to overwhelm me. Compartmentalizing was one thing, but this was getting difficult.

I made my way down into the basement without further interference or missteps, trying to reorganize my brain so it would prioritize some things over others. Like my own survival over Orion's apparent killing spree.

It wasn't until I was standing down there, finally allowing myself to breathe without scanning every inch of my surroundings that I realized what a mistake I'd made.

That I accepted I wasn't alone.

Can you see those? I asked my brain friend, but there was no answer, and for a moment I contemplated the fact that I might actually not be as mentally healthy as I'd previously thought.

Fine. It wasn't talking, but I knew I wasn't dreaming. Was I?

I could hear the sound of machines whirring; the electricity that fed them resounded through my entire body. Soft, lulling, with a slight buzz behind it. Far worse than the tests being calibrated back in the lab. The sound wormed its way into my head like a bee flew inside my ear.

Shivers flickered intermittently down my spine, and a cold sweat began in the small of my back.

Seeing them this time so close was a thousand times more terrifying than when I'd seen them several weeks ago. These weren't my friendly shadows in the wallpaper; these were mechanical. At first, they appeared just like they had back then, shadows with strange robotic or electrical elements to them. The occasional glimpse of steel and electronics through the strange blackness that enveloped them was enough to cement I wasn't hallucinating. There was something very off about them. Hurt my teeth sort of off, as if there was a decibel level they'd reached that I couldn't hear but that I could feel.

Then I realized some of what it was. It wasn't shadows that clung to them, not really, but more like a sort of molasses, tar mixture. It hung off them and made them appear like shadow impersonators in a dripping goo sort of way. They definitely weren't the ones who'd attacked me on the way home with my disgusting burger. Nor were they the shadows that had recently hidden me from the guard.

The other thing I noticed made my skin crawl so much I thought it was trying to jump off my body. They could smell me—or perhaps taste the odor on the air? And I didn't for one moment think these things were sensing my person. No, they could feel my power, and at the same time that aura reading thing that Nya had been so excited to tell me I had?

I could tell these things loved electricity. They devoured it, were built from it, and hungered for it constantly. Their forms leered at me, approaching me from two sides, and I could have kicked myself for not being more alert when I headed down to the basement. These things were loud, loud and dangerous, especially for me. I shuddered to think what might happen if one of them actually touched me.

But they weren't near the lab storage room I'd originally entered through. Not yet, anyway. Making sure not to make any sudden movements, I made my way to the door, like perhaps I hadn't realized the creatures were there.

That element of subterfuge seemed to amuse my would-be devourers. They trailed after me, but gained a step for every five I took. If I could just make it to the door, I should be okay, shouldn't I?

Hey. Are you there?

I tried it again, but there was still no answer. The absence of the voice threw me more than I liked to admit. It didn't feel like it usually did either. I thought I wasn't supposed to be alone in this afterlife thing. Right now, I'd never wanted to be surrounded by people so much. I'd never wanted my afterlife friend to speak to me so much.

Perhaps the frequency from these things interfered with however SC communicated with me. It'd make sense since I felt like they were hunting me.

Along with their appearance, I realized these robot-creatures also had a smell of their own. Something like burning wires and the dust that accumulates around a fan that's never been cleaned. It wasn't pleasant, but it wasn't something others would notice and think something was strange.

I reached for the doorhandle and turned it fast, boosting myself for all I was worth to make it through the door in a split second and slam it shut behind me.

Turning into a flash of speed took a lot of effort and power. Even as I gathered the power within me, I could see the robots begin to react. Violently, immediately, dangerously. They could sense my power building, taste it in whatever way they fed or needed it.

The more power built within me, the more their alertness climbed. Just before I reached the level I needed to push me at the speed I wanted, they went wild. One of them managed to snake a tendril of itself around my left ankle as I pushed myself to shoot through door. I stumbled and fell hard on one knee but made it through. Cold and metallic, the touch acted like a brief conduction wire, sucking at the power suffusing my body until I managed to forcefully swing the door shut, severing the tentacle like appendage. It twitched on the ground, trying to make it to me, and I could still feel its hunger, the life it wanted to take from me.

Outside the door, they clambered against it like they were trying to break it down. The way it heaved, I was positive it wouldn't take long. Not sure what else to do, I fired a hot shot of electricity into the tumbler of the door and melted it. Sure, the lab would need to call in a locksmith, but at least I'd bought me hopefully enough time to get out of here.

My energy was flagging precariously, somehow unable to refresh itself the way it usually did. I couldn't give into the fatigue I knew was building inside, because if I did, I'd never make it home. I wasn't a match for them, not in my current state, not until I figured out just how they'd managed to drain so much from me in so little time.

After sealing the room, I ran to the window, climbed out. I didn't care if someone saw me, and I didn't bother to control my speed as my desperation spurred me on. I didn't care if I drained all of my electricity as long as I got home. They'd picked on the wrong fucking zombie.

6
NOT A ZOMBIE

I practically flew home. And it took the voice until I was almost there to speak to me again. When it did, the surprise in its tone stopped me short. Quite literally stopped me, actually.

What are you doing? How did you get here so fast?

It sounded confused, like it had been in limbo for the last twenty minutes. Which, if I were to think about it, it probably had been. I just didn't know why.

Ideas began to form in my mind, and I realized I'd missed the perfect opportunity to look inside the bag I had stuffed up the front of my hoodie. What had they sent me to get that warranted so much danger, such a risk? Why did they require operatives who were technically on borrowed time to perform all of these tasks? I couldn't understand what it was the Second Chance Organization did. Cloak and daggers, shady descriptions, vague meanings and warnings…

Did they require the threat of termination in order to succeed in their agenda? What was that fucking agenda anyway?

Dare?

The voice pulled me out of my spiraling thoughts just as I shook my head to clear them myself.

Sorry. Tonight was a bit batshit.

How so? Did you get seen by a guard?

I barked the laugh out, heading toward my apartment home with slightly less urgency. *Sure, yeah. It had nothing to do with the swamp monster robots that were after me.*

There was a hesitation in my head. One that if I were to examine it closely wasn't there while I was in the basement of that damned building. So many more questions constantly sprouted up instead of answers, just like weeds.

I believe the reference is that you have been observing too many movies.

Was it…was it making a joke, or was it being serious? *Seriously?*

Yes. I don't believe I witnessed any such thing. There were three guards on the property and four overnight supervisors to keep all the data straight. Seven people in total and none of them robots.

It sounded very certain of itself. For just a moment, I sincerely doubted what I'd seen, doubted myself. But it didn't last long, because the feeling of dread I'd felt had been real, the revulsion and the fear.

Sure, I said, trying to fill the gap in time left by my thoughts going haywire. *That's what it was.*

Exactly. I must caution you, though. Using your abilities to get from the lab to this close to home in such a short time is inadvisable. This action must be flagged in case reports emerge.

I blinked. What the fuck? Since when did they do that?

It was okay. I didn't give it an answer, just focused on getting myself back home in one piece and disposing of this stupid paper bag in the process. *Letterbox drop?*

No. Give it to Orion. He'll get it to the proper authorities.

I blinked. Why was Orion my go-to person? I didn't want to be in the same vicinity as him right now. Had he already ratted me out about the partition thing? The only bright side in my grumbling thoughts was that at least I didn't have to take a detour.

The sooner Nya and Shane could get me out of this, the better. After all,

I didn't really have anything other than family to leave behind anymore. The sadness made my chest constrict. Shane still owed me an explanation about Orion, even if it wouldn't make a difference.

The house was quiet when I returned home, and the only light was the small one in the living room. It cast a golden haze over the area, the fixed television, and the raggedy furniture that managed to be so comfortable I couldn't ever see us replacing it.

Apart from the general electronics in the house, there didn't seem to be any other lifeforms in there. What an odd way for me to check. I could have just called out, but at the same time I realized it was such a waste of what I could do to not use those skills.

What else could I do?

As if in response to my question, a menu popped up for me. It wasn't the same as the more polished one outside of the restricted zone I'd added. In fact, it was very similar to the one that fed me the caution and warning messages that I believed to originate from something beyond the current SC system.

At best, the navigation was rudimentary and clunky. However, upon opening it, I realized it was filled with tenfold the information I'd been given access to so far. There were so many branches that it resembled my scar. Which took that exact moment to ache with a pulsing sensation, like it was saying "no shit."

The amount of weird happening to me…

"Dare?"

I froze. Orion had walked in behind me, and every fiber of my being wanted to run away and never come back. I could, you know. Run away. But as it was, the system would find me and kill me or something like that. Maybe they could just flick a switch and turn me off. I had no clue anymore.

"Are you okay?" He reached out involuntarily to touch my arm like he'd done a thousand times before, but I flinched.

I may as well have punched him in the face for the look of shock that crossed his expression. He couldn't touch me, though. Right now, I was feeling charged, and I wasn't sure how much damage I'd do even to a not a zombie. Plus, my feelings about him and what he could and would do were far too complicated to think I wouldn't react negatively.

"Sorry. I'm fine. I have to give you this." I reached into my pocket and pulled out the bag, placing it carefully on the table. Not that I'd thought about being careful previously. Probably a mistake on my part. If it had been a bomb, though, it would have blown up ages ago.

His eyes darted to the object I unloaded, and a firm scowl crossed his face briefly. Oh, how I wanted to know what that response meant. Shouldn't I be able to read minds if our brains ran on neurons and required electricity?

"Thanks." His words were crisp when he spoke, like the friendship portion of him had disappeared and been replaced by Mr. All Business. Hadn't I insisted on that though? I knew I'd been responsible for some of the distancing.

"I've just been waiting on this. Was expecting you sooner." A hint of disapproval crept in under his words. It grated against my nerves like a block of parmesan cheese. I wanted to bite the hell out of it.

But I didn't. He did outrank me, and I wasn't sure just how it would go down for a lower rank to get into an argument, virtual sparring match, or in this case probably minor case of electrocution…with a higher ranking operative.

So instead, I bit my tongue and forced a smile. "Sorry about that. My mission information lacked crucial details that would have led to me leaving a spot earlier. It's okay, though. That information has already been passed on."

I kept my tone as neutral and indifferent as I could, pushing back on the part of me that didn't want to do this. That just wanted to grab Orion, pop some popcorn, and sit and watch a movie like we used to. A ghost of concern flickered through his eyes when I spoke, but I couldn't let it distract my resolve.

Keeping that smile plastered on my face, I took a wide berth around him and headed to my room.

"Dare!" The note of anguish in Orion's voice almost undid me, and I paused in my surefooted steps, like a cry for help. It took all the willpower I possessed not to turn around and ask him what he wanted.

Warning: Portent Ability activated.

It crackled in my head, the electricity, the power, the ability to use it to alter time, to stop the flow, to kill, to heal, to be everywhere at once. All the futures, all the pasts, all the choices there ever were. Everything darted in different directions, some brighter, and some drenched in blood.

Words and feelings, sensations and conversations flooded my head so fast it sent me spinning. I was sure I wobbled, still standing there debating whether or not I should turn around. But I didn't. Holding strong, I gathered my tattered wits about me and took the next step.

I could practically feel him deflate behind me, feel his frustration and disappointment and a strange need to keep me by his side. While I might want to listen to him, while I might want to return to how we'd been, I wasn't about to give him the platform he needed.

Because now, I knew what he was going to say anyway.

Your assignment has been satisfactorily completed, including hand off to a superior operative. You have received monetary compensation and experience bonuses.

Congratulations, your rank has increased.

You have been moved from Rank J - Novice to Rank I - Apprentice.

Future assignments will be subjected to a 5% pay rise. You will receive further instruction. Your testing phase is complete.

Testing phase? What the hell? I threw myself down on my bed and channeled all my frustration through my body and to my fingertips, culminating in a torrent of electricity being funneled into the balls in my hands. Despite their ability to mute, despite their sturdier than store bought construction, they basically disintegrated.

Damned if I didn't need a better way to expel my excess energy.

What were these stupid ranks anyway? I flicked through my menus, but there was nothing in the older version that I could trace back to the names I'd previously heard. This system was expansive, massive, and decidedly tricky to navigate. The one thing the SC program had going for it was ease of use. Everyone could use it.

Finally, I found the ranking system located under advancement opportunities squirreled down a hole with training completion certificates.

Rank K - Junior
Rank J - Novice
Rank I - Apprentice
Rank H - Senior Apprentice
Rank G - Intermediate
Rank F - Associate
Rank E - Senior
Rank D - Expert
Rank C - Mentor
Rank B - Master
Rank A - Grand Master
Overseer

This hidden piece of information was a gold mine.
Designations of each type of skill as far as I could see.

Runner = Speed/Time Manipulation
Blocker = Decoy/Disguise/Protector
Driver = Spatial Manipulation through Earth
Cleaner = Manipulation of matter through elements
Minder = Mind reset abilities
Healer = Healing powers
Diviner = RARE - See a moment into the future
Enforcer = Assassin/Hit Man/Enforcer

My mind reeled with the information I should have had from the beginning that was hidden behind convoluted walls. I still didn't understand the correlation to the skills we were brought back with, but I figured if I'd found this, the other info would be there if I just kept digging this time. Hopefully.

There had to be more information on just what elements made up each designation, right?

Flickers of light kept irritating my eyes, and I refused to try and catch the shadows that liked to plague me in my room. Even if these ones weren't robots. Only, after a couple of minutes, I realized this wasn't my friendly neighborhood shadow men. This was a notification.

Oddly game-like. Different from the other system that just smacked anything it wanted me to know straight in front of my face. The fact that it didn't appear to understand that I didn't want it to do that was just icing on the cake.

No, this was an informative notification about my Portent ability.

Fascinating.

Portent Ability

Due to increased electricity activity firing through your brain, your brain cells have expanded. There are many abilities that lie dormant in the human brain, and this is one of them.

You are now capable of observing current situations, facts, and/or behavior and extrapolating potential outcomes from those things. This allows you to see the path and possibility for several different choices and the impact they will or could have on the future.

Be careful deliberately accessing this ability. While it appears to work well and fortuitously when dawning naturally, forcing it has previously resulted in dire and worse circumstances coming to pass.

The more this ability occurs, the subtler tones it will pay attention to, and the more dire situations may be avoided due to its evolution.

Wow. Okay. So I could see the future now? Except only involuntarily and with great caution. I mean, way to put a dampener on an otherwise amazing skill, but I understood it. Which was why I sometimes hated my logical brain.

Lots of mays, should, could, might. So basically, if I used it right, it might be a good thing. I wished I could share it with the voice in my head, or with my…with Orion. Right now, I couldn't even reach out to Shane and Nya.

This whole afterlife thing was starting to feel lonelier than my life had been. I couldn't trust Orion anymore, I barely knew the rebels as I fittingly decided to call them, and I couldn't trust the voice in my head.

I wasn't even sure if I could trust myself anymore.

Time passed in a blur for me. At least since Orion murdered that guy. I couldn't even tell what day it was next, except it was a week day, and I had track and field. It was time I told Coach Marth that I couldn't coach the kids from the inner-city schools anymore. Hell, I loved doing it, but with all the assignments they sent me on, the avoiding of Orion, and my own stress levels, I wasn't getting in nearly as much studying as I needed to.

Okay, well…as I wanted to. I wasn't in any danger of failing, but my grades had slipped somewhat. At least I wouldn't have to worry about pay. My bank balance was doing nicely, and any future assignments would be paid even better. I don't think they realized that even before this five percent increase, they were paying me more than I'd earned in life. Typical, really. Now I was dead, I was doing really well for myself.

"You're doing it again, you know?" Neale startled me out of my calculations as he plopped his backpack down.

"Doing what?" I asked, trying to keep my shock down a level. I hadn't heard him walk up to me. Almost like he'd just appeared out of nowhere. Paranoia was coming to get me.

Neale grinned. "You're wearing your thoughts and concentration on your face. Careful. You'll get a worry line right in between your eyebrows." He flicked his finger lightly at the would be crease between my brows.

The gesture was a new one from him, and I laughed, not really thinking anything of it. The tension eased out of my shoulders slightly as Cyan bounced into the chair next to me. Over the last week my friends had been amazingly accommodating. They'd never even once questioned what was wrong between Orion and I. It was something I appreciated more than I think they realized.

I didn't even want to think what this would have been like if it had happened a year earlier, where Orion and I were still in multiple classes together because of the first two years of like every degree. But Cyan and Neale always kept me company anyway. I think I was lucky to have rounded up such a good slew of friends. They were genuine people, each with their very own flaws, as I was with mine.

As Orion was with his.

I frowned, while trying desperately not to do so on the outside. Was that his flaw? He couldn't say no? Nope. That didn't fit in with everything else I knew about him. It was wishful thinking at best. Perhaps death had changed him, though.

Tomorrow night was our Friday get together. If I didn't find out anything this evening, then I would probably find out tomorrow. As long as I didn't get sent on some random case.

Did you not want an assignment tomorrow night?

The voice startled me, because I'd been so sure I was talking to myself. I had to be more careful about that. *If I say that, you're just going to wake me up with an alarm and tell me I have one anyway. Let's just say I'm fine with whatever comes.*

The voice sounded reproachful when it replied. *I didn't mean to do that. I really did try to get you that night off.*

I relented. *I know. I'm just teasing you.* I knew that voice wasn't my enemy.

A few moments passed and I jotted down more notes, watching Cyan and Neale do the same.

You are really taking the killing portion of the previous assignment to heart, aren't you?

I froze. Damn it. I'd even thought about that in its context with Orion while I wasn't in my own headspace. Well, no time like diving into ice cold water. *Yeah, I did. I really did. He's changed, and I hadn't realized it.*

Killing is just part of the job. It can be necessary to insure protection.

I shuddered at the calculated part of my mind delivering me such information. *Well, it shouldn't be.*

I couldn't think of anything else to say. Not killing another person was a basic human tenet. If we didn't adhere to that, what sort of monsters did that make us?

7
RUNNER

Friday night, I arrived home with a couple of bags of snacks. I'm not sure where they all ended up going to. I knew I wouldn't eat more than a few bites of summer sausage and some crackers. Gotta keep those protein levels up. I'd told Cyan to let Sam know I was getting the treats this week. She'd raised an eyebrow but otherwise hadn't commented.

I was grateful for that. Chopping up cheese and sausage was somewhat therapeutic. Cutting things, destroying things—it really gave me an outlet for all the nervous energy that now constantly lived in my body. Restraining myself enough so as not to prepare a full-blown meal had been difficult.

Orion wasn't home yet, but I half expected him to pass on the night's activities. He hadn't really tried to talk to me again yet. Did I even want him to? What I did want was for him to apologize and say it would never happen again. But the point was that it had already happened, not only in front of me, but probably more times than he could count. Before I even got there, before I even knew about the program.

What if the program had deliberately recruited me for some reason? I mean, after all, two other people involved directly in my life were in there.

Coincidences were never really just that.

The thought hit me in the chest, knocking the wind out of me for a moment. Okay, so not the wind, but I did forget to breathe briefly, so it was the same thing.

"Summer sausage and cheese. Going all out." Orion's comment felt just sarcastic enough to be friendly, and the words almost made me shriek out loud. I hadn't been expecting him.

Fat load of good this portent ability was doing me right now. Didn't it know I wasn't ready to deal with this shit yet? At least I didn't need to worry about that train of thought. There was no way it wasn't going to come back and haunt me.

"Yeah. I'm on snack duty." I think I detected a tremor in my voice, despite my best efforts not to let my emotions show. Breathing out a sigh, I returned to concentrating on the task at hand.

"Look." I could see him run a hand through his hair in my peripheral vision, but I kept up my task for all I was worth.

"I realize you don't want to talk. Maybe it's hard for you to accept, perhaps it's not something I should be doing…"

"Oh sure, murder is only something you should maybe not do, a might-want-to-stop-building-it-into-your-schedule sort of thing." Heated sarcasm poured from me. I couldn't let that pass.

"For fuck's sake, Dare. Let me say my piece before you hellfire me." He paused, taking a visible calming breath.

I stayed my tongue, barely.

"The system has reasons that make more sense the higher rank you attain, and it has its finger on the off switch. It can be flicked at any time, and even if I'm not saving the lives I wanted to right now, not in the way I wanted to, anyway—in the end, I will be." His body was rigid, like I could try to push him over and he'd just bounce back like one of those bottom weighted boxing bags. He didn't make eye contact with me either.

I took in the words while he stood there, mulled them over in my head again this way and that. No matter how I looked at it, I still felt like he had made the choice himself. Consciously.

"How did it happen?" I asked softly, methodically placing the cheese around the platter, focusing on a strict geometric design to calm my mind.

"Happen?" He seemed confused, and I let out another sigh.

"How did you figure out that you could kill so easily? And I'm not just talking about your attitude, I mean the way you do it." The words tried to stick in my throat like caramel popcorn.

"Oh." For a moment I didn't think he was going to answer because his shoes appeared to be far more interesting than my question. "I was bored. Playing around with the dishwater, actually, in the sink. Just after my secondary element developed enough to use. Making ice is so much fun. I started spearing the sponge, and of course, since it sees everything I see and hears everything I think…"

He shrugged, like it was all a big mistake but okay. Like it wasn't such a big deal. Though I couldn't ignore the sadness in his eyes. He seemed genuinely regretful, but resigned. Such a tough combo.

"I didn't really figure it out at all. I was just mucking about with the water. It was never my intention…" His voice faded away again.

"I can't forgive you, and I can't forget. Not for this. It's too much, Ri." I spoke the words softly as I put the finishing touches on my geometrically designed snack plate and walked it to the fridge, deliberately avoiding his gaze.

"The you that was, who became my friend, who has been through so much with me—it's not there anymore, and I'm having trouble dealing with that." Keeping the words soft was paramount to getting them out. If I didn't concentrate on it, I was going to scream.

And my body knew it, which was unfortunate, because I was barely holding the tray as it was. My fingers sparked as I opened the fridge, and I was grateful for managing to get it in there without blowing the appliance up.

Finally, I turned around and faced him. His eyes were sunken, like he hadn't slept in nights. My heart lurched a bit, feeling the pain he emitted. This aura shit was no joke, and I didn't think I liked it after all. It was hard to stay mad at him, hard to not see him as the friend I'd always known when I could feel the edge of despair he was balanced on.

"Does it always effect you like this, or are you not sleeping because I'm angry at you?" There, I asked one of the difficult ones.

"A bit of both. It always affects me like this, and well, I mean." For a moment he sounded exasperated. "Your being upset with me makes it ten times worse. I'm already doing something I hate, and your disapproval? How would you feel if I were pissed off at you for something you had no control over?"

He ended on a soft tone. There was no one else in the house, so I wasn't sure why he was being so careful, but I understood the need to keep calm and quiet or else risk me losing my tenuous control.

I looked at him, really examined him. Neither of us needed to mention that he did have control. We both knew it, but only one of us was ignoring it. Casting my mind back, I remembered several times over the last two years where he'd seemed extra tired, and somewhat down. But I'd always chalked it up to him overstudying or else stressing about his schoolwork or some family matter.

The most shocking thing to me, though, was that I wanted to forgive him. I wanted to say I understood even if I didn't, because I missed him and I missed us. Life without my best friend wasn't an option I'd ever thought about, especially not my afterlife. And it had only been a few days.

"I wish I could say don't do it again." I whispered.

"I wish I could say I wouldn't." His voice cracked, but it wasn't because he didn't mean what he said. It was because of the pain I could see him going through. Inside, I realized, he was breaking and desperately trying to plug up the hole.

If he wasn't careful, the whole dam would come crashing down. An unwilling serial killer. This program had a lot to pay for. And I had a lot of work to do to figure out just what it was I could do to accomplish that.

When the doorbell finally rang, Cyan and Sam were the first to arrive. They nodded at me and walked in with drinks and their own sugared snacks. Damned if my mouth didn't water, but I had to limit my self-indulgence with my next competition coming up. Even if my mood left me really wanting something sweet. Instead, I reached out and grabbed myself some summer sausage. Surely, I could take my irritation out on it instead.

I didn't even have time to talk to them before Neale and Levi arrived. Six bodies crammed into our small living space. If I concentrated, I could smell the sweat that beginning of summer made crystalize on our skin.

That and the breeze created by the overhead fan left the whole area feeling alive, with the buzz of energy thrumming. It was our space. I watched them all, chatting, laughing. Even Cyan and Orion. The way they stood together, both with their blue-eyed goodness. What a couple they would make, even if it made my stomach cramp with envy. But Cyan deserved better than a murderer.

Sam, however, was watching the same thing I was. And Sam was nosy even on a good day, able to pick up on things I didn't realize I was broadcasting.

She elbowed me in the side and raised an eyebrow in Orion's direction. "You two okay?" And her words were laden with triple meanings because she knew. Of course, she knew. Even if she hadn't been there, the grapevine always existed in a workplace even if it wasn't supposed to.

"We're fine even if none of this is as I expected." My words felt stiff, and I could feel a headache coming on. I wasn't used to dealing with this much drama on a daily basis. Family drama had never come close to whatever this was. Davin and I got along swimmingly. Sure, we had spats, but…that was all Orion and I had had up until now.

Sam just stood there, sipping on her drink and watching me with knowing eyes like she was waiting for me to say more.

"Fine. I'm not okay with this, and I don't want to be okay with it. But…" I shrugged as my mind flailed how to express myself. Glancing around the room I saw the other four gathered together as Cyan regaled them with something spectacular. Not that I knew what it was, just that her stories usually were.

Sam nodded at me, her face serious for once. "Of course you're not. It's like being friends with a serial killer who is sort of sanctioned, but sort of not, and who has untraceable killing power."

I cringed. Yeah, that about summed it up. Serial killers were notorious, which meant my best friend was notorious now. Though it was likely he'd never be looked for, it was still a stark reminder that normal rules didn't apply to us anymore. That we could kill and get away with it. Maybe that was what bothered me most.

If I was thinking in that direction, then how about the unsolved murders around Philly? After all, there was a high level of drug dealers and other *shady* people that weren't always top priority for crime solving units. How many of those were actually SC related?

"I won't be able to do what he did." I said it quietly, because maybe I'd been more concerned about myself than I realized. "There's no way I can bring myself to do that. Not even if you show me a record of my target being a pedophile or murderer. Sure, hurt them, maybe, but not kill. I just don't think I have the right to be anyone else's executioner."

Sam's brows creased thoughtfully and she shrugged. "That's your choice then, hon. Not everyone chooses to live, and to be honest, I've often wondered if there are some of our operatives who revel in that kind of thing. Surely, they had a fine line to tread with their choices for the program, right?"

The others were about done with Cyan's story. Laughter floated over to us, cushioning Sam's next words to me.

"When it comes down to it—if it comes down to it for you—that's when you make your choice. You either kill someone in order to prevent potential disaster in a specific way, or they get rid of you and any good you could have contributed with your power." She sipped the last bit in her cup, making that horrible straw sapping noise. "Ultimately, they give you a second chance at life, but it's your last chance to live. They're not going to dangle it in front of you again. You choose to go against their orders, and it's pretty much a re-death sentence, but if you look at it that way, you were already supposed to be dead anyway."

Her smile held pity for me, but as the others made their way over to me, I don't think they noticed.

Sam was right. Ultimately it might come down to just how much I was willing to sacrifice and what good I might do in the future. I couldn't let that sort of thinking influence me now, but I definitely needed to talk to Orion about it more, even if only to understand how that part of the system worked.

It was close to midnight before the others left. Maybe we were getting older or else just less prone to partying. But everyone helped pick up and put things in the kitchen and rubbish where they belonged before leaving.

Sam, surprisingly, had leaned in to hug me, despite the fact that everyone knew how much I wasn't fond of it. But that was just it, lately. Lately I'd been going through a lot. Knowing that my friends were there was priceless.

"Can we talk?" I asked Orion quietly as we finished washing the last dish. Twelve-thirty in the morning. The night air still carried a slight chill, but it was getting better. I couldn't wait for it to warm up faster in the mornings, though I knew I'd regret running after ten.

The hope on Orion's face when he looked up at me almost broke my heart. He nodded, like he was too emotional to get the words out.

I figured the living area was a nice neutral place to talk, so I grabbed a can of guava juice and sat down on my usual chair. He joined me a moment later but didn't settle into the sofa. Instead, he sat forward with his knees almost at a ninety-degree angle, his hands clasped between them. I could see the tension in his shoulders, and he cleared his throat.

"I'm sorry I didn't come clean sooner, and I want to make it up to you. Tell me what I can do. Tell me what I *need* to do." The desperation in his voice had a keening undertone to it, and for just a moment, I wasn't sure what to say.

"Look, I get it, but I also don't." I took a deep breath and barreled on before he could interrupt or say anything else. "I don't approve, and I don't think I would do the same in your shoes, but I also don't know your exact consequences, nor am I aware of how they handled your awakening. So I'm just going to leave this there. Talk to me, don't avoid me. But I'm just not quite willing to let this go yet."

"Okay." He sounded a little puzzled. Like he'd been expecting more of a lecture or perhaps more conditions. "I really am sorry you had to see it like that. I should have told you. I owe you that much."

"Yeah. I think that might have been a solid idea. That whole informing me before the fact thing." I managed to get a small smile out of him. Which would just have to be enough for now. "I'm not sure how comfortable I'll be, though. So let's just take some baby steps, okay?"

He nodded, and his relief was palpable. I guess I could sympathize with that, since I felt the same. Fifteen years of friendship hadn't quite made it down the drain. Now all I needed to do was pick past the gunky build up the program was leaving behind and hope it hadn't rotted my best friend beyond repair.

8
AS IT SEEMS

Saturdays were always a little odd for me. There was no huge impetus to get up early because our track training wasn't held later than during the week. I wasn't entirely sure why that mattered, but it did. Still, I managed to wake up after a slight sleep in and basically didn't feel like shit.

My head was a little sore, but I knew I drank that sugary drink too close to bed and needed a good dose of water. I mean, who didn't, right?

The house was quiet when I got to the kitchen, almost too quiet. I frowned and checked to see if Jacob was home, but he didn't appear to be, which would explain a lot since at this time of the morning he was usually making breakfast. Must have been a pretty hefty night at work. Orion's shoes weren't at the front door, which wasn't always a strange occurrence. Sometimes he didn't take them off until he got to his room, but I could remember his being there last night when we said good-bye to everyone.

The things my brain remembered.

My jog couldn't wait though. Sleeping in until just after seven had been heaven for me, but if I didn't make it to the track soon and see Coach Marth, he was probably going to kill me. I knew I hadn't been at my best all week, so he would be concerned. It was just the sort of guy he was behind that rough exterior. If there was always one thing I could be certain of, it was where I stood with my coach. He always told it like it was, whether the person he was talking to liked it or not.

What I didn't expect to happen while I was training was for Orion to appear at the field's edge. I frowned, and tried to turn my attention back to my training, but it was difficult. And I could see Coach getting irritated by Orion standing there distracting me.

He waved us both over, a semi-scowl on his face. "Look. I'm old, but I'm not stupid and I know something is up and bothering you both, and thus it's bothering me. Figure it out. And stop coming to gawk at Dare's training. You're distracting Dare, and I won't have my athlete distracted. Do you copy?"

Orion nodded. "Sorry. Something came up at the house. I'll try not to let it happen again."

"Damn right, you will." Coach Marth was in a gruff mood, and I hoped he was okay. "Both of you go away. Dare, you have two weeks left. Buck it up. Your training has been lacking."

With that comment, he turned and left. I watched him go, somewhat perplexed. Had I really been that bad? I knew I'd stopped feeding my own energy supplies as much since training with Shane. Control had been paramount in my mind. Stopping my mood from souring so much that I began yelling at Orion took a humungous effort. I changed quickly, pulling my jacket over my arms and glared at him.

"What?" he asked, snapping a bit.

"What are you doing here?" It was training. He never came and watched my training. Not even when we were one hundred percent hunky dory, not angry with each other, laughing-and-playing-jokes best friends.

He looked a bit sheepish, his eyes downcast as he kicked at the sanded floor outside of the track. "I don't know, I just...I had trouble sleeping, and I wanted to see you."

That sounded odd, even coming from him. "Why?"

He glanced around, like he was trying to check and see if anyone was listening. All he had to do was ask me. I could have told him no one was there.

Heartbeats give off electricity, auras, and general presence in the world. I was slowly coming to realize just how much innate electricity powered things—things other than microwaves and televisions. And now I was grateful for that knowledge. Perhaps also a little scared by it.

"Can you...does that partition thing you do weaken with time?" He asked me the question, his eyes darting here and there. But even with that rapid movement I could see how nervous he was to ask it. Which made the answer I had to give feel even worse than it already did.

I shrugged. "I'm not sure. I can't really figure out how I did it in the first place. Does it really work for you?"

The words sank to the bottom of my stomach like lead trying to poison me. I already felt nauseated because clever me forgot to eat before leaving the house. But the hope in his face, the light...it faded and disappeared with my words, and now all I could think was that these rebels were wrong. We should be sharing this. We should be rescuing all our fellow SC members. None of us chose this, and none of us truly loved the work we were forced to do.

All I wanted right then was to tell Orion I was joking. But a small part of my mind whispered things I wouldn't usually have thought about. It asked me if Orion was good at acting, did I remember those times he'd fooled his parents into letting him stay home sick when he wasn't? And then he'd come over and brought video games to cheer me up because I was, in fact, sick.

Yeah, sure, I'd remembered that. How could I forget it? How could I forget anything about our friendship?

For a brief second, I could see him in front of me, superimposed over a slightly younger him with wet hair plastered to his alabaster face. A face so pale he looked like a corpse. But the image was gone so fast, I wasn't sure what had happened. My portent ability remained stubbornly silent so I was pretty sure I wasn't having a future ability seeing.

Orion's own expression wasn't shocked, but sad, and the tone in his voice broke my heart. "Oh. I was hoping. It's just been nice having somewhere I can actually think and be me, without having to...never mind. I'm pretty sure the barrier is deteriorating. The window for the amount of time I can think by myself has become almost unusably small. Thanks anyway, Dare."

His wan smile almost undid me.

But I managed to stand firm and keep at it. "I'm sorry."

And I could put all the feelings I had behind those words because I truly was sorry.

Orion did his best to smile back at me and grinned like I remembered. "It's all good. I've put up with it for two years already. All I have to do is not think too much and I'll be perfectly fine again."

Except I knew he wouldn't. Ever since I'd become a part of the program, his personality had undergone a change. Even if he didn't notice it himself, I did. Because he'd somehow lost the hope he'd always had. Perhaps with me not being in the program, he'd seen me as his one normal lifeline, as the mask he'd had to maintain. And if he'd had those thoughts, then perhaps the system had chosen to make those disappear by including me.

Suddenly the pieces of the puzzle slammed into place. Was I targeted because they needed an eel? Sure, probably. But it seemed far more probable to me that they'd targeted me because it was a way to control Orion. Maybe. Or was I just conspiracy theorizing.

"I'll work on it. I'll see if I can remember how to do it. Seriously, I need to not be so tired when I try new things." The words rushed out of me before I could stop them.

"Really?" His face lit up with so much relief that the slight foot in my mouth I'd just committed seemed totally worth it.

Unable to push out the words, I just nodded. That was another thing I was going to have to talk to Nya and Shane about. But I'd have to see them first. Orion and I walked home in silence, and I couldn't believe how much difference my comment or promise had made to his aura. Perhaps he wasn't doing what he'd done because he wanted to. The more I observed, the more I watched, the more it seemed entirely likely that SC was breaking my best friend. I didn't take kindly to that.

It only made me more determined to figure out just what it was that stupid system was up to and either repair it or take it down so it couldn't do that to anyone ever again.

Home was where my ramen was, and by the time I got home, I was starving. Orion peeled off, collapsing onto his bed as soon as he got into his room, and I smiled, feeling some semblance of normalcy return to our friendship. One of us always protected the other. Perhaps he had been doing some of that while I was oblivious to his predicament. I had no idea.

It was nice to see him relaxing, although I knew his barrier wouldn't last for long. One week since the operation that showed me my best friend was a killer, and I'd almost forgiven him. Wasn't it duress or something when you were forced to do something criminal that could result in your or someone else's deaths otherwise? I wasn't the lawyer, but I was pretty sure it worked that way.

Assignment Notification.

Location: Ranlan's Research and Technologies

Objective: This is a close quarters group assignment consisting of:

1 x Runner

1 x Blocker

1x Minder

Your Minder will have more information. Please abide by ranking and SC protocols. Minder is tasked with Delivery. Highly confidential mission. Cannot be discussed outside this direct group of people.

Meeting time: 7 p.m., at the corner of North 3rd and Poplar.

Time Limit: By midnight tonight.

Reward: Dependent on the mission's success.

Caution: Guard patrols and any on site night shift workers.

Well, that was oddly specific in a very strange way. There was no Cleaner, which was Orion's job, which meant he wouldn't be coming on this with me. A feeling of worry washed over me. After all, so far, all of my bigger group missions had included Orion as the Cleaner. Perhaps they didn't expect this one to be messy, but then why would they send a Minder? I mean, wasn't their entire reason for existing so that they could wipe minds and make sure that no one would remember ever having seen us?

I sighed. This only made me wish I could see Nya and Shane five minutes ago. The questions were beginning to crowd my brain leaving little to no room for my silent brooding. After all, as much as I knew eels had their reasons, being able to quasi teleport into a place would save so much on manpower. Also help with my laziness. I guess it meant I didn't get to curl up with popcorn on the couch and just do nothing but think tonight. Excellent. I peeked in at Orion on my way to the kitchen. He was sound asleep, oblivious to my dilemma. And he had to remain that way. Poor guy hadn't slept well in days.

Ramen cup in hand, I boiled the kettle, staring out the narrow window at the city beyond while it did its boiling thing. The view wasn't spectacular or anything, but I could see a part of the city skyline. Sort of. Everything looked different now, even though outwardly all the buildings were the same. Single bricks with small stains on them lent such an appearance of age when put all together.

What would people think if they realized there was this whole version of life after death no one had thought about? How many people out there were so much older than they appeared to be simply because SC allowed us to appear as if we weren't aging as fast? Or was that simply the individual's choice? Wouldn't that mess up that whole maintaining your life thing? What did it do that it could stop or repair death?

Why couldn't it fucking cure cancer? The amount of lives lost to that bastard was astounding. I couldn't help but feel that if this sort of technology existed, then couldn't it do more than just interrupt someone's death and reactivate them or reanimate them? An idea occurred to me. Something that would be so very Orion and probably explain a lot of what he was putting himself through.

Maybe Orion was waiting to see how he could adapt what gifts he'd received to the world of modern medicine. After all, he'd always wanted to be a doctor and had lost his mom to the damned big C. The more I thought about it, the more I realized that was likely at least one of his driving forces. The other was probably access to more advanced technology.

And while I'd been contemplating the fate of my best friend, my water had stopped its bubbling and begun the journey back to being tepid. I sighed and tried to choke down the ridiculous amount of questions I had and put the kettle back on.

I was definitely getting more confident at catching small metal tubes of death since dying. It had never occurred to me before just how dangerous those things could be. Potentially, with the amount of electricity engaged inside of the vehicles and powering the vehicles themselves.., trams and subways and I were just not the best matched transportation methods in history.

It wasn't viable to own a car where we lived. Everything was within walking distance, or jogging for me. Hell, public transport was everywhere. All the trains and buses you could catch. It made life a bit fitter and definitely cheaper, because cars were expensive to maintain. If you tried to factor in parking in or even around the city, you'd probably have to sell a kidney, and then only if you could find somewhere to put your vehicle. Pile on the insurance, registration, and even with the kind of money SC was now giving me, I wouldn't have wanted to afford it.

I could feel the sweat starting to settle in the small of my back as I pushed onto the meeting place on N. 3rd just north of Poplar. There was a bench in an old wooden gazebo underneath tall trees in the tiny park. The perfect place to take a seat and wait for my fellow mission carry-outers.

Me and my fantastic vocabulary. I pulled out my phone and began to flip through to some running wear sites. What I needed was breathable mesh outfits. Ones that could channel my sweat and allow me to remain relatively cool. I cringed at the prices but remembered these were for work and my new source of income, which begged the question of taxes that I wasn't ready to deal with. I still needed to be incognito, avoid any and every one that might be able to follow me.

My balance was healthy enough. There were thousands of dollars in there now because I'd spent as little as I needed to. Apart from some snacks and a couple of items like the microwave, I hadn't spent any of it. It just sat in there, getting bigger and bigger every time I completed a mission. It was difficult to keep my train of thought from running to the IRS. How was I supposed to explain an income of this magnitude? Would they send me a W2? Apparently, since Orion seemed fine financially, it wasn't a problem.

"Runner?"

Sam's voice surprised me. She must be the Minder coming with us on our little spree. I liked working with Sam, and I liked knowing someone on our team. At the same time, I didn't like it, though. There was too much risk. What if I did something stupid while trying to help her in a situation I might not otherwise have helped her in? What if we disagreed on elements of the task at hand? After all, they didn't exactly know my skills in detail, which was sort of my fault, and the fault of the eels who'd tried to break free, and of the system for not maintaining their original information. I wonder if they saw the irony there. Breaking free while still being held to be accountable to an archaic system was just the opposite of being free.

"Hi there, Minder."

She grinned at me, eyeing her watch. "You're early."

"Yeah." I wondered what to say. Should I tell her the actual reason, or just leave it at that. "Didn't want to mistime a tram and end up being late. The punishments they dish out are no joke."

Sam smiled tightly, like she understood exactly where I was coming from, and I had a horrible feeling that she did. She seemed to have an abundance of abilities that I couldn't quite put into words. Being able to wipe minds wasn't something I wanted the responsibility for. And how did she do that if she couldn't harness electricity? All the damn questions just kept mating like bunnies. What other skillset could she have that would allow her to adjust something in the brain?

Water washed over my face, stinging my eyes with salt. My vision blurred. Orion stood up, and I suddenly felt nauseated.

I shook my head, like I was trying to get water out of my ears. Maybe I wasn't getting enough sleep lately. These weird memories that weren't mine were beginning to wear on me.

"How are you two doing?" Sam asked the question tightly, scanning the streets in either direction from the corner, probably to see if our Driver was going to make it on time. We still had twenty minutes to wait and I guess it was up to me how boring that got.

"We're okay. You know, at least as good as can be expected." I leaned forward, mirroring the way Orion had leaned on his knees when speaking to me. Sam nodded.

"It can make and break friendships. I was worried about him when you first got flagged and joined. He seemed so happy but at the same time devastated. You two have been through a lot, and there's no reason to let this affect it. You know, except the occasional killing part."

She said it so matter-of-factly that I cringed. It wasn't what I'd had in mind after all. What I'd been thinking was more of that the system was forcing him to do something against his will because a voice in his head told him that if he didn't do it, he was going to die. Most people would choose self-preservation. Most people would probably include me.

For the first time, I didn't really want to be most people.

I flexed my fingers where they gripped the bench, and flaking green paint came off on them. "I'm not fond of the killing anyone part. It's not something I volunteered and signed up for, and the duress we're under to do what they say sits about as well."

I didn't actually care that they could hear me, that anyone could hear me.

"I just hope it's not a decision I'll have to make, because if I do, the odds are I won't be able to go through with it. I might like living, but so might the person who I take out." I laughed, not feeling humor at all. "Actually, most people I've met do love to be alive, or at least like it slightly."

I grinned at Sam, trying to take the edge off my words.

She smiled tightly, and then we heard footsteps and the conversation ceased. A woman, probably slightly older than I was, approached us. Her hair was a disheveled mop of dark brown curls, and when she smiled at us in greeting, she had deep dimples on either side of her face.

"Sorry, am I late? I try so hard not to be." Her manner was easy going and immediately disarming. I'd have to watch it around her, because I didn't think that was all-natural exuberance.

"I'm...oh wait. I'm the Driver." She put her hand to her mouth and giggled. Like she'd never been on a mission before.

Sam and I exchanged a brief glance. This was going to be entertaining, and I wasn't at all sure it'd be in a good way.

73

9
TECHNOLOGY

Sam cleared her throat as the mission time approached, and I could feel as waves of heightened tension began to surround her. I got the distinct impression she didn't like this assignment. I wished I could sit her down and talk to her and find out why.

The thought occurred to me that perhaps I could activate Aura Detection myself. So I focused my attention on her every move, breath, and the air that surrounded her. It was tricky to activate the other system in my mind without having it spill over past my barrier.

Aura Detection Activated.

Caution: Prolonged use may cause hallucinations.

Great. So glad about that. Sam was definitely worried. The strange combat green that shimmered around her spoke volumes. But all I could see was how she felt, not why. I shut it down, slightly disappointed in what I'd thought would be a really cool ability. Maybe I needed to use it more to get better at it. Although perhaps it could be used as a truth detection spell.

"We have a couple of objectives in here. Getting inside is where you come in—" Sam nodded at the Driver, who grinned again like she should be anywhere but about to break into some large compound. Sam continued. "We need you to give us as much cover as you can. Once we're inside, we'll still require shading and movement concealers. So, make sure you have enough juice left."

The smile faded from the Driver's face, and I could see her personality almost click over to going serious mode. Those modes were night and day, and I couldn't get a read on her aura at all. It fluctuated and pulsed, held tightly against her body so the colors were difficult to define. There was far more to her than met the eye, and I wasn't sure that was a good thing. But I couldn't contend with major doubts right now. I had to concentrate.

"Once we reach the entrance, it's your turn, Runner. You'll need to subvert the alarm and tie off any loose ends. Then, once inside the developmental quarters, we need you to access the terminals and find their main database. Once we access that console, you need to target the specified files. I expect you to be able to do that while I keep a watch and the Driver covers us. Do you understand?"

"No. What do you mean? You want me to hack into it? Or something like that? I'm not a hacker. I have no idea how I'm supposed to access anything you've asked me to do." Better to say it out loud than to have them think I knew what I was doing and therefore fail abysmally. So far, to be perfectly honest, I'd just been winging it.

"What?" Sam seemed genuinely surprised by my outburst.

"Electricity doesn't automatically make me able to speak to machines and ask one to give me some codes, formulas, or their latest technology." Maybe I could have been nicer but I was so over it. If this was how shoddily they ran things, no wonder the eels fled. "Sure, I know about computer code, but I have no idea what fail-safes and security measures they've taken. I can try, but don't expect miracles."

Maybe I'd been a little more heated than I should have been, but they didn't seem to have any idea at all how this worked. Neither did I, but I did know how computers worked from a non-injected with electricity standpoint.

Sam seemed uncertain, but she pushed ahead. "Look, these are my orders, which basically means we have to figure this shit out. I just need to know you're with me in that regard."

You don't have anything to say? I added hotly to my little friend in my head. But the voice didn't say anything, though I swore I could feel its presence.

So I sighed and then nodded at Sam, fully aware of the strange way the Driver was watching me. Like she could see into my soul and find my actual reasoning for saying things, perhaps even motivations I wasn't aware of myself. It wasn't unlike feeling like livestock, uncomfortable and itchy. Curiouser and curiouser.

Moving out, I could feel the difference from one step to the next when the Driver's abilities activated. One moment it was twilight, and the soft reds and oranges permeated everything. The next, it was dark, and I could barely see a hand in front of my face. I walked behind Sam and the Driver behind me; I wasn't so sure I liked being the middle of a sandwich. I could feel the Driver's gaze trying to bore through my skull, and it set all my interpersonal and eel-powered alarms on fire.

The pure adrenaline that shot through my system told me to run and never come back. I didn't need an Aura Detection skill to get those vibes. If it were an option, I'd take it. I wish I had a better handle on what I could do with my Aura skill, but all I could glean was that the Driver's intentions weren't *completely* hostile. At least, I didn't think they were, toward me at least.

The next time I saw Nya and Shane, I was going to have words. It was all well and good to teach me new techniques, and to attune me to the Timewarp, but a little information on I don't know, how to be a super speak-to-electrical-programs hacker might have helped.

The building loomed. The large brick fence around it appeared taller than I remembered from walking past it earlier. But it had been daylight then, and now night was approaching, making everything that bit more ominous. I couldn't sense any guards in the immediate vicinity. I wish that made me feel safer, perhaps better, even. But it only made the trepidation worse.

Sam walked confidently, her stride sure and shoulders squared. Her footfalls were even, and her heartbeat was perfectly normal. I envied her, aware of how my own body was reacting to this stress. Suddenly, she stopped, and I almost crashed into her. She turned and held her finger over her lips, like we'd been noisy or something. I dared a glance back at the Driver, sort of surreptitiously so she wouldn't know.

Her expression was almost vacant, like she was anywhere but here with us. The smile she'd worn in the beginning to disarm us had been replaced by a semi-permanent scowl. Then there were her eyes, so intense it made me want to run, yet they appeared to focus on nothing. The change her appearance had gone through, her outward presentation? It made me think of stories like the bodysnatchers. Then again, she was concealing our presence. Maybe this was a part of it.

Sam turned suddenly to me, startling me out of my observations. She lowered her voice before speaking. "Are you not thinking or something? Because my system asked if you were still here."

I didn't have to feign the shock I felt. It must have shown on my face pretty clearly. "Not really thinking, just sort of drinking things in." I pushed out the words, wondering why my own system hadn't called me out on being too silent to begin with. Perhaps it was on probation or something. I mean, it hadn't answered me when I spoke to it, so I was a bit defensive when I added to my reply. "My system hasn't been answering my questions."

"Odd. Well, I need you fully invested in this. Be thinking. Of ways you can fulfill the role you're supposed to play. Because if we don't manage to complete this task, I am in deep shit." She didn't sound angry but more scared than I thought I would ever hear Sam sound in my life. In her role as Cyan's friend in my apartment, Sam was strong and vibrant, in charge and mischievous, but here it was different. That alone was enough to get me to leave the confines of my own little holding cell and allow my thoughts to roam freely. Except the ones about being an eel—those I locked away in my vault. Nice and safe.

I nodded. "Sorry. I just try to blank my mind so I don't run the risk of getting overwhelmed."

"Good. Let's get on with it then." She turned back around and walked for several more steps.

My lies were getting so much better and falling from my lips much smoother. I wasn't sure why, and I knew I didn't like it, but it was a means of self-preservation. Lying had never been my thing, but now I was getting used to it. The things we did...

Sam stopped abruptly. "I need you to short this out if you can. Don't set off alarms, please? I mean, I've seen you do this before."

Her words had an edge to them, like she'd heard so much about how good eels were, and yet the instructions she'd been given had raised her expectations. Still, how was I supposed to not do that? I mean, I hadn't even been an eel long.

I wanted to reassure her; she seemed very tense. "Look. I'm still new. There's no one to teach me. I have to figure this out by myself."

"Sorry." Sam grimaced and lowered her voice. I got the impression she didn't want the Driver to hear her. "Just not used to my instructions being so vague."

Nodding, I walked softly to the door handle, not that it mattered, because shadows obscured my every move. This brick fence for this old building was solid and well cared for, and this section butted straight up to the building, so it was likely to be well guarded. I couldn't see any security cameras on the outside, which surprised me. The door was old and wooden but sturdy from the days when there was a permanence to how they tackled construction.

Even if there were hidden cameras, I doubted they could see us, considering the density of this Driver's concealment. It was far blacker than I remembered David's being.

I reached out for the strange, knob-like handle and closed my eyes, making very light contact with it. Electrical currents spread before my awareness like singular strands of perfect hair. Every strand led to their source of power, but the trick was in making the system think a fuse had blown and not that sabotage had occurred.

I frowned and hummed a little under my breath. "This'll take a few. It's a complex system. Not as old as this building seems." The system didn't reflect the age of the fence, nor the sight of the building. I was almost excited to see what it looked like inside.

Concentrating, I allowed myself to breathe slowly, to steady my hand and make sure my mind was calm. All very difficult to do under the current circumstances, but I'd like to say I handled it like a champ.

There were several ways to trip me up built into each of the conduits that carried the power to set the alarm off. Almost tripping one, I had to separate myself from the system and take a moment. Their security set up was next level. Nothing I'd ever seen before, with some technology in it that made me want to grab it and take it home with me. This was definitely no ordinary office block. It was like a mimic just waiting to snap.

Finally, I managed to find the right tether and activated a minuscule shock through the system. The alarms remained silent, and the door handle clicked as the locking mechanism opened.

"There." I said it a little smugly.

But the Driver shrugged. "I could have just picked the lock and taken less time."

"Yes, but then you would have set off the alarm." Sam pushed past and opened the door fully. "Shall we?" she asked, ushering us through without waiting for an answer.

Portent Ability Active

Portent Ability Warning

I hesitated, but could almost feel the Driver's breath on the back of my neck and hurriedly passed through the damn doorway. Still, I felt like I needed to turn around and run away. Sometimes I wished I listened to my instincts more, especially when the damned system agreed with them.

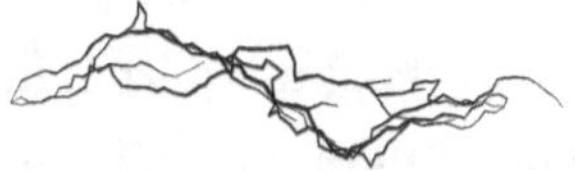

The inside of the compound felt like we'd somehow entered another dimension. Back in the old days, I would have loved this sensation. You know, before death decided I was a human lightbulb.

Right now, though, it was creepy as fuck. The lights that shone overhead seemed older than I would have expected, like they came straight out of the 1950s and flickered on into the now. Their yellow light attracted dozens of moths that flittered around them, lending an oddly surreal tone to the shadows reflecting beneath it. I wanted to reach out and touch it, to feel what old electrical charge had been like, but something whispered in my mind not to. And it wasn't my friendly neighborhood Second Chance system voice.

Maybe it was all a part of the subterfuge, trying to make people think the place wasn't what they'd thought.

"Come on." Even Sam seemed somewhat put out by the seemingly other world we'd stepped into. Only the Driver didn't. She still had that smile on her face, the one that told me she wasn't everything she seemed to be. The one that held the strange scowl just behind it.

You are curious about your Driver?

Yeah, she's a little unorthodox.

How so?

It was sort of nice to have my voice-in-the-head friend back and talking to me. Less lonely, even if it was probably out to trip me up. I shrugged. *Her friendliness was over the top, not genuine, and she isn't one to keep a real smile on her face. She's hiding something. Her mind isn't fully on the task, either. I don't trust people who don't show the world who they really are. It only means they have something to hide.*

Well, that turned out a lot wordier than I'd expected. The voice in my head kept quiet, probably mulling over my words, or else regretting it had asked me a question. I wasn't sure which was the actual option. Still though. We stepped lightly in the shadows, keeping eyes out for guards, but I couldn't see any.

I couldn't feel anything, either. No auras apart from the two flanking me. No heartbeats that didn't belong to squirrels in the trees outside or moles under the ground or the three of us on this mission together.

The area around us was like one huge entrance hall, a foyer. The wooden floors under our feet didn't creak or strain though, and the Driver masked our footsteps anyway. Occasionally there was a scent to the air, too. Like a gentle wafting of rotten meat, left out in the sun too long. But as soon as I identified it, it seemed to disappear.

And a chill that wouldn't leave my back alone. I felt like something kept walking over my grave repeatedly. The sensation was full body, like my bones were being scraped from inside. As nice and bleached as that sounded, I'd never wanted to have it done.

"We're here." Sam sounded relieved, and I wished I could read minds. Wouldn't that be a cool skill?

The Driver doesn't appear to be hiding anything. I wasn't expecting my brain pal to talk to me, and I barely suppressed my gasp in time.

You checked? I didn't think the system would go and run a check for me. After all, weren't we all just spokes in the giant wheel that was SC?

Of course I checked. You are an eel. Your abilities are still out of my range of comfort, and if you feel something strongly, it could be a manifestation of your skills. Or it could just be paranoia. But I can't be too careful.

Why? I sounded like a toddler.

Because if I lose you, I lose my own voice.

I hadn't thought of it like that. If I were to disappear or die, did that mean that this voice wouldn't get the chance to speak again? The thought was sobering. Oddly enough, I found the thought of its personality disappearing somewhat sad. But then, I also found my own imminent punishment if I were found out sad, too.

Well, here's to working together. I lied my ass off, but it seemed to make brain friend feel better.

Everything around us felt like a lure to bring us into a false sense of security. I couldn't be sure, but I was quite certain something was hiding people from me. Something or someone. Was it another eel? Someone not working for SC? Come to think of it, were there other organizations out there like SC? Was it first come first serve?

No. We don't operate like that. We are the only one with that power. Concentrate on your mission.

I am, I snapped back at it as we approached another door. This one was large, about eight feet tall and appeared to be made of extremely thick wood. Its planks were bound by slats of iron. The black kind, sort of like a dungeon door with the bolts around the hinges and the worn feeling to the wooden planks.

It looked impossibly old. Far older than anything in this city had any right to be. The lights and their dim golden light flickered and went out.

I glanced up at the ceiling and balked. Pitch black. There were no fire alarms glowing softly, nor any lights that I could see. We were in a black box that somehow defied my ability to sense anything.

"Sam," I whispered, my mind doing double time and trying to get a handle on what my senses were telling me.

"I know, Dare. I know." She spoke calmly, like she'd been doing this the whole time, every day of her life.

How could she know? "You know? What do you know?" My whisper held a hint of panic no matter how hard I tried to hide it. Because it didn't seem feasible to me that she could know. If she did know, why hadn't she warned us?

"That we've walked into a trap? Yeah, I knew this would happen. I told them not to leave me with an on-loan Driver and an eel. Put those together and bad shit is bound to happen." Her tone sounded irritated, like this was an ongoing problem she constantly had with those who gave her assignments.

We'd walked into a trap, and I had no idea what it would do, nor how to disarm it. And the Driver neither of us knew kept smiling like a fucking clown in a sewer, her eyes softly glowing. The only thing missing was her balloon.

10
TRAP

Pitch black wasn't my favorite way to experience anything, and right then, I felt completely blinded and utterly undeserving of my rank up. There was a fluid sensation surrounding me, like I was moving through water.

Neural Function Detected

Caution, subjects in close proximity.

That was a new one, but I wasn't looking this gift horse in the mouth. I lowered my voice, feeling my mission mate's presence with me. "I can sense them. Four close, and maybe another four further away."

Sam moved at my back, but with purpose and not fear; her body didn't tremble in the slightest. "Trap or not, they don't know who they're dealing with. Stick with me."

She spoke like she belonged there, as if she knew what she was doing as she moved out. But the thing was, though I might be an exceptional runner, I wasn't good at fighting—with words or limbs. I followed her lead, my heart beating so fast I thought it could open its own power station. The Driver snorted behind me, like she encountered apparently empty halls in almost pitch darkness all the time.

Maybe she did. But I was nervous about rounding the next corner because I couldn't feel anything but the beings watching us. Sure, my eyes were used to the darkness now, and I realized I could make out shapes enough to avoid them.

I didn't like the silence. The thing was, sometimes there might be a soft indiscernible buzzing. Coming from the lights, for instance. Right then, though, there was nothing. If I'd tried, I probably could have heard a pin drop. And that's what heightened my good old anxiety.

Sam was already in combat when we rounded the corner. Fighting was her best form of flattery. If she deigned to fight you, apparently it meant you were worth something. The clothes on the guard she fought were straight out of the 1950s movies. He was dressed in grey pants with a dark grey buttoned up coat. It was almost a military uniform, as if the security working here had mimicked it. I'd take a bet it was wool, too.

Her fists flew in ways I didn't realize she knew how to fight. Come to think of it, I had been pretty good in the Tae Kwon Do I took many years ago, but I'd quit when I was nine, letting my love for running take over.

The Driver beat me to it, though. Quite literally. She pushed forward, her shadows flowing from her like a cloak that draped us all in its wake. Her movements were smooth and accurate as she sunk to one knee like it was the easiest thing in the world and swept the leg of the nearest guard.

At first, I thought my eyes had gotten really good at seeing in the dark, but then I realized when we turned the corner a soft light emitted from an upstairs room with glass windows, illuminating the whole fight.

I watched in fascination as they both engaged those guards in combat, preventing them from using the whistles their opponents grabbed at in their time of need. Both of my mission mates were efficient in their own ways. The Driver's job seemed to have a lot more to it than I'd originally thought. They weren't particularly agile or ideal, but they appeared to have the ability to also block out the light from anyone they were fighting and not just the people they were fighting with. This made it far more difficult for opponents to leap in and jump in the middle.

The way the shadows twisted and turned, I swore I could see eyes and claws and hands. For one moment I just stared, trying to see beyond it—to see if these were real shadows or robots. Nothing emerged for me to grip onto, and I shook my head, vowing to get to the bottom of the damned shadow conspiracy before it drove me insane.

Though I wanted to help, I was certain that my trying to would only get in their way. What I did do was sidle around behind them all and make my way to the next door. The only way to get out of this in any way was to complete the assignment. And what better time to do that than when security was otherwise occupied ambushing us?

I took the steps two at a time up to the office that was giving off the light. All doors in this place were hooked up to the same security system, so technically I'd already disabled this one. Its intricacies extended throughout the whole complex. This lock seemed to stick a bit when I twisted it open, like the tumbler was stiff and rarely used. I realized why when I finally got it open and stepped inside.

Before me lay a room of technology. Fantastic, brand spanking new. Making the fans whir like kittens purred new. Or perhaps not new, just updated and lovingly maintained. I had an itch at the back of my mind, needing to meet whoever had set this up.

I scanned the room briefly. Over on the far side was a large desk surrounded by glass. Sort of like a see-through separate office with no door. The machines in there were more like massive servers with a primary access point.

I wasn't sure how long Sam and the Driver could handle those guys outside, but I knew I needed to move quickly. This whole office building set up had me on edge.

My fingers itched to touch this beauty as I raced across the space to it. There was no one in here that I could sense, not even mice in the walls. Granted, I think they maintained the building's aged appearance to put people off what was really in here.

Sitting at the desk, I pushed a sliver of power to my fingertip. While I desperately wanted to access the computer through the keyboard like I would have any other day, I also didn't want to accidentally fuck up. It occurred to me that I wasn't entirely sure if I should go through the terminal to get what we needed or if I should approach the actual servers. Perhaps a bit of both. How was I going to get the information to Sam anyway?

What even was that information supposed to be? May as well just store everything, right?

I took a breath to calm myself and laid out a plan in my head. First get to the information, and secondly, figure out how to remove it and take it with us. My eyes cast around for a thumb drive or something. Perhaps even a portable hard drive.

There was a loud crash against the door, and I cringed at the sound and hoped they could keep the fighting out there away from these machines. From what I could detect, there were a lot of auras out there. Sam and the Driver were known to me. And two of the first four opponents they'd encountered were already down for the count. Thing was, they were about to face a few more.

Urgency threw nerves at me, but I swatted them aside. Standing up, I crossed to the servers. Now, if I were a secret well of information, where would I hide? I didn't even know exactly what I was looking for, but I did know it would be well hidden. The logical thing to do was to search for and find something that either a) appeared innocent and uninteresting or b) was completely hidden and took moving mountains to find.

Taking another deep breath, I placed my hand on the server and did what I can only refer to as diving.

Fine line electrical control.

Do you wish to interface with this terminal?

Yes or No?

I blinked at it. Of course, I wanted to. *Yes,* I directed my answer at the prompt.

You are about to activate an electrical interface with this terminal. Please be advised that you are responsible for maintaining your sense of self for the duration of this interaction. This warning will not be shown again.

I barely had a moment to register what it told me before a shock zinged through my finger and through my entire body, riveting my attention on the terminal.

Currents of electricity sucked me in like I was riding a wave in an ocean of information and code. It was beautiful. Nothing like movies would have you believe at all. There weren't streams of coding falling down from black ceilings, nor were there green lines of code constantly working.

It was more like a series of waterfalls, some small, some large, all gushing over their edges with numbers and codes and algorithms churning fast in the waters as they rushed over. It was beautiful to look at. I could have sat there for hours, but the system warning rung through my skull like a death bell.

Reaching deep, I tried my best to activate that slow mode I seemed to possess, unsure if I could do it while already using one of my abilities. Inside my vaulted mind, I received a pop-up notification.

Timestance activated.

Slow initiating in:

3

2

1

Once activated, it made the digital water run slower, which in turn allowed me to see some of the caves hidden by the cascading falls. Small openings dotted the mountains that the waterfalls fell over. Not in everyone. Some of them were too small, but that definitely counted as hidden data.

Traveling along the stream, I past my consciousness over the information contained within. Some of these were simply maintenance tunnels. Elements that kept the systems running, and performed the daily tasks required by Ranlan Industries. That was good, nothing hiding there. I didn't know what an eel without computing background might do, but I was glad I had it, or else I'd have even less of a clue in here.

Something was off about everything in front of me, and I frowned as I tried to concentrate harder to focus on it. All around me the water speed had slowed, and I could visually see it as well as hear it. Like a metronome trying to tick me to sleep.

Except for one. I could hear it. Not that it sounded over the other ones, but instead, out of synchronization with them. Which shouldn't have been possible. The time slow should have applied to everything, but something sounded out of sync. It was so well hidden and unobtrusive that someone had to have expended a lot of effort to make it appear so unassuming.

Even if the door was bashed in right then, I wouldn't have heard it. I stood next to the servers, for all appearances frozen in time as I searched through the programs contained within. That one little waterfall was so small. I hadn't even tried to see if it had a cave. It was difficult to zoom in on and even more so to stay focused on. Something about it almost told me to not look at it. Which, of course, sent up huge red flags.

Everyone I knew wanted to do something more if told not to. I was no exception.

I plunged into the waterfall, through it, and into the cave. Cold sensations assailed my body, like a last line of defense. The coding in here didn't seem white and frothy but instead glowed a strange yellow gold and smelled different, like fresh soldering on metal mixed with tangy battery acid.

My brain could see how complex the information contained within was. And my coding language balked against what had been used to write it. And yet, I seemed to be able to replicate it. I sent one copy to the mainframe so Sam could download it when she eventually finished her therapeutic beating the shit out of the guards, and on impulse, sent one to myself, storing it inside my mind pocket, safe, just for me. I wasn't even sure if it would work. But self-preservation and curiosity won out.

It took me a lot longer to disengage from the amazing surroundings in that server than it had for me to enter it. There was a lull that pulled me to it, like the power contained within didn't want to let me go. I wondered if perhaps the electricity I put out helped power it.

I blinked as I pulled away from it, a sudden wave of vertigo overcoming me. My mind reeled from the disconnect, and I stumbled to the floor, landing hard on my tailbone. It hurt like buggery and I yelped in pain, louder than I should have.

Suddenly, the door to the computer lab flew open, and a man in a modern black suit stood there glaring at me. Personally, I thought he looked like he'd be better served arresting aliens, but what do I know. My head was woozy enough and my tailbone painful enough that I just wasn't sure how to react.

So I laughed. Perhaps I was a little overtired on top of everything else.

The man paused, looking at me, and spoke one word I couldn't quite hear.

The door, still open behind him, morphed slightly. It went from appearing ancient to revealing a strong and steel exterior. Beyond him, I saw the lights change from what had apparently been their camouflage mode. It was probably all hooked to a hub, but it was impressive.

I stumbled back to my feet, determined not to let Mr. Alien Herder get the best of me. Flashes of Tae Kwon Do came back to me, stances and movements. Though I wasn't entirely certain of my footing, I still fell into an easy fighting stance, my fists raised, and hoped I wasn't just referencing the karate movies I'd watched over the years.

Sam and the Driver were still out there fighting. I could feel how fast their pulses raced, just how much energy they were expending fighting the multiple foes they had. It would be pure luck if they finished their encounters in time to come and help me with mine. Which meant I had to suck it up.

Suddenly, my opponent wasn't standing at the door any longer, but instead right in front of me. I barely dodged in time and could feel the whoosh of his fist as it connected with the outer fringes of my hair, which was pretty short.

Fuck. This wasn't good.

I'm not a fighter, I spat at the voice in my mind.

Without any hesitation whatsoever, it responded, and not in the way I'd expected at all.

Your power is electricity. All you should have to do is touch him.

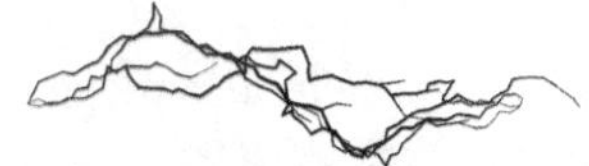

The first punch connected with my jaw before I could process what the system was telling me. It wasn't anything new or anything I hadn't thought of before. It was just in a far more active and real context than I'd ever let it exist in.

Of course, all I had to do was electrocute him. Silly me.

But I'd been punished that way, and I knew how much that hurt, and my death still rung in my ears.

So even as that punch connected with my face and sent me flying over a desk and into the wall, I didn't have the presence of mind to react with an electric shock. All I had to do was touch him, right? And touching him included his flesh connecting with mine. As long as I could channel the pulse into the exact right spot.

It wasn't simple at all, and it wasn't something I had practiced or wanted to do, but the way he leapt over that table and stalked toward me as I barely managed to pull myself up against the wall left me little choice that I could see.

Except I could already feel the blood trickling down from my lip, and the pain in the side of my face refused to subside. I wondered if he'd dislocated my jaw or something. I stared at him as he somehow moved closer to me without actually taking a step. Maybe my mind was blanking out of fear, because I sure as hell was shaking right then. So close to disengaging from the server and that electric adrenaline rush. I was so close to feeling what I should be, to reaching for that element of electricity that I couldn't grasp.

Hairy knuckles flew toward my face. *How did one get hairy knuckles?* was a thought I never realized I'd have. But I realized two things. Way to focus, and...I could slow time. For me, at least. According to him, he was still moving at the same, extremely speedy pace.

Timestance Activated.

Instant Slow Enabled.

I ducked just in time, even through the throbbing of my skull. It was an advantage I needed to take, even if it barely gave me an edge, even if it drained me.

I knew I needed to get myself a vantage point, and perhaps some breathing time to stop my head from trying to disconnect from my body. Bracing my foot against the wall, I used it like a starter block and sprinted.

While I wasn't a sprinter by any measure of speed, I did know how to jettison off those blocks. Add to that an electric boost and my time stoppingness, and I accelerated forward so fast, my attacker probably thought I disappeared.

The thing I wasn't so good on was directionality, but I made it away from Mr. Alien Wrangler, and that gave me enough time to reassess my abilities, my injuries, and my state of mind.

Tell Sam I have the files, but they're on the mainframe, and I'm not sure how she will access them.

There was a pause in my head that felt far too long, even given that I had time quasi paused, before it finally responded.

Done.

At least that was taken care of. It didn't need to know I also had a copy for myself. Sort of. As long as my head didn't get completely scrambled by another connecting punch. My opponent wasn't as slow as I'd hoped even with my cheating. His ability to track me down made me think he'd had some sort of contact with an eel before. Which was yet another question in my huge pile for Nya and Shane.

I was tiring. Holding onto Timestance chipped away at my endurance. Considering I had an abundance of it from long distance running, this was a severely lacking area in my severe lack of eel training.

All I needed was one good connection. Of his fist to my skin. Because the odds of me connecting a punch were close to negative.

Message received: Sam will be here as soon as she can.

Gee, that was comforting right now. I didn't give the system a response because I needed to concentrate on Mr. Alien Big and Beefy. At least he didn't have dark glasses on.

The brighter lighting helped me, probably him not so much. By now I was panting, and my jaw still wasn't working properly. I think I was drooling a bit.

His gaze locked on me, and his strides covered the ground fast, like he was pushing against my abilities. Either that, or my abilities were fading rapidly. Damn it. If I made it out of this, I needed to take my training into my own hands.

And that thought was just enough to get in the way of my escape this time. I tried to dodge the next punch, but he somehow changed direction mid stride and angled the punch differently than I'd anticipated. Instead of catching me in the face though, luckily this time it only caught me in the upper arm, right next to my shoulder. His fists were like iron or bricks or something really hard that could cause a lot of damage.

Like a really thick piece of rebar.

I grunted in pain. Okay, it might have been a scream, but I wasn't very objective. A grin crossed the man's face, like he enjoyed beating up on me. Or perhaps not me, just anyone, and I happened to be handy. I sort of wished he'd give me a bad guy monologue so I could use it to get the upper hand. No such luck.

His grin widened as he saw the shock in my face when I realized the other hand was coming in for a hooked blow and there was nothing I could do to stop it. Not even my speed got me out of there in time.

He didn't aim for my face, no, he got me right in the left side, in the soft gut area, hooking underneath my ribcage. It was all in slow motion, though probably not for him, of course. However, my abilities took that precise moment to show me just how powerful they were. His fist crushed into my side, pushing against my ribs as my body lifted with the momentum. This time it didn't fling me over a desk, but crashed me into the nearest one, hitting my head on the edge and knocking the wind completely out of me.

I tried to gulp air in, but all I sucked in was pain, my head swimming with confusion. For a brief moment, I wasn't even sure where I was.

The grin on my opponent's face turned sinister, and I could hear each knuckle he cracked as he stood over me. Even the faint scent of onion and garlic wafted to me from his breath, lending nausea to my current state of being.

Instead of trying to outsmart him, I gathered all the electrical energy I still had, fueled by fear, and bundled it up to the surface, hoping for some clue as to where he was going to hit me.

Portent Ability Activated.

Situation assessed.

Suddenly I knew where he was going to hit, but I didn't know if I could redirect the power in time. He was aiming for the left-hand side of my face, wanted to connect and show me just how much better physical force was.

Even as I watched his hand inch toward my face, I couldn't move. My body ached too much to do so. But I could push the power around in my body. If I could get enough electricity to the surface, he'd be the one who was blown away.

But I wasn't sure I could do it, and time was running out.

11

SKILLS

I couldn't believe how slowly it happened. Like a time-lapse movie demonstrating how to punch. It was the worst movie I'd ever seen.

The force of the electric shock as his fist connected with my face sent us both flying in opposite directions.

His back crashed into the steel wall behind him with a sickening thud as his body convulsed with the electricity I'd poured into it.

I skidded back along the floor, pushing the desk behind me along for the ride, and came to rest just shy of the other wall. Not that it mattered at all. My body was spent. If he hadn't taken the full brunt of electric force, I was screwed. My entire body ached, and my head felt like a ball of lead on top of a stick, wobbly and precariously balanced. I didn't even attempt sitting up. But I knew I had to.

Blood pooled in the back of my throat, and I was pretty sure one of my teeth was loose. Great. Dental expenses on top of everything else. Now I could see why SC paid so well.

Technically, I should be able to heal it, but I'd poured so much out of me that I felt raw. It hurt to even contemplate channeling more of the beast.

I was sort of proud of what I'd done, only wished I'd managed to do it sooner. A bone weariness began to settle around me, and I had to push myself upright painfully in order to make sure nothing was broken.

I bit down, clenching my teeth to withstand the pain before sending slivers of the remaining electrical build up along my body to help me heal up. There was no getting out of here without my doing that. This healing thing wasn't immediate, nor was it miraculous, but as soon as I'd released the power and given it direction, I could feel some relief wash over me.

"Dare!"

Sam tore into the room, violating one of SC's huge rules, but I really hoped they'd let using my name slide.

"Shit!" She knelt down by my side, her brow furrowed with worry. "Are you okay?"

I coughed as I struggled to sit up straighter and saw the red blobs as they caught the light in the room. Great. I didn't want to see my face in the slightest. "I'll be fine. Working on healing up already."

My voice croaked, and I could feel liquid running down my throat. I didn't need to be a doctor to know it was blood.

She nodded, and I watched as she hesitated, torn between worry for me and worry for her own sake. We'd been sent here to do a job. "Did you get it?"

Fear of the overlord won out.

"Probably. Grabbed a lot of files." I wanted to know why we needed them. Why would a company that specialized in security need files related to an organization like ours? Why hadn't the instructions been more specific? What was in them that was so important? All the questions again.

"That was good work. Rest up. We still have to get out of here." She glanced over at the guard who I'd electrocuted into the wall. "He'll be okay?"

"P'rbly," I muttered, hoping I was right, but my heavy head wasn't getting any lighter, and I thought I might have just slurred my words. "He'sh just resh-ting."

She shot me another concerned look and hurried over to the terminal, picking her way through splintered desks and trashed computers to the mainframe behind its own little glass prison. I couldn't follow her further than that; my eyes and head were having trouble obeying my orders.

Driver leaned against the doorway, watching us. She looked like hell with an air of angry. Her already disheveled hair was an actual mess now, and she sported an emerging black eye and some nice cuts and bruises on her face, arms, and legs. Since she matched Sam so well, I would have to heal them both up a little bit before we talked about the mission. If I could get my mind to work.

Sam was back sooner than expected, or was it because I'd let go of the time alteration? Time passed so fast outside my head. Maybe I was just way too tired for all of this.

Sam insisted on seeing that I got home safely. She bundled me into the car, and I could see the concern on her face. It didn't make much sense to me. Didn't she know about my superhuman healing abilities? Wolf dude, eat your heart out.

Literally? He probably would. I wasn't sure where my mind was going, but I seemed to sort of float between lucidity and some strange notion of Red Riding Hood. The things brains did to try and heal themselves.

Only we didn't end up going home. Sam hopped onto the freeway and sped straight to HUP. I wanted to tell her I wasn't that badly off, but the words I thought I spoke emerged like a gargled cough. Giving up, I watched the city lights blur together in my vision.

I hadn't thought I was that bad off, and a part of me was grateful she didn't just take me to Temple, considering I wanted to keep living. Not to mention Dr. Caroline wasn't there. She'd know what to do.

I swear the hospital was busier this time, and a part of me didn't want to be here. Did I really want to see Dr. Caroline? How did I know that being a part of Second Chance didn't automatically negate the Hippocratic oath? Because it probably did, right? I'm not entirely sure how we got from the car to the waiting area so fast. But I knew it had nothing to do with my own speed.

My head still spun, and it was getting worse. Like that gravitron ride at county fairs. Spinning non-stop.

You're experiencing a concussion. The doctor will be with you shortly.

"Yep. Got it."

Sam looked at me with an odd expression, and I realized I'd spoken to the voices in my head out loud. Come to realize that it was good SC had its own doctors. Or else we'd all probably be on watch lists.

Cyan's friend looked at me. I could see she was concerned. Maybe even a little afraid for me. Truth be told, so was I. My head was doing weird shit. Flickering between moments in the battle to recalling memories I hadn't thought about in a very long time—ones I weren't even sure were mine.

The water splashed on me again, salty and sharp, cold and wakeful as I pushed the heavy bundle up to the catamaran, letting hands and the people with no faces pull it from me.

It felt like my brain was breaking.

Suddenly, Dr. Caroline was standing in front of me a nice little furrow in her brow. She must do a lot of frowning.

"Dare. You've got to stop trying to live up to your name. I don't have enough worry points for this." She sounded like she might mean it. But I'd already been deceived by this program a lot, so I wasn't sure I believed anything or anyone.

"Can' help it." My tongue felt thick. Maybe I'd bitten it during the scuffle. A laugh escaped me. That fight had been so far beyond a scuffle, but I really liked the word. It sounded sort of...cool.

If possible, her brow creased even more. Maybe I should start being worried about myself.

"Slurring words, inane laughter. I knew you had a concussion, but I think it's worse than I first thought. Sending you off for a CT, and I'll find a bed for you. You're staying overnight." The way she said it, I knew it wasn't an invitation. It was more of a command. Sort of like, you don't really have a choice, but for appearance sake I can pretend you do.

"Bed." I just wanted a bed with a soft pillow and a warm blanket. Tiredness kept threatening to close my eyes, but I remembered something about concussions and how it wasn't ideal to let the person sleep without waking them every so often. Didn't matter though. I just wanted to rest my aching head.

Dr. Caroline nodded, and turned her attention to Sam. I could see them talking, and I knew it was about me or maybe the mission. I just didn't know why or what. A nurse came into the room and tried to make me comfortable, offering me a hospital gown. There was nothing comfortable about those damned gowns. I grumpily swatted her away.

"I'll shleep in my clothesh thanksh. Butt cheeksh aren't mah head." I giggled then. Because I was apparently mentally twelve when I had a concussion.

The nurse rolled her eyes, but she let me remain in my dusty clothes and ushered me over to a bed. She reached up with one of those strange tentacle devices that spread out and massaged my head, sort of like hairdressers do. I could feel the whir behind it, the power, but somehow, I didn't think it ran on electricity. What did was my brain, my very tired brain.

The nurse frowned and patted my head like she was an ancient old aunt. "You're safe to go to sleep. We have you alarmed. Rest up, and you should be able to go home tomorrow since you heal so fast."

Her demeanor was great. Friendly and caring. Sort of like the old Orion. The sudden thought assailed me, and I wasn't sure where it had come from. Casting it aside, I flipped onto my side and snuggled my face into the soft pillow.

There were times I wished I was still alive. Who was I kidding? They were all the times. But waking up in the hospital was one of the reasons. I'd never been hospitalized overnight before. And after the weird-ass dreams that ran through my head during the night, I didn't intend to make a repeat performance.

Not with the strange shadows lurking at every turn, bleeding in through the walls, caressing my head. Maybe they'd really been here, but if so, they were pushing the boundaries I was comfortable with. That and the ocean, the catamaran, and Orion. I wasn't sure where the latter dreams were coming from. I hadn't been boating since the beginning of high school.

What I needed was a way to contact Shane and Nya. I needed training, and if they weren't going to give it to me, I'd give it to myself, somehow. I had skills *before* I got my face punched to a pulp. I didn't mind fighting or self-defense if I knew what the hell I was doing.

The grey metal ceiling of the room I was in wasn't lost on me. One day I would figure out just how much of this university the SC system actually contributed to. I had a feeling there was just so much more here, more to the roots. More to everything really.

The nurse popped her head around the corner and grinned at me. Perhaps she'd been the night nurse. For all I knew her power was staying the fuck awake. Okay. I was getting grumpy. I couldn't remember the last time I'd eaten.

"You're looking well this morning. I'll go grab the doctor for you. She'll want to see you to check that we can discharge you." She was gone before I could ask her any questions. Typical.

While I waited, I tried recreating the previous night in my head, but there was something rather off about my memories. They seemed fuzzy, like they'd been messed with, or interfered with. Something about the previous mission, the way we'd been lured in or trapped, grated on me. Had someone known we were coming? And if they did, how had they known? These were questions best left for someone else. But all I had was me.

I was so lost in my own thoughts and possible solutions that I didn't notice Dr. Caroline come in at first. My aura detection was apparently on the fritz. So by the time I noticed, she could have been standing there studying my facial expressions for I don't know how long. The thought was unsettling, and for the first time I didn't feel comfortable around her. It was beginning to be a repeat theme. First the Driver from yesterday. Now the Doctor I'd already met numerous times.

Electricity made my brain more paranoid. Or perhaps just more aware of subtle nuances. which would inevitably drive me crazy when they took over.

"You look at lot better complexion-wise this morning." Her tone was cheerful, upbeat, but I got the feeling it was all forced. How else would a doctor get through a day of losing patients, giving them bad news, and trying to save lives? Don't get me wrong, I was fully aware they didn't lose every patient. But sometimes...didn't the constant obvious mortality wear on them?

"I feel somewhat better. My thoughts are more coherent and don't feature heavily around weird dreams and being punched in the face repeatedly." I joked a little, trying to bring some levity into the situation.

She frowned as she looked at her clipboard. "I'm glad you have a sense of humor about it, but I'd prefer for you to have more self-preservation awareness. I'm putting you out of commission for the next week just to make sure you don't relapse or have a more serious injury."

I was about to protest when she held up her hand.

"Look, I know you can heal quickly—or perhaps quicker is more accurate—but I'd like you to take the chance to have some downtime and perhaps learn how to defend yourself better."

I laughed. "I had to let him hit me. I can't throw thunderbolts yet." Which gave me oh, the best idea, but I had to just leave it for now. That germ of an idea would grow beautifully if I had a week of uninterrupted life after school.

12
ILLUSION

Orion wasn't home when I got there on Sunday afternoon, and I heaved a sigh of relief as Sam walked me into my room. She sat on the end of the bed and helped me arrange my phone on its charger as well as a few other things I needed to have close by. It was nice to have someone taking care of me. Even though she'd tried to do that in the field, too.

"Thanks, Sam," I said softly, and meant every single letter.

She smiled a bit awkwardly. "Yeah, I'm not so used to being grouped up with people I know. I've only ever had a few little missions with Orion too. Like in the last two years."

"How long?" I wasn't sure if asking that was sort of taboo. But I guessed it couldn't be too bad because she gave me a wan smile.

"Four and a half years next month." She looked down at her hands, at her fingernails with a sort of wistfulness that bordered on sadness. I wished I could give her a hug, but my limbs weren't in the most cooperative mood. And I wasn't sure I could handle close physical contact after all that went down. I was far too drained.

"Sorry." I didn't think, gauging from her reaction, that it was the best time or best idea to ask her how she died. Her powers were still a little vague for me, and I wasn't sure if it would be comfortable or not for her to answer.

She stood up, clapping her hands on her thighs. "Is what it is, right?"

I nodded, suddenly feeling extremely tired again.

Sam leaned forward and ruffled my hair. "You take care of yourself, and enjoy your week off. I'll see you on Friday."

I watched her go and suddenly felt all too alone. No one else was in the house; even the mice that ran around inside of the walls weren't making any noise today. I closed my eyes, ready to drink in the beauty that was my very own pillow, when I realized what I could hear. Scraping. Against wood, against metal, against everything.

Shivers crawled under my skin, like beetles trying to break their way out of me. Little legs that pressed against my bones, rasping against them like spines made out of steel. I didn't want that to happen. The itch under my skin turned into blobs that moved, writhing and squirming as they tried to eat their way out of my skin or through my bones, I couldn't tell which.

I blinked, but the blobs were still there. Like ancient Egyptian scarab torture trying to eat me from the inside out. I kept waiting for their little feet to pop out, their pincers, unable to look away. Was I asleep, dreaming, or a weird mixture of in between? The itching began to subside, but then I heard louder scratching. I was grateful it didn't come from within. No, this new noise came from the walls.

If it was a mouse in there, it had to be the size of a small horse, because that noise reverberated through me, ringing in my ears and made my skin tingle. Fear gripped at my throat, making it difficult to breathe, shooting pain through my system that delivered brief paralysis. I shivered, the blankets unable to hold in the warmth I needed. Finally, I managed to move enough to pull another one from the foot of the bed, determined to stop this cold I felt.

And maybe if I hid under the blankets, the terror that shook my soul would back the fuck off. I'd never felt dread this clearly before. It coated me like a blanket of glue that wouldn't peel off.

Then the scratching noise elongated. It pushed outward from the wall. Through the wallpaper, like one of those screaming masks except there was only a hollow where the eyes and mouth should be, and the hands that pushed next to where the head should be obviously had claws. They strained at the wallpaper, through the drywall or planks that kept this house together. My brain couldn't comprehend what it saw. It pieced it together in a series of strange static movements and shapes.

And then, like an elastic band firing backward, it snapped away, gone in an instant.

I lay there, staring at the place where the wall had warped and extended its nightmare. My breath came in ragged gasps, and my heartbeat slowly returned to normal. This wasn't conducive to restful sleep. My pillow was supposed to protect me, and given what I'd just seen, I wasn't sure anything could.

Silence began to weigh on the room. Unnatural in its intensity. I knew there was at least some traffic not twenty feet away. Not the busiest street in Philly, but there should have been some noise. None of that sound reached me up here. Not anymore. Something else was keeping it out. Like it had soundproofed my room without checking with me. Or perhaps despite knowing I wasn't the biggest fan of it.

I heard the skittering next. Like some sort of rodent was running around my wooden floor, deliberately missing the rug that might have muffled the noise of its movements. I laid back in bed and pulled my blankets up to my chin. A whimper escaped me, and I was suddenly very glad no one else was in the house to hear me totally losing it.

Was this a result of the concussion? Or was I just getting overwhelmed and seeing things?

Shadows permeated my room, and I think a lot of time had passed. Like the time slowing ability I had applied the opposite effect right now. It was moving faster, doing more to confuse me. I wanted to hold my hands over my eyes and block out the sight, but I got the distinct feeling that doing so wouldn't be effective.

Except they were real. Hot air whooshed by my face as they passed me. I could smell the sulfur and a faint scent of lavender. Such a stark juxtaposition, and yet ideal. Because at least the lavender let me know that they weren't out to get me. Calming lavender wasn't generally associated with ghost stories.

...not ghosts...

Okay. So that was new. I mulled the occurrence over in my mind and decided why the hell not? "What do you mean?" I whispered the words, determined not to let my head ache too much. Of course, I wasn't a hundred percent certain this wasn't a dream.

There was a long pause. Like it was trying to figure out how to express something.

...Old and new...we are the stolen...

Oh, joy. Cryptic clues were just so much fun. Actually, that was sarcastic. I hated cryptic clues. Still, though. "Are you the same ones who tried to take the burger?" I needed to know who I was talking to.

There was hesitation that floated around me like it wanted to smack me in the face. But eventually I received my answer.

...yes and no. We are many, but we are linked, even though we are individual...

I mulled that over in my mind, realizing that what they'd just said made no sense whatsoever. Trying to wrap my brain about it, I spoke up again. "So you are shadows that have solid form, but you are not robots?"

I could almost see them exchanging a glance together. There was something they weren't telling me, or weren't sure they could trust me to tell me. And damned if I wasn't just dying to find out.

...we were the you before you were there...

Fantastic. I had my answer. Pity it was clear as mud, and the dull throb in my skull wasn't helping. "You're not making sense."

...you are not listening, then. And you are not seeing. See more, learn more...then we shall return.

Their presence suddenly vanished, like it had never been there. And maybe it wasn't, because dang, how much I didn't trust my mind right now. Beaten to a pulp the previous night after a wild ride through strange waterfalls of coding and numbers, of algorithms I couldn't possibly hope to describe to anyone in the course of my life.

My head hurt badly, so I took one of the tablets the nurse had given to me when she sent me home. Maybe I could calm my mind enough to get some much-needed sleep.

This was my existence now. Talking to shadows, defending myself by letting someone punch me so I could electrocute them. I just had to get used to it.

My dreams were filled with shadows, with heads exploding both outward and onto me. Orion sat in the shadows, and the only way I could identify it as him was to hear his voice as he mumbled strange phrases to himself, just out of the reach of my comprehension. His face flickered in and out of focus, once sharp and clear, his hair perfect, his concentration in place. Then an overlay occurred, superimposing skeleton features under his skin, giving him a sickly pallor and sopping wet hair. Confusing didn't even begin to cover how my mind worked in that state, and I think I might have willed myself to wake up.

There was no light in the room when I finally managed to pry my eyes open. The only illumination came through my curtains from the street lamps outside. My head still pounded, but more like a soft bass drum than a loud snare. I knew I should feel hungry, since I couldn't remember when I last ate. But all I could feel was queasiness.

Without my bedroom light on, the shadows seemed even more sinister, even though I knew they weren't. Concussions were such a shitty injury. You could feel fine laying down, and yet as soon as you stood, vertigo smacked you upside the head and laughed. The pain throbbed through it and discouraged actual movement. But I felt the uncontrollable urge to disobey it.

It was probably the longest stretch of time I'd ever gone without running in like, ever. Okay. Maybe about five years would be more accurate. And I wasn't taking that punishment period into account. My feet itched like they needed to be moving, and I wasn't about to disappoint.

Pushing myself slowly, I refused to look around me in the dim lighting, because another part of me suspected shadows might be there, just waiting to see if I wanted to sit down and have a good ole chat. Those shadows and claws, the cryptic remarks, they only made my head hurt more. Finally, after what seemed like an age, I managed to reach the light switch and flick it on.

In hindsight, it wasn't the best decision, because the brightness pierced my eyes like a thousand needles sticking into my irises. Fantastic. Just add a set of cymbals to that good old base drum, and I was going to turn into the whole kit soon.

Not sure why my thoughts were so focused on drums, but they were.

I opened my door slowly, but the light wasn't on in the hallway, and only a dim echo of light shone down the hall from the living area. Sighing with relief, I pushed into the bathroom and drenched my face in some nice cold water, hoping that it would make the headache at least recede a little bit. It worked. Somewhat, anyway. The kitchen would have some pills I could take, although...perhaps I shouldn't mix medications. I'd have to check on that.

Jacob sat in the kitchen, sipping on what looked like a cup of tea. In front of him, he held a journal. I don't think he heard my footsteps as engrossed as he was. Besides, when I pulled the fridge door open, he started a bit in surprise.

"Oh, good. I was going to come in and check on you before I left for work. Sam mentioned you'd fallen and hurt your head. Gotta be careful, Dare, need that brain for thinking and stuff." He grinned at me like he'd just made the best joke ever. I couldn't blame him, after all. He was only measuring against my brother, who was somehow an expert at dad jokes at the ripe old age of twenty-five.

"Yeah, didn't mean to fall and smash my skull, but you know how best laid plans go and all that." I had already stuffed a piece of ham into my mouth, realizing I was severely lacking in protein.

He chuckled at my response. "Can't have hit it too hard if you still have your sense of humor about you."

"Ha. Ha," I said, rolling my eyes. Although in hindsight. Still, I grabbed an apple, a few more pieces of ham and some bread, and slapped the sandwich together haphazardly as I took a huge bite of my tiny apple. I really needed to upgrade myself from those snack box-sized ones.

"At least you have your appetite." Jacob returned his attention to the journal after one last comment. "If you can eat without feeling nauseated, I think your brain is going to be just fine."

He was a good sort, always concerned about friends or family. Medicine was the right field for him. I'd be too busy looking after myself.

I stopped short in the living room, realizing that Orion was napping on one of the old recliners. Unsure how I'd missed that on my way out of my bedroom, I took a few steps closer and settled in the other one. The taste of the ham and nice, soft fresh bread was divine. While the whole Second Chance program was suspect at best, it did let me afford to eat nicer food. I could get used to that, but I would have to remind myself not to sell my soul for it.

Orion looked peaceful for the most part, except that occasionally his eyebrows furrowed, like he was arguing with someone. Perhaps he was. Maybe he was having those awesome shadow conversations I'd got to experience for the first-time last night.

"I know you're watching me." He spoke, only moving his lips. Not even his eyes changed from their sleeping appearance.

Okay, so he wasn't talking to shadows. Perhaps he was talking to his inner voice. "Yep. Watching you and wondering when I could put your fingers in some warm water."

I sighed theatrically as I ripped another bite out of the huge sandwich. "Of course, now you've proven yourself to be awake, and my plans are ruined. Way to go, Orion."

He laughed and pushed himself into a sitting position. Well, sort of. He brought his knees up and draped his arms out across them, studying me with an unusual scrutiny. "You doing okay? Sam told me what happened."

I shrugged, not used to so much concern about me. But I knew I'd do the same in their place, so I couldn't really argue. "I mean, I'm okay. Things just...didn't quite go as expected, planned, or anything in that vicinity. Pure and utter improvisation."

"Oh." Orion grinned. "Nothing unusual, then."

I scowled at him. But I was too far away to bother moving so I could thwap him one. For the first time in a good while, I actually felt comfortable with my best friend. As long as I didn't think about certain instances, it was almost like it was possible for me to push the memories away.

Almost.

I sighed, irritated with myself and my sluggish brain for ruining what could have been a nice moment. "Got a week off out of it, complete with a note for school. There's no way Coach Marth is going to let me run when I've injured myself."

The realization came to me as I spoke the words, and it stung a little. This mission had interfered with my life. Even with my quicker healing capabilities, there was no way to explain that to someone not in the organization.

So I'd have to put up with sticking with the usual. Because the usual is what everyone would expect, and what my coach wouldn't question.

"You'll be fine. If you find yourself lacking a bit in endurance for the regionals, can't you just give yourself some juice?" Orion grinned at me. But I couldn't help the angry thoughts that wanted to leap out and attack him.

It wasn't his fault, though. Sure, I could do what he hinted at; I could totally cheat, but the point was he would never have suggested it before all of this SC crap. "I shouldn't be using my skills when others can't. That's not a fair race." As soon as the words left my mouth, I knew what he was going to say.

He pushed himself up to standing and looked down at me, a soft grin on his face. I knew he was trying to make me feel better. "We both know you rejuvenated your energy levels for that state meet. Maybe you'll have to do it for regionals too. Resetting your energy levels should be fine. It's like allowing yourself to get a really good night's sleep before the competition. Which, so far, you haven't been getting because you've been doing missions.

"So just let yourself. You know?" He reached out and tousled my hair, leaving memories of previous times he'd done that to dance in my mind. As if my brain didn't already have enough to deal with.

I watched him go back to his room, still conflicted as fuck, but perhaps appreciating our friendship a tad more.

Even if he was a killer.

All it took was one stray thought to send me plummeting back to that place of uncertainty and anguish that existed solely to torture me. Ask anyone— I was my own worst enemy. It was like I loved to torture myself.

Shoving the last bite of ham into my mouth, I pushed myself up to standing, marveling at the fact that it was already after seven o'clock and I was still tired. If they'd let me, I could sleep for the whole week. Only I still had to go to school, even if my concussion got me out of training.

13

EXCUSES

Coach Marth accepted the doctor's note for my training purposes. The bad thing was that I didn't want to stop training. I swear, I needed at most until Tuesday to be all right. But as far as the rules for the health of athletes went, my coach wouldn't let me train for a week after receiving a concussion.

He did purse up his lips and tap his foot, glancing at me as if he wanted to ask a billion questions. But instead, it seemed he finally settled on one. "Are you really doing okay then? What were you doing? I mean, concussions don't generally happen when you're jogging."

He was right. I mean I couldn't deny that. I had to mull an answer over in my head. Make sure it would stick for him.

"I just didn't think. It was really stupid." I looked down at my feet, doing my best to express the contriteness I felt inside, outwardly.

"Dare. I only scold you, or I guess push you, because I know what you're capable of. Just please. Take care of yourself. Don't do stupid shit and ruin all the chances you might have in life because of one screw up. Okay?" The sincerity on his face made me squeamish.

Because the thing was, he couldn't know. He didn't know, but I did. I'd already lost that life, and it wasn't through any fault of my own. It was either through really bad luck, or deliberate machinations of SC to create an ability they didn't have enough access to.

And the more I learned, and the more I did for the organization, the more I was certain that the second option was the valid one. But Coach didn't know that. Coach couldn't know that. I looked at him, and I knew I looked guilty, even if it was for a different reason that he'd assume. "Yeah. I know. We only get one life, got to make sure we take advantage of it."

He smiled at me as the lead dropped to the bottom of my stomach, refusing to digest anything in it. "Good. Take a week off, recuperate, and come back stronger and ready to show them who's boss at regionals, okay?"

"Got it, boss." I saluted him, trying to mimic the enthusiasm I'd always had for this sport, even if it was beginning to wane.

Stupid after death ability shit. I kicked an inoffensive rock off to the grass as I walked out of the field. Not through the showers, not through the locker room. Nope, because that might tempt me to get dressed and run anyway.

I got to the lecture hall way earlier than I needed to be there. I was so used to being at the university early, I hadn't even given it a second thought. We were the first lecture in this building though, so it didn't matter. I just got myself one of our favorite seats and sat there, staring at the lectern, mulling over the thousand thoughts running through my brain.

I wasn't sure what the Ranlan Industries even did. They displayed their name loud and proud on their buildings, and their brick walls, so it wouldn't be a weird thing to actually pull up the information on them. Would it?

Pulling out my tablet, I grabbed the keyboard, attached it, and set to researching.

What are you doing?

I'm curious about something.

You shouldn't question your missions.

I'm not, I replied as smoothly as possible, holding the flash of irritation in check. *I'm researching after the fact. That's not questioning, that's curiosity. And I should be allowed that. The mission was performed successfully with minor hitches, I guess. I was just wondering what they did, because it seemed technology based, and we all know I love my computers.*

It wasn't like I was lying. Every single word I said was the truth. It was just stretched to fit the right mold a bit. This whole fiasco was turning me into a pretty good liar. It was sort of scary how easily it came to me.

You will be placed in an appropriate employment location once your education is complete. There's no need for you to research potential jobs.

I hadn't mentioned looking for jobs, and that was the first I'd heard of that. Frowning, I wished it could see my face, because dang I think I looked pretty pissed off right then. *Do you mean to say I don't get a choice in my career?*

Of course you do. After all, you had already chosen the subject of your degree. It would be a waste of time for us to have you start from scratch with something else. Thus, your current studies will be utilized once you have graduated.

I tried so hard not to let my temper get the better of me, but it was difficult. The deep breath I managed to take almost strangled me. *Okay, so I get put in place by you, at a location you choose, but within the skills my degree has acquired?*

Exactly.

That's pretty fucked up you realize, right? Degrees like mine study specifically to specialize. I was planning to work part time and go into cyber security so I could utilize a highly sophisticated set of skills.

You will perform the job SC obtains for you.

If I didn't know better, I would have said the voice in my head was completely different from my usual friend. There were overtones it didn't usually have, and ways it phrased things that felt decidedly off. *Sure. Okay. It'll be a waste though. Just so you know. My degree can be pretty damned selective and exclusive.*

May as well dangle the carrot in front of the...weird alien computer system in my head and see what we got.

There was a pause, another thing that my usual voice didn't do. I became wary. Had they noticed my absences?

Once you are close to completing your degree, we will see how that goes. Should it prove beneficial for us to send you for further education, it will be an option open to us.

The silence that rang through my head after it disappeared felt more final. Had the system perhaps sent a different agent—or whatever these things in my head were—to check in on me when I began researching things? Had they noticed how much time I spent not actually in my head? Or at least not in the head they thought I resided in?

"Dare!" Orion plopped down next to me, scaring the living daylights out of me. He eyed me strangely as I gasped for the air I'd just managed to lose. "You okay?"

"Way to knock five years off my life." I glared at him, but it was only half-heartedly at best. I knew he shared this class with me. It was the only class we still had in common. But my brain was still racing at the possibility of the system already flagging me to be watched more carefully.

"I'm here if you want to talk about it," Orion offered, lowering his voice slightly.

"Talk about what?" Cyan asked as she dropped into the seat on the other side of me.

"Whether or not Dare needs help with the next assignment," Orion offered smoothly, not missing a beat. I wonder how many times he'd had to make up lies on the spot to cover something that had to do with SC.

"Shh. Both of you." I scowled at them. If I wanted any hope of making it to postgraduate success, I had to ace these classes.

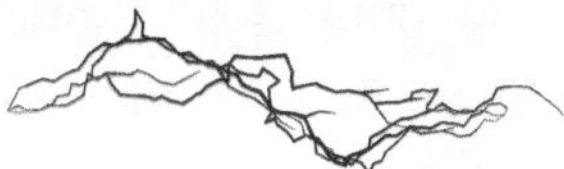

A full day of school had not been the best idea. My head still hurt. It wasn't even getting better like I thought it would. Just how hard had that guy smashed me into the damned wall? I felt like my brain somehow came loose in my skull and wanted to rattle around, or bleed out through my ears.

Perhaps I was just making excuses. I wasn't sure. Was it just nice not to have to get up so early and go for a run? Had I just enjoyed it that much? It was a nice breather for me, even if my coach seemed really concerned. Did I really want to go as far as I always had in track and field now that things had changed? Distance running didn't have to be done with an athletic goal in mind, even if

I did like the bling it ended up giving me. And from what the system had told me earlier, the odds of going to the Olympics now were less than zero.

It was strange how the dream I'd always had could be crushed without a thought. There was an emptiness inside me where it used to be. I knew I couldn't pursue it anymore, not with my powers giving me such an edge, not with a clear conscience anyway. It should have hurt more, but right now it didn't. Maybe I'd gone numb.

Orion had something to do with work tonight, I thought. Perhaps he was meeting the all-knowing SC system and they were figuring out what to do with me. Hi there, imagination, thanks so much for making my night even worse.

Head pounding, I reached for my pills, grabbed them and wandered into the kitchen to get some more food before I took them. I knew they wouldn't be nice on my stomach. I was so preoccupied by the memories of my beating that my head begun to throb more than it had all day. There was something about the attack that I couldn't put my finger on, something far too convenient.

Try as I might, I couldn't push through the haze in my brain to reach it. As I tried, I realized there was an odd sound in the kitchen. Like something had been left plugged in perhaps? A very soft buzzing that I could only hear when standing completely still as I stared inside the refrigerator.

I even tried to close it and my eyes and stand there, listening.

It wasn't a cricket; those things were highly identifiable. Nor was it a mouse or any type of rodent in the walls or ceiling that I could define. Glancing around quickly to see if Jacob's keys were here, I sighed with relief to see they weren't. Which meant he was out. I hoped anyway.

Fridge door shut once more, I stood there, my arms softly dangling by my side and closed my eyes. Balance was difficult to maintain at first, but I dug my heels in. Concentration made my headache recede into the background despite not yet having taken the pain meds that should have helped me.

I frowned, trying to locate the source of the sound. Was it people beneath the window? Was it animals? I didn't think I'd be able to identify insects. Feeling outward from me, away from the appliances and lights, away from the electrical outlets, I pushed my awareness out, past the brick walls, attempting to sense the culprit.

Electricity was everywhere. The way it appeared in my mind was quite beautiful, worthy of being on the National Geographic cover, really. Cascades of light from heavy hubs appeared like volcanos erupting with light. It was easy to spot where the electrical stations were. Their brightness hurt the eyes I didn't even have open. I had to pull my awareness back inside myself, closer to my current location. The sound I was hearing wasn't from outside; it came from inside the house.

I frowned as I narrowed in on our apartment. I could see where the microwave lived, and the fridge, and even the little griddle that wasn't on but was still plugged into the power outlet. The television only had tiny trails of power leaking to it from the walls, and our rooms only gained power when we used the lights or computers therein.

But there was another source, another place I could feel power emanating from. It wasn't pulling from the house's source, though. It had its own small power source, batteries. And it was right above us.

Slowly, I raised my eyes toward the lights, and there, just on the side of the stem that came from the ceiling, was a tiny golden lump. It was so well camouflaged against the old brass light fixture that I had to do a double take to see it all.

It appeared, at first, to perhaps be a bit of excessive brass. Like the fixture itself was just a second and wasn't of the highest quality. It would explain a lot about the place, but even still. Upon closer inspection, both visually and from a power stance, that tiny imperfection was a bug. It sat there, and who knew for how long, listening to all of them. During our Friday night parties. While we all had our day to day conversations.

Just who had put this here and where was it transmitting to?

The thing was, the system could hear me. The system in Orion and myself could hear outside of us. So that could only mean that the bug wasn't from Second Chance. Why the hell would someone put a bug in the middle of our kitchen so it could catch everything we said?

14

I SPY

My days were pretty boring without the threat of missions looming over me and training taking up a huge portion of time in the mornings. Or that would have been the case if I wasn't trying to figure out who had placed that damned bug. The thing was, I couldn't detach it and risk alerting whoever had placed it there to my knowledge of their existence. I had to leave it there and wait for time when no one was in the kitchen to sit there quietly, acting like I was reading, so I could follow the trail of the bug.

Except I hadn't been trained to do that. I hadn't given any thought to how to do that before this. Not that I'd been trained to do anything…the whole system winged everything. Anyway, right now was simply a case of trial and error.

The tiny bug output a signal, which floated on airwaves out into the abyss of radio signal. The trick was making sure I could follow that signal with my mind. The amount of finesse required to perform that task was far higher than the actual power it needed. I was searching blindly with it too, with no clue as to whether or not this would actually work.

Apart from the signal getting weaker as it moved further away, it helped me recognize signatures as I followed it. It struck me that this might even be a training sequence from Nya, but why wouldn't they have told me? Right after I was done here, I planned on figuring out how to send them a message.

There were elements about this whole SC thing that simply made me believe it was all some sort of simulation in my head. Even this weirdly tricky element of sensing felt like a bit of a test to me. And it was irritating. I was irritated!

"Dare?" Orion sounded surprised to see me in the kitchen. Or more accurately, probably to see me sitting down and reading a book in the kitchen. He'd be right too. This wasn't the usual place I would choose to read a book. But following the signal the little spy toy gave off was largely putting me to sleep, and I welcomed the distraction.

"That would be my name," I quipped at him, almost cracking a smile, but I think my tone was off.

"Yes, it would. Why so snappy?" He sounded genuinely concerned. Perhaps he was. "Are you doing an assignment or something else?"

"I'm reading this book on equations of excellence for my own fun factor," I replied dryly, hoping this stopped the game of twenty questions he seemed to have initiated. While I might want to chat, I didn't have time.

"Oh." He threw me a mildly confused glare. "Well, I'll be in my room when you're not as grumpy as you are now."

Great. I'd offended him. Not that it mattered right now. I was still slightly angry with him. Maybe. He probably would still be a great friend if I let him quite literally get away with murder. Which brought me, in a roundabout way, to wonder if he could feel remorse. I really hoped he could. Because that sympathetic side of him, the caring one—it was part of what had always made me so proud to be his best friend.

I didn't have time for these trains of thought. There was too much riding on my finding where this bug went to. Of course, I mean, I thought there was. It couldn't be a good thing to have a bug transmitting information about your house elsewhere, right? At least, I thought there was. Maybe it really was just a lump on the brass after all. It could be a wild bug chase, but a part of me was positive I'd find something. Turning my concentration back toward the bug, I began to focus my attention as acutely as I could.

Try as I might, my reach just wasn't there. My mind was getting used to some of my abilities and was able to reach further than I'd imagine, but it still wasn't enough.

And then I heard the beat. Not a normal sort of heartbeat pulse, but the sort that resonated through your entire body when you feel it. Like a gong had been hit and announced it calling out to me. A pulse like currents in the waves of information floating around in the air. It held so much, information just beyond the horizon, and I couldn't figure out how the hell to access it or understand it.

You realize you'd accomplish much more if you just went into your quiet bedroom and lay down so you could soak in everything around you, the sounds, the smells, everything.

The voice in my head startled me. My old friend had been watching my every move. Apparently, I hadn't been thinking into my private headspace. Still though, perhaps it knew something I didn't.

Thanks, I directed at it, wondering why sometimes it felt like its comments had nothing to do with SC.

Yeah. I guess that might be an option for me. Just let my senses soak everything up. Sounded like a plan.

It wasn't necessarily the best idea to go into my bedroom. After all, it was farther away from the kitchen where the offending little bug was placed. But it would be quieter in here, and there was the possibility that the waves I needed access to flowed nearer to my bedroom than to the actual kitchen.

Or else I'd hit my head harder than I thought.

My bed was comfortable, and with my door closed and this whole concussion thing, at least it would keep Orion out. While that wasn't my goal, it definitely provided an environment that was more suited to me concentrating than brooding over what I was supposed to do with my friendship, my second life, and my moral code.

I closed my eyes and visualized where the bug was. I caught onto the trail of a signal that floated out and around it quite easily considering I'd already latched onto it once anyway. This time it had a glow to it. Sort of gold in nature and luminescent. But it didn't hurt my eyes.

If I wanted to trace this back to its origin, I needed to come up with a better way than I'd already tried. The streets could get noisy out there, and Monday peak hour traffic was no exception. So many cars and other machines existed the further I moved away from our neighborhood. Electrical wires ran everywhere, and differentiating them from the wavelengths I had to find wasn't an easy task.

Meditation had never been my strength. That was something my mother was amazing at. But for me, while it calmed me a bit, I'd never reached a transcendent state of mind. Quieting my thoughts was usually difficult enough. But this time I wrestled them down and shoved them in a nice sturdy cardboard box in my mind. I just had to hope the masking tape was strong enough to contain them, because I couldn't afford to have them distracting me.

I took a deep breath and reached out. Farther than I'd gone before, but in the direction that veered past my room and out toward...toward the street where I'd first realized Shane was indeed a part of this whole SC conspiracy shit. I mean, he'd been in my ambulance for crying out loud. How had he known? Had he been placed there, or was it one of those highly convenient coincidences that seemed to flow around SC?

My thoughts kept tugging at me, threatening to side-track me even more than I already was. From dogs barking in the distance to sirens rounding the corner and music booming out of windows to trail down to the apartments below them and annoy the next set of people. Philadelphia was a busy city. It should have been almost impossible to find the thread I was trying to pick up. Almost impossible to have a hope in hell of discovering who was listening to us and who was watching us that wasn't inside our heads.

And it almost was.

A surge sparked along the line, emitting alarm that raced through my system. It stretched out along the tenuous chord between us, striking a discordant note as it set my teeth on edge. It bypassed my failsafes and plunged right into my mind. Cold assailed me, and I bit down, clenching my jaw even though it still ached from well-aimed punches.

It wasn't just cold though. No, this was like the brain-freeze from hell. Like a who-can-drink-the-most-of-a-frozen-slush challenge that ends up with people rolling on the ground. Each of them going down in pain and agony as their brains react to the intense cold temperature. All I could see was a bright light between my eyes. Gasping in air became painful.

That was the sort of brain freeze. The type I'd never want to have again. It froze me in place with no pun intended, stabbing me through my skull like I'd just had my third eye impaled on a spear. I couldn't breathe, couldn't focus; I couldn't even get a sound out of my mouth. The pulsing assailed my senses, and all I could do was stare at the ceiling. There was knowing in the sensation, like it knew it had caught a spider in its trap and was wondering what it should do with it.

Then, as suddenly as it occurred and assaulted my poor concussed brain, it left. The frigid air whooshed out of my lungs, allowing me to gasp back in pure warmth. It burned as much as the cold had, but in a far better way. A living and breathing way. My eyes stung, like tears had frozen as they formed, and my nose began to run.

Most of all though, my head hurt like it had been impaled on a stake and hammered with a mallet. Like someone had attempted to cleave it with a machete. Perhaps too much of a visual concept, but it was the best I had right then.

It was all I could do to keep my eyes open, and eventually I lost that battle, too.

15
HINT

Dare...

The sound of my name brought my awareness back around to the surface. It was like pushing through sludge-thickened water that threatened to choke me if I breathed it in. Dreams and I didn't get along very well especially not lately with this drowning obsession. Not that I didn't have nightmares, just that I rarely remembered them.

So this didn't smack of a dream but of something I couldn't quite put my finger on. There were things floating with me that I couldn't define.

Warning: Portent Ability unstable.

Gee. Thanks for that not-in-time warning brain. That helped me so much.

At least my biting sarcasm was still working, so I must have been feeling mostly okay. But that didn't help me in this place. The phosphorescent lighting soothed my tired head, like it was trying to make it feel better and forget being concussed. It was working. A tranquil veil attached itself to my thoughts and smoothed out the pain.

Still though, the area around me was blank. Just the shining sludge and myself, floating in oblivion.

Dare...

That sound, those whispers...they felt like the way the shadows had spoken to me. Something desperate clung to the word, the sound. They needed me? Perhaps that was just my imagination, but it felt like they had something to ask me or show me. Perhaps even to answer questions I might have. And I had to admit it, I had so many questions I think my brain was about to explode from keeping them bottled up.

We need you to understand. We need you to see.

Yeah, I'd like to do both. I forced the words out of my head through the pain left over from the damn brain freeze that sent me into this mess. Just what were they trying to tell me. It seemed I could communicate with them now, while I was unconscious or something, so why not just ask them?

I tried to form the words in my mind, but it was more like pictures.

Warning: Portent Ability unstable.

Refrain from overreaching, else backlash could occur.

Fantastic. I'm sure I wanted to know what backlash involved in my still mildly concussed state. Which I didn't, and even through all of my defenses, I was scared. I could die, I'd seen that. Sure, it might be more difficult to kill me considering I could boost my body's healing rate, but...the feeling of David's blood and viscera sliding down my face in the moments after his death played in loop constantly. It whispered warnings to me at a level no one else could understand.

While death might not have killed me, SC could terminate me. But they didn't know about the abilities locked away in the safe haven I'd created. So could those abilities they didn't know of help me avoid their kill switch?

I pushed, just a little more, despite the utter fear I felt at the concept of what backlash might be. The more I attempted to seek it out, the less certain I became that it was a good idea. But slowly, I could hear the voices approaching me again.

You are what we were. Solid. Real.

Before they destroyed us. Before we succumbed.

Well, this was getting dark. The ominous overtones of that statement weren't lost on me. The only thing I really needed was a definition of "they." Opening myself to the possibility that these shadows weren't just a part of me slowly losing my grip on reality apparently triggered the next step in this dreamscape.

The thick sludge water around me changed abruptly, tossing me into what seemed more like a Jell-o version of the ocean. It felt like a stop motion film, complete with clay elements.

Timestance activated. Unauthorized usage excused.

Energy Distribution Initiated. High power mode engaged.

Thoughts raced through my mind, trying to keep up with everything. I could practically see the electrical impulses firing through my brain, correcting the pain and shooting adjustments through my body as if my veins were on fire. The pain it caused was more like the discomfort of stretching muscles before a race. The speed and accuracy activated by my skills astounded me.

Whatever these shadows were and however they'd gotten here, they knew my abilities far better than anyone in SC seemed to and perhaps even better than Nya and Shane. I wanted to know more. Far more about them and how I could access the knowledge they obviously possessed. My brain wouldn't leave the thought alone.

I was fascinated by the intricate knowledge they possessed and how electrical pulses passing through synapses could trigger a whole slew of responses. This was what I needed to learn.

Why have you waited so long? I wanted to know. I'd been at this for like two months now, and my skills and control were still sorely lacking. I had all this power bottled up in me that could probably kill me and anyone within twelve feet, yet they couldn't know. No one out there could know. And I got the feeling somehow, whatever this was is what happened to the rest of the eels.

...you are perceptive.

The overtones of the words in my head sounded infinitely sorrowful. Like a death tolling bell. *It's not perception, it's just matter of factually assessing what you're all doing. Logic, really.*

There was silence for a while as I could feel my body healing itself.

Pushing power in ways I'd never contemplated. I drank in the knowledge with an eagerness that surprised me. If I could harness my own power even half as deftly as they were, it would make a world of difference. What would it have been like if Orion had received my abilities? He knew human anatomy from his studies. Just imagine the things he could have experimented with.

And suddenly, that didn't really seem like such a good idea. Perhaps knowing too much and trying too many differing applications eventually turned this skill bad.

...Orion was not suited for this ability. You think to run. He would try to save the world.

I wasn't sure if they were trying to insult me or not. Of course I wanted to run, faster and faster than anyone, preferably away from imminent danger and death. Orion would heal. He would...try to do things that no one else could. Wasn't that how supervillains emerged in comic books?

I see. And the realization brought me a profound sadness. These shadow things, these souls speaking to me.

You were all once eels, weren't you? I wasn't sure I wanted to know the answer, but the question begged to be asked. What were these? "Figments of my concussed mind" was out, because I hadn't had a concussion when I first encountered them. Was I just losing a grip on reality since being struck by electricity. My scar tingled at the thought, as if it was trying to remind me that hey, I was still alive. In a way, I appreciated it more than I thought possible.

No...

About to apologize for assuming, the words flooded my mind before I could.

...we are still eels. Just incorporeal. Our speed, our ability to move and to survive, to fix and to heal got the better of us. We are here, both in and out of your time, both in and out of your world. But we still exist.

Okay, so I didn't see that one coming. Taking a deep breath, which seemed sort of frivolous in a dream, I opened my mouth to speak.

You are not dreaming. This is a heightened state. Though others will assume you are sleeping.

The hits just kept smacking me upside the head. So much information to digest. *Okay, then.* I began as the questions began to crystalize in my mind.

What are those creatures that seem to look like you but have machine in them? Like a shadow-draped robot. And why did you jump me when I was on that mission? Thinking too much made me realize they owed me answers, and I wanted them now.

We didn't jump you. We were simply trying to prevent SC from gaining the information you held. Before knowing what you now know, you would have reported on us, and we couldn't have that.

*As for the machines...*This voice sounded slightly different. Each word accentuated by the soft ringing of a cat-collar-like bell. *The machines are an attempt to find us, to tap into what we've become. We think long ago that SC realized we hadn't all died, we'd just transcended what it was to be mortal.*

She sounded sad. Like she missed being human.

We are sad, but we are also lucky. We can warn you, and now that you are receptive to our presence, we can also help you in certain ways as long as we avoid detection.

What about Nya and Shane?

Those two are safe, but always remember to analyze everything yourself. Nya has ways you can avoid becoming what we are. But you must listen. You must follow her guidelines because deviating from them might end up with you in our predicament too.

There, you should be much better now. Your head was shaken. Your mind wasn't thinking straight.

The bug! It came back to me, the whole reason I'd been in my room in the first place.

We apologize. It is old, placed there to keep an eye on Orion and any new people who interacted with him, far before your time. The waves lead to us, all around you. Now that you've experienced our wavelengths firsthand, you will be able to see that the signal splits off, to all of us. Since your demise, we have used this avenue to keep an eye on you. To make sure you are safe and not succumbing to the lure that electricity can bring with it.

The lure. That certainly felt like an apt term considering just how entrapped I felt by both my situation and my abilities.

Sleep now. Your body will be fully healed by the morning, and you can pursue your curiosity. It is not a bad thing, and you are not a cat. Stay safe. If you need us, we will attempt to come to your aid.

They were gone, and my mind was suddenly overcome by a distinct fatigue settling into my bones. Perhaps they had guided my hand to use my ability and heal myself. But right now, I was a bit concerned they'd overdone it. This weariness couldn't just be talking to them. Perhaps it was a part of communicating through my mind, and accessing elements of my powers I hadn't realized existed.

Either way, I wanted sleep, and my room was darker than my thoughts. Poetic, really.

Advisory: Portent Ability restabalized.

Advisory: Timestance resuming normal mode.

Well, those were good at least, right?

I began to drift off, my thoughts busy but my everything exhausted. I'm not sure what it was, but just as I slipped off, just as I decided to give in and lose consciousness, I swear I heard the handle on my door click back into place.

The next morning dawned far too bright for my liking. Even though my headache appeared to be completely eradicated, my eyes were still sensitive. I glanced at the clock. Six-thirty in the morning. Seriously? I'd slept in way past my usual alarm, and while I didn't have to be at practice right now, I also didn't like this concussion thing making me feel like I was lazy.

Last night's dream felt much like a blur, almost like I hadn't talked to those eels. But my head felt a thousand times better than it had. Perhaps sleeping in had been worth it after all.

"Dare!" Jacob smiled at me from his perch at the kitchen table, as if he'd been waiting for me or something. He held up a piece of toast with peanut butter and jelly on it before heftily biting into it. Tiny spots of jelly stuck to the outer edges of his mouth; one even graced his cheek. "You're actually sleeping in."

His grin disarmed me as I popped a piece of bread into the toaster, and any notion I'd ever had of him being a part of the program disappeared. He'd have told me, I think.

Jacob has never been a part of the program.

I glared inwardly at my chatty little friend. Besides, Orion had never been close to him, and that hadn't changed in the last two years.

"Yep. Decided to see how the lazy half lives." I winked at him, knowing he was far from lazy.

His mock offense taken made me laugh as he staggered from his chair and into the wall, like my words had shot him. Straightening up almost as quickly as he'd pulled his masterful acting, he brushed the crumbs off his shirt. "And with that, I take my leave. It's been a long week, and I desperately require sleep. Stay safe."

I nodded at him, his words reminding me that I needed to check in with my family.

Something about my night's rather adventurous experience made me realize I felt more at ease with my own abilities now. My body did, anyway. I could close my eyes and see different electric pulses all with subtle color variance. Those shadows had shown me how to navigate the paths of my own body to invoke healing. Perhaps I could transfer that knowledge to other people and help if my friends ever got wounded.

My brain enjoyed this new sense of connectivity, of having control over what I did.

Grabbing my own piece of toast, I sat down at the table, closed my eyes, and insisted on trying to search my brain. Jacob had a distinct glow to him, but I couldn't quite put my finger on what to call the color. It was sort of beige with hints of orange shining through, and it fit him and his personality so completely, I was shocked. It made me fearful to see what Orion's was, not to mention my own.

Aura Detection Activated.

Run in the background?

Yes or No?

Okay, so that was new. Also welcome, still odd thought. I thought a vehement yes at the prompt and realized it lent new colors to the entire world around me.

Intentions waved like electrical pulse flags, as if it was easy enough to see everything if only you looked.

My food tasted good, like nothing had since this concussion. I didn't want it to end, and I also didn't want to run to school, but I knew I had to. Mainly because this colorful array of people around me interpretation might be a fantastic tool, but it was one I didn't know how to turn off. If it stuck with me all day, I'd see it about everyone. I'd be able to read them, and frankly, I wanted to know more. About Cyan and Neale, about Levi and all my lecturers, and of course, about Orion.

The latter was the one killing me. What if I saw something in his aura I couldn't handle?

But he solved that for me by walking straight into the kitchen and grabbing an instant oatmeal pack out of the cupboard.

"Morning. You slept a long time, I even checked in on you, and you didn't move. I was a bit worried." Orion didn't look at me as he spoke, he was too busy preparing his oatmeal, tearing open the little baggie and popping it in a bowl to microwave it with some water.

My mouth went dry. Sitting there, I couldn't help but see the colors swirling around him fighting for dominance. Blackness twisted in and out of all the other colors assailing him, dirtying everything about him.

Reds and blues mingled together to make a pretty purple, but the black twined around it all like raw sewage. It twisted all the colors with a sinister air until the middle of them pooled together in a sickeningly vivid manner. It writhed around him, taunting the other streams, insidiously intertwining in what appeared to be his very being. He seemed oblivious to the obvious torture his soul was being put through.

"Dare?" he asked, his brow furrowed with concern.

"Yeah?" I responded, wondering how I managed to push words past my lips.

"You doing okay? You seem more distracted than usual." He grinned at me, but black slime permeated his eyes, making momentarily monstrous.

I stood up, unsure of how to take this day any further. All I knew was I had to get away. To anywhere but here. Anywhere but around him, at least with this aura thing on. "Of course." I managed to succeed in saying the words smoothly.

Warning: Electrical Pulse Control unstable.

Yeah, I've got it already, I practically shouted at the system. Nerves sparked electricity within me, and I struggled to keep it at bay. I could figure this out, but now while I was so close to him. Not when Orion looked like he'd already sold his soul for his powers.

16
WAITING

Waiting wasn't really my style. If a train, bus, or subway was late, I tended to run to my destination. Sitting on my ass for a week while I waited for them to put me back on duty, or else for Shane and Nya to finally fucking contact me, wasn't my style. Thursdays weren't full of classes, and since I couldn't train, I had time to spare.

There had to be a way to contact them. Shadows flickered in my peripheral vision, more prevalent since I hadn't pulled the blinds up yet.

Are you able to get a message to Shane?

For a few moments there was nothing, and I thought my mind had been playing tricks on me. It wouldn't be the first time. I sighed and swung my legs off my bed, determined to make today count, even if I had to do it myself.

…We can contact him. If needed. With what message?

I tried to push down on the excitement that gave me. A way to communicate that was solely outside of the system was an amazing thing. I mulled over the type of message I wanted to send, just what I wanted to say to them that didn't involve screaming and glaring.

Tell him that I need to see him. Now.

There was a pause, and then the presence of the shadows in my mind vanished, and I could only presume they'd gone to deliver my message. Still, I couldn't be certain. I got up and went about my day.

Except as I finished brushing my teeth, the absence in my mind disappeared, and I waited, almost holding my breath until the sting of the mint made me spit out.

You are to meet. At the corner where you once did. Now.

Well, that was interesting. Short, to the point. I grabbed my backpack, an apple, and rushed out the door, pushing past Orion, who barely had time to register my passing. He was part of the problem, anyway. He was part of the reason I needed to see Shane.

Out past my normal route to school, toward the bridge that started everything whirling around in my mind. I didn't have to be at school until much later, but I needed these answers now, before I drove myself to a breaking point trying to answer them.

Shane stood there, same as always. His hair was blown by the wind, sunglasses pushed right up his nose as he leaned against the traffic light. It was a hot wind, with the edge of the coming summer humidity riding on it like one of the four horsemen.

"Reaching you guys is a pain in my ass," I said as I stood next to him.

He glanced down at me, a grin emerging on his face. "Should have attempted it earlier. You can also access us through the old interface. Anyway, I take it it's urgent. I don't have much time before my shift this morning. Let's do this."

The small alleyway just a short way down provided excellent cover for displacement. At this time of morning there were people around on their way to work, home from work, whatever. I wondered idly if any of them noticed us or if there was somehow a shield of don't look here around us.

Electricity crackled around us, Shane's hand on my shoulder making me an extension of himself, and suddenly we were back inside Nya's office, or eel headquarters, or whatever it was. This time the propulsion only caused me to feel nauseated. I didn't heave, and I didn't fall to the ground gasping for air.

I did stumble a few steps, though.

"Okay." Shane took his sunglasses off and pinched the bridge of his nose. "What's the alarm about?"

I blinked at him, slightly irritated already. There were so many ways I could approach this, but all I could think of was how annoyed I was that I hadn't been given training, that everyone except my little shadow friends thought it was okay for me to just not learn anything. "How about 'I don't know what the fuck I'm doing and I nearly got killed trying to figure it out during an actual fight?'"

Shane at least had the good grace to blush and break eye contact. Yep, that's right, feel a bit careless and ashamed, I'll wait. I even crossed my arms and invoked my trademarked glare.

"Sorry. It's been hectic. In here, out there. The world is a bit of a clusterfuck right now." He sighed and pushed a hand back through his hair. "I meant to reach out to you before this. Before things got this bad. You'd just been limping along on your own so well, I kind of kept putting it off."

Incredulousness overwhelmed me. "That's not a good excuse. Hell, that's not even an excuse." I couldn't get the words out the way I wanted to, and the power inside me began to whip around looking for an outlet.

Calming breaths. That's what I needed to take. Calming breaths. I focused my gaze on the ground so I wouldn't react to Shane's expressions. "Look. I didn't ask for this, and figuring out shit along the way obviously isn't working. Take the bloody time and train me."

I heard the sigh whoosh out of him and could feel the wave of guilt that escaped his shielding. He had to be shielding himself, or that wave of guilt would have been constantly floating around him. Come to think of it. What was shielding?

"Sorry. I know Nya would feel bad if she were here too." He glanced over at the training room entrance I hadn't been permitted to use yet and grimaced. "Look. You're not quite attuned yet. Let's get you to meditate, and I'll see if I can get the attunement finished so we can use the room next time you come."

"Next time like tomorrow, right? Not next time in another ten days, because I could be dead by then. Again." I kept my glare directly on him this time. This was the what, third time they were attuning me to this room? It couldn't be all that complicated could it?

"Now I have some questions," I said as I sat down, patting the stone floor beside me. "While you get this attuning thing seen to. Why don't the eels stay with SC? People like you have effectively emancipated yourselves from the system. I assume you're not the only one."

There was a tugging in my mind, like something was gently pulling on my energies. It felt soft and gentle, as if it was inspecting how I worked. I glanced at Shane, whose brows were knit with concentration, and continued my train of thought while keeping a close eye on my power levels.

"If the eels stayed with SC, it would make missions so much easier. Send in one or maximum two people directly to the spot where they needed to be. In and out in under a minute. Sounds fucking fantastic to me." Dreamlike, really. Even if it meant being a taxi cab for everyone.

Shane let out a dry laugh. "Sounds great. But why do you think I always pick you up at that same spot? It's not like it's my favorite place in town."

I frowned. He had a point there. Were there only certain spots we could displace from?

He offered me a tight grin. "Exactly. I know what you're thinking. Nya is far better at it than I am. I require an open area, with a certain amount of electrical energy available to pull on in case of emergency. Not all eels can displace, and not all of those who can are restricted I the way I am. But if I were to try and port into a building in a tiny space, the electrical discharge I'd create would fry any computer within a ten-yard range and probably short out the alarm system and drop us in deep water." Finally, he sat down with me. "There, done."

"I can go?"

He laughed. "No. You're attuning. Give it half an hour. Should be done, and then we'll get you here tomorrow to use the room. Sorry it's taken so long. It's been a really long week for us."

I eyed him. He did look more tired than I remembered him being last time I saw him. "So. Displacement isn't as awesome as it sounds, right?"

"Got it in one. Displacement might sound like an awesome futuristic scientific ability, but in reality it takes a lot of precision and control to open basically a portal through folded space." He shrugged. "That's about as simplistically as I can put it, even though it's not simple by a long shot."

"Sounds more like a horror movie to me." I shuddered, not really wanting to travel through folded space ever again.

I'd seen that movie. I didn't want that shit to happen to me.

But then my other reason hit me. "Orion. You promised me you'd tell me about Orion."

I glared at Shane accusatorially and he grimaced.

"We can't talk about Orion yet. Not in the way I think you want to. I can't explain to you why he's dangerous, why he's necessary, and what he's done until you understand a few other things about the systems and eels." He spoke softly, the words pulling from him like he didn't really want to talk about it.

"What can you tell me then, Shane?" I asked, suddenly damned irritated. "Can you tell me how better to defend myself so I don't get beaten to a bloody concussed pulp next time I have to go a few rounds? Can you teach me how to channel my power into my body to make me stronger? Can you show me how to release excess power without causing a neighborhood blackout? Oh, and can you—maybe, just maybe—explain what the fuck the disembodied eels are doing floating around in my apartment?"

My voice rose with each question, punctuated by my impatience finally losing it.

He stared at me, and this time regret washed over me like a sudden wave on a beach, pulling back before I could fully register it. "Sorry. Usually it takes us more time to locate the eels, but this time I was in your ambulance. Major coincidence. We just didn't have time to get things in place for you before you were being sent on missions."

I found that so hard to believe, but one thing did stick out to me. "So you weren't deliberately placed in that ambulance?"

Shane shook his head. "Just a very fortuitous coincidence."

"I dunno, Shane." I hugged myself, suddenly feeling cold. "I don't believe in coincidences."

17
REACTIVATION

The next day I woke up to a wonderful notification flashing across my vision.

Assignment division reactivated. Availability for tasks refreshed.

Looks like my little holiday was over already. How sad. I'd almost missed the adrenaline racing bits of my life. Not knowing if I or someone else could be killed. I mean, gotta live life on the edge, right? Some days my sarcasm scared me.

Report directly to Nya for a J class intervention.

What the what? How did they classify them now? That didn't even make sense. It was like they'd been watching too much anime. Although I guess since it was an ancient system, presumably in the bowels of the earth with amazing multitasking capabilities, it had probably had the chance to watch every single anime and television show ever made.

Pushing myself out of bed, I wasn't sure how I was supposed to find Nya. And it took a while as I activated my status information to realize that the message hadn't come through my regular system, but instead through the original portion I accessed when in my right mind. The pun was fully intended;

if I didn't make myself laugh every now and again, I was going to go completely insane.

It gave me more information, but the fact that it was separate from the system that actually rebooted my brain wasn't lost on me. I found it strangely foreboding.

You will be picked up at the same location as the last time you visited. Please make sure to come alone so as not to complicate transport.

I sighed, checked my bag, and walked into the kitchen. Alone. I don't think I'd spent this much time alone, like ever in my life. To be honest, while I often thought I might be an introvert, the lack of constant contact with my coach and my fellow students was really starting to wear on me. Though I did perk up as I headed out of the house after scanning it to realize it was already empty of black and evil auras.

Perhaps the thought of seeing Wick again had something to do with it. He hadn't been there yesterday, which made me wonder if Nya had taken him home. The pup had grown a little on my heart and I missed him. Maybe it was also because the dog was someone I could talk to without any judgement, and without anyone else's questions trying to interfere with the ten thousand I already had about everything going on. I should probably get a goldfish.

Sure enough, Shane was leaning against the brick building at the corner indicated. He had on jeans and a simple light jacket over a white t-shirt. His blue cap was pulled down in front slightly, like he was trying to hide his identity, and he had his sunglasses on again. He might be, too—maybe being around here posed a risk for him. If he died in the area, or perhaps even if he'd worked with people now stationed in the area.

Come to think of it, was his entire brain sectioned off so he could just be himself and not worry? How did they manage to evade the system's recognition abilities? So many questions and so few answers. Yesterday had been an okay start, but I was determined to get more of them answered today. As long as I remembered them while we were training. I hoped this was training.

Shane grinned at me. "Nice and on time. Gotta love a punctual recruit."

I scowled at him. "Look, I don't know what I am, but I'd like to think of it as me auditioning which system might better suit my, oh, I don't know, conscience."

He looked a little taken aback, and I realized I was taking my uncertainty and moodiness out on him. His aura was soft blue mixed with greens and only a streak of reddish purple through it. His energy was calming, and I cringed.

"Sorry." I wasn't in a good mood, even after our talk yesterday. Everything was piling up and trying to itch its way out of my brain. "It's been a rough few days, and it's about time you started coaching me."

This time the crash landing didn't impact me as much. Sure, my stomach still felt like it wanted to heave up everything I'd ever eaten in my entire life. But it didn't. And that's really the defining point. Since the arrival was about the same as yesterday's, I resigned myself to the fact that displacement and I probably just didn't get on.

Nya stood at her desk, reading through something in her hand. I found it strange that she'd use paper, considering the ability to funnel things directly to her sight, but as I took a few steps closer with Shane hot on my heels, I realized it was more like a translucent screen that appeared to be paper.

"Excellent," she said without looking up. Her shoulders hunched ever so slightly, like she was done with everyone and everything but that she had no choice other than to soldier on. She finally looked at me and smiled. "It's good to have you with us. I hope you realize that."

"Nope. Not really." I shrugged. I'd never really been one to sugarcoat things. After all, what use was it? Lying or stretching the truth usually only resulted in either someone getting hurt or a goal not being met. I got the distinct feeling that neither of us could afford that right now, anyway.

She laughed. "I should have known you'd respond honestly. But rhetorical questions are just that: only rhetorical if there isn't really an answer." Nya winked and moved away from her desk. Suddenly she seemed small again, young and vulnerable. Maybe I'd learn how to jump other people's perceptions too.

"Is that a skill? Or do you just change with your moods?" I asked, quite genuinely curious to know the answer.

Her expression softened a little.

"It's good that you can see that." Her brow creased momentarily, and she sighed. "I have been called away, because of course I have. But Shane here will run through the same exercises I would have with you, and I have to warn you. Even though you've been attuned, this will prove tiring and eye opening. And must be done inside the Timewarp."

"Timewarp? Like the dance?" I struggled to understand the term because now I had the bloody song stuck in my head.

"No!" But Nya couldn't choke down her laughter. "I swear the term has been around longer than the dance. I promise."

"Oh, good, because otherwise it was really poorly named." I felt a little foolish. And suddenly tired.

"Timewarps are sort of like bubbles where time passes inside, but not outside at all. This allows us to pause the system so it doesn't realize you're gone, and for you to get more out of the limited time we have here." She paused, reaching down to pet Wick, like she was trying to figure out how to phrase what she said next.

I darted in. "It's like we step in inside of a moment and exit the same way. But while we're inside, it's just fluid?" Wrapping my head around this was going to be problematic. I could see that now.

Nya frowned. "Sort of. That's probably about as accurate as you'll get before you use the actual chamber. We have only have the one room that allows us to train in this way. You'll train inside for hours, but when you emerge, it'll be as if you just left." Nya pushed a few strands of hair out of her eyes. "The terminology gets confusing. Just go in, train as long as you can handle it, and then go to school. Just make sure not to overdo it. Keep your eye on the timer that hangs above the door. Especially for someone as fresh to it as you, I wouldn't recommend more than two, maximum four hours. And then you still might even get side-effects."

"Won't that effectively extend the time I'm here? I mean, won't that still have an effect on my body?" I asked the question knowing that she had to have an answer, right? I mean, it was only logical.

"Of course it will, but it only adds up over time. You could even try to catch up on lost sleep in there if necessary." She said it like she thought it was an obvious thing to do.

"Oh. Okay then." I didn't know what else to say. It looked like I was going to be doing my thing in a room. I hoped the room wasn't too small. I hadn't been able to see inside yesterday.

Nya nodded and left me with Shane, Wick trotting after her adoringly. She was gone in an instant of displacement. Her distortion of time and space even reached me at the other end of the room. It tugged at my stomach, tempting it to empty its contents.

"Just you and me, Dare. You up for it?" Shane had gone all serious. The easy smile he usually wore had disappeared, and I was a bit worried.

"Sure. As long as you can tell me this isn't going to hurt?"

He grinned. "Well, it won't hurt me. But you will probably feel some strain and pain from working your eel muscles. But no, it's not like shock treatment."

"Great." I just hoped I didn't have to port to this room, because I felt another jolt to the stomach was going to finally undo it this time.

Shane nodded and motioned for me to follow him. Over in the far corner, where the screens had been the first time I visited, he stopped and pulled out a weird necklace. The pendant was on a long chain and slotted into the delicate filigree design in the side of the bookcases, like it was the mold it came from. The shelves rose up into the ceiling, leaving those screens I'd seen originally open to the air. Only they weren't screens. They were windows. And they looked out onto a huge room, gymnasium size with strange bronze fixtures in each corner. I only knew they were bronze because of the occasional green in the joints. Brass wouldn't have had as much because it didn't contain as much copper.

"This isn't where you sat me yesterday?" I was hesitant. This looked like it could be a prison, used to hold anyone.

"No." He paused. "I attuned you yesterday through the transfer system. It knows your eel signature now and won't react negatively to your presence."

"So it knows me?" I asked again, pushing for a little more time before I walked in there.

He sighed. "It knows you, it knows your power, and once you enter, the Timewarp will be maintained by a sliver of power it borrows from both of us. Or else it can't operate. You ready?"

I nodded, not really trusting myself to answer.

"Here we are. Welcome to the Timewarp." Shane grinned at me, like he'd just shared the world's biggest secret with the new recruit.

And perhaps he had, because as I looked into the room, I could see the occasional crackling of electricity that kept the whole thing together. If it ever overloaded, it'd level everything within like twenty miles.

18

TRAINING LIKE A MOFO

Crossing the threshold of the room sent electric shocks down my spine, and I cried out from the unexpected pain.

Shane cringed. "Sorry about that. Should have warned you. That's just the room calibrating your electric signature, reconciling it with the records it has, and adding it into the makeup. That way it doesn't accidentally zap you, or I guess you could say, freeze you in time."

I blinked at him. "Thanks for forgetting something as inconsequential as that."

"Sarcasm suits you." He smiled tightly as he moved over to the end of the room. "You stay here. I need to test your reflexes."

"Without any practice?" I asked, nerves starting to get the better of me. I was tired, though I knew I'd slept well, and sort of scared. This whole Timewarp room thing intimidated the hell out of me.

"Yep," he responded, his friendly demeanor disappearing as concentration replaced it. "Without any practice."

Before I could so much as blink, a ball of electricity shot right at me. It was huge, white, and static with the electrical strings that made it up. My brain froze, and I barely reacted in time to dodge out of the way. Or not even, because the smell of burning hair meant at least one of those strands on the outer layer had caught my hair. "Hey, my hair is already short enough, thanks. Don't do that!"

Shane laughed. "If you dodge it quick enough, it won't touch your hair. Good luck!"

His eyes lit up like the balls he was throwing, silver and blue with an intensity I'd not noticed before. Perhaps his demeanor lulled me into thinking he was always laid back. But I'd been so very wrong.

I had to keep my eye on the balls. Each one approached with accelerating momentum. At first, he only threw one at a time, but slowly, as I begun to get used to the pattern each of those exhibited, he began to add in more.

Sweat began to form droplets on my forehead as I focused more than I ever had in my life. The balls grew slightly smaller over time, but denser in their make-up. Each time I narrowly managed to avoid one, the energy that dissipated as it dissolved, tempted me like nothing else. Absorbing it could be so easy. But there wasn't time.

It was like dodge ball times infinity. Jumping left and right, up and down, over and under was exhausting. Shane always made sure the ball zoomed toward me, almost like there was a tracker on me so I couldn't escape. There wasn't time for thinking only for reacting, and I was going to exhaust myself before I got better if this was how he trained me.

Finally, he threw one straight at my face. I'd had enough, and focused a burst of my own energy into my feet, jumping as high as I could. Anger fueled my ability too, because I was frustrated and didn't feel like I was learning anything. Which the whole jumping ridiculously high in the air proved me wrong about.

"Took you long enough." Shane grinned. "Now we just need you to do that consistently."

I blinked at him. "Really? Why didn't you just tell me?"

He shrugged. "Because if we tell you, then you're less likely to activate your brain and solve problems by new approaches to your ability when it really counts."

"When you put it that way...I guess it makes sense." I thought of the electric blast I'd managed to fire through my attacker previously. Would I have thought of that if I knew I could do it?

"Damn right, it does." He winked at me. "Okay, next round is specifically designed for you to do exactly what you just did. Size and speed will vary, so you need to take all of the factors into account in order to keep up with it."

Jumping lightning balls was not how I'd imagined my Friday morning to go. But I did it anyway. Jumping high became easier and something I could do over and over with little effect to my personal energy levels. It gave me a fantastic direction to channel my unspent electrical charge into. The thing was, I couldn't go jumping high down the street every day. Maybe I should pursue pole vaulting instead of long distance running.

The novelty of the whole situation ended up wearing off around minute, oh, say twelve. And now we'd been doing it for half an hour.

Finally, Shane spoke up. "Okay, that's enough of that. Now we're going to work on some offensive abilities, since that's what messed you up last time."

He frowned, like he was sorting through files or something in his head. Maybe he was a robot too? Not sure why the thought suddenly came to me, but there might even be some truth in it.

"Okay. What I need to do is see how you are with hand to hand combat. That's where you're lacking. Whereas both your Driver and your Minder had combat experience, you did not. Electricity is useful, but it won't save you all the time. You need to ground it, push through, and learn to fight your opponents."

"Okay." I tasted the word, slowly digesting what he meant by that. "Then what do I need to do?"

This time he grinned. "I thought you'd never ask."

"Stop it with the one liners. What I care about is understanding what I'm supposed to be learning so I can apply it to everyday problems I've been having."

And oh, hi, snappy mode of impatience. I thought we'd lost you. I took in a deep breath and made eye contact.

"Look. I'm sorry. I just feel so vulnerable out there without back up. There are things I know I should be able to do and things I simply can't." I concentrated on lowering my heart rate before continuing. "Can we just get to this like a business transaction and avoid getting all muddy clear on it?"

"Sure. But I'll have to let you know. Impatience doesn't work well on electrical abilities. It'll feed off that instead of the adrenaline you're focusing into the work right now. It might seem like I'm being flippant, but I'm trying to show you that rushing it isn't going to make these abilities come any quicker than they will. I need you to stick with it and persevere. Is that okay?" His tone was full of genuine concern, and I felt like a heel.

He was right. Hell, it appeared he was often correct. "Fine. But teach me. I felt like I left with more questions than answers last time. And I'd like not to feel that way again, thanks."

Shane eyed me. "You're not like the usual eel."

"What's that supposed to mean?" I snapped out the question, but in my defense, it was a shitty thing to say.

He sighed, and I could feel his aura powering down, like he wasn't going to fling weird electric yarn balls at me anymore.

"Most eels are excited by their abilities, obsessed even. The whole 'omg I'm not dead' thing comes into play a lot with them. Hell, I remember what it was like for me when I first came back. Like the world was new, being seen through a different light. But you?" Shane paused, looking at me with his head cocked to one side. "You. You seem to act like this is all a total inconvenience to you. Like you'd prefer if you hadn't died, or at least hadn't had to interrupt your life, which you wouldn't have had to do if you were actually dead."

I mulled the words over in my head. I didn't see it so much as a benefit or something good and benevolent. What I saw was interference in the life I would have had. "I had goals in my life. Goals I'm likely unable to pursue because of this Second Chance thing. So yeah, I'm angry and resentful and filled with logic that tells me I should know more about this and how my powers work. That if this were any job, their on-site training would be under litigation. It's shoddy and dangerous for workers to know as little about their abilities as I do.

"Not to mention the assignments. What the hell is with those? They make no sense? Killing people when we could have just knocked them out? Nope. Not my cup of shit. Stopping megalomaniac tyrants? Sure, I'd be fully in for that. Do you see what I mean?"

The words tumbled out, and I couldn't help it.

I didn't want to help it. I was tired of keeping it all in and all to myself. And Shane was the only person I felt I could rant to. Sam was holding something back, and Orion was just outright different than he'd been. I needed—no, required—for this to be more organized than it seemed to be. And right now, where we weren't losing time, where I wasn't in danger of having the thin line I was walking be broken, I needed answers, and I needed them yesterday.

Shane didn't seem as shocked as I thought he would. Instead, he looked like he was thinking really hard. I couldn't blame him. When I got this annoyed, I sort of tumbled over my words trying to get them all out of my system.

"Difference isn't a bad thing, it's just an unexpected thing this early in. Cynicism hasn't been prevalent in the people we've had to recruit, and if it was, their non-compliance tended to result in their accidental demise before we could put safeguards in place and help them. When an eel hasn't yet figured out much to do with their abilities, there's really nothing stopping them from accidentally frying to death."

I preferred this side of him. The side that didn't let nonsense interfere in what should be an important conversation.

He grinned at me and put his hands on his hips. "Well, I guess we've got our work cut out for us, then. Good thing we have all the time in the world."

I groaned. "Has anyone ever told you that your puns are dastardly?"

"Never, not once, ever." He winked again, like it held some hidden meaning and I was too tired to find it out. "Okay then. Sit with me for a bit, and then we'll spar like there's no tomorrow. But right now, it's story time, and I don't actually think you're going to like it."

His gaze seemed sorrowful, like he didn't want to tell me it would be bad but couldn't help it.

I sat down, a strange somberness coming over me. Because I knew he was right.

Annoyingly enough, Shane took a while to start his tale. His outward expression changed subtly. Like he wasn't sure how much to tell me and was trying to figure out what he could and couldn't say. He probably thought he had a poker face, too.

My fingers itched, wanting to reach out and throttle him for a moment. Even though I knew we were technically frozen in time in here, and I shouldn't be close to the time limit yet, I couldn't help feel like we were moving too slowly. Also, what sort of ramifications did this whole thing have on the human body? How long could a person stay in this time lock without detrimental effects? All the questions assailing me weren't helping my mood at all.

"We're not entirely positive how the system originated, nor why it was set up with such a unique criterion. But it's been around a long time, and finding out the intricacies is one of Nya's obsessions. We already know a lot more than we used to." He began his lecture with a serene expression on his face, like he'd just imparted wisdom with me.

I rolled my eyes. "Look. I already know it was designed to protect humans from themselves, whatever that means. I also know that eels haven't been prevalent because they can burn themselves out. I also know that not all eels disappearing means they burned out, but some of them are displaced in space and time, and sort of incorporeal because they accidentally put themselves there."

Shane blinked at me, and a wave of sadness seemed to envelop him. "Fine, ruin my awesome story by being knowledgeable and way too cynical. I thought you said you didn't know enough and needed answers."

It occurred to me for the first time, that perhaps these eels with Nya and Shane didn't know everything they needed to either. It wasn't reassuring. We were just a bunch of electric eels bumbling around in the dark trying not to electrocute each other.

"I do need answers. Why are there fake shadows out there? Who made them? More importantly, why were they created, and how come they keep appearing? How can they constantly monitor me without the system knowing? Why are we directed to perform the tasks we're given?" Each question heightened my anxiety and the anger building inside me, which electricity fed off. It was a vicious cycle, and I needed to calm myself down. Standing up, I stretched my legs and my arms, glancing down at Shane and his processing of the plethora of questions I'd just asked.

My feet itched, but in that can't-reach-it, need-to-rip-my-skin-off kind of way where it sank into my bones. I could feel the hairs on the back of my neck start to stand up, and the ones on my arms. Wired. I was totally wired and I needed to burst.

"I need to run," was all I said before heading off. The room was massive, far big enough for me to treat as a track and just go. Concussion and all, it'd been the longest interval ever for me. No running, none of the calming rhythm that kept me going during the days. Nothing like it. The amount I missed being able to channel my own and now this excess energy through and into the sport I was passionate about wasn't lost on me. It was like this ability was made just for me. I ran for what seemed like an age, and slowly my mood bettered. Slowly I began to feel like maybe everything wasn't doom and gloom after all.

Logic seeped back into my angry brain, and I finally understood one thing about my power. It needed to be expelled in the most efficient way possible, all the time. Not a bit here or there, but constantly. It fed off my emotions, grabbing a hold of them and magnifying the ones that produced the most power. In my case, that meant anger, frustration, and impatience.

Excess fuel would end up sending me into oblivion like the poor shadow creatures I'd already encountered. That wasn't going to happen. I came to realize that part of the problem was the splintering of the system. Because obviously, if two segments existed, then at some stage they'd been split. The why and the how were important, but so was the who.

Exhilaration flooded my body as I sat down next to the still-waiting Shane. My mood was already better, more focused, and less likely to blow a gasket. "Sorry about that. With the concussion, I haven't been able to run. All this energy gets bottled up so tightly, and running helps me drain the tank to a manageable level."

He regarded me with something that I hoped was respect. Because the other choice was mild disgust, and I didn't like that option.

"You're fast, even without your power. It's like it was made for you." He spoke the words slowly, like he was still thinking potential greater ramifications over in his head.

"I know." I shrugged, trying not to let the fact that his words so closely mirrored the thoughts I'd had while running affect me. I was a runner who'd been hit by lightning which could coincidentally increase my speed. If I was into conspiracy theories, I'd think it wasn't just a coincidence.

"The shadow remnants are called Demarcates." His expression was serious now, like he was talking to someone older, more in the know. "They're still entities, but no longer human. I don't think you're in danger of their fate, but never give in when the power is trying to coax you, okay?"

I nodded, heeding his serious tone, perfectly sure of what he meant. I'd already had a couple of run-ins with that particular brand of coaxing. Shane seemed to be about to say something else when he shook his head slightly.

He jumped up from his sitting position somewhat ninjalike and grinned. "We're close to your two hours. Don't want to overdo it. The rest of the information is something you can earn by passing the rest of my training. Battle up, Dare. Prepare to be assessed."

19
CURIOUSER

"Fuck!" I screamed as Shane's fist connected with my jawbone for the second damn time. "I'm a runner, not a fighter."

I didn't expect the statement to have him in stitches, so I scowled at him until it subsided. At least he had the common sense to look sheepish.

"Sorry, it's just—you're really bad at hand to hand combat."

His comment was sobering. And also correct.

"Okay, then. How am I supposed to protect myself? How am I supposed to not get smashed in the face?" It was amazing how much good the brief run had done for my system. I was irritated, sure, but I wasn't ready to explode.

He shrugged. "Barricade your skin."

"You mentioned that last time. How about a little bit of showing and less telling me what I should do? There's far too much to learn for me to be wasting time like this." I thought we'd talked about this. At least I had. Apparently, he hadn't listened.

"Hey. It's not a waste of time to figure out where your strengths lie. It's what could mean life or death all over again for you. Stop trying to make less of it than it is, okay? This flippancy you exhibit isn't going to do anyone any good." His voice modulated with his words, and I think it was the first time I'd seen him irritated with me. Good for him.

"Okay. Sorry. I'm ready and listening, coach." And I actually was.

He raised an eyebrow and approached. "Okay, so this is a little more finesse than you've learned up to now, but it's also vitally important. If you get the barricade wrong you could electrocute people around you, never mind your enemies. Of course, if they're all enemies, I guess you'd want to, but that's all part of the control needed to pull this off without exploding people and things."

I nodded, not liking the image of blowing Cyan and Neale up in a fit of impatience that ran through my mind. "Got it."

"Hold out your left hand." He held out his own for me to place mine into.

Complying, I felt oddly worried about what backlash could occur just from training.

He continued as soon as I gave him my hand. "Now, concentrate in your mind and envision the skin. Run the electrical pulses through to the surface and reinforce a line just beneath the dermis."

It sounded so much simpler when he said it in his this-isn't-that-difficult voice. Visualizing in my mind wasn't the problem. That I could do. It was figuring out how to funnel the electrical charge down to my hand with enough finesse that it didn't break out or hurt anyone around me that was the problem.

"Shit!" Shane dropped my hand and shook his own. I swear I could smell a faint scent of fried hair and skin.

"Sorry." I felt pretty bad. Not completely. I mean, what did he think holding my hand in place while I worked this bit of electrical mojo would result in?

"Nope. My bad. With the feistiness of your charge, I should have known better. Let's practice this with less physical contact." He grinned at me, and there was a sparkle in his eye, like he thought he'd found a solution.

I bloody well hoped he was right.

Closing my eyes lent me far better control. Sure, I knew I couldn't do it that way in a battle, but let's actually obtain the skill first, right? The whole idea of reinforcing my own skin was a brilliant bit of thinking. If I was hit, my skin would be harder and thus absorb some of the damage. But if I could get this right, I might also be able to prep electrical charges ready to blow if my skin was contacted in a violent way.

And here I was telling Shane not to put the cart before the electrical shock. "Okay. Ready?" It felt better to ask, just in case he wanted to run and hide.

Maybe he nodded; perhaps he didn't. Closed eyes didn't help with that. But I also didn't really care. I'd given him advance warning. My conscience was clear. Slowly, I released electrical pulses underneath my skin, pushing it all the way to my left hand where it stopped. Then I fed more power to the spot, reinforcing it, visualizing that it hardened. After I was pretty sure I'd covered the entire area under the surface of the back of my hand, I opened my eyes.

I wasn't expecting my hand to glow, but it did. Pale blue suffused my skin, like I was shining a blue torch through it. Reaching out with my right hand, I touched the spot, surprised by how steel-like it made my skin feel. The thing was, I think maintaining it sapped at my energy at a faster rate than anything else, because I was suddenly inordinately tired. But I'd done it, and damn, did I feel a sense of accomplishment.

"Wow." That one word was filled with pride, and Shane looked on like the big electrical brother I'd never had.

"Yeah. It's pretty cool, isn't it?" I asked, my voice soft with awe. "But fuck, this is tiring."

He laughed, and glanced at the timer over the door. "Let that go. It's the first time you've done it, and it takes a lot of concentration to get it initially. I don't think I've ever seen someone get the charge so dense before, but either way, you need to rest a bit. Remember, it's still time as normal out there. You can rest up and relax for a little while. We even have food in here, though that's a bugger to get in and out, I can tell you."

I held my hand in front of my face, frowning at it, totally fascinated by what I'd just done. Concentrating so hard I bit my lip, I pushed a tendril of that solidified awesomeness out a bit further, making it hit my pointer finger. My head got dizzy, and I realized that yes, this was going to need a lot more work than I'd put in so far.

"May as well grab some food and water. You need to replenish your reserves and go to school." Shane grinned as he ran off to what I hadn't realized was a tiny room in the very back.

He emerged with cheese crackers, some beef jerky, and a bottle of water.

"Take it easy though, don't overdo it. This will take time, and practice every spare minute you find. Did I mention practice? Because control is the key. Once you can barricade your body without a second thought, you can move to the next step." He grinned at me, like he'd just told me the world's greatest secret.

"Weaponizing it?" I burst his bubble and it showed on his face.

"That's not fair," he said, pouting a bit.

"Nope." I grinned. "Definitely not."

Class was damned difficult to get through that day. I was still mentally exhausted. Physical exhaustion might be cured, and I could certainly rejuvenate it myself, but that whole brain fog went to a completely different level when it came to being an eel.

I barely remembered talking to Cyan; the only thing that stood out to me was her concerned look as I half-stumbled out of the lecture hall. Neale didn't have classes on a Friday, and I hadn't seen Levi in an age. It was all I could do to stumble home.

My room, on the other hand, felt like the safe haven I needed. Nestled toward the middle of the building, it rarely got direct sunlight and remained mostly cool as the outside heated up. Of course, in the winter that was sometimes horribly detrimental, but right now? It was glorious.

Laying my head on my cool pillow, I closed my eyes, fully intending to practice weaving some electrical intricacies and make the most of my time. Reinforcing was all well and good and might help me not get beaten to a pulp, but I did love the idea of being able to fire a shock back at someone who thought it was okay to hit me.

The next thing I knew, the light from the window receded, signaling sunset. I'd fallen asleep. How embarrassing. Sleep was arguably far better than my own little electro rejuvenation pulses. Maybe I'd harmed my cellular regeneration rate or something by entering the Timewarp. What sort of studies had they done? Were there any side effects? Thanks for nothing, brain.

Still dressed, I pushed myself up and made my way to the bathroom just as Orion came out of his bedroom.

"Dare!" A huge smile broke out over Orion's face. "I was just about to come in and wake you up. You've been asleep since I got home. The others will be here shortly."

Nodding, because words sort of stuck in my throat, I walked into the bathroom. I was still tired, but felt more refreshed than I had been all day. Maybe it was my own bed, perhaps just the comforts of home. Either way, it was good to be here.

I checked both systems to make sure there weren't any other notifications for me that I'd missed. Because it was typical of SC to not care what my plans were and to simply allow whatever assignments it deemed fit to float my way regardless.

Sort of. Not really. I realized I was being petty, or tired, or maybe even a bit of both.

The doorbell rang, signaling the first guest of the evening. Apparently, we were doing this. One night, after I'd been off with injury, I was finally able to come back and actually enjoy being home instead of being sent on wildly weird side quests in a badly coded game.

Had I given that a thought? Yes, I had. What if this was all just one big prank? If it was, I think I was going to have to kill whoever came up with it in the first place.

Sam and Cyan jaunted through the door, their steps in unison, their clothing not. Cyan was dressed as usual. In her namesake, of course. Blue as far as the eye could see, and it could often see pretty far on Cyan.

Sam grinned at me, grabbed a snack that I belatedly noticed Orion had prepared for the little soiree, and dragged me over to the corner to whisper. Cyan raised an eyebrow, and I thought I saw a sickly green aura lurk around her for a moment, but it was gone a split second later. Even so, a part of me wanted to know whom it was directed at.

"So? How did you heal up? Are you okay? I was so worried about you!" Sam was full of life but obviously concerned. "We really need to work on your own defenses."

"Yeah," I responded. "I know, I already am."

She smiled this time; it was a genuinely happy expression, I think. "Good. Got some mega cold feet there. Not only because you were injured, but we didn't even have a Cleaner, and you were there. Hopefully the guys were taken care of. I never wish anyone harm."

"Sometimes you just have to make pain to get progress?" I grinned this time, biting into the smoked gouda cracker Sam gave me.

"Got it in one. Still, though." She seemed thoughtful. "I wonder why there aren't so many eels around anymore. And what to do about having one? Are you finding difficulty accessing information on them? Because I haven't found anything that might benefit you yet and since that whole incident last weekend, I've been looking."

"No need to go to any trouble, I can mostly guess what I need to do. I'm no doctor, but I do know the human body functions because of tiny electrical impulses that fire through the whole synapses thing." The thoughts were clear in my mind from the training I'd already done that day. All I needed now was to apply the principles I'd practiced until I could do it in my sleep. But of course, Sam couldn't know that.

"Hey, you two! Are you planning a surprise birthday party for me or something?" Cyan only sounded half serious about her statement. That sickly green surrounded her again, but it was thinner, closer to her body, difficult to pull away from her bright blue. It didn't flare as she put a hand each on Sam's and my shoulder, so I still couldn't pinpoint the target.

"Nope, no surprise anywhere for you." I realized then that I was going to have to come up with a surprise birthday present or party for her or else be considered a really bad friend.

While we talked, I tested my Aura Detection again, because Cyan was confounding me. From what I could sense she was pretty happy, perhaps curious, and generally just herself. So I switched to glance at the others.

Watching them showed me a few things, among them that it was easy for some people to present an entirely different self to the world than what was real. Like Orion when he wasn't busy murdering people. His aura flickered with darkness, but for the most part, he was himself, and I wasn't sure what to make of it.

You need to let that go, I told myself, scolding myself ferociously. And now I was talking to myself, which couldn't be a good sign.

Assignment Notification.

Location: City Hall Adjacent Museum.

Objective: This is a close quarters group assignment consisting of:

1 x Runner

1 x Cleaner

1x Blocker

Your Blocker will have more information. Please abide by ranking and SC protocols. Driver is tasked with Delivery. Highly confidential mission. Cannot be discussed outside this direct group of people.

Meeting time: 7 p.m., at the Rodin Museum.

Time Limit: By midnight tomorrow night. Must be completed outside of normal Museum operating hours.

Reward: Dependent on the mission's success—experience, skill points, and monetary compensation.

Caution: Guards and a high-level security system.

Just when I thought the night couldn't get any better, I got an assignment for the next day. It's not that I didn't want to do another mission, it's just that it was tomorrow, and that didn't give me much time master the new skills I'd learned. I needed like two weeks of time in the Timewarp room so I could hone them properly.

I was scared. Sure, I could admit it. I could admit that there was a trembling starting in my gut and threatening to make me sick. The knowledge that I didn't feel prepared, and wasn't in fact prepared, bore down on me. The room, and my friends in it, seemed to take on a decidedly grey hue while my mind worked nineteen to the dozen.

Could I manage to slip in another training session? All I had to do was contact Shane, right? I was sure I could do it through the older system. I had to be able to. After all, that's how I'd known to go there this morning, right? If not, I'm sure my Demarcates friends would help me.

Frowning, I searched through the older, clunkier interface. Its design was definitely subpar. Nothing intuitive about it. I found the notification I'd received first thing this morning and backtracked from there. If I hadn't done that, it would have taken me forever to find where this thought it a good place to put the communication system.

"Archaic" sprang to mind.

"Dare?" Cyan's eyes held the faintest hint of irritation when I looked up into them, startled.

"Sorry, what?" I tried to look sheepish, like I'd been miles away at the time, but she didn't seem impressed.

I think it was the first time I've ever seen her truly exasperated with me. Impatient on top of that, totally out of character for the Cyan I'd come to know. I mean, sure, I irritated people frequently. But not Cyan. It twisted my stomach like I hadn't expected and I sighed.

"Sorry, I've got a lot on my mind lately." It was a lousy excuse, but that didn't change its truth.

She appeared only slightly mollified. "Something more than that has gotten into you lately. If you don't have the time for us anymore, you need to let us know. We wouldn't hold it against you. Hell, Neale has to skip the next D&D night because he's got a team to visit who've been scouting him. I wouldn't hold that against him for a second. But if he kept blowing me off or ignoring me while he's right in front of me—now that I could hold against him for eternity."

Her pointed gaze was piercing, and for a moment I felt like she could see through and past everything I'd ever tried to hide.

"I'm sorry." And I truly was, which I think reflected in my words because her demeanor changed.

"I know. And I know you don't mean it. You just take on everything. Most athletes heading to nationals might have tried to turn their four-year degree into a five year. But not you. Never you." She sighed and pushed a hand through her hair.

For just that moment, she looked perfectly vulnerable. Like everything about her was close to crashing down in ruins at her feet. It wouldn't surprise me because sometimes she was just supernaturally perky.

I'd never really thought about it before. But it must be exhausting to keep that persona up. And I knew she did it a lot for me and the other people she cared about. Most people would have to, or I'd realism them into the ground. "Sorry. I don't mean to worry you. And my studies and athletics are going fine. I've just been thinking a lot about life after...school. You know? Getting all up in my own head."

After school, after death...such a fine line. Was the former really a lie? I think not. Or so I told myself.

Cyan giggled, like she was prone to do from time to time. It encapsulated all of her young energy and bottled it up, shaking it so the fizz would explode that cap right off. She flung her arms around me, and for just a moment I didn't completely mind.

The moment passed, though, and I gently stepped away, disentangling myself from her grip. "I see I said something that made you happy?"

"Are you kidding me? You opened up. You actually confided in me, told me something about what's been bothering you. Do you have any idea how difficult it is to get you to say even a fraction of what is on your mind? I mean, I have no problem getting other people to open up, but you, Dare, are a bit of an enigma wrapped in a cast iron wall." Her grin lit up her whole face, and I remembered just why we'd become fast friends.

Her whole attitude about everything—about school, about life, about friendships—it was hopeful, determined, positive, and downright infectious. Sometimes, I wish she could just sweep me away with who she was.

"I'll remember that next time." It seemed like the right response to give. After all, I *was* glad she seemed so happy. I just couldn't figure out what I'd really done, considering I'd basically just lied to one of my best friends.

I was really, really hating Second Chance's impact on my life.

Focusing back on the ancient menu system I had pulled up, I sent a message to who I hoped Shane was, using a chat interface that reminded me somewhat of an older chat system we'd studied in first year called IRC and that one would have been a mild upgrade.

Shane.

Have mission tomorrow night. Am worried about getting beaten to a pulp. Can I train for as long as possible before my mission? Is that okay? Is there still a limit to time in the room for me?

Dare

I mean, it was me. And it was the message I needed to send, and all of the questions I wanted to ask. Okay, so not all of them, but I was asking the important ones and taking it a step at a time.

Willing it to send off, a bone weariness suddenly overcame me, and all I wanted to do was sleep. Perhaps training tomorrow before the mission wasn't the wisest idea I'd ever had, but it was the only option I could guarantee my own safety with. If I could rely on my own devices, then these assignments became that much more manageable for me.

So, whatever the price I had to pay, I'd have to make it worth it if I wanted to stick around long enough to figure out what the hell I was going to do about my predicament.

20
MUSEUM

Saturday morning was unexpectedly chilly, considering it was getting close to summer now. Me and my trusty hoodie stood on our street corner waiting for Shane to show. My message had reached him, and his reply woke me up this morning. So here I was, on the dingy street corner he'd first kidnapped me from, waiting like an idiot.

"Sorry." He panted behind me, and I twirled around to see him bent over his knees, panting out hot air like there was no tomorrow.

"You're not very fit, are you?" I asked dryly, waving a hand at the very obvious lack of breath he had. "Speaking of. Like. Do we get upgraded when we're saved I guess?"

I didn't like the term I'd chosen, but it made more sense than anything else I could think of, so what the hell.

"Like? Fitness levels? Body capacity or whatever?" Shane's gaze was somewhat incredulous. He seemed genuinely amused. I'd never taken kindly to being amusing. It wasn't exactly a compliment in my book.

"Yes. Like everything. Do you get sort of upgraded to maximum peak so that the program gets the most out of you?" I realized my comment to Shane about not being fit was unfair. It was cold, and he could have any number of lung conditions, or asthma, or perhaps even something wrong with his heart. In today's world it could even be lingering aftereffects of a virus.

"No. Not that I'm aware of. I mean. It could. But it doesn't." He paused for a moment, like he was thinking over what he'd just said. "Strike that. I don't think it could do that. It doesn't alter us on a genetic or molecular level. It just resuscitates us. Sort of like a…"

"Mystic defibrillator," I finished for him, sick of the analogy by now.

I was definitely getting used to the displacement travel by now. I barely even retched once after we landed. However, it did feel like I was cheating. I was tired already and wasn't sure how well that was going to bode for tonight's assignment, but I guess I'd find out.

Nya wasn't anywhere to be seen as Shane ushered me through to the Timewarp area. He glanced at me as he activated it, like he wanted to ask me something but wasn't sure how to phrase it, and it was driving me absolutely bonkers.

"What?" I asked it in as nice a tone of voice as I possibly could. Thought I could see it didn't have much of an effect on it.

"You wanting to do this. I mean, I realize you don't want to be beset like you were last mission, but most of the missions you've been on haven't been violent, right? Have people attacked you in every one or something?" His brow furrowed, the concern not only in his voice, but also his expression.

I shrugged. "Well, not so much. Although it's been a close call once or twice. You know, like having your Blocker's head blown up all over you. Gotta love the mess bullets leave behind."

It'd be so much easier if we could just zap them and make their hearts stop. I realized I wasn't any better. Bullets let us know cause of death and probable ability to trace the crime to the perpetrator.

My way? It'd be seen as a heart attack. Being an eel seemed the perfect recipe for a serial killer. Another aspect I wasn't fond of in the slightest.

"Odd. You should have some skills to help you, and while this is a form of training, it's not something they would usually have implemented, so the fact that you have access to it is a good thing, don't get me wrong, but the system shouldn't be relying on you working by yourself on a skill that you're basically required to have in order to survive the very missions they're giving you." His concerned face was starting to wear on my patience.

Not the least of all because he was completely correct.

I sighed. "I know. Hell, I'm far more aware of it than you'd believe. But I'm here now and ready to learn. Because I have to. Not only for my own protection, but for those I have to group up with." I was proud of myself for sounding so mature and so in control when I was secretly part boiling angry and part scared shitless inside.

This time his gaze bore into me, like he knew the amount of bravado I was putting up in front of the terrified me inside but wasn't sure how he should broach the subject.

It seemed like he gave up. "Okay. First up. I can't let you spend all day in here. Nya would kill me."

I scowled at him. "Fine. How long do I get then?"

"Just a few hours, and be glad I'm bending the rules and letting you do that. Since you practiced yesterday in here, you really shouldn't be in here again so soon." He bit his lip as he ushered me through the door. "Let's keep doing this drill until you can't do it anymore. You need to learn to expand your awareness to keep yourself and others safe. So first you need to be able to push the electric charge into a skin barricade in your sleep and upside-down while being attacked by spiders."

I raised an eyebrow. "Really? Upside down now?"

He shrugged. "Any which way. The point is, it must be second nature for you. All the time. So natural it's like breathing."

Shane made sense, and I didn't like it at all. I concentrated, pushing the power inside me through my veins and tissue, reinforcing the outer layer, making myself like a tank. Except it was exhausting. Concentration and the redistribution of my own strength took more out of me than I liked to admit. Perhaps this hadn't been the best idea I'd ever had. I opened my eyes, aching as they were from my scrunching them shut, and looked down at my body.

What was I thinking? Sure, of course my like second time ever was going to enable me to reinforce the entirety of my body at once. Not. My left forearm was all I'd managed. And I felt like I needed to sleep for a week. Fuck.

"You didn't expect to get it straight away, did you? Not after last time, surely," Shane asked, a hint of humor underlying his words, because we both knew a portion of me had totally been thinking exactly that. At least wishing for it anyway.

"Yeah, yeah...don't rub it in." I glared at him. I could do this. Regenerating my abilities with Shane hanging around wouldn't be a problem. I mean, anger-fueled electricity, and he was already pissing me off, so win-win, right?

Taking in another breath, I concentrated again, expelling the energy slower, more refined and even than I had before. My legs began to shake slightly, like I'd just run fifteen miles at a full-on best per mile pace ever. This shit wasn't for the weak.

"I never thought I'd lack stamina for anything. Turns out I was wrong." I panted the words out, unable to remember the last time I'd ever felt so winded in all my life. The only time that came to mind was when I fell off the jungle gym at school, belly flopping onto the ground and whooshed all of the air out of my lungs when I was seven. That's the kind of hurt I experienced.

"Maybe thinking isn't your strong suit then." Shane danced out of the way of my halfhearted punch.

Who was I kidding? I wouldn't have been able to make the punch if he leaned down and offered his eye to me. "Yeah, yeah...just you wait until I have enough energy to do this. I'll make you regret picking on me."

Shane laughed and headed toward the kitchen at the back of the Timewarp gym while I gathered everything I thought I had left in me and tried to fuel it into another attempt to harden my skin. This was the only way I could begin to protect myself properly. I wasn't a fighter; I couldn't take weapons with me when we went on assignments, and my ability was often best served straight to the skin through direct contact.

I had to get better at this. Just like I'd had to qualify for regionals. Just like I needed to go to the same school as my best friend. I would make it happen. I was completely certain of that. Closing my eyes again, I dug deep, completely determined to do what I needed to do.

I could feel the way the power reinforced the tissue nearer to the surface of my skin. Like it was lending it a cohesiveness that ended up appearing like electrical thread, binding all of me together, making me stronger. Like when you darn a sock that has a hole, you bring the parts together to make sure the hole closes. That's all my power did. Instead of trying to force my power where I wanted it to go, I just let it flow to where it was needed. It wasn't nearly as exhausting as trying to squeeze it into areas where there essentially wasn't any space.

Slowly, I opened my eyes and looked down at my body and let out a small gasp of surprise. Just like my hand had done previously, my body was glowing, very subtly. All the power I'd fed into my body was spread evenly throughout my torso.

There was a weariness that lingered on, and yet at the same time a sensation of rejuvenation that clung to every pore in my skin. It looked like my very own suit of armor, shining brightly to my eyes. It was heady and powerful, almost scary, but fear didn't drive me. For the first time since getting my scar, for the first time since dying, I finally felt like I had some control over my life.

Time began to lose all meaning, but even then I knew Shane wasn't going to let me stay in here indefinitely. He'd seemed reluctant to let me in here at all today. But I'd needed to. Best pleading face ever. It worked, but the sense of urgency nipped at my heels. Even with a Timewarp on my side, I was going to have to take that step to the right sooner rather than later.

Nya had mentioned a maximum of four hours inside. I was hoping Shane gave me a little more. Perhaps he felt pity for me. I'd milk it for all I could.

The room—though hall was more accurate, sizing-wise—didn't feel like it was a pocket inside of an instant. Everything in here felt normal. My metabolism, my abilities, my hunger. If I hadn't experienced it yesterday, I'd have thought it was a joke.

Give me a computer and some code, technology I could understand, and I was a happy person. Talk to me about quantum physics, and I'll quote the good Doctor. My head ached slightly. Maybe I'd already been here too long, but I couldn't afford a nap, not with a limit imposed on me.

While I wasn't yet super confident about my new-found abilities to reinforce my skin and provide myself some meager protection, I was happy that I'd done what I could in the time that I had. For a while during the last mission, while being bloodied up and sent flying through the room, I'd had a few flashes of my life pass me by. I'd legitimately feared for my life. Frankly, when that electric shock actually worked, I thought I was done for. Now I was still here and could do something about that.

I would never be put in that situation again.

Even if my attacker had just been doing their job. Perhaps if we'd been stealthy enough, none of that would have happened. But it honestly felt like they'd knew we were coming. Like they'd been lying in wait.

"Okay." My bones ached, like they could tell the time far better than anyone else could. My brain hurt with all the different minor tweaks I'd made to the exercise or spell that I'd created.

Now I could push the reinforcement through to one particular spot fairly quickly. I'd probably stick to just reinforcing all of me until I knew exactly how to direct the power the fastest and most efficient way I could. Right now, though, I didn't feel like I'd die. Nor did I feel in imminent danger.

This ability needed to become second nature to me. It had to. Now that I had a good amount of control, I could practice it anywhere and probably not burn down my surroundings.

Shane came out of the corner he'd been curled up in as he leafed through several textbooks. Never understood the thrill of old textbooks, after all. I could fit so many more on my tablet and didn't have to lug a heap of weight around either, which let me run faster, too. He seemed tired, but curious.

"How long have we been in here?" Suddenly I was worried. Should we have done this?

He shrugged. "Too long. But I've been in here longer a couple of times. Sure, it's a bit jet laggy at first, but you'll be fine. You can always shock yourself awake anyway." His joke fell as flat as my cooking. "Pretty sure Nya will have my hide for letting you hole up here for six hours on your second day."

"Should I take a nap at home before I head out on my mission?" Suddenly I'd lost some of the confidence I'd gained. Sure, I might feel like I'd achieved a bit of an advantage considering I could now protect myself at least, but there always seemed to be a catch. And right now, I was so deathly tired, I didn't think a cat nap was going to help me in the slightest.

"You should definitely sleep. Give yourself like four hours and then have a shower or something before you head out. You're going to be useless if you don't try to get some actually good rest. Cat naps or no naps aren't going to do you any good. So don't say no, and just do it, okay?" He seemed concerned, and maybe he should be. Hell, maybe I should be too.

"Thanks." I glanced around, my mind focusing on things I needed to stuff back in my backpack before leaving.

Shane chuckled. "Go home. Make sure you get some decent sleep. Maybe you'll be lucky and the jet lag will avoid you."

He didn't have to tell me twice. I was out of there in two shakes of whatever. The sooner I got home, the sooner I could sleep off this bone weariness.

The air still had a coolness to it, but there was an underlying muggy feeling like it was lying in wait. Once outside the Timewarp, everything around me seemed dreamlike. I pulled my hoodie tight, barely able to tone down the chattering of my teeth. The air might be about to turn humid, but I, for one, felt freezing.

Our apartment was eerily empty, like it wasn't quite in sync with the rest of the world. Or maybe that was me. I could feel this strange chill seeping through me. Like it searched for the center of my body so it could fill it with ice and begin to freeze me from the inside out.

Even colors appeared subdued. It had to be aftereffects. Curling up and going to sleep until the afternoon was the only thing I thought might help. Chugging down some electrolytes and a PB&J that tasted decidedly like cardboard, I allowed myself to fall onto my bed.

Dreams chased me, unable to catch me because I was outside of time. In them, I laughed and pointed, telling them they could never catch me. But Orion appeared and touched my shoulder, saying one word so soft I barely caught it: tag.

I dragged myself out of bed when my alarm went off, thinking there was no way it could actually be after three in the afternoon. But it was, and I had places to be.

As I passed people on the street in the budding summer air, I couldn't fathom how they managed to only wear a t-shirt and shorts, with no jackets or anything else. The only upside was it shocked my brain into the semblance of a sort of working order.

At least if I had fire as an ability I could warm myself up and set shit alight. Wouldn't that be a far better ability?

No. You are highly mistaken. We have very few pure fire abilities because most people burn up beyond reparability before we can revive them.

Good to know, I told the system, very glad I'd only been partially fried instead.

You seem out of sorts. Again. Are you ill? Or coming down with something?

The genuine concern in my little friend's voice was rarely lost on me. *No, not that I'm aware of.* But even so, I began to do a self-diagnosis, because it was inside me at all times, surely it would know if something was wrong with me, right?

Tiredness seeped through my entire body no matter what I tried. Tired and worn out. That's all the help I'd gotten from the Timewarp. Making sure my thoughts stayed within my barriers was essential, and currently exhausting. I couldn't forget again. But the weariness wore away at me, and right then all I wanted to do was turn around, go home, sleep and just dare SC to switch off my contract.

You might have to hurry a little. It appears you may be late. It sounded confused, like that couldn't be possible, but something was off.

Of course, it could tell something: I'd been awake too long. I shook my head, totally aware that it couldn't see me, though I did know it could feel me. So, either way, I won. *Look. I'm not late. I'm just not as stupidly early as I usually*

Even so, I was hyper aware of everything around me. Like my senses had been magnified, and just defining them and separating them from each other was all I could do to maintain sanity. Electricity was part of nature, right? So maybe being in that room, perhaps pushing the limits I'd pushed had managed to tip me over some sort of barrier and into...

I couldn't even make that shit up.

The outside of my body sensation that ran through my mind wasn't helping the situation either. But I pushed on. Because despite the utter fatigue I felt, I still really wasn't ready to give up on this life just yet.

I plopped myself down on a bench lining the parkway, just off to the side of the Rodin Museum. Closing time should be just around the corner, even if I still felt like I was quasi astral projecting. Even taking just that weight off my feet helped immensely. My face sort of hurt too. I leaned back and looked up at the sky and its darkening colors. How the clouds shifted from the white of day into the grey of night, and the light bled red and orange into the navy of night. There'd be no stars to see, or at least not many. Too many of the city lights interfered with the natural scenery up there. But if I closed my eyes I could imagine all of the heavens twinkling down on us.

Stars were so peaceful, so far away. I envied their ability to be oblivious to us. Coldness gripped me again, and I had to wonder why with my hoodie and a t-shirt on underneath it all. My eyes wanted to close, but I forced them to remain open, to endure this weird state of apathy with me.

With another wave of fatigue washing over me, I realized I'd resigned myself to the inevitable. At least until such a time I could figure out how to free myself from this afterlife prison. Keeping those thoughts to myself, I repeated them like a mantra to myself and only myself. And then I leaned back and waited for my task partners.

21
HALF THE OLD

"Excellent, just the Runner I was hoping for." The voice was familiar and full of good cheer. I couldn't help but crack a smile before I even opened my eyes.

"My favorite Blocker." And I actually meant it, because Adam had seen me at my best when I healed him, albeit accidentally. And of course, at my worst, after I'd watched Orion explode that head. He'd let me go, signaled that it was okay for me to run off after my portion of the job was taken care of. I had a soft little spot in my chest cavity just for him.

He laughed and let himself fall into the seat next to me. "Still owe you big time for this." He motioned to his entire body and winked at me.

I laughed at his comment suddenly feeling a thousand tons lighter. "Thanks. Laughing really does heal the soul, am I right?"

Adam grinned, but this time I could see those shadows of concern underneath his expression. He looked me over in a different way now, like assessing if I was okay, or if something wasn't right. "You taking care of yourself?"

That was such a loaded question, and while I knew he didn't really mean anything by it, I also knew that he did.

I know, right? Talk about convoluted conversations. "Yeah, of course. That concussion I got last time is gone now. Always makes me restless when I don't get to jog. Gives me too much time to think."

I hadn't lied. In fact, some of that was a little too close to home and felt uncomfortable. The Cleaner still wasn't here, and we only had about another fifteen minutes. I frowned. It wasn't Orion, couldn't be. He'd not even mentioned this mission to me. Although, if I thought about it, I didn't really see him after I got this mission given to me.

"Runner?" Again, Adam's tone was filled with concern and I sighed at my brain.

"Sorry. It's been a rough couple of weeks. Just going over the minor self-defense shit I've drilled into myself over the last week. Not about to make a habit of being anyone's punching bag." And I really meant that. Because even with all the shit, that one mission had caused things I never wanted to experience. And I was never going to experience them again if I had anything to do with it.

"Perfectly understandable." He nodded at me, but I could feel from his aura that there were parts of what I'd said that he didn't mesh with. His piercing gaze followed me like he could pull my thoughts from my head. It made me retreat into my little sanctuary all the more.

I turned around, suddenly aware of another presence. It was heavy, not unlike the feeling of shadows when they inundated my room, but still not the same. All I could think of was a being, watching me, weighing me down with whatever was on its mind despite not being visible to me yet. It didn't have that same harmlessness as my shadowed friends often did though. The Demarcates had purpose, and helpfulness to me and how not to become what they were was paramount to that.

"Hey there, Blocker, Runner, I presume." The voice was unfamiliar and yet lingered in the back of my mind like something I should have remembered. There was an oily quality to it, but I couldn't place where I'd heard it before.

Adam glanced up, and for a brief instant I was sure I saw annoyance flash across his gaze. But it was gone so fast, clamped down on and sucked away, that I could also have imagined it. Not.

"Hey there." His tone was neutral. I'd never heard him speak in a neutral way before. You know, in all of our three encounters.

Our Cleaner, I presumed, smiled, but it felt more like a gloat. Oh, how I wanted to reach into their thoughts and find out why. They were about as tall as I was but hunched over slightly, with their dust jacket pulled tightly. Their head was hidden beneath their hood; the shadows played off the loose strands of hair that whished across the darkness that had to be their eyes.

A sudden tug at my brain, or from my brain, had my back slamming into the bench. Like my power really did want to know the Cleaner, to figure out what they were hiding underneath that hood. I'd never felt such a stark reaction from my power before. It startled me, and I coughed, the winded sensation in my chest only slowly subsiding.

"Oh, sorry. Did I surprise you? I have to remember not to hide my footsteps from my allies, after all." Again, that silky smooth voice with those words that sounded nice, but were filled with double meanings I had no clue about.

"No, just swallowed a bug." Of course, the part that would jump out and save me would be my sarcasm. "Sorry, who are you?"

Not sure how I managed to include that last line, my audacity levels were peaking. Something about this person with the aura and voice that were familiar and not at the same time really irritated me. The slight crease of suppressed laughter around Adam's eyes made it all worth it though. At least I was entertaining someone.

"I'm your Cleaner." Their tone momentarily lost that overconfidence that plagued it at first. Pity their demeanor didn't.

"Oh, good. Then we're all here. Lay it on us, Blocker." I turned my back to the Cleaner, deliberately, hoping I wasn't just being a foolish twat, and gave my entire focus to Adam.

He cleared his throat and tapped his chest a couple of times before speaking. "Sorry, must have been a bug or something. Anyway. It's a simple in and out...if you'd call disabling a rather tricky alarm system and breaking into a complex without alerting anyone simple, that is."

I rolled my eyes. Oh joy. He was in a comedic mood tonight. I probably hadn't helped.

"Sure, sure." Cleaner waved a hand at Adam, like he'd heard it all before. "Where do we go, what do we break into, and why are we here tonight? I hate short notice assignments."

On a whim, I accessed my interface to pull up information on the Cleaner.

Name: Cal

Designation: Cleaner

Rank: H - Senior Apprentice

Skills: Fire Major, Earth Minor

Second Chance Affiliate

Point of Contact: System influence.

Not as much information as I'd have liked, not even as much as I'd got on the good doctor, but far more than I would have thought, considering we were supposed to use code names. Though maybe that was more for if someone alerted the authorities or something. Seriously, they needed an employee handbook.

Also, I couldn't help but noticed they were only one level above my ranking. Considering their aura, that felt weird. There was more strength about them than I thought someone of that level should have. Maybe I was just weak or slow in developing perhaps? Something about this person, this whole situation, wasn't sitting well with me.

Adam's eyes narrowed, and I could see his irritation building. There was something about Cal that he didn't like, but my own leanings were more curiosity. Something about him just…reached out to me. How I wished I could read minds.

Warning: Portent Ability activated.

Inadvisable given current predicament. Disengage and reset for a later time.

What the fuck? Notifications everywhere and not a drop to drink. I still didn't even know how to activate the damned thing.

I'd missed something Adam said, because the glaring match going on between those two was undeniably vicious. Great. Just what I needed.

"Hey, you two. Sorry to interrupt the glare-off, but I want to get this done so I can go back home. Not to mention, could we put our hatred away for tonight? My last assignment ended with a concussion and a week off everything. I'd really like to just get in and out without requiring medical attention. Thanks?"

Adam blinked at me, and Cal's expression was unreadable, but at least they stopped arguing with their eyes.

"Sorry about that, Runner. Won't happen again. We just have a bit of history."

No shit. How I wished I'd been a fly on the wall in the past and knew all about that undeniably juicy bit of history. But we had things to steal and places to be. "Obviously."

I gestured at the Thinker statue behind us. "Before we turn into that guy, can we get a move on?" Pretty sure both of them barely avoided laughing.

"Runner. You disable the alarm, and open the window the second from the left in the basement. The bars should just pop off. Safety protocols. Patrols run on the nine-minute mark, with the security guard stopping to have a cigarette every third round. We should be good to go in about fifteen minutes. Down the basement entrance stairs once we've accessed the security box on the side of the building. I'll cover us with shadows." Adam sounded all business, and I glanced around to see if I could see any of my own shadows, but for once, they seemed alarmingly absent. Not even a glimpse, which gave my overactive imagination more food for thought.

"Then it's a pretty easy in and out as long as we remain obscured. Runner needs to disable the system and insert the virus, while we maintain lookout. Cleaner is to fix any trace evidence left behind, and on the off chance we fuck up and someone sees us, takes care of their memory too."

A shiver ran up my spine, and I wondered just what that "taking care of" meant. Originally, I'd assumed it meant wiping their memory, but after Orion's last stint, I wasn't so sure anymore. Not to mention I was sure Adam was a Blocker, wasn't he? Since when could he perform like a Driver? And wasn't a Minder supposed to do the mind wipes? It was all starting to get very confusing, running into each other like that.

"Any questions?" He looked at me, ignoring Cal.

"Virus? I don't have no virus, and contrary to what appears to be popular opinion in this organization, I can't just magic anything to do with electronics to appear out of thin air." It was odd to feel stereotyped in death like this, but here we were.

"Oh yeah." Adam reached into his pocket and pulled out something tiny, handing me what appeared to be a mini thumb drive. "Here. Sorry."

"Stupid question time." I ignored Cal's snort of laughter. "Why can't they just send it in an email, hidden behind innocent words? I mean...this feels so unnecessary."

Adam shrugged. "I just run the missions they tell me to, do what I'm briefed to, and get paid damn well. As far as I know, it has to be entered into the system through the mainframe, which is usually what we have to do when we get assignments like these."

"But they're doable without an eel, right? I mean, you don't have many." I wanted to know why this had to be me. Why me? Why not just give it to Adam? They seemed to be needlessly complicating things. And I made sure I allowed my little buddy in my head to see all the thoughts I was having because I found this highly suspect.

"Well, yeah, but you make everything easier. Not many of us out there could hack through a security system with the time and accuracy it takes you. Being an eel makes the electronics all friendly with you. It's like they want to be your best buddy." He grinned at me, and I realized I wasn't going to get anything more out of him. "Okay, we got it then?"

Both Cal and I nodded, even if I wasn't completely ready. The thing was, Cal seemed to throw a lot of glances my way now. Like they were trying to catch my attention. By the time we moved out, I had no idea what to think, only that I really didn't like being under such scrutiny. Especially not when I was about to commit breaking and entering.

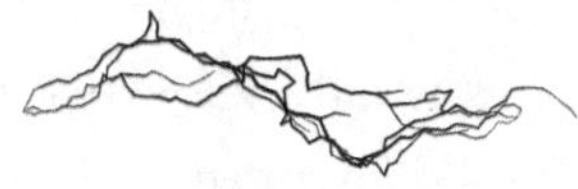

The security system required me to completely redirect the electricity and leave a loop in place that essentially faked that the system was still online. It involved me having to move the current into its own little circle so it could continue, oblivious to the fact that the window had been opened.

Speaking of windows, I was getting very tired of entering buildings through them. There had to be better ways than this.

But also, worse.

What do you mean? Of course, as soon as I thought the words, I regretted it.

Sewers. You really couldn't come up with that one?

I groaned softly, and Adam and Cal both turned their glares on me. At least they weren't glaring at each other though, right?

We pushed through the museum, and I had to wonder just why we'd need anything in here. It wasn't like this was one of the world's most prominent research facilities or anything. It was just one of the many museums around here, and far less popular than the big museum of art just down the parkway. It was a bit creepy, though.

The bronze sculptures cast shadows that made me think people were standing around every corner. I just couldn't see a reason why we had to be here, why we couldn't have just hacked the damned system. So what did this museum have that needed to be eradicated?

You ask so many questions.

Because you keep sending me on so many assignments that make no sense whatsoever. I snapped the words in my head. Not only angry with the system, but irritated at myself for continuing to participate in something I didn't understand.

With no answers forthcoming, even after I'd been participating in this crap for more than two months now...I didn't even have words for how irritated I was with myself. Or how much I'd apparently overestimated my will to die for a principle.

Maybe I didn't stand for anything anymore. Being a pawn. Being willing to do anything to stay alive? How did I know that this file wasn't going to— and then I remembered. What I'd forgotten in all my concussion.

I almost forgot to switch my thoughts over. Here, somewhere in my mind, this separated little section, I'd downloaded a copy of that file I'd given to Sam. My body tingled with anticipation, and it was all I could do right then not to turn around and go, "Hey! I'm out for the night!" so I could go home and examine just what it was we were doing. Breathe. I had to breathe.

Just what could my brain store, anyway? I had a sneaking suspicion it was more than I could imagine. As we approached our destination, I ran over a few ideas in my mind. The halls were empty, and I'd rerouted the cameras so they played on loop. Why, yes, some of the movies got some aspects absolutely correct. Which was a thing I never thought the alive me would experience.

The museum was nicely free from interference. Except for all the creepy shadows cast by the damned statues littered all over the place. The basement was standard fare, storage, boxes, shelving. But coming up to the ground level that we had to navigate in order to access the mainframe was another story. Avoiding the security guard in the front was easy. He spent most of his time looking at his phone with an occasional glance up at the monitors.

But the statues sent tendrils of shadows that I couldn't be sure weren't Demarcates floundering around us in the dim lighting. The soft buzz of the lighting didn't help my imagination either. Maybe I was the only one, but there were too many of these statues that looked far too like crying angels until I got up close. I really didn't need the vision of them clawing off my face that kept running through my head.

When we finally made it through that room, regardless of shadows woven to hide us and statue figures stalking us to the end of it, I finally breathed a sigh of relief.

Cal still surveyed me like I was a piece of meat hanging from a hook, but I could deal with that later. Right now, I was trying desperately to figure out just how I could download the information I was about to wipe out with this virus before I wiped it out with the virus. Because I needed to figure out why the hell we were doing this in the first place.

I definitely could. If I could figure out how to upload that amount of information to my head. If I didn't know better, I'd think I was an android.

The systems room was empty. I didn't feel guilty as I scouted for the USB slots on the big server rack. I mean, honestly, there was a fifty percent chance every time you tried to put in a drive that it wasn't going to fit. These guys didn't have upgraded models yet, nor anything fancy, so at least I had the right drive.

Which meant I could *accidentally* access the outlet and therefore the files with a single strand of electricity. In theory. With any luck—and I might be being too wishful in my thinking—I was fairly certain I'd be able to speed download what I needed.

Nothing really stood out to me in those files, but I knew there had to be something. So I just tried to access most of them. I wasn't foolish enough to attempt accessing the virus first. Who knew what that could do to a human mind? But I kept an eye out for anything that seemed so mundane it could be hiding in plain sight. I'd figure out the rest of it when I had time to go over everything in my head later. From what I could tell at a glance, most of it looked like names. Maybe a list of donors or something.

Adam tapped my shoulder, like he was asking what the holdup was. I rolled my eyes indicating the difficulty I was having in inserting the thing. Adam's laugh almost escaped him when he nodded his understanding. A tiny worm of guilt crept through me.

Finally, I allowed the tiny virus drive to slot into its little connection and ran the info on the stick. Loading it through all of the data contained there, I felt like a terrorist. That's what this clandestine operation resembled. After all, why were we constantly destroying things? Having lives held over us, required to perform specific tasks or else be essentially killed, maybe terrorism under duress. Still, though…

There was undoubtedly something here. But maybe, just maybe, if I played my cards right and figured some shit out, I could become a double agent and fix all of this.

22
COMPLICATIONS

Sometimes, I think I got ahead of myself. Not necessarily that I made mistakes, just that I discounted pertinent information that would have made all the differences in how I read and judged situations. If nothing else, my time with Nya and Shane had taught me about auras, that they had meaning and a purpose, and that being able to see these things could give me a bit of an advantage.

Apparently, eels needed all the advantages they could get.

As I exited the mainframe room, I had a sudden feeling of foreboding.

Warning. Portent Ability activated. Shock mode initiating. Defensive Cycle slowdown has begun.

Timestance Initiated.

Okay, so...

But I didn't really have any more time to think, because there, just in my peripheral vision, I could see a shadow waiting. This wasn't a statue or a Demarcates. This was something I couldn't identify. It was almost like I stopped time in that instant. There were two choices, and neither of them were preferable for me. Hell, I'd already saved Adam's life once before. Him dying wasn't an option, or even just him coming to harm wasn't an option I was willing to entertain. Damn my moral code.

I only had a split moment, even in this time slow that I'd placed us in. Hoping against hope that my brilliant extended training session had paid off, I focused all of my skin barricade to my back and pushed Adam ahead of me, getting ready to take the brunt of the attack on myself. Reinforcing my shielding with a bit of electrical bite, I made sure there was enough energy to overload the attacker and stun them, at least temporarily.

Or so I hoped. Couldn't exactly measure it, right? No directions like "Add one cup of electricity. Do not mix with water."

Warning: Timestance about to expire.

As soon as I touched Adam, time returned to normal, and I rolled with him like a wrecking ball, indeed taking the full force of the attack meant for him on my back. Air whooshed out of my lungs as electricity sang through the air. I could even feel where the damned blade tried to bite into my back. I'd have a welt there in the morning at the very least. I heard a screech behind us and for a second thought we'd caught a banshee. But as I rolled clear of my Driver, I realized our attacker was none other than trusty old Cal.

"What the fuck, Cal?" Adam apparently didn't give a shit about code names or anything anymore. "What the hell was that?"

But Cal was still convulsing on the floor. Perhaps I'd overdone the electrical shock a tad. I mean, it's not like I'd had much of an opportunity to practice how much of a charge to let off, right? Disabling an assailant so they were disoriented versus disabling my attacked into a catatonic state wasn't something I'd had the opportunity to practice. All things considered, Cal still appeared to be alive. If I didn't have this nifty little combat option, at least one of us would have been dead.

A thousand questions flooded my mind. Among them, and definitely not the least, was why? Why the hell had Cal attacked us? Or attacked Adam. Perhaps they'd attacked me; I couldn't tell. And it was fucking frustrating.

All I knew was that amount of noise wasn't going unnoticed despite the security overrides I'd done. I could hear and even feel the energy of the guard coming to check out the noise. Adam was still glaring at Cal, so I grabbed his hand and tugged. "We need to go before security gets here. Job is done. But I'm not going down for this crap."

Adam blinked once, like I'd pulled him out of some deep memory. "Right. Got this."

He bent down and dragged Cal back toward a corner. They'd stopped convulsing now, which secretly relieved the hell out of me. I had to learn to control that ability far better than that. Adam closed his eyes, and shadows appeared. Not that it worked that way, precisely. Just that Cal was already in a corner, and he sort of pulled the existing coverage to extend over the Cleaner. "Exit alarm."

It was nice to know that I could jump on command. But compared to everything else, the door alarms were simple. As soon as Cal was covered, we exited the building. I was grateful for the accessible entrance. I would have hated having to drag him to the main door with all those steps. Adam cushioned our footfalls as we exited, through what I suspected had to do with manipulating the concrete. Perhaps it had some relation to earth. His abilities were a mystery to me because it seemed he held multiple roles.

"Okay. We should be good then," he whispered as we exited through the door, after I indicated there didn't seem to be any presence on the other side.

The moon shone down, like we hadn't just broken into a museum, infected their computers with a virus, and been attacked by a person who was supposed to be on our side. Obliviousness would be nice, but that was something we just didn't have.

We didn't speak until we were well clear of the building. Dragging Cal to the bushes at the corner of the block, we left him on his side. He should wake up shortly, or at least I hoped he would. On the bright side, his chest was moving. There were enough homeless on the streets that him being here wouldn't arouse suspicion.

"Is it okay to just leave Cal here?" I asked, because I felt the guilt trying to gnaw at my stomach. My shock had pretty much put Cal out of commission, and I wasn't sure what would happen.

Adam shrugged, his face grim. "Oh, it's more than all right. We should have just left Cal inside to be found and rot in prison. But the system doesn't like having to tie up loose ends. And we are to attempt to keep the secret of SC at all costs, blah, blah. So yeah. Cal will be fine there. They'll probably send a retrieval team. Considering the report I've filed, that's highly likely the case."

He was angry. I could almost touch the feeling that radiated out from him. The way thoughts and emotions emanated from people fascinated me. How I could see them?

"Why did Cal do that?" I couldn't help asking. It wasn't normal to discuss anything about the mission outside of the mission, but I figured this was a bit of an exception.

"No idea." Adam's eyes weren't focusing properly. He had to be busy in his HUD. I kicked at the ground, waiting for him to be done, even though I was fairly sure I could go already.

"How did you know?" Adam turned to me finally, but he didn't seem angry, more curious.

"Oh?" I shrugged. "I don't know, I just felt it. Like this gut feeling that tried to get me to vomit up food from lunch."

Adam laughed. "Sort of like ESP?"

I shook my head. "No, more like sensing something was waiting for us. Not really all supernatural or anything. Just luck, I guess."

He studied me a moment. "Perhaps. Or maybe you knew because you're an eel. We don't know enough about eels."

"Nope. No, you do not. Which makes it doubly difficult for me, because I'm learning from you." I took a step back though, because for a moment there I envisioned myself stuck in a cage and being poked and prodded so they could understand me.

Adam smiled and ran a hand through his hair. "Guess I owe you another life, right?"

"Totally. I'm marking you down, and one day you're going to have to pay up." I meant it as a joke, but there was a portion of me that was partially serious too. I needed to know more about the ins and outs of the business. And one way or another, I was going to have to get it.

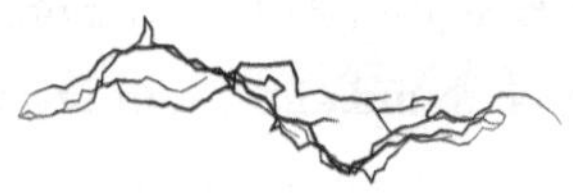

I didn't have to worry about drop off. We didn't acquire anything to be delivered, but Adam did take the virus drive from me and headed out. He had been out of my sight for a bit while we were inside. For all I knew he'd been sent to retrieve something completely different.

Come to think of it, Cal had been trying to catch my attention there a couple of times, after originally being an insufferable jerk. I hadn't paid that much attention at the time as I was going through my own instructions. Hindsight was unfortunately twenty-twenty. What I desperately needed to learn was how to regulate my abilities. And I needed to figure out why Cal had been so vicious toward Adam. Was he a bad guy and I'd been fooled?

The trudge home was just that. And I was tired already from the day that never ended. Naps aside, I knew I'd punished my body. Those extra six hours in that concentrated space had done a number on me. Maybe I could think clearer after I woke up. I couldn't help the feeling that somehow, I'd already made my moral choice though. What if my discharge had killed Cal? I mean, it obviously did a little more than shock them. Still, though, that me first attitude didn't entirely apply, did it? Hadn't I reacted to save Adam? Did that count for something?

My feet found the steps all on their own, just like I'd been going through the motions on the way home. Here I stood, suddenly in front of our door, wondering just how much stuff had gone through our mail system before. Had Orion been the one to pick up that first package? Was that why he was on the steps so long ago?

Finally, after managing to jiggle the door open, I closed it behind me and turned around.

Orion sat on the stairs, just watching me silently. His blue eyes weren't properly visible through the darkness, and I had no idea why he hadn't turned the light on in the hallway. Maybe it was burned out again. But even so, there appeared to be a slight glow around his iris. Maybe it was my imagination; perhaps it was simply a reflection of something. All I knew was that it sent shivers down my back that made me want to run.

"Hey," he said, and I realized he was leaning forward with his hands over his knees. That thoughtful way he got when he was contemplating bigger things.

"Waiting for me now?" I half joked, trying to turn the situation to the humorous, because I had to admit that after the whole Cal incident, I was on edge. And I couldn't stop the feeling eating at me that something wasn't quite right with Orion. I'd never seen him so somber before. No, that wasn't the right word. Resigned was more accurate.

"You just couldn't tone it down, could you?" He asked the question like I should know what he was talking about, but I found myself standing there, trying to peer into his mind to understand where the hell those words came from.

So I did the next best thing, I employed my copious amounts of talent in the sarcasm industry and shrugged. "Nope. Never can, you know me. Toning it down is the last thing I'd do...if I even had a fucking clue what you were talking about."

Okay, so maybe I wasn't playing it cool. And my voice had risen enough that it echoed through the entire building. The stairwell was apparently acoustically constructed.

The look on Orion's face was priceless. Like a bit of "what the fuck" mixed with "I should have known." And really, knowing me as long as he did? He should have known. He only had himself to blame.

"Let's go upstairs. Jacob isn't there. It's more private." He spoke like he was giving me an order. And if there's one thing I didn't like, it was orders from someone or something that wasn't visibly threatening my life at the same time. Okay, I didn't like any orders.

"Is it now? And why the fuck should I care?" So yeah, I was sort of throwing a tantrum, but my feelings of irritation, of not understanding anything, they all welled together in the middle of my chest trying to push out in one massive and fiery electrical charge.

Orion's gaze raked me over. Like perhaps he'd misjudged something. I'd give him misjudged.

"You aren't in charge of me, regardless of what your ranking might suggest. So fucking ask nicely, or I'm going to taze you."

His eyes widened, and an involuntary laugh burst out from him. "Yeah. I imagine you would do just that." Then he sighed, like my words had only just sunk in. "Sure. Come on. Please come up stairs with me so we can chat."

"See," I said as I pushed past him on the stairs, reinforcing the skin barricade over my back yet again. I could see it now: paranoia and I were going to become best buds. "That wasn't so hard, was it?"

He didn't answer. In fact, he didn't say anything until we were sitting in the living room and I was slouched on the couch with a Nutella sandwich. I rarely indulged and kept the jar in there purely to test my willpower, but right now was definitely a hazelnut treat eating sort of time. And a couch time. Full-length, only-me-on-it, stay-the-fuck-out-of-my-personal-space couch time.

Orion eyed me from the chair he sat on. Leaning forward in that way again, his fingers steepled and his knees pulled up to a ninety-degree bend.

"Spill. I'm tired, and starting to apparently get a reaction headache, so just get this lecture or whatever it is over with so I can go to bed, okay?" I was impatient. Hell, I needed to go lie on my bed and process what the mission entailed. And sitting here, waiting for Orion to speak, wasn't going to accomplish that goal in any timely manner.

He sighed, and I wanted to throttle him, but instead I ripped another gooey bite of my sandwich off with my teeth, imagining it was a steak instead. Damn, could I go for a steak.

"Okay. Well. I wasn't expecting you to electrocute Cal." He looked up at me, making eye contact for the first time since I saw him in the stairwell.

His eyes were rimmed with sadness, and he looked positively worn out.

"How do you know I electrocuted Cal, and why should that bother you when it wasn't your mission, and Cal wasn't attacking you or your other task partner?" It's amazing how non-combative words sound when voiced over a mouthful of chocolate.

But Orion cast his gaze around, and this time it felt like he was scared someone was listening in. Instinctively, I searched, finding the bug in its place and deactivated it. More than that though, I gave it a surge that should seem natural, and placed monitoring it in my interface so I could keep an eye on it and see if it came back online. If it was listening in, it wasn't via an electronic means, and I said as much. "No one can hear us through any normal tracking abilities. I can't do much about others though."

Also, just in case this was Orion trying to weasel info on eels out of me, I'd covered my basis by telling him electrical devices were what I could shut down. Precautions were always good.

A brief flash of relief crossed his expression. "I hope you're right."

"Usually am," I replied, popping the last of the bread into my mouth before sitting up properly and fixing my gaze on Orion. "But you really need to start explaining, because I'm tired, and I'm drained, and I'm pretty much a honey badger right now."

Clever Orion didn't even laugh. "Well, I mean, I'm not even sure you'll believe this—"

"Try me. I mean, I recently died, came back to life as a superhero with electrical powers, and now practice breaking and entering." I crossed my arms and glared at him. "But this had better be good."

The look he gave me in return made me question whether the good it was going to be was actually something I wanted to know.

23

COMPLICATED

"I believe, though I don't yet have proof, that you're being deliberately misled." His voice was soft, and I'm not sure why, because couldn't our friendly neighborhood brain friends hear us anyway?

Also, not what I expected him to start off with. I blinked at him, which he took as a sign to continue, so that was good, all things considered.

"You've sort of gone off the radar a couple of times, and I'm worried. Even putting aside how shocked you were on our last mission, even though I know you might not get me and my motivations right now, blinking out of existence, even temporarily, worries me. I've seen too many operatives disappear that way." He looked away from me, like he was trying to find the right words but looking at me was distracting or something.

Bully for me. I was still trying to process the fact that he knew I'd disappeared somewhat, and that he was worried. I really had figured after our arguments about the fundamental morals we both stood for, that he'd be less inclined to care.

Should have known though, it's not like I cared any less.

"So I've gone off the grid? How so?" There, play dumb and test the

185

waters, see what he's really after. Because right now I wasn't sure. He might seem concerned but it could all be a ploy.

You're doing it again.

My blood ran a little colder this time. Because the voice was right. I had just directed my thoughts to myself, which meant I was leaving it out of the loop, which meant Orion probably knew because the system communicated with all of its subsidiaries. I was one of them. And if my thinking wasn't able to be observed or monitored, then I must be checking out. Forgetting to set that thought loop wasn't the brightest lack of judgement I'd ever had.

"Yeah. Off the grid. Unfindable. Unable to locate you. Unable to see where you are or send aid if you need it." He ran a hand through his hair. "I'm not as high up in the rankings as I'd like to be, but there are a few Cleaners around. I didn't think you'd feel comfortable with me there tonight, not yet. So I asked Cal to go with you."

Oh, wow. So that was a bit of a twist I hadn't seen coming. Maybe that was why Cal kept staring at me. I frowned, trying to play the events of the evening over in my head again. I'd expected Orion to be a part of it. I wasn't aware he could request a replacement. Did that mean I could request a replacement? "So wait. Why would Cal have been going to attack Adam? I don't understand."

Because I didn't, and Orion's gaze shifted down to his feet, a clear sign that he didn't really want to tell me why. I mean, he'd been there when I saved Adam's life.

"I'm not entirely sure, and I won't know until Cal wakes up." He sounded unusually emotionally involved, and a stab of pain flared in my chest at the thought. I pushed it down, concentrating instead on what he didn't say.

"But you have an inkling, or you'd be entirely sure. So what is this bit you might know?" Yep, that was the ticket. Let's just attack our best friend because we were feeling insecure for our own reasons.

He eyed me for a moment. "Well. I did ask Cal to watch out for you."

It was my turn to raise the eyebrow. "You realize I can fully take care of myself, right?"

"Well, I realize that *now*." He pouted. "But I was worried back then, and

I didn't know why you kept disappearing. No one else I know goes off the grid that way unless…I was worried that playing with too much electrical energy would be unhealthy."

"How would you know?" Okay, here we go, let's do a bait and switch or something, because he was clearly more in the know than I was, and I needed to know more than him.

"Because you were disappearing." He said it like I should know what he meant. When I didn't change my expression to one that indicated a lightbulb had gone off, he continued. "I've been researching in the archives. And the reports all say that before eels disappear or die, they all go into a semi-permanent off mode. Like none of their thoughts were audible, and nothing they did could be predicted or else seen by their companions."

"Wait, there are archives?" I blurted out.

My little companion seemed slightly sheepish at my outburst. *Sorry for not telling you sooner, I just thought you'd figure it out. And then I could barely hear you or see you. I may have alerted Orion.*

Just Orion?

After a very brief pause I got my answer. *Just Orion.*

I wasn't sure how to feel about that.

Orion ignored my outburst, and I partially ignored my companion in that I didn't give it any reasoning. My head was still reeling. "Okay, so archives, and you figured out that most of them are out of touch for a while first before they disappear?"

"Yep." But there was hesitation in his voice, like he knew more and didn't want to tell me in case it alarmed me. Which, of course, meant I had to know.

"Come on, Orion. You've been holding out on me, and you shouldn't have been. What else are you not telling me?" I barely managed to keep my temper under control. Because right now it was being fed by panic, and that was an emotion I never had much control over.

"Well, you did mention that you'd been seeing shadows, too. And that seems to have some correlation in these 'sudden disappearances' too. So I just wanted to check in on you, make sure you were okay, even if I wasn't the one directly keeping you safe." He sounded almost embarrassed.

Normally I would have found it sweet as hell. Normally, I might even have tried to read anything and everything into those words. But right then, all I could focus on was the shadows, and the fact that going off grid hadn't meant anything good for eels in the past. Because, let's face it, not everyone made it to the stage Shane was at right now. Then how could this whole clandestine rebellion thing be any good for the present? How could it be any good for me?

My mind was reeling. My brain just wasn't prepared for that information. I'm not even sure how much time passed before I registered exactly what it was he was saying to me.

But there he was, kneeling next to me, that same concerned expression on his face that he'd shown me thousands of times in our lives together. The old Orion. The one I knew before the whole mission debacle. For just that one instant, I wavered. Beneath that expression was a hardness that hadn't been there before. A determination to do what needed to be done at all costs. I wish I could say I'd misjudged him, but he'd still killed a person and obviously more before the one I saw. A wave of nausea overcame me.

Fighting it down I tried to open my mouth and speak, but at first all that came out was an odd sort of sob. Great. Emotions now? What sort of timing was that? I tried again. "Okay, I think I get it. I think."

I was mumbling, muttering the words out loud so that maybe I could try and get a more tangible grip on the fucked-up situation I now found myself in.

"Sit down properly, before you fall down—probably on me—and electrocute me." Orion used his firm, doctor-type voice and gently pushed me back into a lying down position. Then he sat on the edge of the couch, and I could practically see the thought patterns running through his mind. Like he was considering different options and discarding them just as fast.

"It might have been remiss of me to inform you of all this crap in this way. Truth be told, it's not exactly easy to talk about any of this. There are so many watchers, so many ways for them to hear us." He looked scared. Like maybe he'd lost someone else due to this before. And for all I knew, perhaps he had. He'd been dead forever and a day. Or two years, but that was close enough.

"Maybe it was remiss of you not to tell me sooner." I grumbled the words out, because of course I couldn't show him how much I still cared. No, that would be a disaster after all. Almost rolled my eyes at myself in all of my sarcasm.

For a few moments we sat in silence. Jacob was on a night shift, as usual, so there was no danger of interruptions right then. I was dead tired and trying hard to ignore the pun. But the thing was, I had no idea how to approach the information he'd just given me. Had he really said what I thought I'd heard? Because if he hadn't, then I was having some other major problems right now.

"Guess you have a lot of questions?" he asked softly, and I could see the caution in his eyes, like he believed someone would break the door down at any moment and shout "Freeze! You're under Second Chance arrest!"

"You could say that," I snapped. But he didn't deserve that, and we both knew it. So I took in a breath, and pointedly directed a thought to my friend in my brain.

Are you attached to the mainframe at all times?

Yes.

So everything you experience is transferred? I didn't like the knot that formed in my stomach. I always knew I'd had a spy in my head, but I'd never actually asked it before.

Technically.

Define technically. Haha! I threw back some of the frustration it had given me when it first booted up in my brain.

If I hadn't known better, I'd almost have thought it smiled. *I am required to keep the connection open at all times, but as you know, there are always ways to circumvent orders such as those while technically still following them.*

I got the distinct impression I probably shouldn't press the question. Okay. So that meant what I was speaking to Orion about right now wasn't technically making it to the mainframe. I liked that word. Technically. My brain was hyper-focusing on it now.

Orion sat there, staying still and watching me quietly, even though I knew his brain was going nineteen to the dozen. I wasn't really ready to talk yet, but there were too many questions not to. The days of being oblivious were over. They'd stopped when I got that damned wire dropped on me.

The scar on my skin began to tingle, like it was trying to tell me something more than "hey, look at me, I'm a scar that would be a pretty cool thing except for how you came by me."

"So, you're not the goody-two-shoes teacher's pet I thought you were being, then?" Great way to phrase the question there, Dare. Not offensive at all. I could have kicked myself, but I was pretty tired and that took a lot of effort.

Orion chuckled. The sound came across distinctively sad—mournful in a way. Again, it made me want to reach out and give him a hug. Which was something I rarely ever wanted to do. But I waited for him to be ready to talk, despite the impatience trying to claw at my throat.

"I do what I need to do to get through this and survive. So that maybe, just maybe at some point in all of this, I'll do something necessary, an action that means something to the world at large. It's all I've had to cling to for two years." He looked up from where he was studying the intricate knotting of his fingers he'd attempted. "And then you died."

I burst out laughing, unable to help it. At first, he looked offended, but then his eyes crinkled at the corners, and the laughter poured out. We both pretended not to hear the hysteria in one another's laughs. As a tension release, I swear laughing had to be one of the best forms. Right then, we desperately needed it.

It took a little for us to calm down, but I felt more at ease with him than I had in weeks, and now I was ready to hear him out. There were, after all, two sides to every coin, even if it was a trick one.

While Orion made himself some food, I scanned the surrounding area as best I could with my sleep deprived brain. I couldn't tell him about the eel territory, the Timewarp, or any of my training. At least not yet, not until I was completely certain that this wasn't all some elaborate ruse to put me into a false sense of security so I would give away any eel secrets I possessed.

But what Shane had, or more precisely hadn't said, stayed with me. It wasn't the time to discuss Orion. Which made me think that what I'd be told at least wasn't bad.

Orion still seemed to be somewhat uncomfortable, but I didn't think that had anything to do with me, more about the subject matter we were attempting to discuss. When he finally came back into the room, a thick sandwich in his hands, some of the tension had melted off him. Maybe he'd been scared I wouldn't listen.

"So. Tell me everything." Cliché perhaps, but it was true. He needed to let me in on everything he knew and whatever was giving his forehead premature wrinkles if this was going to have any chance of convincing me he'd made the choice he had to. Not to mention getting to the bottom of why Cal attacked Adam.

The options of why he'd done what he'd done were black and white for the most part. You or them. Your friend or them. But the more I knew about SC the less I thought that elimination was as easy as flicking an off switch.

Orion, however, didn't seem to know where to start. It took a good few minutes of him munching on his food in silence, with varying expressions of thought crossing his face, like he was weighing pros and cons. And it took me all the patience I had to spare not to jump up and grab him by the collar and scream in his face to hurry the fuck up so I could go to sleep. I'd discharged a lot of electricity today. The day that never ended. That felt like it started a good day or two ago.

Finally, he cleared his throat. "I sent Cal because I didn't think it a good idea to go with you. Cal is very astute but often difficult to get along with, and I didn't realize at the time that your Driver was going to be Adam. If I'd just dug a little deeper..." He ran a hand through his hair, shadows haunting his eyes.

"I take it they have history?" Because I was brilliant at stating the bleeding obvious. I made a note to ask about Adam's roles a little later, because that was hella confusing.

"Yeah, sort of. You could say that, but it's a lot more complicated." He half laughed as he said it, without even a hint of amusement.

"Of course it is." I kept my face as impassive as I could.

"Yeah." Orion sobered up and pressed on. "Adam was there when Cal's partner died, and Cal blames Adam for being negligent."

"And was he? I mean, was Adam negligent?" Because come on, that was the crux of the matter. And considering the two times I'd pulled Adam's ass out of the fire, also completely believable.

Orion nodded slowly. "Adam was being reckless. He'd just been reprimanded and gone through punishment. And let's face it, I don't know about you, but it certainly never makes me want to toe the line more, only to destroy as many things as I can."

I nodded, because that applied to me in so many ways.

"Anyway. He wasn't doing his job properly. His concealments were shoddy, partial at best, and he spent most of the mission on his phone. He was deliberately stirring up his leader because they were the one who reported him for the instance that got him punished." Orion hesitated and I tapped my foot impatiently.

"Go on," I ground out.

"You've got to understand how it works. There are only so many of us around here. We have to work together a lot of the time. Adam was always strong, quite opinionated, and very resilient. When they were on a mission together, no one thought anything of it. And well, while we can all die, it's not like it's easy to kill us. Basically, it has to be a kill shot. We're not just going to die from excess blood loss. Sections of our body will be stimulated until we heal more, close the wound, produce more blood. It's sort of complicated."

He looked down at the floor.

"Now, Cal's partner wasn't an eel like you, but they were fairly rare because Diviners become, they sort of aren't born, so to speak."

I held my hand up, interrupting him. "Diviner, say what?"

"Oh, not like you're thinking. Nothing that powerful. They often fulfill other roles, too. They have to possess multiple elemental skills and can catch a glimpse of potential futures. It's not an exact thing, but when there's hesitation for an assignment, it's usually good to have one of them with you. That whole gut feeling thing." Orion took in a deep breath before barreling on while I tried to sort out all of my thoughts on the matter.

"Anyway, Shauna had stopped Adam, grabbed his arm or something, halted the whole group's progression. Presumably it was to give them a warning, but in his irritation, Adam let his control of his abilities waver. A headshot took her out. Right between the eyes, exploding out the back of her skull like a bowling ball. No way to salvage that." He sounded like he was repeating something he'd learned verbatim. Going through the motions, trying not to think.

I didn't really want to interrupt him, but I had to, and I tried to be gentle. "Okay, wait. So I get that, but I mean, Dave died instantly too. Did they know where to shoot him or something?"

Orion blinked at me. "Guard was probably nervous."

"And a very good shot." I glanced at Orion, whose expression had turned thoughtful.

"Not much is going to bring you back from that, just shy of necromancy. And despite everything you probably think, we're not actually zombies." He attempted a light joke, but I could still see he was thinking over what I'd said.

I rolled my eyes. "Fine. Carry on."

He had to spoil all my fun. The least I could get from this was a zombie uprising.

"Anyway. Shauna died. Adam fucked up and dropped his concentration at a really crucial point, and Cal has never forgiven him." Orion cringed, and I could almost feel the sensation in my bones. Damn that overactive imagination. "Adam was reprimanded and punished, but let's face it, nothing was going to bring Shauna back. It was a stupid mistake, though some people think it was a bit more than that, Cal included. Anyway, it was my fault for sending Cal in before I knew who your Driver was going to be. I thought Cal had finally accepted that accidents happen, but apparently I was wrong." Orion seemed convinced.

The thing was, I wasn't. Because Cal hadn't seemed angry. They hadn't appeared to be unreasonable. Sure, it appeared as if Cal was attacking Adam, but at the same time, if I ran the memory over in my mind, he wasn't. Cal wouldn't have known who the Driver was going to be, so it wasn't a premeditated anything. Twisting that memory in my mind, Cal wasn't looking at Adam, but past him instead. My brain itched with the need to know why, like my abilities were annoyed I couldn't get more by examining what I'd seen.

"Are we able to go visit Cal at all?" I asked, trying to sound nonchalant.

Orion eyed me critically. He knew me far too well to take what I said at face value. "Technically no, but I'm sure the doctor would let you if you asked nicely."

I couldn't tell how much of that was sarcasm and how much was real, but I chose to assume the latter. "Look, you're thinking Cal was just too distraught. How long ago did this whole accidental death thing occur?"

"About nine months ago?" Orion asked me, like I'd know.

"Okay." I mulled it over. "That's soon enough to still be fairly raw, but also perhaps allow for some rational thinking to intrude. In my opinion, Cal wasn't acting recklessly. They were acting with deliberate speed to execute something, I just have no idea what. Perhaps it wasn't even aimed at Adam, though it at first seemed like it. Maybe there was something I didn't notice, and so I thought Adam was being attacked.

"Not to mention you've all heard of eels and not really worked with them, but know electric shocks suck. So discounting me didn't seem smart either, you with me so far?" I knew there was more to it, and the more I spoke it out loud, the more I realized I was right.

"You don't think Cal was aiming at Adam at all then?" Orion seemed highly unconvinced.

And if I'd just been looking at the aftermath, I'd agree with him.

"Not necessarily. I just think that whatever Cal was doing, there was more to it than we're giving credit for. Cal wasn't panicked or angry; their aura didn't let off anything that might indicate a premeditated murder attempt. They were reacting within the scope of their duties, but I just don't know why." And the why was what puzzled me the greatest.

I should report this back. Would you be okay with it if I were to phrase it as my own observations through your eyes during the operation?

What the what? My friendly neighborhood system was actually asking me if it could report something. It confused me a little, but I could see that maybe it was trying to gain my trust. Okay, I'd see where this took us. Because thinking to myself constantly in that area of my mind was obviously sending up red flags. And right now, I didn't even want to think about the complications that Shane and Nya presented.

Sure, I answered cautiously. *Just don't give away what I can do. I'm seriously fearing for my second life right about now.* With any luck, that would remind it that if I was gone, so was it.

Noted.

Orion still looked thoughtful, like he was having his own inner conversation and it was going about as well as mine was. Now all I had to do was figure out just why and what Cal had been doing. Sure, maybe one day I would get those amazing mind reading skills, but today was not that day. I'd have to resort to good, old fashioned, sleuthing.

24
RABBIT HOLE

Orion and I stood on the sidewalk outside the hospital, looking up at the levels as they towered above us.

"You're sure you want to do this?" he asked, gently. Like he'd totally forgive me if he had to walk all the way home now.

It was dark, and the wind had a distinct "Haha, I fooled you into thinking summer had come" chill to it. The sky wasn't showing us any stars, but it was about as clear as it got in the city.

"Yeah, I'm sure," I answered even though the words got partially stuck in my throat. I was ready to go in and see if I could get some answers, but at the same time, something kept trying to hold me back. Like a part of me was certain I wouldn't get any of the answers I wanted to get. Maybe it was right, too, but I had to try, didn't I?

"Let's go in, then. It's chillier than I expected." Orion hadn't brought a jacket with him, while I stood there in my trusty hoody that I hadn't removed since my ill-fated mission ended a few hours ago.

I pushed away the pure fatigue that threatened to break my bones. Occasionally I felt like I was made out of spaghetti. While I loved the idea of spaghetti monsters, I didn't want to be one.

As we approached the entrance, a nurse in a blue pair of scrubs appeared as if by magic. Dr. Caroline must have an alarm system that showed her when people were nearing. Or, you know, a whole system at her beck and call.

The nurse wasn't one I'd seen before. His black hair was neatly braided back, and the light in the driveway entrance made his skin shine healthily. "What can we do for you? There seem to be no injuries I can detect."

There was a note to his voice, like he was tired of people coming in who didn't actually need any help.

"We're here to see Dr. Caroline about our conditions." Orion phrased it in a way I wouldn't have, but immediate recognition popped into the nurse's eyes.

"Excellent. I'll let her know you're here. Follow me into the waiting room."

So we did.

The only way I'd entered here before had been on a stretcher. So I hadn't really seen the whole set up before. To be honest, when I'd left previously, I'd been far too preoccupied to care about surroundings. While we came in through the normal side entrance where the emergency area was, the path veered off to the right. As we followed our nurse down two separate corridors, we finally came to a door titled:

Dr. Leigh Caroline

Research Specialist

Call for appointment

Well, that was eerily unspecific. I wasn't sure I liked that. Research specialist. Perhaps that allowed her to do a whole mess of things. Keep it nice and broad so that people don't begin to question or some such?

The seats were just like any other waiting room seat. Uncomfortable and deliberately too close to one another.

You complain a lot. Maybe I liked it better when you kept your thoughts from me.

I'll remember that. It was nice to hear my head friend again. Even if it appeared to have gained some attitude. It got lonely talking to myself.

We waited for about twenty minutes, not saying anything to each other. Frankly, that's probably because I kept half dozing off and falling onto Orion's shoulder. Being shorter than me, it didn't seem to bother him. He just let me get the rest I obviously needed.

After what seemed like an age in the waiting room all by ourselves, the doctor pushed open one of the three doors along the right-hand side and came out. She looked a bit haggard herself. I swear that's all this organization was good for. Tiring its people out.

"What's up you two? I have a busy night." She didn't seem so much impatient as just busy and preoccupied.

"Can I see Cal, please? I was on the assignment too, and needed to ask a question." I tried to keep the desperation out of my voice, as well as the concern and remain professional. I was actually proud of myself for the control over my words considering I was so tired I almost couldn't see straight.

"Ah, yes." She looked me up and down like she was scanning me in her own right. "That's your handiwork in there. Nice, by the way. No serious burns, nothing permanent. Good control there. I'll talk to you about how you handled it at a later date. Get some details. Right now though, I'm trying to get Cal to heal up from the shock so I can put them through their next…treatment."

"Treatment?" I asked, even though I'd known it deep down, I still didn't want it to happen to him. I guess SC had to come up with some terms so that no one overheard them using punishment as a treatment method.

"Of course. Cal endangered a fellow operative. It's not like we can just throw our opinions around willy-nilly." She seemed surprised by my question and extremely adept at adjusting the terms she was using to sound less threatening. "And, well, electricity did a number on Cal, considering their other affinities. But I'll have them operational again in no time."

"Just in time to…treat them?" To inflict pain on them was what I wanted to say, but managed to bite my tongue in time.

"Of course. Can't let him get away with that sort of insubordination."

"Whatever was I thinking?" I muttered, before clearing my throat to speak louder. "Thing is, I don't think they meant to attack us."

Dr. Caroline paused and turned back to me, eyeing me curiously. Like she was fighting with herself about whether or not she should let me speak or tell me to go home. Finally, the former won out. "Okay, I'll bite. What do you mean?"

I took a deep breath. It was either now or never, as long as I left out that wee bit about the Timestance activation. "Okay, so. I can run that information through my mind and check things that happened while I was there right smack bang in the middle. Like sort of a rewind button. First up, in hindsight, I don't even think Cal was looking directly at Adam. There was something they were focusing on past him. It was like Cal trying to tell me what to do, or what they were going to do in a split second of time before I reacted. So this whole thing could have been my fault."

I carried on before anyone could stop me from being an idiot.

"I don't know Cal, and so I had to just go with what I did know, and that's how to listen and how to read people. Cal seemed upset, and perhaps even worried. But for my safety, not for any amount of revenge or leverage or anything personal. More like it was something mission-related. The thing was, their aim, in my eyes in that instant without the benefit of analysis, was focused directly on Adam." I shrugged. "I guess what I'm here to say is that you should maybe wait until they're awake and can tell their side of the story before you follow Adam's suppositions and angry report down the rabbit hole to oblivion."

Me and my analogies. Dr. Caroline looked thoughtful. "I haven't been able to get anything out of Cal yet. So this is all sort of subject to speculation right now. But I promise I will ask. Is that all you needed?"

It wasn't though, and Orion was quicker than I expected to exert a little pressure. "We really did want to see Cal, if that's okay?"

I watched myriad expressions flit over Dr. Caroline's face before she finally sighed and gave in. "You can go and wait for Cal to wake up. Then you have five minutes. Not a second more. Don't push it, or I'll think up some kind of treatment for you because you're taking advantage of the fact that I actually care a little bit."

Orion grinned, and we followed the doctor back to the area I'd come to know fairly well. The same machines blipped now that had blipped when I was here, and the sounds sung out to me, like a weird chorus of insects that shouldn't exist.

There were several doors with long, narrow windows just above the door handles. I peeked in all of them only to see every single one occupied. I guess operatives really did get injured on the job fairly often. The realization left me with that queasy feeling I get when I taste fake sugar.

Finally, Dr. Caroline pushed a door open. Here in the decent-sized hospital room, with IVs and wires coming from all different areas of their body, lay Cal. Their face appeared much paler than when I first saw it, and it looked like they'd lost weight in the last few hours. Frankly, I was appalled.

"That was me?" I wanted to say something to lighten the moment, but the words died in my chest, so I cleared my throat, waiting for an answer.

"Mostly. The fall to the floor helped with a bump to the head, but that electrical shock you gave Cal? That's what did most of the damage. Nothing permanent, though. Like I said, well controlled." The doctor still seemed quite impressed, even if she wore her business face.

"Oh." I wasn't sure how to respond to the slight note of pride in the doctor's voice. Though I was sure she had like four hundred questions for me.

"I have rounds to make. If you're still here when I'm done, you need to leave. Understood?"

I nodded my answer, hoping that would suffice. Moving closer, I reached out for Cal's hand. It felt clammy and cold, like they were fighting off some illness. Electrical aftershocks for the win. Am I right?

"It's okay, you know. At least a shock didn't kill Cal. Most other operatives wouldn't have had that control." Orion's words were meant to comfort me, but I felt like shit because I should have had more control over the damned ability than I did. But instead, I'd barely got any sleep while practicing my ability to project my shock through my barricaded skin. Who cared about a little thing called shocking others without killing them if I could do that?

"Dare?" Cal's voice broke through my thoughts, his eyes suddenly open. But there was a tiredness in them as well. They smiled at me, like relief flooded through them and made it easier to breathe.

And then they spoke words I'd simply not expected to hear.

"Thank the gods you're okay. I was worried."

I wasn't sure what to think of the way Cal reached for me. Their entire demeanor toward me from the very beginning had been strange. At least, not friendly, and not particularly happy to see me. Perceptions could always be misinterpreted, but I was slowly learning that auras couldn't be.

Intentions, on the other hand, sent up a huge red flag. And the intentions I'd felt, I'd experienced while watching Cal were a mixed bag. None of them evil, but some of them were probably questionable. The words Cal spoke rang alarm bells in my mind. Not for their true meaning, but because on some level, I actually believed them.

"What do you mean?" Orion's tone was harsher than I'd expected. All things considered, I was secretly happy to see that level of emotion in him. Maybe this was salvageable.

Cal blinked like they'd only just noticed Orion was with me. "Sorry. Didn't see you. What happened?"

They appeared to be groggy and uncertain, like I'd reset their brain or something. Their brow furrowed, and they seemed to be gathering thoughts, or perhaps memories.

"You tried to attack Adam." Orion crossed his arms, his stern expression in place. It was like he was trying to shock his fellow Cleaner into admitting something or anything.

Cal laughed. "I most certainly did not." But they looked at me and, realizing that I was also oblivious to what they'd done, their face went pale.

"You didn't see it?" Now they sounded scared. I could almost hear their thoughts whirring around in their minorly concussed skull. Like they was running through every thought they'd had, and everything they'd seen. But their results were obviously different than I'd expected because they squared their jaw, looked right at me, and spoke with confidence.

"They were all around you, leeching onto Adam too. These strange spidery things. Sort of spiders anyway. They winked in and out of my vision.

At first I couldn't be sure I'd even seen them, but about halfway through the mission, I started noticing them more." Struggling to sit up slightly, Cal continued. "Actually, they were very fond of you. If I hadn't known I was awake, I would have thought I was dreaming. Like skittering robots with camouflage. I say spiders because they had tiny legs and moved like arachnids. They resisted my fire cleansing and only appeared to grow stronger from the power, like they sucked it into themselves. Like they grew with it. I'm exceptional with controlling my fire, and I didn't want an explosion on my record. So I followed them."

Cal seemed totally confused, and I wished there was a way to tap into their brain and check and see if they'd really observed something like that. Maybe there was, but I had no clue how to go about it. I needed to start experimenting on my own. Screw all these people trying to tell me how to use my ability, and what I needed to do.

"No," I finally answered, after wracking my brain searching for anything I might have seen that could put Cal at ease. There was nothing there. I hadn't even seen my usual shadows, let alone some strange robot spider shadows. "No, I didn't see anything like that."

For the first time since coming in here, since waking up, a flicker of doubt passed over Cal's face. They took a breath, like they were trying to remember if it had all been a dream, but that look of determination didn't wane. "I know what I saw, and my system should be able to verify it."

Can it do that? I asked mine immediately.

There was a brief pause. *Technically. Though I'm not sure why it wouldn't already have done so. It would save both their system and their body a lot of potential trauma. Perhaps there are reasons.*

I didn't say anything more, wondering if the system realized that a cover up had been performed? Did it know it just sort of said that to me? If Cal was certain of what they'd seen, then the system had seen it too. Cal wasn't an eel and couldn't partition their thoughts, so their system had observed it and neglected to pass it on. That was major food for thought later.

"It hasn't yet, though, has it?" I asked the question gently, and fear passed through their eyes.

"Not yet." They bit their lip, like worry was beginning to gnaw at them. "No, not yet. Perhaps the electrical charge screwed something up. I've never been electrocuted before."

I couldn't imagine they had. And their thought process wasn't too far from the truth. After all, electricity could disrupt their thought pattern. Perhaps it could affect memory as well.

That same old flash of waves against the hull of a catamaran flickered in front of my vision again briefly. I was about to resort to hypnosis to figure out what the fuck it all meant.

What if eels could adjust memories? Made sense. We could probably fry sections of the brain with accuracy given enough practice. Had I accidentally jumbled something, or was the system deliberately holding information back and sending one of its agents to punishment?

Furthermore, what were these robots? They didn't sound like the shadow creatures I'd encountered and whose appendages I'd jammed in doors. The only thing I could admit was that I was floundering more than usual. And I wasn't happy with that at all.

25

THICK AS SLUDGE

By the time we got home, I wasn't just irritated, I was angry. And my little friendly voice was being unnaturally absent in its commentary.

So many elements of the last couple of months began to click together. The strangely fortuitous appearance of the mechanical shadows I'd been shown in my very first mission. Just enough to rouse my curiosity. Nothing referenced them, and my inner watcher didn't appear to notice them. My eel powers were uncontrolled, and I almost burned myself out several times. But no information was available.

My head was aching like it was trying to tell me something, but I couldn't see what it was through all the bullshit I had to wade through. There was something not clicking right, but it was just out of my reach. With all my concerns about keeping the secret of the eels from the authoritative figures, I'd been overlooking something, even if I couldn't quite figure out just what that thing was.

Frankly, I didn't think that eels were rare. I thought they were pretty frequent, but the speed with which the electricity could overwhelm them and burn them out or render them incorporeal made it so few were left with functionality. And here I was, lucky me, still a living and breathing human. If my head would stop pounding.

I shook my head, trying to clear my thoughts, which was essentially a bad idea. The pressure in my skull compounded, threatening to explode.

David's face exploding toward me. Like a watermelon hit by a sledgehammer.

Nausea began to overwhelm me as the memory replayed on a loop in my mind. Thinking hard shouldn't cause a reactionary headache...unless I was reaching for something.

What are you hiding? What are they hiding?

My little friend, with whom I thought I'd come to an understanding, remained silent. So much for the friendly neighborhood keeping-my-secret internal voice. Fine. I could work around that. I'd done it before. Disappearing might set them on edge and worry them, but it no longer worried me. If I couldn't trust the counsel of others, I'd just have to rely on myself once the room stopped spinning.

And if SC had trouble tracking me, maybe Shane and Nya would too. Right now, I didn't feel so trusting of anybody around me, including Orion. Maybe especially him.

"Dare?" He sounded concerned, but was he really? I looked up at him, trying to study his face and see if it was the same one I'd been watching since I was five.

I couldn't be sure. Hell, I couldn't even be sure of my surroundings. It felt like the walls were bleeding in and out of each other, occasionally opening up to the outside and allowing the city to leak through. Like the traffic was actually driving through my living room, or else through the hospital. Showers of electricity from broken power lines cascaded through the space, like loose snakes with their venom spurting out for all to see.

Wavy electrical wires. Something about it struck a memory chord within me, but I couldn't quite focus on it. Every time I tried, it slipped right out of my grasp. The pounding in my head increased, like that good old bass drum, except this time it had funeral overtones. Visions passed through my mind so quickly I couldn't grasp them, foreign and yet familiar at the same time. My head spun like a top, reaching through to my stomach and trying to pull my intestines through my mouth.

"Dare?" Orion's voice came from everywhere at once, and his face spun around in my vision, in this cave-like existence that flashed through so many memories I couldn't get a grip.

Pain shot through my head like someone hammered a stake right through my brain. It hit electricity in only the way metal could, conducting it throughout my entire body and sending me into a convulsing heap on the ground. I couldn't fight anything; I could barely move. So when they picked me up and moved me away, all I could do was pass out.

What the fuck, Shane. Orion sounded angry in the strangely lit atmosphere I found myself in. I think I was awake, but I couldn't be sure. And how did Orion know Shane? Wait, were they all in on it somehow?

Look, maybe you should have paid more attention in the first place, and you could have prevented them targeting your best friend at all. As it is, you're lucky I happened to be on shift in the ambulance, or this whole thing would have blown up in our faces. Shane's voice was even more heated, if that was possible.

How you let this go under your radar when everything else puts you on high alert, I'll never understand. Shane grumbled the words, and I was sure they'd make Orion scowl, if I could just see his face. Perhaps.

But the light kept flickering in and out, and I had no idea where I was, nor a clue what was actually happening. It was like my brain was stuttering through time, trying to grasp at straws to fit things together. Right now, I seemed to be missing half of the puzzle pieces.

None of what I heard made sense, so it stood to reason that perhaps I was just imagining it in all my wishful thinking.

How long did you spend in there? The anger in Orion's words brought me back from whatever precipice I'd been dangling over in this weird fragmented vista. What long spend in where? Not even my thoughts were clear.

Just over six hours, I think. Shane seemed nonplussed as the two of them,

I think, pushed me through an opening.

Are you fucking kidding me? What did you think was going to happen if you kept Dare in a Timewarp for that sort of duration before properly attuned? Now I could sense the breaking point for my best friend. He had this thing where he lowered his tone of voice to such a level that it made anything he asked sound like the person on the receiving end was a complete and utter idiot.

Knowing Shane as little as I did, I suspected he wasn't going to take kindly to it.

I don't know, Orion. I thought, hey, how about I fuck Dare right up just to piss off water boy? There was silence for several seconds as shapes and breaches in the walls decided to inundate my awareness.

I almost thought I could hear them glaring at each other. Full with background villain music to boot. My brain and I really needed to talk.

Orion sighed, but I think I missed something, because the air where we were felt different. Cleaner, fresher, easier to breathe.

Stop taking it so hard. It's not your fault they dragged Dare into this. We just have to figure out the best way to circumvent their intentions. Shane's tone had changed. Dropped with a softness I'd not expected of him, like he actually cared. So how did he even know Orion, and how did Orion know Shane? And what the fuck was going on?

But none of the questions floating around in my head made it past my lips. In all honesty, I wasn't even sure my eyes were open or if I was in some sort of trance. And what the hell did Shane mean by it not being Orion's fault? Why would it be his fault?

I moved slightly, my left elbow suddenly hurting me. But the ground beneath me wasn't hard, nor was it my mattress. I wasn't in my own room, nor was I anywhere in our apartment.

How did they move me? How did any of this happen? My limbs suddenly felt heavy, like they'd gained thirty pounds of weight each. My head was still booming along like a bass drum, and all I wanted to do was sleep.

If I'd known what could happen, I'd never have agreed to maintain my life as it was. It would have been better for me to leave than to see Dare go through this. They've effectively taken those dreams away.

From all of us, though. Shane prodded with his words, such a gentle reminder. Perhaps they'd been friends all of the last two years. Wait, I thought Shane was going to tell me Orion was evil.

My head swam, and I sought out my little safe haven in my own head. It was still there, beautifully reinforced, secure, and all mine. Where I could be me and have all the thoughts I needed to have, witness everything I'd seen and not have to worry about anyone looking in on me.

Orion's voice leaked through to me again, his words filled with melancholy. *It's my fault. I need to toe the line better, for now at least. Rebellion got my best friend killed, and now I have to live with having ruined Dare's career. At least I can still be a doctor, but the more Dare's ability expands, the less that running speed is going to pass for normal human capabilities.*

I'm not sure what Shane was doing, nor was I sure what Orion was thinking because my brain latched onto those last words he'd spoken. Normal human capabilities? Of course, I'd thought along those lines some, because if I wanted to push more electricity through my running, I could. And it never seemed to run out. The more energy I put into my body, the more it produced, so it was a sort of evil circle that fed off each other.

And here I was overhearing, or maybe reaching into their minds. I had no idea, but here I was finding out that maybe I was right.

What are you going to do then? This time it wasn't Shane, and it wasn't Orion. It was Dr. Leigh Caroline's voice. I might not know her that well, but you don't forget the voice that patches you up, you don't forget the voice that explains the whole damned system to you, and you definitely don't forget the voice that meters out punishment when you've really done nothing to deserve it.

The next thing I knew, I was groggily starting to wake up. There were no more splinters in the perception of my surroundings, and the reflection of the sun didn't try to stab my irises when I opened my eyes. In fact, for the first time in a long time, I actually felt quite rested. Body-wise, anyway. My brain on the other hand? It was full of so many questions I needed to hold a press conference.

First up. Orion had been forced into something because of me? Or was that simply a manifestation of my wishful thinking that he was coerced into killing and thus still my dear friend underneath that tortured exterior? I mean, that would solve all the problems, right? It would simply mean we had to remove him from that situation, and everything would be fixed.

Except that wasn't right. Was it? Rebellion? Too long in the Timewarp. Dragged into it. All of the words echoed around through my head trying to break free of the confines of my limiting thought.

Also, I was starving.

My eyes didn't want to open though. Not fully, not now they'd finally had some rest. Cautiously, I forced them to comply. Strange. I was sure I'd heard the doctor's voice. But she wasn't in the room with me, and I didn't appear to be in the hospital either. Nor was I at my apartment or anyone's I'd ever visited. I tried to sit up, but the room obligingly spun around me and I made myself lay back down, trying to stop my stomach from throwing up its lack of contents.

Whatever had happened, my head wasn't having any of it right then. I tried my best to take stock of the room I was in without actually moving. Eyeballs were my limit and even those felt sore. What had I done to myself?

The room was fairly nondescript. It had a simple desk and chair in the farthest corner from me. From what I could tell I was on a full-sized bed with a pretty damn nice mattress from its comfort level. There was a small window up high to the left of me, so I surmised I must be in a basement bedroom or apartment somewhere.

When I'd finished my trusty evaluation, I noticed it had actually sapped some strength from me.

I didn't like being in this place, being in this area where I didn't know who had taken me and hidden me away here. Sure, I'd overheard three people I knew in my delusions, but that's all they could be. What if this place was where SC operatives came to die?

Great. Scare the shit out of myself.

"Dare?" Orion popped his head around the plain door directly opposite the bed.

I don't think I've ever been so relieved to see anyone in my life. His smile reached his sad eyes, lighting them up for a moment, and he closed the door behind him as he pulled up the chair and sat next to the bed.

I waited. Not that I wanted to, but it seemed he had something to tell me, and I got a distinct feeling that I wasn't going to like what he had to say even if I had an inkling I already knew. Not that I thought he'd done anything wrong, just that I was pretty sure I'd be pissed he'd taken this long to tell me it. Probably could have avoided a lot if they'd just included me from the start.

"So." He studied his fingers like they were the most interesting things on Earth. And he did indeed have very nice fingers, but that wasn't what he came here to talk about, and we both knew it.

"I have questions, so many of them." My voice was raspy as I tried to push the words out, and he eyed me, concern passing through his gaze. "But you seem to have something on your chest, so it's probably a better idea if you just say what you came to tell me, and then if I still have questions, I'll go. Sound okay?"

Orion nodded, and I could feel the relief that passed through him, like a wave of cool air tempering the heat. He paused for a few moments before finally looking up at me. A dark shade of mixed colors lingered around him like a shroud of guilt. At the same time though, brighter colors sparked around him, daring the darkness to take more. Like he was proud of what he was about to tell me.

On some level I knew what I'd heard hadn't been a dream, but a part of me was scared to hear it come from him.

26
CONFESSIONS

"It's my fault you're in this predicament. I did something I shouldn't have, and this was my punishment, I guess." The sorrow in Orion's voice almost undid me. Surely there'd been more to it than that. I'd heard this much in my fevered dream state, so there was no real need for me to digest the information he was giving me.

He might not have expected me to respond. Hell, it probably would have done me better if I'd thought things over and processed his actual words before speaking. But I wanted this awkwardness, this alienation I felt from him to be over.

"Did you cut the line?" I asked, trying to sound as serious as possible.

He blinked at me. "What line?" His confusion almost made me laugh.

"The electrical cable that fell on me and gave me this wondrous gift." Perhaps I wasn't as okay with this as I'd first thought. My sarcasm was already creeping in and suffusing my words. But if nothing else, that seemed to put Orion at ease. Like he saw his same old Dare emerging.

"No, I didn't cut it." He sighed and chuckled softly. "I get what you're saying and what you're trying to do. And there's no need for you to try and take the blame away. The fact is that ice is one of the rarer talents that emerge. Ice users, it turns out, are pretty indispensable. About the same as an eel who survives initial ability awakenings. Both ice and electricity can cause results and often look like something else, or a complete accident."

I digested the information and nodded my head slowly. That actually made more sense than I'd anticipated. But it also sank into my bones as it proved one of my theories correct. My death hadn't been an accident, it had been a controlled situation in which they produced an operative with an ability they needed in order to punish another of their agents into toeing the line.

"What did you do?" I asked the question to nudge him along so he'd hopefully get the rest of the information out before I exploded with curiosity and anger.

He eyed me with an unreadable expression. "I questioned orders given to me. Almost every time they gave them to me. I even deliberately disobeyed direct orders. Methods of containing situations that I didn't agree with, that seemed too extreme. Things I didn't want to do and didn't agree with doing because I believed there were other ways to accomplish those, which I then went ahead and did. I was your regular little rebel."

Orion sighed, like it was all a part of a bad dream and he didn't want to remember it. Still, I waited for him to continue, knowing he would, because he had to. "The last mission was killing someone who I really didn't understand the need to silence. I mean, they weren't doing anything that could have given us away. Sending someone to sleep is just as easy with the abilities I manifested. I can lower them into a deep sleep and they wake up once they warm up." He shook his head, clenching his eyes shut like he was fighting to forget shit.

"Hey, if it's too difficult..." I left it open, knowing he wouldn't take me up on the offer, but at the same time sort of hoping he would. The pain reflected in his eyes was real, and there was more I wasn't entirely sure I actually wanted him to tell me about.

"It's not just that it's difficult. It's that it's the reason you're here with me, knowing about this, participating in this..." He looked around the bare room. "This is a safe space, not even your friendly neighborhood voice can reach you in here. You'll be off the grid. They'll worry. Hell, they'll worry more with it being the both of us. Hopefully that'll be where it stops. I can't afford to have any other friends die. I don't think I'll survive that."

Okay, now I was getting a little worried. This kicked dog routine he was pulling just seemed so unlike him. Like he'd given up on doing what he deemed to be right. And that wasn't the Orion I'd grown up with. "No. Stop this."

He looked up at me. My clear and crisp words apparently confused him, because his next words were questions. "What? What do you mean by that? I don't think you understand."

"I understand perfectly well. You feel responsible for my death, and maybe you are, in a way, but you didn't kill me." I took a deep breath because this was going to be difficult to say. I needed to make him believe even when I didn't really mean it right now with all the feelings warring around inside me. But it was what he needed to hear, and I hoped it would help him be more like his usual proactive self.

"But this way, we have each other to work with. You should have looped me in from the beginning. If they can't hear us in here, then this is a safe haven, and that's something we need." I held up a hand to stop the speech I knew was coming. We didn't have time for this if the system would get suspicious. "Stop moping. I'm dead now, there's nothing we can do to reverse it, but perhaps there are things we can do to change how it impacts us."

The more I said, the more I felt good about what I was telling him. There were parts of it that I'd only ever said to myself, thought deep down and away from anything that might pry. But letting the words out there, allowing him to hear them, perhaps that was the key all along.

He watched me, his brow creasing slightly as he contemplated my words. "Then you understand now? Why I've been doing what I've *had* to do?" The way he spoke made me feel guilty for having judged him without knowing all of the facts.

Sure, he'd killed a person, but it was different if he'd done so under duress. From everything I'd found out, he'd not done so willingly, and not even to save his own life. Now, it was to save others from being consigned to this pitiful version of an afterlife. The relief that swept through me lifted the last vestiges of aching from my bones.

"I understand, but I wouldn't have done it in your place. At least, I don't think I would have. Your inability to defy them any longer makes sense. In this case, you put the life of your friends above the life of the person in question. That isn't something I'm happy about. And knowing me as well as you do, I would think you'd be aware of that." I let the words sink in, and saw his expression fall. He knew I was right, even if it hurt. "I understand why you did it, but I don't think I'd make the same choice."

"I didn't know what else to do." He pretty much just mumbled the words so I had to strain to hear him. "It's why I didn't greet you at first, it's why I didn't talk to you about SC before we had that first mission, because I didn't want you to be in it. I didn't want to admit what had happened. But when they threw you in my face, as my Runner on a mission, there was no more denying it."

His expression was filled with sadness. It tugged down at his mouth, destroying the half smile I loved so much. It ached to watch him struggle with what he'd done. All his life he'd wanted to help people, heal people, the opposite of killing people. That his ability had morphed in such a way as to make him an ideal killing machine was just irony at its finest.

"I'm sorry for judging you. I'm sorry that I can't say I would have done the same. But maybe, from here out, we can work together to stop this. To do something about all of this." I waved a hand around randomly, indicating the room and the situation we found ourselves in.

Orion's smile reappeared, and he looked like new hope had been breathed into him. "I was so hoping you'd say that. Because there is so much I have to tell you, hell, that we all have to tell you."

"Yeah, how about you start with exactly how you know my ambulance buddy Shane, and just why does Dr. Leigh Caroline know anything about my this?"

From the surprise on his face, I'd say my overheard conversations had been real and not a part of my imagination. I don't think I've ever been so relieved about something in my life.

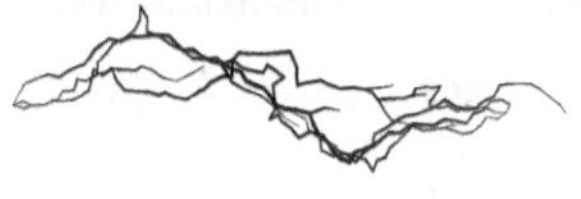

I was more tired than anticipated, and I couldn't really help falling asleep shortly after my conversation with Orion. All in a day's work, as long as I could sleep to recuperate. My dreams were contrarily awful. Electrocution appeared prominently in them, my own. In every form I could conceive of. From the toaster to a light switch, even down to while I was running.

But each time I didn't jolt awake, I just switched to the next one. Running from it didn't help; it was all I could do to stay even with it and not get gobbled up by the rain of electrical storms behind me. Restful definitely wasn't the word I'd use to describe my sleep, but it was less shocking than waking up to find a few people gathered around your bed staring at you when you woke up.

Which is what happened.

Orion sat where he'd been earlier, Shane was by the door, his arms crossed and his expression one I could only describe as gruff. Dr. Caroline sat with her legs crossed, examining that same tablet type thing I'd seen Nya working on that one day. I closed my eyes, hoping a couple of things. Perhaps they hadn't noticed I'd woken up, and that maybe they were a figment of my obviously over active imagination and would be gone when I opened them again.

No such luck, though.

"Come on, Dare. I don't have all day to hide here. It might be one of my rare days off, but I have other work I need to perform." The doctor seemed impatient, but her voice still held kindness. And she was probably right. I wonder how much sleep she got considering the amount of work she needed to do if she was going to keep SC happy and do whatever she did for this little rebellion sort of thing.

"Sorry," I said, still feeling groggy and somewhat overwhelmed. My head hurt, but I was feeling more rested than previously, so it was a win in a way. I shot a trickle of healing through my body, attempting to relieve the tension in my neck and at the base of my skull. Again, it wasn't instantaneous, but I could feel it slowly begin to take effect. "So. Why are you all looking at me with grave expressions?"

"Grave expressions." Shane snorted back a laugh, but I could see it still twinkling in his eyes. It must be awesome to be so amusing.

Orion clenched and unclenched his fists, cleared his throat, and was, I think, about to speak, when the doctor got bored of waiting.

"Well, you know now, so we need to talk to you about what else there is to all of this. you're probably not going to like it much." She held out the strange electro clipboard in her hands, and I took it from her.

Once it had left her possession, she began to shift. It was subtle. Hair color darkened ever so slightly, and her body shape changed subtly. To be honest, they were minor adjustments, but they made her bleed into Nya.

"What. The. Fuck" was pretty much the only vocabulary I could express right then.

She chuckled. Which, in its own way, was infuriating.

"Wait, so who are you?" I whispered, suddenly afraid that the people all around me were shapeshifters and I actually had no idea at all who any of them were. "What are you?"

The Nya-Caroline doctor grinned a little sadly. "I'm really just the doctor, but Nya helps me keep my two jobs separate. One of which can't be discovered, and that one is Nya."

"But how do you—" My words were not working.

"Refraction of light through electrical charges reflecting skin level differences." She shrugged. "To put it in less technical terms, it's basically a close-to-the-skin molded illusion or disguise."

"Can all eels do that?" I still couldn't wrap my head around it.

Nya shook her head. "I don't think so. It could just be a time thing. I've been around for a good long while, and I certainly couldn't do it at first." She seemed sad, if her tone was anything to go by.

I blinked, still trying to digest it. "But I've had missions that have sent me to you, you *as* Nya. I'm really confused right now." Because I had been sent to Nya. I remembered that clear as day.

"Nya is the name of one of the programs I initiated. It's a check in and check over, but it's also an easy way for us to get our little rebels to see me and receive information without alerting the SC portion of the system to our presence prematurely." She grimaced. "It's getting tricky to work around."

I nodded, not understanding if the name was an acronym or if she'd just called it that on a whim. It made sense the way she described it, and yet it didn't at the same time. I was done with this constant beating around the bush. I wanted answers now, or preferably yesterday, but I'd take either.

"What is this whole SC portion of the system thing, and why do I receive two different sets of information? How are there even two systems? What is it we're supposed to hide from our supposedly benevolent benefactor who has magnanimously brought us back from the dead to serve a higher purpose?" There, I think that was about all the information I could digest right now. I just had to sit back and wait for someone to answer all my questions.

All of them exchanged looks with one another, and Nya slowly bled back into Leigh Caroline. I must admit I liked the doctor persona far more.

"Don't all rush to answer at once," I half joked, but they didn't seem to take it that way.

"It's not that," Orion began. He glanced at the other two. "It's more you've sort of answered your own question. Are we really here to serve a higher purpose, or has that purpose been corrupted? Think about it for a moment, we've got some time."

I looked at him, incredulousness overwhelming me for a moment. Sure, the system told us that we were needed to protect humanity from itself. And let's face it, humans are destructive beasts. We kill each other and everything else. Sometimes I wonder if we were dropped here because we already blew up one planet. Still though, why were we monitored, and just what did the system count as protecting us from ourselves? Who set the parameters, and if it had been around for so long, wouldn't the limits have changed over time?

"It can carry out the threat, right? In the TOS? That if we don't fulfill our obligations, then we will be terminated from the program?" I could hear the hesitance in my voice. This was the main thing I wished wasn't really true.

"Correct." The doctor watched me intently, and I really wished just one of them would answer my question, because this figuring it out myself while there were other people who obviously knew the truth was getting a little bit old. "Technically."

"Correct me if I'm wrong, which I doubt you'll do, but I'm going to wish for anyway." I could hear the snide irritation in my voice, but I was so done with this cryptic bullshit. It had been going on since this whole thing started. "The SC program is a splinter of the original."

I noticed their acknowledgement in their eyes. None of them seemed surprised that I'd got this far. Considering my major, I'd be shit at my future job if I didn't. "At some stage in history, or at some specific event, this program received a knock on the head and fractured. Or perhaps even a loop, or virus…" I could see it coming together in my thought process. And though it seemed more like a science fiction story, I pressed on.

"When it began malfunctioning, someone or something noticed and took advantage of it. Where the consequences are punishment, and where the operatives don't have a choice between life and death, and where the deaths aren't always accidental, but instead are engineered to produce the types of abilities the system is lacking overall."

Okay, so that was as far as I'd gotten with my logical train of thought.

"So. Am I right? Do I pass? Are you going to fucking tell me what the hell is going on in all this afterlife?" My words were heated, and I just wanted to know so I wasn't in the dark, and so I could simply figure out my next move on my own.

"You're very right. But you are missing one crucial piece of information." The doctor leaned forward, and Orion looked like he was about to burst at the seams from excitement.

The suspense wasn't quite killing me, but if they kept this up, it was certainly going to kill someone else soon.

"We've figured out a way to circumvent the system for the most part, and with our research, it means we can stop the cycle and return the system to what it was intended to be." Dr. Caroline sounded so eager, and so determined at the same time that I didn't have the heart to correct her in any way. But something about it bothered me, like there was a supposition there that no one had considered.

I couldn't quite figure out how to phrase it properly so as not to offend my new friends who'd apparently accidentally triggered my death. I took a deep breath and just went for it. "How do you know what the original intention was? I mean, with time and weather, and earthquakes, and geographical locations, adding in climate shifts, how do you know it can even be fixed?"

27
ANCIENT

"Well, the old system can't be any worse than the splintered one, can it?" There was raw energy in Shane's words, like it was the only hope he was clinging to.

I changed the subject. "So you all know what the shadows are then? Not the disembodied eels, but the mechanical ones." I might have sounded slightly accusatory. But considering I'd asked him about them before and he hadn't really elaborated, I felt like I was justified in doing so.

"Yeah. As far as we can tell it's their attempt to mimic an eel." Orion nodded, and Shane jumped in straight after the statement.

"Those things are creepy as fuck. And if we're right, a version of those is what Cal saw when they went to attack Adam. Or, what we thought was attacking Adam." He sounded almost gleeful, and I was surprised he wasn't rubbing his hands together in anticipation.

Except what he said didn't sit right. Their attitude toward the shadows didn't have any overtones of concern in the way I thought it should. "I've seen the shadows of the eels. I've spoken to them. You don't seem to be worried that we'll end up that way."

"What way? Able to exist on multiple planes, perhaps even travel dimensions?" Orion's smile lit up his face. He'd always loved science fiction. But it was very apparent he was missing the much larger picture.

"Maybe, but that's not how they get there, you know that right? It's not their choice. It's a number of aspects of dealing with electricity that all run in together and create the set of circumstances that separates them from their earthly bodies." My lingo surprised even me as I spoke the words. But I realized how correct I was, and how sad I felt for the eels who'd already gone on their irrevocable path.

"What do you mean it's not their choice?" Leigh Caroline suddenly sounded like I felt. As if she'd misjudged her understanding of the process entirely. As a doctor, that must really piss her off.

I turned to watch her expression as I spoke, because sometimes tone doesn't convey everything we feel.

"They're trapped. Disembodied. Only able to creep around in the shadows and try to warn those of us who can understand that we can't let the power we have go uncontrolled. Eels need control as soon as they're created." I looked from the doctor to Shane and back again. "Please tell me you've actually taken the time to speak to them before?"

Shane shook his head. "It's not the time that was the factor, but more the ability. I've never been able to communicate with them except to see them and to realize that what SC is making is pure imitation. Not to mention I have no idea why they want to."

Dr. Caroline pursed her lips. "I've spoken to them, to an extent, and I realize they're not happy in their incorporeal states, but I didn't realize just how it occurred. I always wondered if it was natural progression and why I hadn't reached that stage yet." The last was said more to herself than to the rest of us, but I could understand the sentiment.

"I'm not special as an eel. Right? There's no difference to my power levels?" I glared at them. They were being too slow for my liking. "Come on. I'm not slow on the uptake, just tell me all the information so I know what to do with what I'm becoming."

I was at the end of my patience. End of my everything right now, and I just wanted to go home and sleep and run through this all in my mind on my own.

Dr. Caroline squared her shoulders. "Sorry. We all went into protective mode once we realized what SC had done to Orion's best friend. We've been trying to protect you and are realizing only now that it's probably not the best way to go about things with you."

"Yeah. Especially with you." Orion seemed sheepish, and wouldn't make eye contact with me. Good. Because he didn't fucking deserve it right now. Keeping me in the dark like that.

"Okay, here we go. Get that overcharged brain ready to remember things." She grinned at me and winked. "I shall only say this once. SC has created eels before, planned their deaths so as to recruit an eel when they've lacked them firsthand. Your life, however, seems to have made you ideal for this power, I guess. A runner, with a knowledge of how electricity acts in conjunction with computer systems and how their body functions on a primal level is probably more ideal than they intended." She paused, and I gave her a nod to let them know I was with her so far.

Not like it was difficult. After all, I'd pretty much come to the same conclusion all on my own.

Dr. Caroline glanced at the watch she wore, and I realized she probably had so much to do in the real world that her time was truly precious. Still, she continued for me. "Eels, for the most part, tend to burn out fast. A lot of people who receive electrical abilities don't know the first thing to do in order to discharge them safely and frequently."

I held up my hand confused. "But the original system has a complete guide on it. At least, far more helpful than the one that woke me up."

I could feel the hesitation more than see it, but the doctor pushed on. "Exactly. We aren't precisely sure when the system's schism occurred, but at some point, a wedge was driven between the pure intentions of the system and allowed it to become corrupted. And we don't even think they can detect one another."

That didn't sound plausible, and I'm pretty sure my scowl echoed my skepticism.

"Hear us out. You have to understand that everything that happened was before any of our times. It was all already in place, and it's only through some damn fortuitous thinking that we've managed to build up any type of a resistance to this system that took control over our lives.

"It can kill you. It can terminate the TOS you've agreed to and actively send you back to death. As long as you can't yet stop it, you can be killed on a whim, or..." She paused and looked at Orion, who wouldn't stop staring at his feet. But her voice grew stronger as she continued. "Or you can be used as a hostage tool for someone who doesn't want to toe the line."

Well, that made sense. Orion was the one who continued though, still studying the floor, not making eye contact with any of us. "I was hoping they wouldn't go through on their threat. I thought it was just a test, to see what I would do. But then Shane alerted me, and I had to calm down before I could see you. This is all my fault, only I think they've bitten off more than they realized."

Now he looked up at me, his eyes bright with determination. "I think they wanted to create an eel so they'd at least have someone useful even if I didn't do what they need me to do. But they didn't realize they'd given you a power that's, like, made for you. And if we're lucky, that might just be the key to getting all the answers we need to fix this."

I pretended to sleep while the others went their separate ways, but my brain was busy. There was no aspect of control over how the resurrected reacted to the abilities they received. Just like with food, hair, body types…everyone was unique.

I could deal with that. A master plan gone wrong. If only the damned questions I asked hadn't led to more. My curiosity began to get the better of me, and I wanted to explode with all the unknown.

Why had the system splintered? What were all these weird missions for? Did that ledger back at the bakery have blackmail information? Why were we necessary? The lists went on, bombarding my brain gleefully.

I wanted to understand the voice that was in my head. The one who'd been there with me since the start. The one that'd disappear if I did. As time passed, it became less mechanical and far more individual. Yet another series of questions waiting to be researched.

Trying to find a comfortable spot, I sighed as I rolled over. Wick was the only real highlight about being in the basement I found myself in. He jumped up on the foot of my bed, turned in circles until he'd made the patch nice and soft for himself, and then promptly dropped down, curled into a dog ball, and watched me, a tiny bit of his tongue sticking out from behind his teeth. Like it didn't fit in his mouth.

It was undeniably cute, and I regretted immediately having said he could stay with Nya, the doctor, whoever she was. A dog of my very own to listen to all my ramblings would come in very handy right about now. But he seemed content and happy, and who was I to take that away from anyone?

It all boiled down to what I needed to do. I needed to trust these people because Orion did. Figure out a way to restore the ancient system and grant those dragged into the program free will. Sure. That sounded like an easy enough quest.

There was a knock at the door. Relief flooded through me because all my thoughts were doing was running me around in circles. I knew Orion was coming to pick me up, so I swung my tired legs to the side of the bed and attempted to rise, only to see it was the doctor and not my best friend.

"Sorry to disappoint. He'll be in shortly." She hesitated, like she wasn't sure how to phrase what she needed to say. "You overdid it. No Timewarp for a while, okay? Shane shouldn't have let you use it for as long as you did. It's the sort of thing you need to ramp up to, and let's just say you did a bit too much all at once. Hopefully the control you've learned will stand you in good stead and you won't need it for a while."

"What sort of danger does it pose?" I asked since being direct always seemed to be the best route to take.

She paused, narrowing her eyes slightly. "If you spend too much time in it prematurely, it can hasten cell degradation instead of prolonging it like the system allows." She left me sitting there on the bed trying to process her words.

Since she'd told me at our first meeting that our lives were basically extended and we'd live past our usual years, that must be some whopper of cell degradation. Also, they'd obviously figured it out somehow. It made me wonder just how many people they'd lost before they realized what the cause was.

"Dare?" Orion startled me out of my conspiratorial thoughts.

"Sorry. Off with the…I have no idea. Just lots of thoughts running rampant." I grinned and pushed myself to standing. My legs still felt oddly stiff, like I'd overworked the muscles. Maybe I had somehow due to the whole having taken time off because of the concussion. Still, it was an easy fix if I just stretched.

"Really?" Orion raised an eyebrow, clearly unimpressed. "You're going to do that now when you could have been stretching and getting ready for the last hour?"

"Well, yes." I grumbled. "Nya, Leigh, whoever she is came to visit and warn me temporarily away from the Timewarp. Would have been nicer to know that a bit ahead of time, but better late than never, right?"

He eyed me and grabbed the bag of medicine that sat on my bed. "Let's get you back to the house so you can be all grumpy in your own environment."

Even his grin was the same as before. Before all of this death, and these missions, and this strange intrusion of privacy. Had he forgotten already? Or was he just doing his best to push down the memories that threatened to keep him awake at night? I know I'd be doing the latter. There was no way I'd be able to sleep.

"Jacob called and asked where we'd been. I told him we got caught out with some friends and we'd be back in time for school tomorrow." There was a tightness to Orion's voice, and I knew he hated lying. Hell, we both did, and yet we'd lied to each other more in these past couple of months than we had in the entire thirteen-odd years before that.

Well, I had anyway. He'd been lying to me for two years.

I decided to change the subject to something I knew he loved. "You going to be ready to take the MCATs? They're coming up, aren't they?"

He looked at me with surprise. "Yeah. I should be able to." A ghost of a smile crept across his lips as his thinking turned to something he was far more passionate about—finding cures.

Sometimes my best friend was easy to read. As long as I put the effort in.

The trek back home was exactly that, and while I loved running and walking, Orion usually took a bus, or train, or anywhere he could sit and read a book while traveling.

"Spill. What's up?" It was more anonymous, more private on the streets where people be everywhere but no one actually paid attention to anyone else. Big cities were the perfect place to hide in plain sight.

"Am I that obvious?" He stuck his hands down in his pockets and scuffed his foot at the ground. With a sigh, he finally spoke. "Look. I'm not the best with words or emotions, we all know that. But I was so worried about you and about how you would take this whole thing, what it would do to our friendship, and if you could ever trust me again. It might seem very woe is me, but I really did feel alone for a while there. I'd dragged you into this, and now you have to fight to survive as well. Overall, I haven't been the best friend I wished I was."

I had to take a deep breath because I didn't want to alienate him or offend him, but right then the poor me attitude wasn't working. "I'm sorry you were worried, and you were affected, but you have to remember you weren't the only one, and other people are allowed to deal with things at their own pace." There, I was sure I'd been at least partially diplomatic.

It took a few moments, but a rather sad laugh emerged from him eventually. "Yeah, you're right. Again. Stop being so insightful, it's like you can see what I'm thinking, and I don't feel comfortable with that. I've got enough going on in my brain."

I laughed softly, trying not to let him see how distracted I became. Sure, I couldn't listen in, and I couldn't hear what he was saying to himself or thinking, but the more I used it, the more I tapped into it, the more these auras let me see the gist of what people were thinking about. There were so many ways for me to use that; I just had to figure out the finer points.

Guessing wasn't going to help anyone.

28
UNDERESTIMATED

The house was so clean I wondered if Jacob had got someone to come and do it professionally. Although I looked at Orion as we walked through the door. He was doing that tense shoulders thing he did when he was stressed. Which meant he'd probably stress cleaned the entire apartment.

"Thanks for cleaning up," I said softly as I made my way to my room and threw down my hoodie. The surprise in his eyes as I spoke was enough reward for me. Now I would try to stare through the ceiling and see if I could gain control of these weird aura sensing abilities I'd managed to pick up. Granted, it was an electrical thing.

Everyone was made up of a charge, some used more dependent on size and activity, and others used less with the same criteria. The point was, everyone varied. Their thoughts varied too, and just like with strength and size, activity and appearance, the charge could change color depending on what the person thought about.

At least, I was pretty sure that's how it worked. Theoretically.

"Seriously, I turn my back for one second and you're off on your own again." Orion stood, leaning on my doorframe, watching me with unreadable eyes. From the strained tone of his greeting, I could only assume he was half kidding, like he thought there was a grain of truth in there somewhere.

Maybe there was. My own thoughts were better company than the constant rainbow that danced around my friend. "Sort of. I'm tired, and I've missed my bed. So here I am, and there you are, and shouldn't we just leave it at that?"

There, complete avoidance. I was about to say more when an alert flashed passed my vision.

Assignment Notification.

Location: Abandoned Railroad Yard, southern portion of the Schuylkill River near Gibson Point.

Objective: This assignment consists of four roles.

1 x Runner

1 x Cleaner

1 x Blocker

1 x Diviner

More information will be available at the task site. There is no drop off required, but the task must be undertaken successfully.

Please be aware that this operation is a task first and a competency test second. You will be assessed and your rank adjusted accordingly should you be deemed unworthy.

Meeting time: 9 p.m. Monday, outside the old railroad station.

Time Limit: Determined by the performance of the task given.

Reward: Dependent on the mission's success—experience, skill points, and monetary compensation.

Caution: Guards must be passed to gain entry. They are the only security system.

I sighed. It was good in a way and very bad in another. Maybe we would get to go on this mission together. It would help us figure out some of the shit we still needed to. Though I couldn't help but wonder why they needed me if there were no monitoring systems for me to bypass and no wires for me to reroute so the alarms didn't go off. So far, the only use I seemed to have for them was hacker slash alarm specialist.

He raised an eyebrow at me. "I take it you're the Runner, then," he said with a wink, and it was like his earlier consternation had disappeared. Once again, he was the aloof, yet somehow approachable friend I'd met all those years ago, and I wasn't exactly sure if I'd get a chance to undo that again. This ability to change like a switch had been flicked bothered me more than I'd like to admit.

Before I could comment, say anything that might get us back to what we were talking about, he dipped his head in a shallow bow, and left his station by my door.

Monday's school day started out badly. As I sprinted as fast as I could without rousing suspicion to the field, I cursed myself for not double checking my alarm. Not to mention, a Monday like this didn't bode well for the mission. Hell. Missions should be forbidden on Mondays.

Coach Marth glanced at his stop watch as he started the rest of the team on drills when I finally arrived. "Go warm up."

I couldn't tell what his mood was, but I wasn't about to ignore that order.

Running did it again. That feeling of control, of contentment, of just living in the now. I missed it. Almost a whole week without it left a hole. I'm not sure what I'd do if I lost running, but some fragment of conversation I'd overheard made me realize that was a probable outcome.

When I was done warming up, Coach pulled me to the side, looking at me over the clipboard he insisted on using. "What's up? You've been different since just before States, and this isn't like you. If there's something going on, we can work with it. You've put in so much effort and worked so hard for this, Dare. Don't let a shitty occurrence or situation ruin your life."

I stared at him realizing he was right. I'd been preoccupied, late twice now, injured myself and unable to train. This wasn't aiming-for-the-Olympics Dare, this was scatterbrained me. "I know. I'm not keeping things bottled up, I've just had a few things to deal with lately." I tried my best winning smile, but he still looked skeptical.

With a sigh, he tugged on his cap. "Fine. But remember, I'm here if you need me, now go run."

The rest of training passed with a bittersweet taste in my mouth. I was going to have to do something about this eventually. I couldn't keep competing if there was even a chance I might inadvertently cheat.

After changing in the locker room, my mood was foul. What with finals coming up, regionals just around the corner, and this damn static headache that wouldn't go away. I sighed, and threw myself into my seat in the hall a lot earlier usual.

No one else was in there, and a weight of loneliness bore down on me so suddenly, I could barely move.

You seem very melancholy.

The voice almost whispered into my mind, like a conscience nestled on my shoulder. *Yeah*, I answered it, curious just how intertwined it was with my thoughts. Was it supposed to do this?

I started when a person dropped into the seat next to me. Looking up, I realized it was Neale and opened my mouth to greet him, but stopped short. My Aura Detection ability listened to my turning it on and off about as much as I listened to my friendly SC pal.

Neale's aura was inexplicably hostile. I'd never noticed it before. Like he was angry at me and everything around him. Dark red frayed the edges, barely holding olive greens and intertwined blacks at bay.

Just as suddenly as I'd noticed it, it was gone. I blinked, quickly checking my skills. It hadn't been activated, which meant it had somehow leaked over into my general perception.

"Hey. How's that concussion coming? Scouts should be attending the regionals, right?" Regardless of what his aura might say, Neale seemed to be his old self, and his anger didn't appear to be directed at me, anyway.

I smiled, but I think it turned into more off a scowl. "Sure, they probably will be. Not sure if I'll make it, through."

"Thought you were doing well, especially lately." His eyes narrowed ever so slightly. Did he know something? I was sure the system had told me he wasn't a part of SC. I double checked.

But could it lie to me? Or was I just becoming totally paranoid. I weighed my words and chose to grimace. "Yeah, I've been doing okay, but with the concussion and all, I'm not sure I'll be at the top of my game for regionals." It wasn't exactly a lie; I just omitted some of the truth.

"You'll be fine." He reached across and tousled my hair, but there was something about him that gave me pause. He was definitely not acting like his usual self, even if it was only subtle. Yet another thing for me to worry about.

"Why the scowl, Dare bear?" Cyan plopped down next to me and for a moment I was irritated that Orion couldn't sit next to me now, but it didn't last long. She nudged me with her elbow. "Spill!"

"Oh, nothing," I said, not knowing what else to say.

"Dare here is pretty sure no scouts from the national training center are going to be there for the regionals." Neale grinned sideways at me like he'd just let my biggest secret out there for all to see.

"Shut up." I could play along with that.

"I know what'll make you feel better." Cyan's grin grew impossible wider. "That Faster movie you were talking about a year or so ago? It hits theaters in a week. We should go together!"

I smiled. It was good to have friends who remembered the things I liked. To be honest, I think my life had been filled with a lot of things I took for granted. With what time I had now, I needed to remedy that.

"Sure," I answered happily.

"Excellent." Cyan winked at me. "It's a date, then."

"Sure." Orion was suddenly behind me, leaning forward from his chair. "Sounds like a great idea Cyan. It'll be an awesome group date."

She scowled at him, and he smiled back. I wasn't entirely sure what their problem was, but going to see a movie sounded like a nice bit of escapism for me. "Great. Let's go see it next Friday instead of having our game night."

Cyan transferred her gaze to me, her smile measurably smaller, and her words sounded a little forced. "Great. Can't wait."

29
TRAPPED

Monday night wasn't an ideal mission night. Especially not after the weekend I'd had Timewarp sickness from or whatever. I still didn't feel like I was at peak energy levels. I also didn't understand why I was being sent on this assignment. It said security guards were their only security system. In which case, why did I need to be there? Hand to hand was very obviously not my forte.

Orion eyed me with concern as we approached the meeting point. I'd never been to this part of the river before. It was a ways down and across the river from the place Orion had exploded that guy's head in. Fun memories. Good times.

But here, right now, the skeletons of trains loomed over us, like ghosts in a graveyard of metal and electricity. Pushed to the back of the railyard, weeds sticking out from in between the gravel, some types even began crawling over some of the older machines. Technically, I could probably power some of these, but several of them seemed old enough to need coal. Good old steam trains. I wonder why steam never took off as a source of power?

The lights flickered overhead, streetlamps probably as old as the rusty railroad it attempted to illuminate. If I let my imagination get away with me, I could see ghosts around every corner.

There's no such thing as ghosts.

That's what you think, I shot back at my companion. *If I can come back from the dead because a computer type being says it needs my abilities, then what do you think ghosts can do? With unfinished business here, and there, and everywhere. Bam, you have an entire influx of ghosts.*

I could hear myself panting and knew I needed to calm down, but it wasn't until Orion gently placed his hand under my elbow that I finally did. Fog began to roll in. It seeped from the riverbanks, up and over the gravel, into the crevices between the tiny rocks, and spread like the fingers of hell trying to grasp everything in their path.

It twined itself through the gaps between the old and rusting black oil tankers that lined up on forgotten tracks like the remnants of an army. Only the dim light of sunset lingered in the air, spreading a reddened haze over the scene. It reminded me of blood, of waste, and that many things in life were out of my control.

Right then. The first time ever, even in all of this craziness we were going through, I just wanted to turn on my heel and run as far as I could away from everything. I was always dressed to run.

Especially in this line of work. I was about to turn around and berate Orion and tell him this whole area had another thing coming when I saw it.

The glow to the fog held a distinct green air, like someone placed a green light behind a fog machine in a haunted house. I heard skittering, like something running along the rocks strewn over the path. Something with a lot of legs. Spiderlike. Pieces of the puzzle floated just beyond my reach, and I wished I'd have been facing the other way two nights ago so I could have seen what Cal saw.

I grabbed Orion's arm and squeezed. "We have to go," I whispered, my voice hoarse with realization all of a sudden. There was no way what we'd walked into was a good thing. Maybe we hadn't been safe in that room and we'd said way too much. The skittering continued, getting louder, but slowing down, like they were aiming for our position.

Grey fog shrouded my vision, obscuring the ground thickly. All I could identify was what looked like a sea of shadows swimming toward us.

Not us.

The voices rang clearly in my mind. I nodded, not caring who saw me. These shadows weren't the Demarcates. And all of us wanted to know how they worked.

As far as I could see, scattered across the ground in front of us, between us and the rest of the trains, was a sea of shadow arachnids, floating just beneath the fog, waiting. The thing was, I couldn't really see them, only those slight peeks here and there, but I sure as hell could feel it. Even small as they were, they gave off tiny sparks of electricity and scattered in front of me, stretching back the way the fog had come. Perhaps they were even waterproof.

Thing was, I couldn't sense anything bad from them. Nothing at all. No auras, no intentions leaking through to harry my gut. These were small robots, much smaller than the ones I'd witnessed in my first twenty-four hours as an SC member.

Orion stubbornly stood his ground with me. Neither of us spoke as we assessed the situation in front of us. There appeared to be many of these creatures or robots hiding just out of our line of sight, using the fog to disguise their whereabouts. They were likely very stealthy when alone, but en masse, not so much. I didn't think anything could approach stealthily when there were fifty-odd of them. But maybe they weren't even trying to.

I wondered why they were here. Why had they been in place at that last assignment? Who made them?

Orion's angry voice broke me out of my question spiral. "I can probably disable them with water or ice."

"They're electric, though. Be careful it doesn't connect to you and fry you through the water—but maybe wait and see first? I mean, they haven't swarmed us yet, and there's got to be at least fifty of them." And from what I could tell, they weren't about to pounce, but we're still waiting…like we were.

He nodded, and I could feel his energy building as he gathered the power at his fingertips just in case he needed it.

Aura Detection Upgrade

Aura Detection has entered passive mode. Aura Detection is now a passive ability that will always be active.

You're welcome.

I wasn't too sure how I felt about that, but right now it definitely made some things a little easier.

"Hi!" A happy voice rang out over the top of the friendly neighborhood arachnids. I recognized it, or thought I did as it tugged at my memory. But I wasn't about to take my eyes off our little friends, simply sitting there. They weren't moving; they weren't doing anything. Just, it seemed, watching us. And I was getting nothing from their auras.

"Runner! I remember you." It was all I could do not to look away from where my eyes remained fixated on our impending doom. After all, a good shock of electricity should put them all out of commission for a while at least if I could overload their systems, which was a possibility.

"Hi." I said, not taking my eyes off the creepy little shit staying just out of my comfortable reach. "Watch out, we have company."

It seemed like the creatures were just sitting there and observing us; occasionally I could see a flash of red spots where the eyes must all be located. Definitely not my cup of tea, coffee, or even alcohol.

Orion's voice was very soft when he spoke, and I had to strain to decipher the words. "You can see those too, right? Like, I'm not going marginally crazy and seeing things?" Of course, he was confused, because he couldn't sense their presence like I could. That whole electricity thing.

"Eight-legged remote-control Roombas?" I asked, trying to bring some levity into the situation.

"Yeah, apparently with a shadow affinity," he joked, obviously relieved that he wasn't the only one who could see them.

"What you all doing?" Our Driver was loud, and I'd never managed to get her name on that assignment with Sam. Just that she was loud, proud, and relatively unpredictable or at least not originally from this area. Apparently, she couldn't see our little robots.

"Scouting out the area," I replied, shortly, as I stood straighter watching the bots retreat. Though it looked more like they were pulling together in the middle. Tightening their ranks. More questions splashed through my mind.

"Just waiting on our leader to get here, so we even know what the task is."

Even I could hear the impatience in my voice.

"Fantastic. Huey, Duey, and Moe." Sam's voice was unmistakable. Perhaps Philly wasn't the rife old hunting grounds that I'd assumed it was for SC. I mean, a lot of people died here—accidental deaths, freak accidents, sad circumstances, gun violence. There should be a heap of corpses to choose from when filling up the ranks. So why was I often stuck with the same people?

Surely Philly had more dead agents than this? Were some of them too badly disfigured by the accidents? My scar itched like it was trying to tell me something. Maybe they saw how people meshed together and just let the ones that worked well continue to do so.

Sam surprised me with a tousle of my hair. "What you doing, daydreamer?"

"Dreaming about you," my smart mouth retorted without actually connecting to my brain, as I stepped to the side out of her reach.

At least she laughed. I wasn't sure what I'd do if she hadn't laughed. Her eyes narrowed as she scanned the area, and she scowled briefly, before turning around to the rest of us and putting her hands on her hips. "What on Earth did you do to make this happen?"

I blinked at her. "Nothing. It was like this when we got here."

Sure, I sounded defensive, but if even Sam hadn't been expecting this then I wasn't sure how to process it.

"Dare's right." Orion shrugged, his attention not wavering from his focus on our little friends.

I wasn't sure if any of the others could tell how nervous Sam was, but it didn't make me feel any better. Maybe this permanently passive Aura Detection ability wasn't a good idea after all. Too late now, though. She seemed more nervous than I'd seen her before, and I didn't like that she was the only one in this little group who seemed to know what was going on.

"So what are we doing here, boss?" Maybe she could hear the tremor in my voice, hell, maybe the others could too, but Sam didn't show it in the slightest.

She cracked her neck from side to side, a determined expression coming over her face. Her eyes took on that sort of half distance trance look that happened when one of us read our instructions. Being the group leader, I knew she'd have commands and information we didn't. Sam cleared her throat. "We're here to clean out the vermin and get as many spare parts as we can."

"Vermin." Orion rolled the word around on his tongue, clearly not agreeing with the term for robotic creatures. "And why do we suddenly have a Driver who isn't also a Blocker?"

It was like he tasted something foul, and I didn't blame him. This all felt so off, so set up, that I wasn't sure what to say. The Driver being here, our opponents being coincidentally cloaked spiders that even surprised Sam. None of it added up.

Sam shrugged, like she didn't care about the discrepancy, but everything in me screamed that we should all care very much about that. Not to mention I got the feeling she was deliberately putting on a front, considering I could see her freaking aura. From her stance and the way her aura flickered every time she glanced at the Driver, there was something she wasn't saying about that person in particular.

"And the vermin is?" I had to ask, because all I could see that I thought they were referring to was those blasted spider troopers. In which case, weren't they from SC laboratories in the first place? And if so, then why were we now destroying them?

Was it because of Cal? Did they not expect Cal to be able to see them last time and had to make up some shit so we exterminated them and didn't question what had been seen?

It was getting way too convoluted for me. A discordant sound lingered in my ears, like hundreds of whirrs coming together to make a musical note.

"No." I said it, a sudden calm washing over me. "I'm not doing this, and I don't care how many threats I get, who says they'll do what to me, and how wrong it is to question what I'm doing."

I took a deep breath and crossed my arms. The moon shone through a scattering of clouds overhead, like it was illuminating my point in fine exclamation mark fashion.

"What?" Sam blinked at me, like she hadn't heard me, or else had and didn't actually believe what she'd heard. "We need to do this. It's part of the assignment. You know, finish the job, get paid, don't get punished and all that." Her expression was trying to implore me to see reason, but all it did was the opposite.

I dug my heels in, both figuratively and literally, and the gravel crunched beneath my weight. "Why? Those are the things that Cal saw, that no one believed they saw, and that Cal was punished for destroying behind Adam. They exist, and I'm not about to be the one to destroy something that proves a person innocent. So no. I don't want to be doing any of this until I can tell that what I'm doing has a good reason." I kept going, on a roll I didn't want to stop. Adrenaline coursed through me. It was more thrilling than being in a fight, headier than winning a race.

I'd started now, let all of the irritation and frustration boil over, and it didn't want to stop spilling out of my mouth.

"And another thing, I'm not a soldier, and I'm not a slave. You cannot, SC cannot, command me to go against my own morals, to defy my own sense of judgement, and force my hand to act outside of my free will." I was angry now, and I could see the tiny sparks starting to flicker through my veins, some of them pushing their way out through my pores. I moved away from Orion as the electricity around me, inside me, came alive.

In fact, I was pretty sure my hair was standing out straight from my head, which was comical and ironic in so many ways. Anger fueled me, and the power inside me acted like I'd just woken it up. In fact, those little vermin dudes, they walked straight toward me. Legs down, shuttling like good little spiders should. Like good little electrically affiliated robots should.

I'm not even sure how I managed that; I'm not even sure if it was me. But it appeared to be. They gathered around myself and Orion, completely unthreatening. At least toward the two of us. The lights in their eyes changed from a sharp red to a dull pink, more like a glow than a piercing laser.

Electricity charged the air around me, but the crackling of my power was the only noise since the tiny feet of those minuscule robots had stopped moving all at once. They waited, as if they were seeing what my commands would be. Each whir they made sounded in unison with my breathing, like they'd become an extension of myself. Just what would I do with a spider army?

There were whisperings in my head. Something like voices, but not quite there yet, and still something like code that tried to penetrate my mind. It was distracting, and confusing, and yet I could almost understand it. Almost understand what they were asking me to do and what they wanted to do for me.

They like you. They are no threat to you. But the others might not be so lucky.

I could handle that. I nodded briefly, knowing the Demarcates would see I was sincere.

"Okay. So this might change things." Sam's tone held its own secrets, but her expression gave her surprise away.

This ability, this eel current that ran through me, it pushed elements of my personality to the fore. And I wasn't about to back down, not if I had the power to back up my words. Or so I thought.

"They like you." The Driver suddenly stood next to me, her giddy happiness gone with a moment's notice. Her eyes gleamed, and I couldn't tell if it was just a reflection of the moonlight or not. "Strange. They're not creatures; they shouldn't be able to feel anything with you. They're just made of mechanical bits and pieces."

Her detached tone rubbed my nerves the wrong way, but I tried to distance myself from whatever her double meaning implied. I could see the little spiders around me becoming agitated, swinging with my moods. Experimentally, I took a step to the left. It served two purposes. To remove myself from Driver's direct proximity and to see what the spiders would do. Almost as one, the entire swarm of bots moved with me, like I'd pulled them with puppeteer strings.

The time I'd spent examining them had obviously allowed them to conduct their own observations, and like it or not, I believe they resonated with me. It was nice to be understood, even if it was by something non-human. I wanted to know who made these. Who had turned me into a puppet master?

Puppeteer.

It's not necessarily a puppeteer. You gave these ones a sense of respect instead of immediately attacking when you strove to understand them before harming.

I nodded slowly, it made sense in a weird way. All I knew right now was that these bots had been subdued and were no danger to anyone as long as I stayed close to them.

"So we're done here, right?" I'm not sure where the danger in my tone came from, but I wasn't about to chase it away. A surge of protectiveness rose up in me, and I wasn't about to let it go. I could feel as the bots warmed to me with a mutual sharing of protection.

Sam nodded slowly, her eyes holding a new respect for me. At least I told myself that. It could have been fear, but I'd go with respect for now.

"Yeah. It said to contain them, not to destroy them, and I don't really see how much more contained they're going to get." Her gaze grew distant as she obviously received feedback of some kind. Her brow knit together with a brief flash of anger, and then she sighed. "Apparently having them whole is better than blown apart anyway. Can you like pied piper them somehow back to one of the entrances?"

"Entrances?" What the hell was that supposed to mean?

The Driver shot Sam a look, a little too late of course, and none too subtle. I could see the effect it had on Sam, like she'd just put her foot in the largest pothole in the world and snapped a bone in the process. She hit herself in the head with her hand and leaned against one of the rusting train skeletons.

But it seemed like she'd dived in and was going to take the brunt of it. "There are entrances scattered around, down to parts of the system. Antechambers, that sort of thing. The place where all the orders come from." She shrugged.

So it would be easier for me to take these there.

"Sort of like the bakery?" I asked but didn't expect an answer, eyeing my new little friends, the rats that I'd piped away.

They seemed like they'd attuned with my wavelengths and simply adopted me. I didn't really want to give them up.

All of the questions stopped dead in my throat when the ground rumbled so hard beneath my feet that I fell to my knees. Tiny spider thrumming surrounded me, like a cushion of protection, as if they were standing up for me. I could feel an aura pressing down. Nothing human, but not animal either. No, this was something entirely electrical, and it could smell me, it could taste me, and damned if it didn't want to gobble me right up.

In the immortal words of my favorite marshmallow, I breathed out. "Oh, no."

30
TARGETS

I could feel the origin of the rumbles came from behind me, and I spun to face it. But there was nothing there but a shimmering of the fog-laden air. The only thing that contradicted the lack of anything visual was the old train tracks.

Not the actual tracks, but the metal that would have been used in making more tracks. It was rusted and old now, degrading in the emptiness of the abandoned train yard. Rust devoured the strength of it, making it brittle. Spans of these railings moved, making an entirely loud crash as whatever it was pushed through them.

Finally, the shimmering air rose up, towering above us. And then it uncloaked.

It rose up, easily twice my height and stood in front of me. Stomping one of its eight massive metal legs again, it made the ground rumble in protest. Its body was like a dome of silver robotics, giving the illusion of one massive electronic spider. One of the old trains closest to it creaked alarmingly, and I was willing to bet the next rumble would bring it to its ruin.

Strange thought to have while you're facing imminent danger. The voice in my head held dry overtones, like it was attempting sarcasm but wasn't sure how to go about it.

Not helping, I mumbled at it, half out loud and half in my head.

Analyze it. Don't panic.

Odd, it truly sounded like it wanted to help me. To help us. I had to remember that without me, it had nothing. I scanned the creature like I would a human. While there was no meat suit, I got a series of diagnostics and electrical information so far beyond my comprehension it made me momentarily see stars.

Which was long enough for it to move one of its legs forward and quake the ground again. The train car I'd observed earlier groaned as it heaved itself to the ground only narrowly missing me because Orion grabbed my upper arm and yanked me to safety.

"Focus!" he snapped at me, and if I'd had the time I would have told him that was exactly what I was doing.

Except arguing wasn't going to tame this huge electrical beast. Its system didn't follow any logic I could see, and the electrical pulses that wavered around in front of it just didn't seem to be refined or calibrated correctly. Like the poor thing was confused, which would explain the hostility.

Especially since I seemed to have taken its babies from it.

A sudden instinct made me want to help it, to tap into it and understand it. What I didn't know how to do was communicate with it, and I should know that, I should know how to use this fucking power already.

Electrical shocks powered around it, dripping onto the ground, dying on the gravel. From everything I could sense, I think it was scared. Sadly, being scared probably made it more dangerous.

Anger seeped through me again, the fuel my currents so desperately clung to, but I wasn't angry at our opponents. I was angry that this was an obvious set up. My anger fueled my power, and I easily channeled the excess into a skin barricade. Okay, perhaps not easily, but easier than before, and I'd take what victories I could get. It was so overwhelmingly beautiful, so much power inside me, around me. Everything had this stream of electricity connecting it, the way life breathed and ended. The way everything resounded with one another.

I could feel power building inside it, like it was trying to defend itself, from me of all people. But I didn't want to preempt it, I wanted to figure out how to help it. "Careful. Get to safety."

The electric pulse hit me like a freight train, but my skin held it at bay. Anyone else would have been torn apart. Instead of renewing its attack, and instead of ordering its fellow robots to swarm me, it sat back on four of its legs, studying me with blinking electronic eyes. A low thrum echoed through my brain, lending me strength and a new sort of understanding. Everything around me glowed with life, except for the dead trains. Those loomed like the dark and lifeless husks of metal they were. The rotting ones, anyway.

Everything around us, from the lights overhead to the tiny spiderbots crouching at my side, the massive one observing me, Orion, Sam, and the Driver. All of these had their own unique signature. Such a beautiful picture, painted with different auras, on a canvas of the black of night.

"Dare?" Orion whispered, and for that split second I wasn't sure who he was talking about. Did he mean me? Was he asking if he should do something? But then it all clicked into place, and the luminescence around my vision dulled slightly.

"It's not going to harm us." I cocked my head to one side, and the massive bot mimicked me. I think it was in tune with me. I couldn't tell. But I could sense that Orion stepped back from me slightly. It made me wonder why. I mean, it's not like I exploded a guy's head off with an icicle shot.

The rush of power wouldn't leave me, and even though it quieted somewhat, it clung to my very nerves, lending me a heightened awareness I could get far too used to. It felt like I was sitting up on top of the clouds looking down on the entire situation. That my mind was capable of seeing it all.

Except it wasn't, and I didn't understand, despite the insight this gave me, just what we were supposed to be doing with these bots. Why were they here? Was this supposed to be a trap? I got the distinct impression that we'd been intended to fight these creatures, creations, whatever they were.

You are correct. The voice in my head held no hesitance. But it did sound slightly smug when it continued. *I told them it wouldn't work.*

So you knew about this? What we were walking into.

Of course I did. That's a part of my job. I need to get you to where you're going, and this was your destination from the beginning of this mission.

No remorse, no feeling of guilt. It had been designed to keep its person in check, to make sure we toed the line. Could they really kill me? Or did they have to rely on some other type of manipulation in order to have the operatives terminated? Surely, with my refusal to cooperate, with Orion's refusal, they could have just terminated the TOS, right? Wasn't that the threat? Wasn't that in the damned contract?

The idea that sprang up in my mind was shocking, and also nasty. My large spider bot moved slightly as if reacting to my own thoughts, focusing its attention on the Driver instead of me, although I could still feel its thrum in the back of my mind, waiting to communicate should I want to.

I took a couple of steps forward, the tiny spiderbots following me like ducklings follow their mother. They nipped at my heels but never close enough to touch or to interfere with my ability to move. The large spiderbot angled its eyes down to look at me, and suddenly most of it became invisible as some sort of cloaking device activated. My idea was germinating, and I couldn't shake it.

While Orion and Sam's voices faded into the background, memories of the software company raced through my mind. Of the virus mission, of the guard breaking through to me. How hard his fists were, how much it hurt each time his fist connected with my face. The feeling of the brick wall smashing against my skull, almost as if my brain hitting my skull was tangible. How had he gotten through? Sam would never have let him through, would she? And neither Sam nor the Driver had been defeated, right?

Shadows accumulated around the large bot, hiding it well against the backdrop in the old train yard. There was an intelligence in those eyes that I couldn't deny, like it had a soul, that it wasn't just electronic. All because it aimed to become an eel, to wield that power. All because humans wanted to harness power again.

It folded into itself, becoming smaller, so it finally compacted to stand about the height of a Great Dane. And as it did, the thrumming in my mind became pictures, clarifying so many different things, and proving that all my suppositions had been accurate.

A total wave of calm washed over me. I got it now. At least, I thought I got it now. But there were factors here that I couldn't control, nor did I know them well enough to do anything. I touched the dogbot with my left hand, willing my command to get through to it. Electricity jumped from me to it, binding us, and transferring the command I needed it to follow.

Go. Go now and stay hidden. I'll come and get you later.

It barely hesitated before vanishing fully, taking the rest of the tiny bots with it. Their small feet vanished in a cacophony of gravel being lightly tapped by steel.

The Driver let out a theatrical sigh. "You really shouldn't have done that, you know."

It wasn't a question, and she seemed quite put out, but then, I'd been expecting that.

"Nope. I should have realized it sooner, should have done it sooner." I could feel my adrenaline rushing through my veins, just waiting to get out and nail her, to make her realize what she'd put herself up against, and just why it wasn't going to go down the way she wanted. They wanted.

"Bit cocky for a fresh eel, aren't you?" The Driver cracked her neck from side to side. "I mean, you have no clue how to use your abilities yet. Still. I mean it takes most people a few months at least, but you take the cake for being irregularly slow."

"And how would you know what I can and can't do?" I wanted to know, and even put a hint of danger into my tone.

She shrugged. "I don't, but I do what I'm told, and I live a very good life."

"Second life," I corrected. "You live a coerced, forced other life that you've sacrificed everything for."

From the scowl on her face my barb hit home. I raised my right hand, tiny shocks jumping all around it as my body fought to contain the electricity. "I've decided that I don't like this program. And I think you already knew that, because I'm pretty sure you're here to kill us, aren't you? Or at least me. You know, after you failed with me on that last mission. Wasn't only supposed to get a concussion, was I?"

I'd like to think I looked imposing, that I seemed in total control of what I was doing, but the truth was I was winging it all the way. Just this feeling in my gut, wrenching nausea that made me want to scream.

The Driver laughed and removed something from the pack she had around her waist. "Guess that makes my job a bit harder. It's always so much easier to just sneak up from behind and take a person out."

"Like you did with Dave." I ground the words out, knowing how right I'd been not helping that it still hurt like hell he'd been killed in front of me.

She grinned and raised a gun like none I'd ever seen before. "Just like I did with Dave."

Dive.

The command shot through my head in an instant, and I dove to the floor, executing a rather clumsy dive roll and only narrowly avoided a shot of something that hit the area I'd stood in but a breath before.

I didn't even have time to think, before she locked whatever that was and loaded again.

Focused EMP shot.

The implications of that name sent shocks up my spine. If that hit me, it would totally disable me if it didn't kill me first. Frying my electrical conduits would mean my veins and blood, my entire lymphatic system. That wasn't good. Not in any way. I was electricity now. An EMP could wipe me out.

The spiderbots reappeared and scattered around me, as if they'd formed a protective unit. I wasn't sure what they were reacting to, but it was sweet and heartbreaking at the same time. And, if they had any sense of self, it was brave, too.

Why are you helping me? I asked the voice, my logic not able to figure it out on my own.

I am a part of the SC system, but I am unique to you. Should you no longer exist, I too will cease to exist. It is in my own best interests to attempt to keep you alive.

You are self-aware? I had to ask, because it really seemed to have grown.

I am becoming more of an individual. The longer I have presence, the more possible it is.

Driver moved in such a way that I couldn't place her precisely. Her movements took on a liquid type of form, and I had to wonder what her elements were. Thoughts flashed through my mind, making me run through that entire previous mission. Had she given anything away back then? What was she capable of?

After all, I came out of that with a nasty concussion and a week off. It wouldn't have taken that beating much more effort to be fatal. Cold suffused me, but it wasn't a shiver down my spine and didn't come from inside me. It answered my questions. I knew how the assailant got through now.

Orion stood next to me, icicle spears in each hand. The look on his face could have frozen fire in an instant. He was angry. Anger wasn't something Orion usually expressed, but I could feel it floating off him in waves, see all of it directed toward the damned Driver. She cocked an eyebrow at him, full of confidence.

Probably should have told her it was the wrong move, because Orion's expression added a smirk to it. Ice bullets shot out of the spear in his left hand, and I had no idea how he did that, but they sped toward the Driver as she released another shot, forcing me to scatter. I barely made it this time, and one of my spiderlings took the blow for me.

It lay there, sparks coming off it as its little eyes dimmed. I wanted to feel, but I didn't have the time. The Driver yelled in frustration, coming to a skidded halt after barely dodging the icicles.

"You don't want to do this, Orion," she ground out from between her teeth and all I could think was that I was probably the only one of us who didn't know her name. "You know what the consequences are. You'll go on the list this time, too."

But Orion laughed. "Actually, I do want to do this. You do realize that you're attacking the only reason that kept me from destroying everything about you?"

She blanched slightly, her eyes darted to Sam, and then back to Orion, like she was expecting back up. Sam shrugged. "Not my fight. If I had known this mission's intention, I wouldn't have come. I don't let friends get killed."

Orion's face held a calm assurance I'd never seen in him before, like there wasn't someone standing there purely intent on killing us both—or us all. I had no idea what her orders entailed, but I was pretty certain keeping us alive wasn't a huge part of it. Her own abilities were still a mystery to me. I could glimpse aspects of fire, but something else, the thing that made her a Driver. The ability to manipulate shadows and bend them accordingly.

Only I could hear her gasp with irritation. Her abilities obviously weren't working the way they were supposed to, not complying to her commands, not serving her will the way she needed them to. The fog was taking up precious room on the ground that she could have used for shadows.

I grinned, a calm suddenly suffusing me as well. "Did you pick the wrong side then?"

She scowled up at me, and for once I was pretty happy to be on the taller end of the scale. "There is only one side. I'm on it, and you're not."

The sudden force and heat of the flames that ejected from her hands was intense on a level I'd not encountered before. I watched in fascination as Orion swept his hand around in an arc in front of him, his facial expression not even twitching as he did so.

A wall of water rose up and out from him, pushing toward the Driver and putting the flames out.

"Think about it, Selene," he said in that easy voice he used whenever he had to give an oral presentation. Calm, controlled, precise. "Do you really want to pit your powers against mine?"

But that line. Not that line. Danger filled those words, making me take an involuntary step backwards. There was nothing about those words that were good.

Selene seemed to sense that, but she smirked. "You think far too highly of yourself. They don't need you that much. Your best friend was supposed to make you cower, not reinforce you."

Another whoosh of fire barreled through the old train graveyard, swooping in along the tracks, focused and exact. This one had more force behind it; I could already feel the heat emanating from it. The smell of sulfur burned strong, like she'd plied it with mass amounts of fuel.

Only fire needed more than that to burn. It required oxygen to breathe and expand. And air was something Orion could use with a skill that surprised me. A loud pop echoed around us, ricocheting off the metal all around us in an oddly discordant manner. I could see it as it happened, as the air entered a vacuum, stealing away from the fire, cutting off its reliant flame. In less than a second, the fire went out.

Selene glowered at Orion. I couldn't fathom why they would send a fire wielder to battle against someone who not only wielded water, but also air. To me, that was a mismatch made in hell and would never result in anything productive.

Come to think of that, the more I saw and heard, the more I realized just how SC managed to enforce their breaches of contract. They didn't just flick a switch and kill you. Which meant there was no flick of the switch. While she'd already admitted to it, I didn't realize that her willingness to assassinate a fellow agent meant that the TOS was a smokescreen.

They sent a certain rank of their recruits to kill others. They made us toe the line by making us believe that the system itself could actually kill you on a whim? That was pure genius.

You've got it. Well done. The only problem is that now you'll have to run.

Defeating Selene will mean they'll hunt us down, then? I asked, keeping my eyes on the panting Driver, and Orion's almost sinister smile.

You are a danger, to many things. It's why you were targeted. But Orion and you together? Together you're both a danger to everything.

Is that why you're on my side? I wanted to be sure.

Precisely. I want to exist. Therefore, I want you to exist. If lucky, it'll probably come true.

I was about to reply when pain shot through my left thigh, causing my knee to buckle. My scream rivaled the sound of the vacuum earlier and distracted Orion momentarily. Looking down, I saw a spider limb sticking out of my wound. The mechanical creature was shuddering on the other end of its appendage, its silver visage masked by shadows and its eyes blinked in an array of red and orange colors.

I should have been paying more attention to my surroundings. Sure, the little buggers were adorable, but their programming was essentially simplistic, and I should have realized many frequencies could take control over their primitive brains. Smart, yet super inconvenient. In that moment, I had no delusions about Selene. She did what she had to do to stay alive, to secure her station in life. Who was I to know what her reasons were? But apparently, they were enough to stab me, and anyone else, in the thigh or back or hell, shoot them in the head.

This whole system, this whole coming back from the dead thing was ridiculous. My head thrummed with power, and my anger built as I tried to breathe. Pulling the appendage out of my thigh wasn't my most wise decision in life, but it helped me focus through the pain. Helped me channel my abilities to healing that which she'd injured.

She shot Dave. It hadn't been an accident, or a part triggered by the breach of the TOS. It had been a command. For some reason, rephrasing this in my head gave it gravity that I needed to focus. I should have questioned more. I shouldn't have just taken things at face value. And while I was at it, I should have delved into those files I had riding around in my brain.

I knew she'd done this the moment I'd realized why she was here with us. Ways to deal with Selene, ways to deal with the program, began to flood my mind. Yet the only thing that truly stood out to me was what I could do right then.

Testing my legs, I bounced on my toes. It appeared my healing had improved, because I was fighting fit, and she was going to pay for subverting one of my little spider friends. And for splattering Dave's brains all over my face.

31
OVERLOAD

Energy crackled around me, flowing through the air, from the ground beneath us, from the spiders around us. As if everything understood how angry I was, how much I needed to borrow the energy. Had I wanted to, I could have plucked it from Sam and Orion as their own anger levels rose.

Red tinged both their auras, black like blood, thick as sap. Realization and anger teamed up to give me powerful allies, yet I wanted to do this on my own.

Selene and her purpose, SC and its splintered understanding of what it was meant to be. They both needed to be stopped. I was a result of that malfunction—a failed attempt to keep my best friend in line when threatening his own life hadn't worked.

My arms began to feel heavy, but at the same time light enough to fly with. Everything about the power around me lent me a sense of confidence I'd never had before. Sure, I'd only got these abilities because of the system, but no one was my master now. I would be my own.

Calm down.

Did the voice in my head sound scared? It probably should. I could short out more than a city block like this. There was enough capacity inside me to hold far more power than I was attempting. To pull it in and mold it, so that when it shot out, it would be a blast of pure energy. Balls of lightning, never mind great balls of fire.

I think I giggled, but my brain was focusing on other things and I couldn't quite tell. Although Orion's eyes looked at me with pure shock. Strange though that was, I thought he'd be overjoyed to have me jump in on his cause.

Dare!

His mouth was moving, but the voice sounded like it spoke in my head. Maybe that was Orion and not my system companion. I couldn't tell anymore. Everything around me was far too bright, burning with power, electricity zapping anything that tried to get near me.

I blinked as Orion mouthed something else, yet I could see the fear in Selene's eyes, and it only added more fuel to my ever-growing power well.

Suddenly, I felt a hand on my left forearm. It was cool and sort of sandy, drawing my attention away from Selene momentarily as I looked down. Earth. Soil. Rich, dark soil coated my skin, like I was soft and newly watered, ready to plant spring blooms in. I couldn't tell where it had come from. Just for a few moments I had a wave of disembodiment wash over me, like I was looking down on myself and this whole situation.

I shook my head to try and clear the sensation out, and then I looked up.

Sam grinned at me, her own fear desperately hiding behind a kind smile. Her determination won out, and her expression assured me we'd all get home in one piece, even Selene. I might not like that plan, but as the crackling energy around me began to quite a bit and dissipate, clarity descended on my thoughts once again.

I'd been so close to disembodiment. So close to losing myself in the power. The thought sobered me right the fuck up. There might be a lot of ways for me to kill Selene and leave no evidence, but I'd almost burned myself out.

Shit.

My train of thought wandered, filled with the tenacity that electricity fed into my soul, and I'd thought about murdering a person and forgotten it was possible to lose myself. My mind reeled, and I glanced up at Sam, shock on my face.

Her smile was sad, and she gave me a very slight nod. Here I was, judging my best friend, and others on just what they'd done for the system, to preserve their own lives, when my using my power to its full capacity wasn't even *for* the system, but for my own sense of morality. My sense. My judgement. Aren't we supposed to be kind? Aren't we supposed to not judge?

My body began to shake, and I watched as Selene's face fell when Orion stepped in front of me, determination etched into his features once again. It was almost like I could see his thoughts, perhaps read them in a way. With the tension in his body, and the way he held himself, I knew he was prepared to hurt her, to terminate Selene, and that he wasn't taking any more crap from the system that had lorded it over him for the last two years.

Selene glowered at us and pulled herself upright. Her impatience shone through; she was tired of waiting for us. "You're all *so* fucked now, you realize that, right?"

Orion shrugged. "Perhaps, but it's better than just taking death lying down the second time around."

He moved a step back and crouched down with me where I'd collapsed into a ball, crouched while hugging my knees, trying to understand my homicidal rage.

Sam crossed her arms. "I never realized us letting you go made us the bad people."

"You let me go, I report back. You don't let me go, they know how I die, and you're on the run anyway. Either way you lose, may as well just go out with a bang." Selene's tone sneered, begging to be wiped off her face while she practically juggled fireballs with one hand.

Orion stood up after checking me once over, and I don't know how he managed it. I was still feeling particularly fragile due to almost giving into murderous intent, due to almost losing myself. My thoughts raced, clashing into one another.

"The choice is yours. You know as well as anyone that there are ways, so many ways for us to beat the system." Rainbows of light refracted off him at odd intervals, like they were broken beams becoming whole again. If I didn't know better, I'd have thought I'd been drugged.

Selene stopped her juggling, and for just an instant I thought maybe he'd gotten through to her, but wishful thinking and I never got along, it wasn't about to start now. She laughed, and the hysterical sound reverberated through the ghostlike yard, echoing off the dying metal skeletons of trains surrounding us.

"Why beat it, when you can get so much more by joining it?" Instead of throwing the fireballs nonchalantly up into the air, she began to mold them into a sphere. Her control over the flames she produced was phenomenal, making me wish I had such control over my own abilities.

And then she launched it. The crack as it left her hands sounded similar to a baseball bat hitting that true home run. It sped toward us, feeling on the air, on her power, hungry to devour everything in its path.

The heat from exploded over me like a hot breath of high summer when the one-hundred-degree heat smacks you in the face as you open the patio door. The humidity tried to suck all of the moisture from my body in an attempt to render me useless and exhausted. But my power was electricity based, and I wasn't about to let her overwhelm me when I wasn't thinking straight.

Selene's hair fanned out around her like flames of an uncontrolled blaze, and her eyes glowed like embers after bonfire night. Her hands wielded the element with such power flowing from her that she could have been made of kerosene. Such a simple beauty and lurking danger about her in that instant. I wanted to close my eyes and hope I was dreaming, but I knew I wasn't. I was sweating way too much for that. Any closer, and I'd begin to blister.

Orion stood unbothered by the heat. Looking close, squinting even, I spied a sliver of ice covering his entire body. Perhaps that took constant exertion of energy to maintain, but it kept him protected from the flames' heat at least. Meanwhile he wove water deftly, directing it in as many places as he could to prevent the fires she cast from spreading. The thing was, there was no way he could maintain that sort of energy consumption for any length of time. He was going to run out.

But you can heal.

I definitely can.

Then heal.

Wasn't fatigue just the body running out of something it normally had? So wouldn't healing just help replenish that energy? Logically, it couldn't hurt. Wearing down of oneself always counted toward making oneself ill. Self-care 101. It didn't only apply to academics.

Getting to my feet was more of a stagger than anything else, and Sam reluctantly let the cool earth around me go so I could move easier. It had done its job though, lent me perspective and the ability to naysay the power fluctuating inside me. She raised an eyebrow, and I shook my head, holding up a thumb in the age-old indication of *I'm fine.*

She rolled her eyes but didn't say anything, biting her lip as she watched the battle. Maybe she was trying to figure out just what she could do to stop it. Orion would reach capacity soon, because he was stuck trying to protect me at the same time. Always trying to protect me. I wasn't a little kid. I wished people would stop doing that.

Electrical Current Manipulation is currently blocked.

Do you wish to expand knowledge in this area?

Yes, No, or not at this time?

This wasn't the current system prompting me. The font across my vision was subtly different, and the wording resembled those guides and not the tutorial from the current one. What the fuck? I didn't have time to consider it. What if it limited some part of my abilities and Orion needed me?

Right now, I had to keep my eyes on things even if my entire body screamed at me to get the fuck out of there. Watching Orion and Selene stand off left my heart in my throat. I only wanted to help him, especially now I'd seen so many different ways I'd misinterpreted events. I was the newbie, I was the one who had no clue, and right now, I was the one not wanting my best friend to be burned to a crisp before I could figure out what the fuck was going on.

Disorientation swept over me as I stood up, and this time the electricity didn't crackle around me like it was trying to escape me. No, this time it just waited there silently, having seen what my intentions were, perhaps. It gave me strength in a slow burning way, lent me the tenacity I lacked. It was so much quieter than I'd imagined. If I'd just decided not to fight it earlier and accept it, perhaps none of this would have happened.

It crept along my veins, empowering me instead of electrifying me. It bolstered my natural defenses, suffusing into my very skin like slow moving molasses. Only it wasn't slow; it was caught in my Timestance with me, churning within me, making me stronger so we could be formidable together.

If only I'd realized it sooner.

Power Absorption Activated.

Electrical Grounding Activated.

The notifications clamored for my attention, but I dismissed them. Fighting the power wasn't going to get me anywhere, and I shouldn't have done it from the start. Understanding the power was the key, what it wanted, how it operated, and what it needed to remain contained. After all, there was so much more it could access if I let us cooperate instead of fight.

Excellent observation.

The voice changed subtly this time. Now it was full of understanding and knowing. Its timbre resonated with me, and I was suddenly convinced I knew what had gone wrong. Perhaps not with the system as a whole, but here, right here, and all around me. The shadows that hid in the darkness created by the old trains, the fake cloaking that covered the spiders still hovering and waiting for me to give a command. Everything was connected, through the earth, through the air, and the electrical currents that made life possible.

Now all you need to do is embrace it.

I'd opened something between my systems, somehow giving them access to one another. Though I could be wrong, the voice in my head had evolved. It was right in a way, but I needed to do a whole lot more than embrace it. There was so much potential in what I could do. I watched Orion as if through slow motion. The way he twisted and commanded the water mere milliseconds before it became ice. How he deftly wove each and every creation his mind spoke to him.

My abilities weren't like that, but the paths they could travel were just as delicate, and just as dangerous. One misstep, and I'd blast us all to smithereens.

Tendrils of electricity wove their way over my skin and down my forearms. They twisted around me like a type of armor, set to protect me from any harmful attacks. Not just reinforcing my skin but providing me with a forcefield of sorts around my body.

Cool.

Orion needed energy, and I could back up his regeneration rates, just like I'd healed him so long ago. There was no way I could fling a bolt of rejuvenation at him without fucking up. I needed to push this healing power into more of a heal over time. Something like in a tabletop game with limitations, but constant replenishment.

But I had to try it on myself first. Taking a deep breath, I channeled the spell into myself, giving it a trigger word as my finger touched my chest. "Replenish." I said it softly, so only I could hear, but the effect was instantaneous.

It zinged through me, chasing away the fatigue I'd begun to feel. Surged through my veins and up to my brain making me heady for a moment while everything settled down within me.

Regeneration skill founded. Replenish activated.

Replenish is a skill in the Regeneration family and allows you to heal an ally or yourself over time. While this could also be applied to opponents, it's inadvisable to use this in its current form. Keep in mind this will sap ten percent of your available energy per application. Do not run your reserves dry, or this will prove more dangerous than beneficial.

Skill unlocked.

Experience gained.

Okay, so *that* happened.

Stepping forward shakily, I approached Orion. "Hey, let me touch your back. Middle."

Orion obviously didn't have much free time right then, but he did nod slightly, and I noticed the ice barricade thin and disappear in just a large enough area for me to rest my hand. I just hoped this would do. Touch transferred the power way back when; it should do it now.

I placed my hand between his shoulder blades, pressing lightly. I could just see over the top of his head, and the visage of Selene in full fire get up, was utterly terrifying. I looked back down, closed my eyes, and concentrated.

"Replenish," I whispered in front of me, as my brain took in his overall health status.

His energy levels were dangerously low, and here he was, standing like the hero he'd always wanted to be. If this could just supercharge his inner healing abilities for a short duration, it should be fine. The electrical pulse I released to power the ability was overjoyed. It riled up the rest of the power in my body, and I had to contain it again.

Wrestling it back into my grasp, I channeled it down and through his system, sparking nerves and muscles from their gathering lethargy, and infusing them with renewed strength. The slight shock I sent through him made him shudder for a moment as he stood there, but I could feel his energy levels spiking and see his pallor shift back to a healthier version.

I was about to heave a sigh of relief, even as he managed to produce a massive ice spear to fire back at his attacker. And I was about try and mesh with him so I could assist his attacks, but my body began to shake, like it was thrown into a tumble dry cycle, and the world began to swim as the voices in my head grew louder.

Dare, are you coming with us?

You could make us stronger.

But we need you more.

The shadows were here, calling to me to come and join them, to come and be a part of them. But that last voice had nothing to do with them. They didn't have these clumsy bodies and could still perform all sorts of tasks, but the best thing was, they could go anywhere, and avoid any damage.

I blinked, not understanding why they seemed to be wanting me to join them.

Re-center yourself.

I listened and tried to get my head back into the battle. And then Orion's ice bolt hit Selene in the side, deliberately placed there, from what my woozy head could see. She was thrown back about twenty feet and left dazed up against the old chain link fence. Then, somehow, she turned sideways. Or at least, until my head hit the ground, that's what I thought.

Time appeared to slow again, as Sam ran toward Selene, shouting "I'll see to her, you take care of Dare."

I could see Orion out of the corner of my eyes, moving so slowly and deliberately toward me like his life depended on it. Maybe it did. Hell, perhaps mine did.

I could taste blood in the back of my throat, feel the electricity crawling through my veins like it was hammering in little grips so it wouldn't be flung out so harshly again. My head spun, and I was dizzy, tired, and utterly ready to just sleep for a week so the nausea couldn't envelop me.

Sleep forever.

It sounded like such a good idea, though I had no idea where the comment came from. My body grew cold and heavy, but in light of how much fire had been thrown around here, I thought it should have been warmer. From the sheen on the skin of the others, it must have been. So why was I so cold? My vision began to fragment. As the train yard broke into shattered pieces I could hear the soft whir of my little robot friends and wondered what they were concerned about.

Soothe away. Sleep away. Let me take over.

That sounded like a great idea.

32
TWISTED

My vision swam with images of a large cavern.

Bright green phosphorescent moss clung in places to the stone walls that rose up so high I could barely see a ceiling. It painted patterns that lingered in my thoughts, like memories tugging at the back of my mind. The area was huge, and the rock had been hewn to level the floor. It held large capsules that appeared to be full of a bright whitish-blue liquid, as if the moss had somehow bled into them. The area was cavernous and took up so much space I couldn't fathom where it might be.

Consoles were positioned in front of those capsules, their lights glowing, beating out strange lines that reminded me of life monitoring, but that wasn't it. More lines than any human would need to be monitored for. If only I could get close enough to see, but my head pounded and I wasn't sure I was in control of anything here, let alone my body.

There was more down here though. Skittering around me, and not like a spiderbot. This was sneaky and sly. Something controlling everything, perhaps someone, but every time I thought I'd be able to catch a glimpse, they were gone. This had to be a dream, a weird sort of mind conversion of everything I'd witnessed in the last few months dream. There was no other explanation for it, and yet, there seemed to be something tugging at my awareness, a memory or an action, something I'd done before, seen before that wouldn't leave me alone until I remembered it.

Remember...

I'd remember if I could! I wanted to shout the words out, but all that resulted in was a hoarse whisper trying desperately to escape my throat. Laughter echoed off to the side of me, like someone having a good old joke at my expense. If there was one thing I hated, it was being made fun of.

Actually, there were a lot of things I hated. Especially being kept in the dark about things that were pertinent to me and my friends.

Dare?

I'm here, I called out, looking this way and that to find whoever was calling my name yet only silence greeted me. My head swam again, and the view in front of me blurred for seconds, excruciating seconds that pounded against my head like it was trying to smash the visions out of it. Which only made me more determined to see them in the first place.

I checked myself over, or I tried to. Everything around me distracted from my tasks. I caught a glimpse of my hand and started. It was my hand, yet it wasn't my hand. The skin appeared slightly loose and translucent like I was covered in a thin mesh of incandescent slime, like the stuff that glowed in those capsules. It gleamed in ways that made me wonder if it was trying to speak to me. Silly, I know, but...

Dare...

That is my name, I grumbled, but I'm not sure if I said it in my head or out loud. Creatures flashed across the floor, so fast I couldn't follow them, at least I think they were creatures. I couldn't really tell. Maybe they were cockroaches. This whole dream was getting old.

Sometimes dreams are real...

Gee, thanks for that Mr. Cryptic Head Voice. I was getting irritated because I knew there was something I should be doing, that I was obviously not getting done while I was wasting time here being all...cryptic-fied.

Down here. Down where? Like, sort of in those labs where I'd originally seen the SC made shadows? Was that a thing?

Deeper. Older...

Great. Cryptic-er. It was all so confusing, being in my head and yet being somewhere else. Maybe I was getting sick. Perhaps I'd put too much pressure on myself and finally snapped. But no, the burns, the difficulty, the shocks—those were all things I definitely did. I could remember those.

And Orion was involved.

Suddenly I caught sight of him. Pushing through miasma at the end of the hall. Except that end seemed excruciatingly far away. Like everything else, just beyond my reach. I pushed through, needing to follow him, needing to figure out just how this was going to work. My electricity had regenerated him, rejuvenated him. Hell, it had rejuvenated me. Why would anyone not want to use that ability for good?

There was so much I might be able to stop with it. So much I might be able to discover. Hell, if doctors took my blood, would it help heal others? Was there a way to use the electrical impulses in the human body to speed up any type of self-healing the body contained?

I was ahead of myself, and speaking of which, my headache compounded nicely. But I had to reach Orion. To reach him and make it to the end of that rope, to the end of that hall, and to reach the end of this area and figure out how this could all make sense for us.

For a moment, I panicked, glancing at my hands. Was I in one of those capsules?

The effort it took to push through the visage around me left me breathless, but the panic subsided as soon as I could breathe in actual air, and I left whatever I'd been incased in behind me and didn't look back. The surrounding air here was suffocating as well though, so I hadn't gained much.

Replenishment applied.

Healing beginning in 3...2...1...

The way it soothed my nerves, the channels the electricity went through, and the way it momentarily made my head stop pounding was sheer delight. But it appeared I could only move through the thick atmosphere when said regeneration was active. If that was it, then that's what I'd do. Because I had to, so I could reach him, and we could figure all of this out together.

Replenishment applied.

Healing commencing in 3...2...1...

My power grew stronger each time I used it.

Timestance Activated.

With each movement closer to my goal, I noticed more about my surroundings. There were beings, creatures, or something in those capsules. Not kept alive as such, but also not dead. They moved languidly in the Jell-o type substance they found themselves in, and the small spiderbots I could now see clearly in my peripheral vision flitted around the whole area, taking notes and checking settings and readings on the machines.

They ignored me for the most part. Perhaps it was that kindred spirit thing we had going. But they let me pass, the occasional one only looking up like it was making sure I was the one they were letting pass.

Finally, I reached Orion and tapped his shoulder. But when he turned around, the lock in his hand clicked, and the double doors swung open, toppling us both out and into a dark room, where the floor apparently sloped like a drain and plummeted us down its sides until we shot out of the opening down the bottom.

I was waiting for the penny to drop, for us to hit the ground, for it to hurt more than humanly possible. But it did none of those things. In fact, I felt okay, finally freed from the strange atmosphere we'd been in, and for once like I understood some aspect of why we were here.

We were here because I was fucking dreaming. If my brain could just stop being a mysterious shit and give me a straight-assed answer for once, I'd much appreciate it. All at once there was ground, something solid, or sort of solid beneath me, but everything around us was still black, dark, nothingness. And Orion, well, he wasn't more than a ghost, like a figment of my imagination. Perhaps it was a version of him trapped in time leading me to something I'd forgotten. Something about him that I'd forgotten.

Whoa, that was way too profound for me.

Remember...

Yeah. Yeah, I get it already, I yelled at myself. *Remember what?* I couldn't think of things I might have forgotten. I stopped in my tracks. Wait, hadn't Nya mentioned something about memories? Or was it Orion, or Shane...or somebody. All the information tried to overwhelm me, make me forget where I was and what was going on.

All up, there was no way for me to dig in and find the memories that might have been wiped. Right?

Remem...

"I get it already!" I screamed the words my throat already hoarse, frustration building in me like a bonfire. There was nothing about this whole thing that I wasn't trying to remember, I just didn't know what it was supposed to be and how I was supposed to go about it.

Bubbles appeared in front of my face, like I was under water. Underwater where Orion had been on that boating trip.

But I hadn't been there with him. I was sure I'd been at home, at home and working on...something, right?

Except the bubbles danced around me, as if taunting me with their very presence. *Sure, they said. You were at home. You're always at home when the good stuff happens.*

Fragments of fractured visions flashed in front of my face, trying to drown me in their confusion.

Orion being hit in the head with the catamaran's boom. Blood immediately spattering everywhere, even all over me. Down my chest, in my hair, across my face...my shirt glowed with its wetness. Vibrant and red, droplets of Orion, like dying stars on a white backdrop. I remembered that t-shirt. Where had it gone?

His eyes glazed over even before he hit the water, and I knew, without even having to dive in and haul him out.

But then I was in the water, clothes still on, trying to drag him up from where he desperately tried to sink. His body was limp and heavy. Our friends gathered around, offering hands, trying to steady the boat. I dragged him back with me.

The body in my arms was lifeless. His eyes stared straight up at the sky, that white film of death began to creep through them.

My head raced, my heart broke, and still, he was dead. Such a freak accident, such a loss, it couldn't be true, could it? But I'd seen it with my own eyes. His dead ones, the severe hemorrhage, everything about that smack in the head was wrong, everything was bad. Orion was dead.

I could feel my limbs numbing as I let our friends haul him up and away from me.

But as they did, his eyes took back their blue, regaining his unique coloring from the white that sought to silence him, and finally he blinked. The head wound was gone by the time they managed to reach in and pull me out, and no blood dripped from his hair anymore.

He'd been dead. I knew it. He'd felt dead; I'd seen it. But now here he was, whole, in front of me...

And then everything went blank.

There was still darkness around me, but the memory was back. It was part of my story again. I'd been there when he died. It had been an accident, unlike mine. And unlike the mind wiping they'd done on me. A sigh echoed throughout this inky surrounding, and I thought it might have been me, but was fairly certain it wasn't. There was something in here with me, something watching me and seeing what I would do.

"I really didn't want you to remember that." The voice sounded achingly familiar, like it was something I'd heard my entire life, as if I should know who spoke those words. And I should, because of course I should. But there was something about it that slipped past my recognition.

"Weren't you telling me to remember?" This whole thing was very confusing.

"You're talking to remnants of the system. You were never supposed to contact them. They were never meant to meet you."

I furrowed my brow, not understanding what this even was. Wasn't I already in this program? Didn't everything about it connect in one way or another? "Why would you wipe my mind?"

Steps came from all directions around me, louder and softer than I expected, many more than I wanted to see. Orion disappeared after the vision left me. All I knew was that the urge to find something diminished. The hunger to know what it was had vanished. That memory was real.

Was this voice even a person?

Now you're asking the right questions.

But this time my friendly helpful voice didn't sound so sure of itself. No, static filled in the space between the letters making the message appear garbled and old. Was it a person, was any of this real? Had we ever left my head?

Well, now you're just being silly.

I wanted to laugh with it, to let it know I did appreciate it attempting to keep me as safe as it could, but I knew we were being listened to. I knew we weren't alone.

Of course we haven't left your mind.

The visage that came into focus around me did my head in. I couldn't process it, couldn't understand why they were here. Was my brain just being a dick again? Was it trying to make me worry, attempting to throw wrenches into everything I'd ever believed?

"You're really our most worrisome child, you know." Alina Harvey stood in front of me, a sad smile on her face. I'd never seen my mother truly sad before. Was my brain simply playing on the fact that I felt guilty for not calling her as often anymore?

Her eyes glowed in a strange and sickly green manner, and her hair took on overtones of moss and mold, but her face was still my mother, the only one I'd ever thought I'd known.

The only thing was, I knew, right down into my bones. "Fuck off. You're not my mother."

The molasses-like walls began to lighten in color and close in on me. I could feel anger directed at me, as if whatever it was had thought it could fool me.

Fool me about my parents? Never. Family was something I knew intrinsically.

My trust had vanished. I wasn't taking shit at face value anymore. No more belief until it'd been proven before my very eyes. I heaved in a massive breath of oxygen, trying and failing to steady my nerves even and I ran.

Rebel without a fuse.

I laughed, and the voice in my mind mouthed words I couldn't hear. Which made no sense at all. Neither did the fake mother appearing in front of me. Had the system reached into my mind and pulled out my worst fears? Had it mixed the memories I assumed it took along with those?

It was clever, I'd give it that. Playing on my fears, on my worst nightmares...

Wait.

I didn't need to run. This was my brain, my thoughts, myself. I stopped and tried to focus.

Astute. You're thinking more clearly again. Now listen to me...

Surprisingly, I wanted to.

You need to focus.

The voice in my head held overtones of static and Orion, like they were both speaking to me at once, a crescendoing sound that culminated in a harmony. It shook me out of the stasis I'd somehow entered, making the darkness bleed back into color around me. I wasn't sure I wanted to, but my Orion head voice coaxed me closer, telling me how much better it would be to just know what was in them.

I approached warily.

The capsules sat suspended vertically, their slim glass windows glowing with that aquamarine blue we all wish our lakes secretly were. Machines around them spat out readings that I couldn't understand, not that I was a premed major or anything, but I thought maybe I could at least notice a heart rate, or blood pressure, or something.

Except that wasn't what these held.

Instead, as I looked into each of the capsules in turn, I saw a different variation of myself and Orion. Younger, older, and all ages in between. All of them asleep, and from the way the bodies within shone, crackled, and sparked, all of them wielding power.

And then I snapped out of it.

33

FISSURE

My eyes flew open, and I sat up. My thoughts were crystalizing quickly. I'd been there when Orion died, but they'd wiped my memory and fabricated a whole new one for me. When I broke through, they tried to use my mother to keep me in denial.

As I surveyed where I was, my mind surprised me with its calmness. I realized Orion was seated at the bottom of my bed. I was tired and relieved to see him there and not in one of those tanks. Not as one of those versions of us. His eyes rested on mine thoughtfully, with a hesitance I knew came from wanting to know what I'd seen but being too scared to ask about it directly. I knew that feeling so well.

"What did you dream?" He asked it softly, as if afraid of the question or of making my ears hurt with his volume.

I looked at him, truly drinking in everything he was. From the tips of his black hair, to the toes of his...toenails, since he had no shoes on. He seemed somewhat disheveled like he'd not slept well, and he was wearing a tracksuit, which is something I'd never really seen him in. I think it was one of mine.

Tiredness flowed off him in waves. But he was worried about me, about everything, if I was any judge.

"I'm not entirely sure." I watched his reaction and saw him suck in a breath like he wished I'd have said something different.

"You were muttering, thrashing around. I got worried." He looked away from me. Silence fell between us, not nearly as uncomfortable as I'd have thought. "It's okay, then. I was sort of hoping..."

But he left the words dangling there as he searched for new ones.

"Hoping I'd see, oh, I dunno see the memory of your death?" Still, I watched him, and he couldn't hide the flash of surprise that passed over his expression.

"Yeah, that." He leaned forward, fidgeting with his hands while he mulled over whatever it was he had on his mind.

"Look. I'm not sure why they did that. I mean, I am. Since I knew you'd died. But...still." Maybe bliss was ignorance, maybe I was foolish to want that small bit of peace of mind.

"Who did they use to prompt you, to attempt to push you over the edge and believe what you were told instead of what you remembered?" He wouldn't make eye contact with me, but instead stared at his bare feet on the floor, as if he could will them to be covered in shoes.

I paused, not wanting to relive that portion of it, not wanting to admit that I'd had my moments there, thinking that maybe nothing in my life was real. Because I still wasn't sure it was. "You first, and then my mom."

Orion tsked with a painful look on his face. "Ouch. That's not nice."

"No, it isn't." I remembered everything. The files I'd taken, the files I'd stored. The pain in Orion's bearing, his unwillingness to kill overridden by his need to preserve those he loved. Oh, I got it now.

"What?" He raised an eyebrow. "You've got that look about you."

"Look?" I stalled for time as my thoughts all mashed together.

"That 'I have a secret about something I probably shouldn't have done, but it'll all work out in the long run' look." Orion crossed his arms, but I could see the ghost of a smile starting at the corners of his mouth. He knew he was right.

"Look. How much do you trust Nya and Shane? What about Sam?" I trusted Orion. Regardless of how I felt about his personal choices, I could see the reasoning that tore him apart. I'd known him as long as I could remember, but I'd barely known the others for two months.

"Shane is…Shane is good people. I don't know Nya as well, and I'm proud of Sam for standing up against Selene. I probably trust them about as far as I could throw them." He pursed his lips thoughtfully. "Why?"

I took a breath, not sure how exactly to go about this other than come out and say it. "Because I may have copied some of the files they made me steal and destroy, because I wanted to know what the hell they were doing."

For a few moments Orion looked remarkably like a goldfish. He simply sat there with his mouth open. Slowly, it turned into a grin. "I say we share it."

And his aura flickered into a strange navy sort of blue. Not the color of revenge, but of determination to see things set straight.

Transferring the files was both easier and more difficult than I'd expected. The stone of the room we sat in seemed colder than I remembered. I shivered.

"How are you feeling?" Nya asked me, tiredness reflected in her tone.

"Okay? Bit drained, slightly irritated, but about a hundred percent determined." And I was.

This wasn't okay, none of it was. Lying to us about being able to end our lives with the flick of a switch. That was such bullshit. Instead, they coerced assassins within the ranks to kill others they'd been paired with.

Nya nudged Wick over to me, and he leaned against my leg before promptly putting his head on my foot. He was definitely a calming dog.

"It's okay to be angry at them, but anger feeds your ability, and you've already exhausted yourself with it once today. We need to build up your stamina." She spoke kindly, even if she threw a nasty look Shane's way, who pretended not to notice.

"Yeah. I get it." And I did. Because I was going to need a whole lot of energy to remain undetected. After what we got away with, there was no way the system was going to let us just go.

Very correct.

Thanks for the obvious.

The voice in my head didn't seem to care that I was being sarcastic. *It's about time someone pushed through. There have been so many chances and no success. This is as far as anyone's gotten.*

"How did you do this?" Shane said with a bit of awe. "Like it never occurred to me…"

I shrugged. "IT major, maybe? The irritation at never being given a why? I've never done well with orders. And anyway, no one told me not to try and copy the files, right?"

Orion laughed. "Is Sam coming?"

Nya hesitated. "Sam got caught."

"What?" I said incredulously. "And you're only just telling us this now?"

"I'm sorry. I'm still trying to play the double agent role, and I have to be even more careful now. I think I'll have to withdraw soon, and that'll severely limit our resources."

I could see why she was torn. Hell, I could feel it. What we were doing, what we were about to do was important, but at the same time, she had a lot to lose.

"Fuck." Shane kicked at the ground.

"Damn it. Can we get her out?" Orion's voice was laced with guilt.

Nya shook her head. "Not right now, but give me a day. I've mimicked punishment. It should hold them at bay for now, even if it's not exactly nice."

And that's the straw that did it. It broke the camel's back like someone snapped the cigarette in half.

"Fuck this. They're not nice. The Second Chance system is a fucking asshole." The words flowed out of me like rainwater into a drain.

I didn't know how to calm that down, how to accept what it had shown me and work from there. It aimed at the best and worst parts of me, made me question my sanity, and then left me to figure out stuff on my own.

"Whatever this system is, I want no part of it. I wish it had never brought us back." I growled the words out, knowing that it was blasphemy as far as this whole Second Chance was concerned.

A sudden whirring sounded around us all, like some massive computer was booting up, feeding off the energy around it. I heard multiple machines waking up, making that sound a gaming rig does when you first hit the on button, pushing through the confines of whatever held them.

All four of us stood up, looking around, trying to find the source of the sound.

Final Chance activated. System booting in.

5

4

3

2

1

Momentary darkness swarmed my vision until the next message hit my screen in bright green lettering.

Second Chance system overridden by user choice. Last Chance system calibrating.

Deactivating imposed limitations.

Deactivating safety protocols.

Deactivating learning blockages.

Deactivating seat belt mode.

Z class bioelectric ability engaged.

Z class Timestance ability engaged.

Z class healing potential activated.

Z class foresight enabled.

Warning: You are your own master within parameters. Staying alive serves the program, dying does not.

Welcome to the Last Chance program. Thank you for re-establishing the link lost over time. We are counting on you and others like you. You were brought back for a reason.

Orion grinned at me, sat there like the Cheshire bloody cat, as if nothing and no one could hurt any of us anymore. He'd obviously gotten the same type of slew of notifications. They all had if the looks on their faces were anything else to go by.

"How…?" I asked, trying not to sound scared and thrilled at the same time.

Nya's features showed the first unencumbered smile I'd ever seen her with. Even Shane smiled.

Orion looked relaxed and excited for the first time I could remember in the last two years. "I think this is how the program was supposed to be, this is what we were supposed to feel like. And now, SC has no power over us."

I took a deep breath, inhaling that first beautiful scent of freedom. "And now, now we can rescue Sam."

FROM THE AUTHOR

Hi there! K.T. Hanna here.

I want to thank you for taking a "chance" on my Last Chance Series. Go the eels! My fascination with electricity has only deepened. I can't wait to pen the final book for you all to read!

If you enjoyed the book, I ask you, *please* take a moment to leave a review. *Reviews* are an author's lifesblood. Without them, our books sink into obscurity. With them, most algorithms allow well reviewed books to self-promote in some way.

Want to find out more about Last Chance and my other series? Here is how you can keep in contact with me:

Sign up for my Reader's Group (login.somnia-online.com/) and get a short story for free!

If you'd like to contact me, my email is:

kthannaauthor@gmail.com I'll do my very best to get back to you

If you'd like previews of what I'm writing, or art I'm commissioning then join my Patreon (facebook.com/groups/SomniaOnline/)!

I can be found in my FB group (facebook.com/groups/SomniaOnline/) fairly often, and also on Twitter (@KTHanna) & Instagram (@kt_hanna).

If you LOVE LitRPG don't forget to join:

The GameLit Society! (facebook.com/groups/LitRPGsociety/)

And of course don't forget LitRPG Books!

(facebook.com/groups/LitRPG.books/)

To learn more about LitRPG, talk to authors including myself, and just have an awesome time, please join the **LitRPG Group** (facebook.com/groups/LitRPGGroup/

ACKNOWLEDGEMENTS

I have a lot of people to thank, who in at least some way encouraged me to write in general, or else to write this book specifically.

Love of my life, Trevor, and my little Kami. It's his fault I found the genre, and her fault I never give up on writing.

I wouldn't be here without the Jami Nord and Owen Littman. I must thank Dawn Chapman, Luke Chmilenko, Michael Chatfield, Tao Wong, and Bonnie Price for their friendship, guidance, and company on an almost daily basis. And of course Andrea Parsneau for being such an amazing person to go through this with.

Of course, I have to thank a few other people (hope I haven't forgotten anyone)

M. Andrew Patterson
Kylie B.
Amanda W.
Quinton Shyn
Stephen Morse
Cait Greer
M Evan Matyas
Ian Mitchell
Marko Horvatin
Dave Willmarth
Charles Dean
Daniel Schinofen
Anthea Sharp

Patreon, I thank all of my patrons. You make so much possible and bring me so much joy! Thank you especially to:

Ma & Pa
Robert
Phoenixblue
Wisp
Daniel

www.ingramcontent.com/pod-product-compliance
Lightning Source LLC
Chambersburg PA
CBHW051653180726
48284CB00006B/1979